THE GUNS OF TANITH

THE MEN ROPED out. Milo led the squad out of the port, his hook whizzing down the cable until he slammed into the curving roof and tumbled off. Domor was behind him, then Bonin, then Ezlan.

On the starboard side, Haller came out, followed by Vadim, Reggo and Nirriam.

The men thumped down onto the roof, scrabbling for handholds, desperate not to slide off into the night. Twenty men down, twenty-five. Thirty. Thirty-five.

The drop's engines failed. Clinging to the curve of the roofing panels on his belly, Domor heard the pilot scream. He looked back. The drop-ship simply fell out of the air and smashed into the roof, crushing a half-dozen of the roping men under it.

Then it began to slide.

A WARHAMMER 40,000 NOVEL

Gaunt's Ghosts

THE GUNS
OF TANITH

Dan Abnett

For Ben Stampton, with thanks for Larkin and the Angel

A BLACK LIBRARY PUBLICATION

BL Publishing,
Games Workshop Ltd.,
Willow Road,
Nottingham, NG7 2WS, UK

First published in the US in 2002.
This edition published September 2003.

10 9 8 7 6 5 4 3 2 1

Distributed by Simon & Schuster
1230 Avenue of the Americas
New York, NY 10020

Cover illustration by Adrian Smith
Map by Ralph Horsley

ISBN 0-7434-4304-7

Set in ITC Giovanni

Printed and bound in Great Britain by
Cox & Wyman Ltd, Reading, Berkshire, UK.

See the Black Library on the Internet at
www.blacklibrary.com

Find out more about Games Workshop
and the world of Warhammer 40,000 at
www.games-workshop.com

It is the 41st millennium. For more than a hundred centuries the Emperor has sat immobile on the Golden Throne of Earth. He is the master of mankind by the will of the gods, and master of a million worlds by the might of his inexhaustible armies. He is a rotting carcass writhing invisibly with power from the Dark Age of Technology. He is the Carrion Lord of the Imperium for whom a thousand souls are sacrificed every day, so that he may never truly die.

Yet even in his deathless state, the Emperor continues his eternal vigilance. Mighty battlefleets cross the daemon-infested miasma of the warp, the only route between distant stars, their way lit by the Astronomican, the psychic manifestation of the Emperor's will. Vast armies give battle in his name on uncounted worlds. Greatest amongst his soldiers are the Adeptus Astartes, the Space Marines, bio-engineered super-warriors. Their comrades in arms are legion: the Imperial Guard and countless planetary defence forces, the ever-vigilant Inquisition and the tech-priests of the Adeptus Mechanicus to name only a few. But for all their multitudes, they are barely enough to hold off the ever-present threat from aliens, heretics, mutants – and worse.

To be a man in such times is to be one amongst untold billions. It is to live in the cruellest and most bloody regime imaginable. These are the tales of those times. Forget the power of technology and science, for so much has been forgotten, never to be re-learned. Forget the promise of progress and understanding, for in the grim dark future there is only war. There is no peace amongst the stars, only an eternity of carnage and slaughter, and the laughter of thirsting gods.

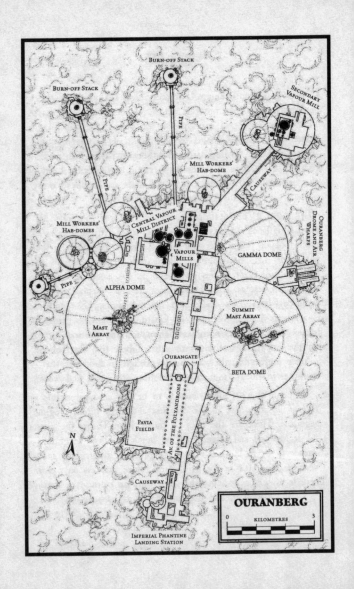

BURN-OFF STACK

BURN-OFF STACK

SECONDARY
VAPOUR MILL

MILL WORKERS'
HAB-DOME

PIPE

PIPE

CAUSEWAY

OURANBERG
DROME AND AIR
WHARFS

MILL WORKERS'
HAB-DOMES

CENTRAL VAPOUR
MILL DISTRICT

PIPE

VAPOUR
MILLS

GAMMA DOME

ALPHA DOME

SUMMIT
MAST ARRAY

MAST
ARRAY

OURANGATE

BETA DOME

AV. OF THE POLYANDRONS

PAVIA
FIELDS

N

CAUSEWAY

IMPERIAL PHANTINE
LANDING STATION

OURANBERG

0   KILOMETRES   3

L ATE IN THE *sixteenth year of the Sabbat Worlds Crusade, Warmaster Macaroth's incisive advance on the strategically vital Cabal system, which had been so strong and confident in its initial phase, juddered to a halt. Three-quarters of the target planets, including two of the infamous fortress-worlds, had been taken by Imperial Crusade forces and the occupying armies of the Chaos arch-enemy routed or put to flight. But, as many Navy commanders had warned, the push had overreached itself, creating as it did a salient vulnerable on three sides.*

'Orlock Gaur, one of the arch-enemy's most able war-lords, making good use of the vicious loxatl mercenaries, drove an inspired counter-offensive along the advance's coreward flank, taking, in quick succession, Enothis, Khan V, Caius Innate and Belshiir Binary. Vital supply lanes, especially those providing fuel resources for the stretched Crusade fleet, were cut. Macaroth's valiant gamble, which he had hoped might win him the campaign outright, now seemed foolhardy. Unless fresh supply lines could be forged, and new fuel resources made available, the hard-won Cabal Salient would crumble. At best, the Imperial advance would be forced into retreat. At worst, it would collapse and be overrun.

'Warmaster Macaroth hastily redeployed significant ele-ments of his spinward flank in a make or break effort to open up new lines of supply. All those involved knew the outcome of this improvised action would certainly decide the fate of the Cabal Salient, and perhaps the war itself.

The key target worlds were the promethium-rich planets of Gigar, Aondrift Nova, Anaximander and Mirridon, the forge world Urdesh, Tanzina IV and Ariadne with their solid fuel reserves, and the vapour mills of Rydol and Phan-tine...'

— from *A History of the Later Imperial Crusades*

PROLOGUE: STRAIGHT SILVER

COMBAT DISPERSAL DROGUE NIMBUS, WEST CONTINENTAL REACHES, PHANTINE, 211.771, M41

'I don't think any of us knew what we were getting into. Feth, I'm glad I didn't know what we were getting into.'

– Sgt. Varl, 1st Team leader, Tanith First

A CHOKE-HOLD was the last thing he expected.

Trooper Hlaine Larkin landed with a jarring thump in a place so dark he couldn't even see his hand in front of his face. He immediately got right down like the colonel had told him in practice. Belly down.

Somewhere in the dark, to his right, he heard Sergeant Obel scolding the men in the fireteam to hug cover. That was a joke for starters. Cover? How could they find cover when they couldn't even see the arse of the man in front?

Larkin lay down on his front and reached about until his fingers found an upright surface. A stanchion, maybe. A bulkhead. He slithered towards it, and then unshipped his long-las from its soft plastic cover. That he could do by touch alone. His fingers ran along the nalwood furniture, the firing mechanism, the oiled top-slot ready to take his nightscope.

Someone cried out in the darkness nearby. Some poor feth who'd snapped an ankle in the drop.

Larkin felt the panic rising in him. He pulled his scope from its bag, slotted it into place, popped the cap, and was about to take a look when an arm locked around his throat.

'You're dead, Tanith,' said a voice in his ear.

Larkin twisted, but the grip refused to break. His blood thudded in his temples as the choke-hold tightened and pinched his windpipe and carotid arteries. He tried to call 'Man out!' but his throat was shut.

There was a popping sound, and illumination flares banged off overhead. The drop area was suddenly, starkly lit. Pitch-black shadows, angular and hard, stabbed across him.

He saw the knife.

Tanith silver, straight, thirty centimetres long, hovering in front of his face.

'Feth!' Larkin gurgled.

A whistle blew, shrill and penetrating.

'GET UP, YOU IDIOT,' ordered Commissar Viktor Hark, striding down the field line of the bay with the whistle in his hand. 'You, trooper! Get up! You're facing the wrong damned way!'

The roof-lamps began to fizzle on, drenching the wide bay with stale yellow light. In amongst the litter of packing crates and corrugated iron, soldiers in black combat fatigues blinked and got to their feet.

'Sergeant Obel!'

'Commissar?'

'Get up here!'

Obel hurried forward to meet the commissar. Behind Hark, harmless low-pulse las-fire flashed in the gloom.

'Stop that!' Hark yelled, turning. 'They're all dead anyway! Cease fire and reset your position to starting place two!'

'Yes, sir!' a voice floated back from the enemy side.

'Report?' Hark said, looking back at the red-faced Obel.

'We dropped and dispersed, sir. Theta pattern. We had cover–'

'How wonderful for you. Do you suppose it matters that eighty per cent of your unit was facing the wrong way?'

'Sir. We were… confused.'

'Oh dear. Which way's north, sergeant?'

Obel pulled his compass from his fatigues. 'That way, sir.'

'At last. Those dials glow in the dark for a reason, sergeant.'

'Hark?'

Commissar Hark snapped to attention. A tall figure in a long storm coat walked across the bay to join him. He looked for all the world like Hark's shadow, drawn out and extended by the bad lights.

'How do you think you did?' asked Colonel-Commissar Ibram Gaunt.

'How do I think I did? I think you slaughtered us. And deservedly.'

Gaunt covered a smile. 'Be fair, Hark. Those men there are all behind cover. They'd have soon realised which way was up if that'd been real las-fire.'

'That's generous, sir. I figure it a good seventy-five point win to the passive team.'

Gaunt shook his head. 'No more than fifty-five, sixty points. You still had an opening you could have used.'

'I hate to correct you, sir,' said a tall, lean Tanith in a camo-cape who wandered casually out of Obel's lines. He was screwing the top back onto a paint stick.

'Mkvenner?' Gaunt greeted the grim scout, one of Sergeant Mkoll's elite. 'Go on then, disabuse me.'

Mkvenner had the sort of long, high cheek-boned face that made everything he said seem chilling and dark. He had a blue half-moon tattoo under his right eye.

Many reckoned he looked a lot like Gaunt himself, though Mkvenner's hair was Tanith black where Gaunt's was straw blond. And Gaunt was bigger too: taller, wider, more imposing.

'We heard them drop in during the blackout, and I got five men in amongst them.'

'Five?'

'Bonin, Caober, Doyl, Cuu and myself. Knives only,' he added, gesturing with the paint stick. 'We splashed a good eight of them before the lights came on.'

'How could you see?' asked Obel plaintively.

'We wore blindfolds until the lights went out. Our night vision was adjusted.'

'Good work, Mkvenner,' sighed Gaunt. He tried to avoid Hark's stern look.

'You had us cold,' said Hark.

'Evidently,' replied Gaunt.

'So... they're not ready. Not for this. Not for a night drop.'

'They'll have to be!' Gaunt growled. 'Obel! Get your sorry excuses for soldiers up into those towers again! We'll reset and do it over!'

'Yes, sir!' Obel replied smartly. 'Uhm... Trooper Loglas snapped his shin in the last exercise. He'll need a medic.'

'Feth!' said Gaunt. 'Right, go. Everyone else, reset!'

He waited for a moment as medics Lesp and Chayker carried the moaning Loglas out of the bay. The rest of Obel's detachment were clambering up the scaffolding of the sixteen metre tall drop towers and recoiling the rappelling cables, ready to resume drop positions.

'Lights down!' yelled Gaunt. 'Let's do this again until we get it right!'

'YOU HEARD HIM!' gasped Larkin. 'It's over! We're going again!'

'Lucky for you, Tanith.'

The choke-hold relaxed and Larkin fell sideways at last, panting for breath.

Trooper Lijah Cuu stepped over him and sheathed his silver blade.

'Still, I got you, Tanith. Sure as sure.'

Larkin gathered up his weapon, coughing. The whistle was shrilling again.

'Fething idiot! You nearly killed me!'

'Killing you was the point of the exercise, Tanith,' Cuu grinned, fixing the flustered master-sniper with his feline gaze.

'You're supposed to tag me with that!' Larkin snapped, nodding at the unopened paint stick hooked in Cuu's webbing.

'Oh, yeah,' marvelled Cuu, as if he'd never seen the stick before.

'Larkin! Trooper Larkin!' Sergeant Obel's voice sang across the bay. 'Do you intend to join us?'

'Sir!' Larkin snapped, stuffing his long-las back into its cover.

'Double-time, Larkin! Come on!'

Larkin looked back at Cuu, another surly curse forming in his mouth. But Cuu had disappeared.

OBEL WAS WAITING for him at the base of one of the towers. The last few men were clambering up the scaffold, encumbered by full assault kit. A couple had stopped at the foot of the tower to take sponges from a water can and smear away the tell-tale traces of red paint from their fatigues.

'Problem?' asked Obel.

'No, sir,' said Larkin, adjusting the sling of his gun-case. 'Except that Cuu's a fething menace.'

'Unlike the actual enemy, who is soft and cuddly. Get your scrawny butt up that tower, Larkin.'

Larkin heaved himself up the metalwork. Overhead, the lighting rigs were shutting off, one by one.

Sixteen metres up, there was a grilled shelf on which the men were forming up in three lines. Ahead of them was a scaffolding arch that was supposed to simulate the size and shape of a drop-ship's exit hatch, and which led out to a stepboard ramp that someone had dryly named 'the plank'. Gutes, Garond and Unkin, the three point men, were crouching there, drop-cables coiled on their laps. One end of each cable was secured to locking clamps on the gantry above the plank.

'In line, come on,' Obel muttered as he moved down the fireteams. Larkin hurried to take his place.

'Dead, Larks?' asked Bragg, making space for him.

'Feth, yes. You?'

Bragg patted a red stain on his tunic that he hadn't managed to sponge out.

'Never even saw 'em,' he said.

'Quiet in the line!' barked Obel. 'Tokar! Tighten that harness or you'll hang up. Fenix… where are your fething gloves?'

The last of the lights were going out. Down below somewhere, Hark was blowing his whistle. Three short bursts. The two minutes ready call.

'Stand by!' Unkin called back down the waiting rows.

Larkin couldn't see the men on the neighbouring towers. He couldn't even see the towers themselves. The gloom was worse than even the most moonless night back on Tanith.

'Make way,' whispered a voice behind them. A hooded flashlight cast a small green glow and showed another man joining them on the tower shelf.

It was Gaunt.

He moved in amongst them. 'Listen up,' he hissed, just loud enough for them all to hear. 'I know you're new to this drill, and that none of you like it, but we've got to get it down by the numbers. There'll be no landing at Cirenholm. I can guarantee that. The pilots are first class, and they'll get us in as close as possible, but even then it might be a lot further than sixteen metres.'

Several troopers groaned.

'The drop cable's thirty metres,' said Garond. 'What happens if it's further than that, sir?'

'Flap your arms,' said Gaunt. There was some chuckling.

'Hook up and slide fast. Keep your knees bent. And move. The drop-ships can't stay on station any longer than is absolutely necessary. You're going out three at a time, and there may be more than one man on a cable at any time. When you reach the deck, move clear. Is that a bayonet, trooper?'

'Yes sir.'

'Put it away. No fixed blades until you're down, not even in the real thing. Weapons on safety. If you've got folding stocks, fold them. Get all your harness and webbing straps tight and tuck them in. And remember, when the real thing comes, you'll all be in gas-hoods, which will add to the fun. I'm sure Sergeant Obel has told you all this.'

'It tends to sink in when you repeat it, sir,' said Obel.

'I'm sure it does.' Gaunt took off his storm coat and his cap and buckled on a hook-belt. 'Loglas is out, so you're a man short. I'll stand in.' He took his place in the number four slot of the right hand squad. Hark's whistle wailed out one long note. Gaunt snapped off his lamp. It was pitch dark.

'Let's go,' he hissed. 'Call the drill, sergeant.'

'Over the DZ!' Obel instructed, now speaking via the vox-headsets. 'Deploy! By the front! Cables out!'

'Cables away!' chorused the point men in the dark, spilling their lines down expertly from the plank. They were already hooked up.

'Go!'

Larkin could hear the abrasive buzz of the cables as they went taut and took the weight of the first men.

'Go!'

Drizzles of low-pulse fire twinkled in the darkness below. Larkin stepped up under the arch, holding the tunic tail of the man in front. Then the man was gone.

'Go!'

He groped for the line, found it, and snapped his arrestor hook around it.

'Come on!'

Larkin pulled his harness tight and went over into space. He swung wildly. The hook bucked and whined as its brake disk clamped at the cable. He could smell nylon burning with the friction.

The impact seemed even harder than the last time. The deck smacked the wind out of him. He struggled to release his hook, and rolled clear just before the man after him came hissing down.

He was on his belly again, like last time. His shoulder nudged a hard surface as he crawled forward and he moved his back against it. Where were the flares? Where were the fething flares?

His long-las was out of its cover, and the scope in place. Someone ran past him and his vox ear-piece was busy with man to man signals.

Larkin sighted. The night scope gave him vision, showed him the world as a green, phantom swirl. The enemy gun flashes were hot little spikes of light that left afterimages on the viewfinder.

He saw a figure in cover to his left, down behind some oil drums.

It was Mkvenner, with a paint stick in his hand.

'Pop!' said Larkin, and his gun fizzled a low-energy charge.

'Feth!' said Mkvenner, and sat back hard. 'Man out!'

Flares burst overhead. Crackling, blue-white light shimmered down over the DZ.

'Up and select!' Obel ordered curtly over the vox-link.

Larkin looked around. They were in place, facing the right fething way this time.

Men moved forward. Larkin stayed put. He was more use to them static and hunting.

He saw Bonin stalking two of his team and popped him out of the game too.

Flash charges went off down to Larkin's right. The bay rang. Some of Obel's squad, along with men from the neighbouring tower, had engaged full-on with the passive team. Larkin heard the call 'Man out!' five or six times.

Then he heard someone cry out in real pain.

Hark's whistle was blowing. 'Cease! Cease and stay put!'

The lights came on again, slowly and feebly.

Hark appeared. 'Better. Better, Obel.'

The men began getting up. Bonin moved past Larkin. 'Nice one,' he said.

Gaunt walked out into one of the pools of light. 'Mkvenner?' he called. 'Score it up.'

'Sir,' said Mkvenner. The scout looked unhappy.

'You get tagged?' Gaunt asked.

'Think it was Larkin, sir. We got about thirty points that time, all told.'

'That should make you a bit happier,' Gaunt said to Hark. 'Medic!'

Everyone turned. Bragg stumbled out from behind some empty munition boxes, clutching a deep red stain on his shoulder that wasn't paint.

'What happened?' asked Gaunt.

'Cuu stuck me,' growled Bragg.

'Trooper Cuu, front and centre!' Hark bellowed.

Cuu emerged from cover. His face, split by an old scar from top to bottom, was expressionless.

'You want to explain?' Hark asked him.

'It was dark. I tussled with the big f... with Bragg. I was sure I had my paint stick in my hand, sir. Sure as sure.'

'He jabbed me with his fething blade,' Bragg complained sourly.

'That's enough, Bragg. Go find a medic,' said Gaunt. 'Cuu. Report to me at sixteen hundred for discipline detail.'

'Sir.'

'Salute, damn you.'

Cuu made a quick salute.

'Get into line and don't let me see that blade again until we're in combat.'

Cuu wandered back to the passive unit. As he passed Larkin, he turned and glared at the sniper with his cold, green eyes.

'What are you looking at, Tanith?'

'Nothing,' said Larkin.

'LET ME EXPLAIN,' said Sergeant Ceglan Varl. He laid his guard-issue lasrifle on the counter of the Munitorium store and brushed the backs of his fingers down the length of it like a showman beginning a trick. 'This here is a standard pattern mark III lascarbine, stamped out by the armourers of Tanith Magna, God-Emperor rest their oily fingers. Notice the wooden stock and sleeve. That's nice, isn't it? Real Tanith nal-wood, the genuine article. And the metalwork, all buffed down to reduce shine. See?'

The Munitorium clerk, a paunchy, dimpled man with greasy red hair and starchy robe, stood on the other side of the counter and stared back at Varl without any show of interest.

'Here's the thing,' said Varl, tapping the weapon's ammunition slot. 'That's a size three power port. Takes size three power cells. They can be short, long, sickle-pattern, box-form or drum, but they have to be size three or they won't fit. Size three. Thirty mil with a back-slant lock. With me so far?'

The clerk shrugged.

Varl took a power clip from his musette bag and slid it across the counter.

'You've issued my company with size fives. Size fives, you see? They're thirty-four mil and flat-fronted. You can tell they're not threes just by looking at the size of them, but if you're in any doubt, the fething great "5" stencilled on the side is a handy guide.'

The clerk picked up the clip and looked at it.

'We were instructed to issue ammunition. Eight hundred boxes. Standard pattern.'

'Standard size three,' said Varl patiently. 'That's standard size five.'

'Standard pattern, they said. I've got the docket.'

'I'm sure you have. And the Tanith First-and-Only have got boxes and boxes of ammo that they can't use.'

'It said standard pattern.'

Varl sighed. 'Everything's standard pattern! This is the Imperial fething Guard! Standard pattern boots, standard pattern mess-tins, standard pattern bodybags! I'm a standard pattern infantryman and you're a standard pattern no-neck, and any minute now my standard pattern fist is going to smack your nose bone back into your very sub-standard pattern brain!'

'There's no need to be abusive,' said the clerk.

'Oh, I think there might be,' said Sergeant Gol Kolea quietly, joining Varl at the counter. Kolea was a big man, an ex-miner from Verghast, and he towered over his Tanith comrade. But it wasn't his size that immediately alarmed the clerk. It was his soft tone and calm eyes. Varl had been spiky and aggressively direct, but the newcomer oozed potent wrath held in restraint below the surface.

'Tell him, Gol,' said Varl.

'I'll show him,' said Kolea and waved his hand. Guardsmen, all of them the so-called Ghosts, began to troop in, lugging ammo boxes. They started to stack them on the counter until there wasn't any more room. Then they started to pile them on the deck.

'No, no!' cried the clerk. 'We'll have to get counter-signed dockets before you can return these.'

'Tell you what,' said Kolea, 'let's not. Let's just swap these for boxes of size threes.'

'We… we don't have size threes,' said the clerk.

'You what?' Varl cried.

'We weren't told to carry any. On Phantine, size five is the–'

'Don't say standard pattern. Don't say it!' warned Varl.

'You're saying the blessed and hallowed Munitorium has no ammunition for the entire Tanith regiment?' asked Kolea.

'Feth!' Varl cursed. 'We're about to assault… what's it called?'

'Cirenholm,' said Kolea helpfully.

'That's the place. We're about to assault it and this is what you tell us? What are we supposed to use?' Varl pulled his Tanith knife from its sheath and showed the clerk the long, straight silver blade. 'Are we supposed to take the city using these?'

'If we have to.'

The Ghosts snapped to attention. Major Elim Rawne had wandered silently into the store. 'We've had to do worse. If Tanith straight silver is all I have, then it's all I need.'

The major looked at the clerk and the clerk shivered. Rawne's gaze tended to do that. There was a touch of snake about him, in his hooded eyes and cold manner. He was slim, dark and good-looking and, like many of the Tanith men, had a tattoo. Rawne's was a small blue star under his right eye.

'Varl, Kolea… get your men back to the billet. Round up the other squad leaders and run an inventory. I want to know just how much viable ammunition we've got left. Account for all of it. Don't let any of the men stash stuff in socks or musette bags. Pool it all and we'll distribute it evenly.'

The sergeants saluted.

'Feygor,' said Rawne, turning to his sinister adjutant. 'Go with them and bring the count back to me. Don't take all day.'

Feygor nodded and followed the troopers out.

'Now,' said Rawne, facing the clerk again. 'Let's see what we can sort out…'

TROOPER BRIN MILO, the youngest Ghost, sat down on his cot and looked across at the young man on the next bunk.

'That's very nice,' said Milo, 'and it will get you killed.'

The other man looked up, puzzled and wary. He was a Verghastite by the name of Noa Vadim, one of the many new Ghosts recruited after the siege of Vervunhive to replenish the ranks of the Tanith regiment. There was still a lot of rivalry between the two camps. The Tanith resented the new intake, and the Verghastites resented that resentment. In truth, they were slowly fusing now. The regiment had endured the fight for the shrineworld of Hagia a few months before and, as is ever the case with war, comradeship and a common goal had alloyed the Tanith and Verghast elements into one strong company.

But still, Verghastites and Tanith were breeds apart. There were so many little differences. Like accents – the gruff

Vervunhive drawl beside the sing-song Tanith lilt. Like colouring – the Tanith were almost universally pale skinned and dark haired where the Verghastites were a rather more mixed lot, as was typical with a hive city of such size. The Verghastites' weapons had folding metal stocks and hand-plates where the guns of Tanith had sturdy nalwood furniture.

Vadim held the biggest difference in his hands: the regimental pin. The recruits from Vervunhive wore a silver axe-rake design denoting their home world. The Tanith wore a gold, wreath-surrounded skull backed by a single dagger that carried the motto 'For Tanith, for the Emperor'.

'What do you mean, "killed"?' asked Vadim. He'd been polishing his axe-rake pin with a hank of vizzy-cloth until it shone. 'There's a dress inspection at twenty hundred.'

'I know… and there's a night assault in the next day or two. Something that shiny will pick up any backscattered light.'

'But Commissar Gaunt expects–'

'Gaunt expects every man to be battle-prepped when we fall in. That's what the inspection's for. Ready for war, not ready for the parade ground.'

Milo tossed his own slouch cap across to the Vadim and the young Vervunhiver caught it. 'See?'

Vadim looked at the Tanith badge pinning back the brimfold. It was clean, but non-reflective, dulled like granite.

'A little camo-paint and spit. Or boot-wax. Takes the shine right off.'

'Right.' Vadim peered more closely at Milo's pin. 'What are these rough edges here? On either side? Like something's been snapped off.'

'The skull was backed by three daggers originally. One for each of the original founded regiments. The Tanith First, the Tanith Second and the Tanith Third. Only the Tanith First made it off the home world.'

Vadim had heard the story secondhand a few times, but he had never plucked up the nerve to ask a Tanith about it directly. In honour of his service to Warmaster Macaroth's predecessor, Gaunt had been given personal command of the Tanith forces. That in itself was unusual, a commissar in command. Commissars were political officers. It explained why Gaunt's official rank was colonel-commissar.

On Tanith, about six years earlier, on the very day of the Founding, the legions of the arch-enemy had swept in. Tanith was lost, there was no question. For Gaunt, there had been a choice: stay and die with every man, or withdraw with what strengths he could save to fight another day. He had chosen the latter, and escaped with only the men of the Tanith First. The Tanith First-and-Only. Gaunt's Ghosts.

Many of the Ghosts had hated Gaunt for that, for cheating them out of the chance to fight for their world. Some, like Major Rawne, still did. But the last few years had shown the wisdom of Gaunt's decision. Gaunt's Ghosts had chalked up a string of battlefield victories that had significantly helped the Crusade endeavour. He'd made them count, which made sense of saving them.

And at Vervunhive, perhaps Gaunt's most lauded victory so far, the Ghosts had benefited from new blood. The Verghastite recruits: scratch company guerillas, ex-hive soldiery, dispossessed civilians, all given the chance to join by Warmaster Macaroth as a mark of respect for the shared defence of the great hive.

'We snapped the side daggers off the crest,' said Milo. 'We only needed one piece of Tanith straight silver to remind us who we were.'

Vadim tossed the cap back to Milo. The billet room around them was a smoky haze of men lolling in bunks or finessing kit. Domor and Brostin were having a game of regicide. Nehn was playing a little box-pipe badly.

'How you finding the drills?' Milo asked Vadim.

'The drop stuff? It's okay. Easy enough.'

'You think? We've done rope deployments before a few times, but not in the dark. And they say the drop could be a long one. I hate heights.'

'I don't notice them,' said Vadim. He'd taken a tin of boot-wax out of his kitbag and was beginning to apply it to his pin as Milo had suggested.

'Why?'

Vadim grinned. He wasn't much older than Milo, perhaps early twenties. He had a strong nose and a generous mouth, and small, dark mischievous eyes. 'I was a roofer. I worked repairing the masts and plating on the Main Spine. High level stuff, mostly without a harness. I guess I'm used to heights.'

'Feth!' said Milo, slightly impressed. He'd seen Vervunhive Main Spine himself. There were smaller mountains. 'Any tips?'

'Yeah,' said Vadim. 'Don't look down.'

'TWENTY-THREE HUNDRED hours tomorrow night will be D-hour,' said Lord General Barthol Van Voytz. He folded the fingers of his white-gloved hands together, almost as if in prayer. 'May the Emperor protect us all. Field muster begins at twenty thirty, by which time, given advance meteorology, the drogues should be manoeuvring into the dispersal field. I want drop-ships and support air-ready by twenty-one thirty, when mount up commences. First wave launch is at twenty-two hundred, with second wave ten minutes after that and third wave at twenty-two thirty.'

He glanced around the wide, underlit chart table at his officers. 'Questions?'

There were none, not immediately anyway. Gaunt, two places to Van Voytz's left, leafed through his copy of the assault orders. Outside the force-dome surrounding the briefing session, the bridge crew of the mighty drogue manned their stations and paced the polished hardwood decks.

'Let's remind ourselves what's on offer,' said the lord general, nodding to his adjutant. Like the lord general, the aide was dressed in a crisp, emerald green Navy dress uniform with spotless white gloves. Each gold aquila button on his chest twinkled like a star in the soft, white illumination. The adjutant pressed a button on a control wand, and a three dimensional hololithic view of Cirenholm rose from the chart table's glass top.

Gaunt had been over the plans a hundred times, but he still took the opportunity to study this relief image. Cirenholm, like all the habitations still viable on Phantine, was built into the peaks of a mountain range that rose dramatically above the lethal atmospheric oceans of pollution covering the planet. It had three main domes, the two largest nestled together and the third, smaller, adjoining at an angle on a secondary peak. The domes were fat and shallow, like the lids of forest mushrooms. Their skirts projected out over the sides of the almost vertical mountains. The apex of each dome was spined with a cluster of masts and aerials, and a thicket of flues, smoke-stacks and heat exchangers bloomed from a bulge in the upper western slopes of the secondary dome. It had a population of two hundred and three thousand.

'Cirenholm is not a fortress,' said Van Voytz. 'None of the cities on Phantine are. It was not built to withstand a war. If it was simply a matter of crushing the enemy here, we'd be doing it from orbit, and not wasting the time of the Imperial Guard. But... and I think this is worthy of repetition... our mission here is to recapture the vapour mills. To drive out the enemy and reclaim the processors. The Crusade desperately needs the fuel-gases and liquid chemicals this world produces.'

Van Voytz cleared his throat. 'So we are forced into an infantry assault. And in infantry terms, Cirenholm is a fortress. Docking and hangar facilities are under the lips of the domes and well protected, so there is no viable landing zone. That means cable drops.'

He took out a hard-light pointer and indicated the narrow decks that ran around the rim of the domes. 'Here. Here. And here. These are the only viable drop zones. They look small, I know. In reality, they're about thirty metres broad. But that will look small to any man coming out of a drop ship on an arrestor hook. The last thing we need tomorrow night is inaccuracy.'

'Can I ask, sir, why tomorrow has been chosen as a go?' The question came from Captain Ban Daur, the Verghastite fourth officer of the Tanith regiment. Gaunt had brought him along as his aide. Corbec and Rawne were busy readying the men and Daur, Gaunt knew, had a cool head for strategy and soaked up tactics like a sponge.

Van Voytz deferred to the person on his immediate left, a short, fidgeting man dressed in the black leather and red braid of the Imperial Tacticians cadre. His name was Biota. 'Long range scans indicate that weather conditions will be optimal tomorrow night, captain,' said Biota. 'Low cloud, and no moonlight. There will be a crosswind from the east, but that should keep the cloud cover behind us and shouldn't pick up. We're unlikely to get better conditions for another week.'

Daur nodded. Gaunt knew what he was thinking. They could all do with a few more days' practice.

'Besides,' said the lord general, 'I don't want to keep the drogues out in open sky any longer than I have to. We're inviting attack from the enemy's cloud-fighters.'

Admiral Ornoff, the drogue commander, nodded. 'Every day we wait multiplies the chance of interception.'

'We have increased escort patrols, sir,' objected Commander Jagdea. A small woman with close-cropped black hair, Jagdea was the chief officer of the Phantine Fighter Corps. Her aviators had been providing protection since the drogues set out, and they would lead the raid in.

'Noted, commander,' said Van Voytz. 'And we are thankful for the efforts of your flight officers and ground crews. However, I don't want to push our luck.'

'What sort of numbers do the enemy have at Cirenholm?' Gaunt asked quietly.

'We estimate between four and seven thousand, colonel-commissar,' said Biota. 'Mostly light infantry from the Blood Pact, with close support.'

'What about loxatl?' Daur asked.

'We don't think so,' said the tactician.

Gaunt noted the number down. It was vague, and he didn't like that. The Blood Pact was the backbone of the Chaos forces in this sub-sector, the personal retinue of the infamous warlord Urlock Gaur.

They were good, so the reports said. The Ghosts had yet to face them. Most of the opposition the Tanith had met so far had been extreme fanatics. The Infardi, the Zoicans, the Shriven, the Kith. Chaos zealots, demented by their foul beliefs, who had taken up weapons. But the Blood Pact was composed of soldiers, a fraternal military cult, every one of them sworn to Gaur's service in a grisly ritual that involved cutting their palms against the jagged edges of his ancient Space Marine armour.

They were well-drilled, obedient, efficient by Chaos standards, blindly devoted to both their dark daemon-gods and their twisted warrior creed. The Blood Pact elements on

Phantine were said to be commanded by Sagittar Slaith, one of Urlock Gaur's most trusted lieutenants.

The loxatl were something else. Xenos mercenaries, an alien breed co-opted by the arch-enemy as shock troops. Their murderous battle lust was fast becoming legendary. Or at least, the meat of barrack room horror stories.

'As you have read in your assault orders, the first wave will strike at the primary dome. That's you and your men, Colonel Zhyte.'

Zhyte, an ill-tempered brute on the other side of the table, nodded. He was the field commander of the Seventh Urdeshi Storm-troop, a regiment of nine thousand men. He wore the black and white puzzle-camo of his unit like he meant it. The Urdeshi were the main strength of the Imperial war on Phantine, if only numerically, and Gaunt knew it. Numbering little more than three thousand, his Ghosts were very much light support.

Urdesh, the famous forge world, had fallen to the arch-enemy several years before. Gaunt's men had already fought the products of the captured weapon shops and tank factories on Hagia. The Urdeshi regiments, eight of them, were famously good shock troops, and, like the Tanith, were dispossessed. The difference was that the Urdeshi still had a home world to win back.

Even now, the Urdeshi Sixth, Fourth Light and Tenth were engaged upon the liberation of their world. Zhyte's filthy demeanor was probably down to the fact he wished he and his men were all there, instead of here, fighting to free up some stinking vapour mills.

Still, Gaunt wished his men had been given the main assault. He felt in his bones they'd do it better.

'Second wave goes here. The secondary dome. That's your Tanith, Gaunt. The secondary dome houses Cirenholm's vapour mill, but, ironically, that's not your primary objective. It goes against what I said earlier, I know, but we need to secure Cirenholm as a staging position. It's vital. Our real trophy will be Ouranberg, and we don't have a hope of taking that unless we have a base in this hemisphere to operate out of. Cirenholm is the doorway to victory on Phantine, my friends. A stepping stone to triumph.'

Van Voytz pointed his stick towards the smallest dome. 'Third wave takes the tertiary dome. Major Fazalur's Phantine Skyborne will lead that one in, supported by Urdeshi storm-troops.'

Fazalur, next to Gaunt, smiled at last. He was a weathered man with shaven hair. He wore the quilted cream tunic of the local army. Gaunt was aware of the terrible loyalties being stretched in this force-screened room. Zhyte, longing to be in a war elsewhere, a war that actually mattered to him and his men. Daur – and Gaunt himself – wishing the Ghosts weren't going in so underprepared. Fazalur, yearning for his men to have the honour of leading the liberation of his own fething world. But the Phantine Skyborne numbered less than six hundred. No matter how brave or driven, they would have to allow others to win back their high cities for them.

'Any other comments?' asked the lord general.

There was an uneasy pause. Gaunt knew that at least three men around that table ached to unburden themselves and complain.

No one spoke.

'Right,' said the lord general. He waved to his aide. 'Let's collapse the force screen now and bring in some refreshments. I think we should all drink to D-hour.'

THE DRINKS AFTER the briefing had been intended to be convivial, to break the ice between commanders who knew little about one another. But it had been stiff and awkward.

Turning down the lord general's vintage amasec, Gaunt had withdrawn early, walking down the hardwood floor of the bridge deck and up a screwstair onto the drogue's forward observation deck.

He stood on a metal grille suspended by tension hawsers inside an inverted dome of armoured glass. Outside, the endless skies of Phantine boiled and frothed. He looked down. There was no land to see. Only millions of square kilometres of dimpled, stained cloud.

There were fast moving ribbons of pearly sculpture, dotting puffs of yellow fleece, iridescent bars of almost silver gas. Murky darkness seeped up through parts of the cloud, unwholesome twists of smog and venting corruption. Far below, occasional flares of ignited gas blossomed in the dense, repellent cloud.

Phantine had been an industrial world for fifteen centuries, and now it was largely inhospitable to human kind. Unchecked resource mining and rapacious petrochemical overproduction had ruined the surface and created a lethal blanket of air pollution five kilometres deep.

Only the highest places remained. Spire-like mountains, or the uppermost tips of long-dead hives. These spires and tips protruded from the corrosive gas seas and formed remote islands where mankind might just continue the habitation of the world its greed had killed. Places like Cirenholm and Ouranberg.

And the only reason for those precarious habitations was so that mankind could continue to plunder the chemical resources of Phantine.

Sliding under the handrail, Gaunt sat down on the edge of the walkway so that his boots were dangling. Craning out, he could just see back down the vast underbelly of the drogue. The pleated gas sacks. The armoured canvas panels. They glowed ochre in the unhealthy half-sun. He could see one of the huge engine nacelles, its chopping propeller blades taller than a warlord titan.

'They said I'd find you up here, Ibram.'

Gaunt glanced up. Colonel Colm Corbec hunkered down next to him.

'What's the word, Colm?' asked Gaunt, nodding to his second-in-command.

The big, thick-bearded man leaned against the handrail. His bared forearms were like hams and decorated, under the hair, with blue spirals and stars.

'So, what did Lord General Van Voytz have to say?' said Corbec. 'And what's he like?' he added, sitting down next to Gaunt and letting his legs swing off the grille.

'I was just wondering that. It's hard to know, sometimes, what a commander is like. Dravere and Sturm, well, they don't fething count. Bastards, the both of them. But Bulledin and Slaydo… they were both fine men. I always resented the fact Lugo replaced Bulledin on Hagia.'

'Lugo,' growled Corbec. 'Don't get me started on him.'

Gaunt smiled. 'He paid. Macaroth demoted him.'

'The Emperor protects,' grinned Corbec. He plucked a hip flask from his trouser pocket, took a swig, and offered it to Gaunt.

Gaunt shook his head. He'd abstained from alcohol with an almost puritanical conviction since the dark days on Hagia several months before. There, he and his Ghosts had almost paid the price for Lord General Lugo's mistakes. Cornered and frustrated, and tormented by an over-keen sense of responsibility invested in him by his mentors Slaydo and Oktar, Gaunt had come closer to personal failure than at any time in his career. He'd drunk hard, shamefully, and allowed his men to suffer. Only the grace of the Emperor, and perhaps of the beati Saint Sabbat, had saved him. He'd fought back, against the forces of Chaos and his own private daemons, and routed the arch-enemy, driving back their forces just hours before Hagia could be overrun.

Hagia had been spared, Lugo disgraced, and the Ghosts had survived, both as an active unit and as living beings. There was no part of that hard path Gaunt wanted to retrace.

Corbec sighed, took back the flask and sipped again. He missed the old Gaunt, the commander who would kick back and drink the night away with his men as hard as he'd fight for them the next day. Corbec understood Gaunt's caution, and had no wish to see his beloved commander turned back into a raging, drunken malcontent. But he missed the comradely Gaunt. There was a distance between them now.

'So… this Van Voytz?'

'Van Voytz is a good man, I think. I've heard nothing but good reports about him. I like his style of command–'

'I sense there's a "but", Ibram.'

Gaunt nodded. 'He's sending the Urdeshi in for first kill. I don't think their hearts are in it. He should trust me. And you. The Ghosts, I mean.'

'Maybe he's on our side for once.'

'Maybe.'

'Like you said, it's often hard to get the measure of your commander on first sight.'

Gaunt turned to look at Corbec. 'Meaning?'

'Look at us.'

'Look at us, what?'

Corbec shrugged. 'First time I saw you, I thought I'd been saddled with the worst bum-boil of a commander in the Imperium.'

They both snorted with laughter.

'Of course, my planet was dying at the time,' said Corbec as their amusement subsided. 'Then it turned out you were–'

'What?'

'Okay.'

Gaunt toasted Corbec with an imaginary glass. 'Thanks for that underwhelming vote of confidence.'

Corbec stared at Gaunt, all the laughter gone from his eyes. 'You're the best fething commander I've ever seen,' he said.

'Thanks, Colm,' said Gaunt.

'Hey…' said Corbec quietly. 'Look, sir.'

Outside, the sun had come out and the noxious clouds had wafted away from the ports. They looked out and saw the vast shape of the drogue escorting them, a kilometre long dirigible painted silver on the belly and white on the top. It had a ribbed, hardwood frame and extended out at the front in a fluked ram the size of a giant nalwood. They could see the eight motor nacelles along its belly beating the air with their huge props. Beyond it, in the suddenly gleaming light, they could see the next drogue in formation.

Floating islands, armed and armoured, each carrying upwards of four thousand men.

'Feth!' Corbec repeated. 'Pinch me. Are we aboard one of them?'

'We are.'

'I knew it, but it takes seeing it to know it, you know what I mean?'

'Yes.'

Gaunt looked up at Corbec.

'Are we ready, Colm?'

'Not really. I'm not even going to tell you about the ammunition situation. But… well, we're as ready as we can be.'

'Then that's good enough for me.'

DZ OR DEAD
CIRENHOLM, WEST CONTINENTAL REACHES, PHANTINE
212 to 213.771, M41

'There was a lot of shouting, a lot of jostling, a lot of activity at first. After that, everyone just went quiet. We knew what was coming. Then we went in. Down the rope. Gak! Holy gak! That was a ride.'

– Jessi Banda, sniper, Tanith First

One

NIGHT HAD FALLEN three hours before. Moonless, as Tactician Biota had promised. A light easterly. The immense gloom outside was a profound black, broken only, from far below, by the faint foam of polluted cloud bars and lustrous mist.

The lumbering drogues, running dark with blackout shutters closed, blinds drawn and rigging lights off, swung slowly around over a six hundred square kilometre cloud bank designated as the dispersal field. They faced north. They faced Cirenholm. It was twenty-one ten hours Imperial.

* * *

COMMANDER JAGDEA, DRESSED in a bulky green pressure suit, her crimson helmet on the deck at her feet, finished up her final briefing, and clasped hands with each of the Halo Flight personnel in turn. They had been grouped around her in a huddle at the edge of drogue *Nimbus's* secondary flight deck, and now they rose from perches on jerry cans and cannon-shell pallets to take her hand.

The secondary flight deck was brightly lit, and throbbed with noise and activity. Deck crews ran back and forth, releasing anchor lines, uncoupling feeder hoses, and pushing empty munition carriages out of the way. Pressure-powered drivers and ratchets wailed and stuttered as the last few plates and panels were screwed into place. Ordnance teams moved down the chevron of waiting warplanes, arming and blessing the wing-slung munitions. A group of deck servitors followed the tech-magi, collecting up the priming pins, each marked with a tag of yellow vellum, that the armourers left in their wake.

The six Marauder fighter-bombers of Halo Flight were set in a herring-bone pattern down the length of the deck in greasy locking cradles. Three faced port, three faced star-board, all of them raked at a forty-five degree angle from the rear.

The flight crews, half a dozen for each forty tonne beast, ran down the centre line of the deck and climbed into their designated aircraft.

A buzzer sounded, followed by a quick whoop of klaxons. Cycling amber lights in a row down the centre ridge of the bay roof began flashing.

Jagdea scooped up her helmet and retreated to the far end of the deck, behind an angled blast-board.

The main lighting went off abruptly, as the buzzer had warned. Lines of low-power deck lights winked on, casting their feeble glow up through the grille of the floor. Deck crew with light poles moved down the line, flagging signals. Hatches and canopies began to close, techs leapt down and rolled away the lightweight access stairs. The massive thrust-tunnel turbines, four on each ship, began to turn over. A whine rose, shaking the deck.

Jagdea pulled on her vox-earpiece so she could listen in.

'Halo Two, at power.'

'Halo Four, check.'

'Halo Five, at power now.'

'Halo Three, power, aye.'

'Halo Six, at power.'

'Halo Leader, confirming I have power. Twenty seconds. Standby to mark.'

The roar was bone-shaking now. Jagdea could feel every organ in her torso vibrating. She loved that feeling.

'Control, Halo Leader. The word is Evangeline. Deck doors opening.'

'Halo Leader, control. I hear Evangeline. Praise be the Emperor. Flight confirm.'

'Halo Two, the word Evangeline.'

'Halo Five, I hear it.'

'Halo Six, aye, Evangeline.'

'Halo Three, Evangeline.'

'Halo Four, I hear Evangeline.'

'Halo Leader. Go with grace.'

The deck doors opened. Shutters peeled back along both sides of the deck, and hydraulic doors yawned underneath the cradles. The tumultuous inrush of high altitude wind and exterior prop noise drowned the engine roar.

'Control, Halo Leader. Execute.'

'Halo Leader. We have launch execute. Set to release cradles. Count off from three. Three, two–'

There was a lurch, and a series of concussive bangs. The huge warplanes tilted as their cradles tipped and disengaged, sliding them out of the deck space, dropping them like stones. Three dropped out to port, the other three to starboard. The huge drogue barely trembled as it released the weight.

They fell for a second into the blackness and then fired their engines, belching thrust, pulling hard G's as they took lift and climbed away from the airship.

The deck doors began to close. Jagdea took a last, wistful look at the retreating specks of afterburner glow that twinkled out there in the dark, like stars.

Another thirty minutes and it would be her turn.

* * *

CIRENHOLM WAS ABOUT fifty minutes' flying time from the dispersal field at a comfortable cruising speed, but Halo Flight were pushing their tolerances. In a long, vee formation they burned north, gaining altitude in the lightless air.

A little turbulence. The airframes rattled. On Halo Leader, Captain Viltry made a miniscule adjustment and scribed a mark on his thigh pad chart with a wax pencil. There were wind-whorls at this height. Counter-turning cones of cold, super-fast air.

There was frost on his canopy, stained yellow by air pollutants, and his limbs were stiff with altitude shock and air-burn.

He sucked hard on his mask.

To his side and just below, his navigator Gammil was hunched over his station, studying the hololithic charts by the light of a hooded spotlamp.

'Turn two two zero seven,' Gammil voxed.

'Halo Leader, Halo Flight. Turn two two zero seven. Make your height forty-four fifty.'

Viltry's sensors showed the first hard returns of the Cirenholm promontory. Nothing by eye.

'Halo Leader, Halo Flight. Make ready.'

Viltry noted with satisfaction the ten green lights that flashed live on his munition screen. Serrikin, his payload officer, had done his job perfectly.

'Two minutes,' Viltry announced.

Another patch of turbulence. Harder. The cabin shook. The glass on a dial cracked.

'Steady. One minute twenty.'

Viltry kept glancing at the locator. An enemy cloud-fighter now would be disastrous.

'Forty seconds.'

Something blurry crept across the sweeping display. An interceptor? Pray to the God-Emperor it was just a falling ice-cloud, echoing on their sensor patterns.

'Halo Two, Halo Leader. West quadrant. Nine by nine by six.'

'I see it, Halo Two. Just an ice-cloud. Twenty seconds.'

The Marauder bucked again, violently. The bulb in Gammil's spotlamp burst and the cabin below Viltry went dark.

He saw the snowy pleats of the filth clouds below, violet in the night. He made the sign of the aquila. He thumbed back the safety covers on the ten release switches.

'At ten seconds! Ten, nine, eight, seven...'

Halo Flight banked a tad, holding pattern.

'...three, two, one... drop! Drop! Drop!'

Viltry threw the release switches. His Marauder rose with a lurch as it loosed the weight. He nursed it back.

Halo Flight banked away west, turning and reforming for the run back to the drogue.

Behind them, colossal clouds of feathery nickel filaments bloomed out in the air, blinding the already half-blind sensors of Cirenholm.

THE MUSTER-DECK of the *Nimbus*, lit a cold, merciless white, was thronging with Ghosts. They were arranged by squad in rows marked by pew-like benches. It was twenty-one twenty-five hours.

Ibram Gaunt entered the muster hall and walked down the rows, chatting and exchanging pleasantries with the men. He was dressed for the drop in a hip-length, fur collared leather jacket, his cap still on. His bolt pistol was holstered under his left armpit in a buckled rig, and his power sword, the trophy weapon of House Sondar, was webbed across his back. He already wore his drop-harness, the heavy arrestor hook banging against his thigh.

The Tanith seemed ready. They looked fine. No one had the nervous look Gaunt always watched for.

Each Ghost was prepping up, and then turning to let his neighbour in the squad double-check his harness and couplings. They were all buttoned up and beginning to sweat. Lasguns were cinched tight across their chests. Gloves were going on. Each trooper had a balaclava and a rubberised gas-hood ready to pull on, his beret tucked away. Camo-cloaks were rolled like bedding into a tight tube across the backside.

Gaunt saw Obel checking Bragg down.

'How's the arm, Try?' asked Gaunt.

'Good enough to fight with, sir.'

'You can manage that?' Gaunt indicated the autocannon and tripod that Bragg was to carry down the rope. Support weapon troopers and vox-officers would have the hardest time tonight.

'No problem, sir.'

'Good.'

Caill was Bragg's ammo-humper. He had drum magazines strung over both shoulders.

'Keep him fed, Caill.'

'I will, sir.'

On the far side of the chamber, Gaunt saw Scout Sergeant Mkoll closing his final briefing with the Tanith scouts, the regiment's elite troopers. He made his way over, passing Doc Dorden and Surgeon Ana Curth, who were inoculating every trooper in turn with altitude sickness shots – acetazolamide, their systems more than used to it since the Holy Depths of Hagia – together with counter-toxin boosters and an anti air-sickness drug.

Dorden was tossing spent drug vials into a plastic tray. 'You had a shot yet, colonel?' he asked Gaunt, fitting a fresh glass bulb into the metal frame of his pneumatic needle.

Deliberately, Gaunt hadn't. The venerable doctor had visited him in his cabin half an hour earlier to administer the shot, but Gaunt considered it more appropriate for him to be seen taking it in front of the men.

Dorden was just acting out his prearranged part.

Gaunt peeled off his glove and hauled back his sleeve.

Dorden fired the delivery spike into the meat of Gaunt's exposed forearm and then swabbed the blood-welling dot with a twist of gauze. Gaunt made sure he didn't flinch.

'Any shirkers?' he whispered to Dorden as he slid his sleeve back down.

'A few. They'll bayonet anything, but the sight of a needle–'

Gaunt laughed.

'Keep it going. Time's against us.'

Gaunt nodded to Curth as he moved on. Like Dorden, she wouldn't be making the drop. Instead, she'd have the unenviable task of waiting in the *Nimbus's* empty, silent infirmary for the wounded to roll in.

'The Emperor protect you, Colonel-Commissar,' she said.

'Thank you, Ana. Let him guide your work when the time comes.'

Gaunt liked Curth, and not because she was one of the most attractive things in the regiment. She was good. Damn good. Fething good, as Corbec might say.

And she'd left a rewarding life in Vervunhive to tend the Tanith First.

Delayed slightly by goodwill exchanges for troopers like Domor, Derin, Tarnash and the stalwart flame-trooper Brostin, Gaunt finally reached the gathering of scouts.

They stood around Sergeant Mkoll in an impassive circle. Bonin, Mkvenner, Doyl, Caober, Baen, Hwlan, Mkeller, Vahgnar, Leyr and the others. Not necessarily the best fighters in the regiment, but the reason for its reputation. Stealth. Special operations. And, so far, all Tanith-born. No Verghastite recruit had yet displayed enough raw ability to join Mkoll's elite scouts. Only a few, Cuu amongst them, had shown any real potential.

Gaunt stepped in amongst them and they all drew to salute. He waved them down with a smile.

'Stand easy. I'm sure I'm just repeating what Mkoll has told you, but I have a gut feeling this will be down to you. The lord general, and the other regimental commanders, are looking at this like a nut to crack by force. Wrong. I think it's going to take smarts. This is city fighting. Cirenholm may be stuck up on a fething mountain, but it's a city nevertheless. You've got to kill clever. Lead us in. Make the place ours. The lord general refused the idea of giving anyone under command rank the city plans, but I'm breaking that.'

Gaunt handed out tissue-thin copies of the schematics to the scouts.

'Feth knows why he doesn't want you to see this. Probably doesn't want troopers acting with initiative over and above command. Well, I do. Here's the thing. This won't be a fight where command can sit and shout orders. This isn't a battlefield. We're going into a complex structure full of hostiles. I want it closed down and secured in the name of the God-Emperor as fast as possible. That means on-the-hoof guidance. That means scouting and recon. That means decision making on the ground. When we've won the day, burn those maps. Eat them. Wipe your arses with them and flush them away. Tell the lord general, if he asks, you got lucky.'

Gaunt paused. He looked round, took them eye by eye. They returned his look.

'I don't believe in luck. Well… I do, as it goes. But I don't count on it. I believe in tight combat practice and intelligent war. I believe we make our own luck in this heathen galaxy. And I believe that means using you men to the limit. If any of you… I mean, *any* of you… voxes an order or instruction, I'll make sure it's followed. The squad leaders and commanders know that. Rawne, Daur and Corbec know that. What we take tonight, we take the Ghost way. The Tanith way. And you are the fething brains of that way.'

He paused again. 'Any questions?'

The scouts shook their heads.

'Give them hell,' said Gaunt.

The scouts saluted and strode off to join their squads. Gaunt and Mkoll shook hands.

'You're first in,' said Gaunt.

'Seems as if I am.'

'Do this for Tanith.'

'Oh, count on it,' Mkoll said.

ALERT LIGHTS WERE coming on. A buzzer sounded. The Ghosts, squad by squad, rose up and began to file out into the departure bay. A last few shouts and good lucks bounced between drop-teams.

Gaunt saw Trooper Caffran break ranks for a second to kiss the mouth of the Verghastite Tona Criid. She broke the kiss and slapped him away with a laugh. They were heading for separate drop-ships.

He saw Brostin helping Neskon to sit his flamer tanks just right over his back.

He saw Troopers Lillo and Indrimmo leading the Vervunhivers in one last hive war-chant.

He saw Rawne and Feygor marching their detail through the boarding gate.

He saw Kolea and Varl, each at the head of his own squad, exchanging boasts and dares as they filed to their designated ships.

He saw Seena and Arilla, the gun-girls from Verghast, carrying the light support stubber between them.

He saw the snipers: Larkin, Nessa, Banda, Rilke, Merrt… each one marked out amid the slowly moving files by the awkwardly bagged long-lasrifles they carried.

He saw Colm Corbec on the far side of the muster room, clapping his hands above his bearded head and raising up a battle anthem.

He saw Captain Daur, joining in with the singing as he rushed to pull on his balaclava. Daur left his cap on one of the vacant benches.

He saw them all: Lillo, Garond, Vulli, Mkfeyd, Cocoer, Sergeant Theiss, Mkteeg, Dremmond, Sergeant Haller, laughing and singing, Sergeant Bray, Sergeant Ewler, Unkin, Wheln, Guheen, Raess… all of them.

He saw Milo, far away through a sea of faces.

They nodded to each other. That was all that was needed.

He saw Sergeant Burone running back for the gloves he had forgotten.

He saw Trooper Cuu.

The cold, cat eyes.

Ibram Gaunt had always believed that it was a commander's duty to pray for all his men to return safely.

Not Cuu. If Cuu fell at Cirenholm, Gaunt thought, God-Emperor forgive me, I won't mourn.

Gaunt took off his cap and pushed it into his jacket. He turned to follow the retreating files out of the muster bay. Passing the entrance of the Blessing Chapel, he was almost knocked down by the shambling bulk of Agun Soric, the old, valiant Verghast gang boss.

'Sir!'

'As you were, sergeant. Get to your men.'

'I'm sorry, sir. Just taking a last blessing.'

Gaunt smiled down at the short, thick-set man. Soric wore an eye-patch and disdained augmetic work. He had been an ore-smeltery boss on Verghast, and then a scratch squad leader. Soric had courage enough for an entire company of men.

'Turn around,' said Gaunt, and Soric did so smartly.

Gaunt patted down Soric's harness, and made a slight adjustment to the buckles of his webbing.

'Get going,' he said.

'Yes sir,' said Soric, lurching away after the main teams.

'Hold on there,' said a dry, old voice from the Blessing Chapel.

Gaunt turned.

Ayatani Zweil, wizened and white-bearded, hopped out beside him, and put his hands either side of Gaunt's face.

'Not now, father–'

'Hush! Let me look in your eyes, tell you to kill or be killed, and make the sign of the aquila at least.'

Gaunt smiled. The regiment had acquired Ayatani Zweil on Hagia, and he had become their chaplain. He was imhava ayatani, a roving priest dedicated to Saint Sabbat, in whose name and memory this entire crusade was being fought. Gaunt didn't really understand what made the old, white-bearded priest tick, but he valued his company.

'The Emperor watch you, and the beati too,' said Zweil. 'Don't do anything I wouldn't do.'

'Apart from killing, slaughtering, engaging in firefights and generally being a warrior, you mean?'

'Apart from all that, naturally.' Zweil smiled. 'Go and do what you do. And I'll stay here and wait to do what I do. You realise my level of workload depends upon your success or failure?'

'I've never thought of it that way, but thank you for putting it into such perspective.'

'Gaunt?' the old, ragged priest's voice suddenly dipped and became stifled.

'What?'

'Trust Bonin.'

'What?'

'Don't "what" me. The saint herself, the beati, told me… you must trust Bonin.'

'Alright. Thanks.'

The final siren was sounding. Gaunt patted the old priest's arm and hurried away to the departure bay.

THE DEPARTURE BAY was the *Nimbus's* primary flight deck. Down its immense, echoing length lay drop-ships. Sixty drop-ships: heavy, trans-atmospheric shuttles with a large door hatch in each flank. The deck crews were still milling around them. Engines were test-starting. The previous day, each one of the drop-ships had been wearing the colour pattern of the Phantine Skyborne. Now each one was drabbed down with an anti-reflective pitch.

The Ghosts were mounting up.

Fifty drop-troopers were appointed to each transport, two squads of twenty-five per ship. The squads mounted, in reverse order, via the hatch they would eventually exit through. Staging officers held up metal poles with stencilled number plates on the end so that the Ghosts could form up in the right detail, at the right ship, and on the correct side for mounting.

There were still a few minutes to wait for some squads. They sat down on the apron next to their appointed craft, daubing on camo-paint, making a last few equipment checks or just sitting still, their minds far away. The point men from each squad were checking, and in some cases, re-tying the jump-ropes secured above the hatch-doors. The ground crews had already done this perfectly well, but the point men took their responsibilities for the ropes very solemnly. If they and their comrades were going to depend on a knot for their survival, it had better be one they had tied themselves.

It was twenty-one forty hours. By now, on two of the *Nimbus's* sister drogues, the Urdeshi storm-troops would already be aboard their drops.

Gaunt checked his chronometer again as he walked down the deck to his drop-ship. Admiral Ornhoff had just voxed down that the operation was still running precisely to schedule, but there was a report that the cross wind had picked up a little in the last thirty minutes. That would make transit rough and roping out harder, and it would clear away more quickly the sensor-foxing chaff that Halo Flight had spread earlier on.

Gaunt called in Hark, Rawne and Corbec for a final word.

All of them looked ready, though Rawne was eager to get to his flight. Hark was still very unhappy about the disastrous ammunition situation. After rationing out all the size threes held by the regiment, and scouring the Munitorium stores of all the drogues, the Ghosts had a grand total of three clips per trooper. Due to a mis-relayed order, the taskforce Munitoria had stocked with size fives, the type used by both the Urdeshi and the Phantine. There had not been time to send back to Hessenville for extras, and no way of rearming the Tanith with alternative weapons.

'It could kill morale,' said Hark. 'I've heard a lot of grumbling.'

'It may actually focus them,' said Corbec. 'They know that more than ever, they have to make everything count.'

Commissar Hark didn't seem too convinced by the colonel's take, but he had not been with the regiment long enough to fully appreciate Colm Corbec's instinctive wisdom. Hark had been attached to them on Hagia, essentially as the instrument of a command structure bent on bringing Gaunt down. But Hark had redeemed himself, fighting valiantly alongside the Ghosts at Bhavnager and the battle for the Shrinehold. Gaunt had kept him on after that. With Gaunt's leadership role split between command and discipline, it was useful to have a dedicated commissar at his side.

A buzzer began sounding. Some of the men whooped.

'Let's go, gentlemen,' said Gaunt.

IT WAS TWENTY-TWO hundred. The first wave of drop-ships, carrying the mass of the Urdeshi forces, spilled out of their drogues into the high altitude night.

Colonel Zhyte, aboard drop 1A, craned to look out of the thick-glassed port. He could see little except the inky volume of the sky and the occasional flare of thrusters from the drop-ships around him. The drogues were blacked out and invisible. There had been a tense last few moments between final boarding and launch as all lights on the landing deck shut down so that the launch doors could be opened without giving away position. An uneasy twilight, oppressive, ending only with the violent thump of gravity when the drop-ships plunged away.

Zhyte moved forward into the cockpit, past the rows of his troopers sitting in the craft's main body. In the low-level green illumination, their faces looked pale and ill.

In the cockpit, visibility was a little better. The lightless, limitless cold ahead was punctuated by sudden and swift-passing curls of smoky cloud or little darting wisps. Zhyte could see thirty or forty wavering, dull orange glows spread out ahead and below: the engine glares of the drop-ship formation.

The ship rattled and vibrated sporadically, and the pilot and his servitor co-pilot murmured to each other over the vox. That crosswind was picking up, and there was a hint of headwind now too.

'Over the DZ in forty-one minutes,' the pilot told Zhyte. The Urdeshi colonel knew that estimate would creep if the headwind got any stronger. The heavily laden drop-ships would be straining into it.

Zhyte studied the sensor plate, looking at the milky display of formation ships, scared of seeing something else. If an enemy cloud-fighter lucked onto them now, it would be a massacre.

TWENTY-TWO TEN Imperial. The exit doors of the drop-ships had been shut and locked three minutes before. Everything was vibrating with the noise of the massed transporter engines.

In drop-ship 2A, Gaunt took his seat, a fold-down metal bracket at one end of the row of men. Someone was muttering an Imperial prayer. Several of the men were turning over aquila symbols in their shaking hands.

A curt voice spoke over the vox-link. Gaunt couldn't make out what it said over the roar, but he knew what it meant.

There was a gut-flipping lurch as they seemed to fall, and then a slamming wall of gravity that threw them backwards.

They were in flight.

They were en route.

This was it.

COMMANDER JAGDEA PULLED a hard left turn and her two wingmen swooped with her. The three Lightnings of the Imperial Phantine Air Defence banked sharply and swept in alongside the dispersal drogue *Boreas*.

Jagdea had eight three-wing flights in the air now, escorts for the wallowing shoals of drop-ships lumbering and climbing away from the stationary drogues.

Visibility was so bad she'd been flying by instruments alone, but now she could see the twinkling burner flares of

the troop transports, hundreds of them glowing like coals
against the boiling darkness below.

'Control, Umbra Leader,' she said into her vox. 'I see a little
spread in the troop formations. Urge them to correct for the
crosswind.'

'Acknowledged, Umbra Leader.'

Some of the drop-ships had wandered on release, driven by
the gathering turbulence. They were straggling out to the east.

Keep them tight or we'll lose you, she willed.

Every few seconds, she scanned the dome of sky above for
contacts. As far as they knew, Cirenholm had no idea what
was coming its way. But enemy aircraft might blow that
advantage at any moment.

Not while she was airborne, Jagdea decided.

HALO FLIGHT HAD circled around to the west for the return
loop to the drogue hangars, following a wide arc to avoid
crossing the massed, inbound formations of drop-ships.

Captain Viltry adjusted the airspeed of his Marauder. They
were running into toxic smog banks, and nuggets of dirt were
rattling off his hull armour.

There was a brief vox blurt.

'Halo Leader, say again.'

Viltry waited. He felt himself tense up.

'Halo Leader to Halo Flight, say again.'

A few answers came back, all of them confused.

'Halo Leader. Halo Flight, double up your visual checking.'

'Halo Three, Halo Leader. Have you seen Halo Five?'

Viltry paused. He glanced down at Gammil, and his navigator checked the scanner carefully before shaking his head.

Shit. 'Halo Leader, Halo Five. Halo Five. Respond. Suken,
where the hell are you?'

White noise filled Viltry's ears.

'Halo Leader, Halo Four. Can you see Suken from where
you are?'

'Hold on, Halo Leader.' A long pause. 'No sign, Halo
Leader. Nothing on the scope.'

Where the hell had–

'Contact! Contact! Eight eight one and closing!'

The shout came from Halo Two.

Viltry jerked around, searching the darkness, frantic.

There was a flash to his port. He looked round in time to see a little chain of tracer fire sinking away down into the clouds like a flock of birds.

There was another wordless fizzle of static and then an airburst ignited in the sky two hundred metres to Viltry's starboard wing.

Something very bright and fast passed right in front of him.

'Halo Three's gone! Halo Three's gone!' he heard one of his gunners yelling.

'Break, break, break!' he ordered. The world turned upside down and Viltry was pressed back into his grav-seat by the force of the spinning dive. He saw the dying fireball that had been Halo Three streaming away in the headwind in bands of blue flame.

His control console lit up and alarms blared. Viltry realised he was target locked. He cursed and flipped the Marauder over, hearing Gammil squeal in pain as he was thrown headlong out of the navigator seat.

They were tumbling. The altimeter was spinning like a speeded up chronometer. They were dropping fast, almost beyond the point of recovery.

Viltry hauled on the squad and fired the burners, slamming the Marauder back up and out of its evasive plummet. He tore off his breather mask and vomited as the extreme G forces pumped his guts empty.

His pounding ears suddenly became aware of a screaming on the vox-link. Halo Four.

'He's behind me! He's on me! Holy God-Emperor, I can't lose him! I can't–'

A wash of white fire blistered across the clouds behind them.

'Halo Leader to Control! Halo Leader to Control! Enemy raiders in the dispersal field! I say again, enemy raiders in the dispersal field!'

The target lock alarm sang out again.

Halo Leader slammed forward so hard Viltry bit through his own lips. He saw his blood spiralling away and spattering against the canopy as the stricken Marauder went into a lengthways spin.

He could smell burning cabling and a cold, hard stink of high altitude air.

He leaned into the controls and levelled the warcraft out.

One of his engines was on fire. Over the vox, he could hear his aft gunner wailing. He turned to look down at Gammil. The navigator was crawling back to his seat.

'Get up! Get up!' Viltry barked.

'I'm trying.'

Viltry's hands were slick with sweat inside his gloves. He looked up, searching the sky, and saw the lancing shadow right on them.

'For god's sake–' Gammil began, seeing it in the same instant.

White hot cannon shells sliced down through the cabin, mincing the navigator and his station in a welter of steel splinters, blood and smoke. The entire lower fuselage of Halo Leader sheared off, shredding into the freezing night. Viltry saw Serrikin tumbling away in a cloud of debris, dropping into the corrosive darkness far below.

The freezing air howled around him.

He reached for his ejector lever.

The canopy exploded.

Two

ANA CURTH WASHED her hands under the infirmary's chrome faucet for the third time in fifteen minutes and then dusted them with sterilising talc. She was fidgety, restless.

The infirmary hall was a quiet vault, well-lit and ranged with rows of freshly laundered beds.

Curth checked a few drug bottles on the dispensary cart, then sighed and walked down the length of the bay. Her boots rang out cold, empty beats and her red surgical gown billowed out behind her like a lord palatine's cape.

'You'll drive yourself mad,' said Dorden.

The Tanith chief medic was lying serenely on his back on one of the beds, staring at the ceiling. Swathed in green scrubs, he lay on top of the well-made sheets so as not to disturb them.

'Mad?'

'Raving. The waiting quite addles the mind.'

Curth paused at the end of the bed Dorden occupied.

'And this is how you deal with it?'

He tilted up his head and looked down the length of his body at her.

'Yes. I meditate. I consider. I ruminate. I serve the God-Emperor, but I'm damned if I'll waste my life waiting to be of service.'

'You recommend this?'

'Absolutely.'

Curth hesitatingly laid herself out on the bed next to Dorden. She stared at the ceiling, her heels together, her arms by her side.

'This isn't making me much calmer,' she admitted.

'Patience, and you might learn something.'

'Like what?'

'Like… there are five hundred and twenty hexagonal divisions in the pattern of the ceiling.'

Curth sat up.

'What?'

'There are five hundred–'

'Okay, I got that. If counting roof tiles does it for you, I'm happy. Me, I have to pace.'

'Pace away, Ana.'

She walked away down the length of the bay. At the stern door, the regiment's medicae troopers Lesp, Chayker and Foskin were grouped outside the plastic door screen, smoking lho-sticks.

'Can I cadge one?' she asked, joining them.

Lesp raised his eyebrows and offered her one.

She lit up.

'They'll be almost there by now,' Chayker reflected. 'Right at the DZ.'

Lesp looked at his wristwatch. 'Yup. Right about now.'

'Emperor help them,' Curth murmured, drawing on her lho-stick. Now she'd have to wash her hands again.

TWENTY-THREE SIX Imperial. Not a bad delay. The pilot of drop 1A listened to his co-seat for a moment over the headset and then turned to give Zhyte a nod.

'Three minutes.'

The Urdeshi commander could still see nothing out of the front ports except vague cloud banks and the light-fizz of other drop-ships surging their engines. The headwind was climbing.

But Zhyte trusted his flight crew.

He moved back into the carrier hold and threw the switch that lit the amber light over the hatch. Make ready.

The men got to their feet in the blue gloom, nursing out the slack on their arrestor hook cords and pulling on their gas-hoods. Zhyte took his own gas-hood out of its pouch, shook it out, and fitted it over his head, adjusting it so the plastic eyeslits sat squarely and the cap didn't foul his vox-set. He squeezed shut the popper studs that anchored its skirts to his shoulders and zipped the seal.

Now he was more blind than ever, shrouded in a treated canvas cone that stifled him and amplified the sounds of his own breathing.

'Count off,' he announced into his vox.

The men replied quickly and efficiently by squad order, announcing their number and confirming that their hoods were in place. Zhyte waited until the last few had fastened up the seals.

'Hatches to release.'

'Release, aye!' the point men crackled back over the link.

There was a judder and a lurch as the side hatches were slid open and the craft's trim altered. Air temperature in the carrier bay dropped sharply, and the light took on an ochre tinge.

'Ready the ropes! Ninety seconds!'

The point men were silhouettes against the gloomy yellow squares of the open hatches, their battledress tugged by the slipstream.

Zhyte took out his bolt pistol, held it up clumsily in front of his face plate to check it, and put it back in his holster.

Almost there.

THE HARD SNAP of the inflator jerked Captain Viltry back into consciousness. His head swam, and his body felt curiously weightless. He had no idea where he was.

He tried to remember. He tried to work out what the hell he was doing. It was cold and everything was pitch dark. Drunkenly, his neck sore, he looked up and saw the faint shape of the inflator's spherical sac, from which he hung.

He'd ejected. Now he remembered. God-Emperor, something had taken his bird apart… and his wing men too. He looked around hoping to catch a glimpse of another aircraft. But there was just the high altitude void, the filmy cloud, the curling darkness.

He checked his altimeter, the one sewn into the cuff of his flight suit. He was a good two thousand metres below operational altitude, almost at the envelope of the toxic atmospheric layer. His inflator must have fired automatically, the pressure switch triggered by his fall.

The safety harness was biting into his armpits and chest. He tried to ease it, and realised he was injured. His shoulder was cut, and some of the harness straps were severed. He was lucky to still be wearing the rig.

Parachutes were pointless on Phantine. There was nowhere to drop to except corrosive death in the low altitude depths, the Scald, as it was known. Flyers wore bailing rigs that inflated globular blimps from gas bottles that would, unpunctured, keep them drifting above the lethal atmospheric levels of the Scald until rescue.

Viltry was an experienced flyer, but he didn't need that experience to tell him the coriolis winds, savage at this height, had already carried him far away from the flight paths. He tried to read the gauge on his air tanks, but he couldn't make the dial out.

Windwaste, he thought. That was him. Windwaste, the worst fate any combat pilot on Phantine could suffer. Drifting away, alive, beyond the possibility of recovery. Flyer lore said that men caught in that doom used their small arms to puncture their inflators so that they could have a quick death in the Scald's poison acid-gases below.

But there was still a chance he'd get picked up. All he had to do was activate his distress beacon.

A toggle pull would do it.

Viltry hesitated. That simple toggle pull might bring him rescue, but it would also be heard by the enemy at Cirenholm.

They'd know that a flyer was in distress. And therefore that at least one Imperial aircraft was up tonight.

He didn't dare. Ornoff had told the pilot fold that surprise was the key to storming Cirenholm. Short range ship-to-ship vox chatter was safe, but powerful, ranged transmissions like the amplified vox-blink of his distress beacon might ruin that surprise. Alert the enemy. Kill thousands of Imperial Guardsmen.

Viltry drifted through the cold air desert, through the dark. Ice was forming on the inside of his goggles.

He had to stay silent. Even though that meant he would be windwaste.

'UMBRA LEADER TO flight, pickle off your tanks,' Jagdea said into her mask.

Umbra flight was threading the rear echelons of the troop ship formations. They were almost over the DZ now. The raised bulk of Cirenholm was a loud blur on her instruments.

The three Lightnings dumped their empty fuel tanks and rose above the drop-ship flocks. They were running on internal tanks now, which meant they had just another sixteen minutes of range left... less if they were called to burn hard into combat.

Jagdea was jumpy. Halo Flight should have made the return run by now, but there had been no sighting of the overdue Marauder flight.

Commander Bree Jagdea had fifteen thousand hours of combat flight experience. She was one of the best pilots ever to graduate from the Hessenville Combat School. She had instinctive combat smarts that no measure of training could ever teach. Those instincts took over now.

'Umbra Leader to Umbra Flight. Let's nose ahead for one last burn. Chase the Urdeshi formations. I've got a sick feeling there's opposition aloft tonight.'

'Understood, Umbra Leader.'

The trio of Imperial fighters swung west. Hundreds of lives were about to be lost. But, running on instinct, Jagdea had just saved thousands more.

* * *

'FINAL PREP,' SAID Sergeant Kolea, walking down the carrier hold of drop 2F at the trailing edge of the Tanith formation.

'Three minutes to the DZ. I want hoods in place and hooks ready in thirty. Door duty to active. Point men, stand by.'

The amber rune had not yet come on. Kolea strapped on his gas-hood, and went down the line checking his Ghosts, one by one.

THE SIDE HATCH of drop 2D was already open. Trooper Garond shivered in the slip-stream blast, and made ready with the rope as Sergeant Obel gave the signal. Outside, he could see cloud whipping past and several drop-ships lying abeam, men crouched in their open hatches, ready and prepped.

ABOARD DROP 2B, Colm Corbec fitted his gas-hood and ordered the hatches open. The squads took their positions, on their feet. Mkoll was at the head of the second squad, ready to lead the scout fireteam in.

Corbec nodded to him and uttered a final prayer.

IN DROP 2X, Sergeant Ewler looked over at Sergeant Adare. The two squad leaders shook hands.

'See you on the far side,' said Adare.

VILTRY WOKE AGAIN and found his face and shoulder were beginning to burn with the cold. He didn't want to die like this. Not alone, discarded, like a wind-blown seed. His numb fingers closed around the toggle.

He snatched his hand away and cursed his selfishness.

Unless…

If dispersal command-control heard his distress beacon, they'd know that something had happened to Halo Flight. They'd realise there were hunters loose.

He'd be warning them.

Filled with a sense of duty, Viltry pulled the toggle. It came away in his hand.

Shrapnel had ripped away the beacon's trigger switch.

SUDDENLY, THERE WAS a creamy glow below them. Available light was reflecting off the primary dome of Cirenholm in frosty midnight shine. The drop-ship's braking jets wailed so loud Zhyte could hear them through his hood. They were stationary, as stationary as the headwind allowed, right over the drop zone. Zhyte prayed they were low enough.

The green rune lit up.

'Deploy!' Zhyte growled.

There was a bright flash outside. Then another.

Shener, Zhyte's starboard point man, looked out and saw the drop-ship beside them splinter and fall apart, cascading luminous debris down into the darkness.

'Interceptors!' he screamed into his link.

Another Urdeshi drop-ship suddenly became visible in the night as it caught fire and burned down like a comet. A moment later, Cirenholm's defences woke up and lit the air with a ferocious cross-stitching of tracer fire.

Shells whacked into drop 1A's fuselage next to Shener. He had been coiling out the rope. A terrible, exposed cold filled his legs and lower torso and he looked down to see that there was an extraordinarily large, bloody hole in his gut.

Shener toppled out of the hatch wordlessly and fell away into the gloom below.

Zhyte reached the hatchway, battered by the wind. Shener was gone, and the two men first up the squad had been exploded across the bay. There were punctures in the hull.

Outside, a storm of enemy fire bloomed up at them.

Zhyte clipped his arrestor hook to the rope. He should have been last man out, but his point was gone and the troopers were milling, disorientated.

'Go!' yelled Zhyte. 'Go! Go! Go!'

He leapt into space.

DROP 1C ROCKED as its neighbour exploded. Whinnying scraps of outflung debris punched through the drop's hull. Sergeant Gwill and three other troopers were killed instantly. Corporal Gader, half-blinded in his hood, suddenly realised he was in charge.

The green rune was on.

He ordered the men out.

Two thirds of the squads had exited when cannon shells ripped drop 1C open. Gader was thrown out of the hatch.

He gestured tragically with his arrestor hook as he fell. But there was no rope.

Gader dropped like a stone, right down the face of Cirenholm's primary dome, bouncing once off an aerial strut.

DROP 1K MISJUDGED the headwind and came in too low, mashing against the side of the dome in a seething blister of fire.

Just behind it, drop 1N braked backwards in a flurry of jets and then trembled as a rain of cannon shells peeled off its belly, spilling men out into the darkness.

Drop 1M faltered, and tried to gain height. Its men were already deploying out of the hatches. Sliding down the ropes, they discovered that the drop was not only too high, it was also fifty metres short of the DZ. Each man in turn came off the end of the dangling rope and fell away into the void.

The pilot of drop 1D saw the enemy cloud-fighter with perfect clarity as it powered in, weapons flickering. He had no room to either pull up or bank. His troops were already on the ropes and heading down. Drop 1D exploded under the withering fire of the passing interceptor. Men were still hooked to the ropes as they snapped and fell away from the detonation.

'TARGETS! TARGETS! TARGETS!' Jagdea urged as she swept down across the Urdeshi troop ships. Drops were exploding all around, picked off by the Phantom interceptors or hit by Cirenholm's defence batteries.

The night had lit up. It was flickering hell here, beneath the vast dome of Cirenholm's primary hab.

Jagdea smoked in wide, avoiding a drop that blew apart in the air. She had target lock on a spinning cloud-fighter and the guns squealed as she let rip.

It was turning so hard it evaded her fire, though her marching tracers pummelled their way up the curve of the dome.

Jagdea inverted and, pulling two Gees, flipped round onto the cloud-fighter's tail. It was heading out to pick off more of the vulnerable troop ships in the van of the flock.

She jinked, lined it up, and hit the afterburner so that her streams of gunfire would rake its length as she swept past it.

The enemy fighter became a fireball with wings, that arced away down into the poisonous Scald below.

Jagdea banked around. Her wingmen were shouting in her headset.

Halo Two had just splashed an enemy interceptor, dogging it turn for turn and chewing off its tail with sustained cannon fire. The stricken fighter tried to end its death dive by ramming a drop, but it missed and trailed fire away into the clouds.

Jagdea hung on her wingtip, and dropped, hunting visually and instrumentally for targets. She powered down through the drop-ship fleet, her target finder pinging ever more rapidly as she bottomed out and swung in on the tail of a cloud-fighter that was flaring around to fire up at the bellies of the troop ships.

Jagdea killed it with a fierce burst of fire.

She yawed to port, out-running the tail of the troop ship dispersal before banking back to come in again beneath it. Her Lightning screwed over and her instruments wailed as cannon shots battered into her flank.

Red runes on all systems. She'd been killed.

She peddled out, pulled back, and gave the dead craft all the lift its wingspan would permit. She was now gliding towards the bulk of Cirenholm, about to stall out.

Jagdea squeezed the weapon toggles on her yoke and emptied her magazines into the dome, for what good it would do.

Her engines blew, and fire streamed along one wing.

She ejected.

HELL WAS REACHING up to them with thousands of fingers made of fire. The night was a strobing miasma of darkness and flashes. The wind was screaming, a dull roar through the gas-hoods. Every few seconds, there was a shell burst so bright the descending Urdeshi could see forever: the great domed face of Cirenholm; the swarming drop-ships; the dangling strings of men, hanging like fruit-heavy vines from the tightly packed ships.

Zhyte came off the rope end hard and slammed sideways into a balustrade. It ran around the lip of the dome's lowest outer promenade, and Zhyte realised that a few metres to the left and he would have missed the city structure entirely.

He'd cracked a rib on landing. He winced a few paces forward and troopers thumped and rolled around him. The vox-lines were frenetic with distorted chatter.

He tried to marshal his men and group them forward, but he'd never known confusion like it. Bitter, hard fire rained down from an elevated walkway twenty metres west, and dozens of his men were already sprawled and twisted on what had once been a regal, upper class outer walk with stratospheric views.

'Singis!' Zhyte yelled into his vox. 'Move them in! Move them in!'

Singis, his young, cadet-school trained subaltern, ran past, trying to get the men up. Zhyte saw a two-man stub-team attempting to erect their weapon, hampered by the men who were dropping all around them and sometimes on top of them. Indeed, there were so many men coming down now that the immediate DZ was filling up. Penned in by the city wall, the edge of the balustrade and the defending gunfire, they were rapidly filling up every precious metre of the drop area. Deployed troopers were being knocked down by the wave behind them. One man was pushed out over the balustrade, and was only just clawed back by his desperate comrades.

Zhyte could feel the powerful downwash of the drop-ships as they came in overhead, jostling for position.

The Urdeshi commander could see for about a kilometre along the length of the curving promenade. All the way along, drop-ships were clustering and roping out the strings of his puzzle-camoed troops. He saw a firefight around a hatchway fifty metres away as his fifth platoon tried to storm entry. He saw the flash of four grenades. He saw a drop-ship pummelled by tube-shot rockets, saw it burn as it tilted sideways, tearing through the drop-ropes of two other ships, cascading men to their deaths. As he watched, it exploded internally and fell, glancing off the promenade with enough force to shake the deck under his feet. A fireball now, it pitched sideways and fell off the city shelf into the abyss.

A trooper to Zhyte's left had lost his gas-hood in the descent. He was choking and frothing, yellow blisters breaking the skin around his lips and eyes.

Zhyte ran forward, ignoring the las-rounds exploding around him.

He got into cover behind a low wall with four of his squad's troopers.

'We have to silence that position!' he rasped, indicating the elevated walkway with a gloved hand. The man immediately right of him was suddenly hit twice and went tumbling back. A second defence position had opened up, raking 50-cal auto-cannon fire into the unprotected throng of the landing troops.

They were dying. Dying so fast, Zhyte couldn't believe what he was seeing. They were packed in like cattle, without cover, with nowhere to move to.

With a curse that came from somewhere deep in his guts, Zhyte ran into the open towards the walkway. Tracer fire stippled the ground at his feet. He hurled a grenade and the back blast knocked him down.

Two men grabbed him and dragged him into cover. The walkway was on fire and sagging. Urdeshi troops poured forward from the dense, corralled mob at the DZ.

'You're a bloody maniac,' a trooper told him. Zhyte never did find out who it was.

'We're inside!' Singis voxed.

'Move up, by squad pairs!' Zhyte ordered. 'Go!'

IBRAM GAUNT WAS the first man out, the first onto the ropes. The secondary dome of Cirenholm lay below. A huge fog of light and fire throbbed in the night sky behind the silhouetted curve of the more massive primary dome. The Urdeshi assault had been met with huge force.

Gaunt hit the DZ clean, and ran clear of the rope end as his men came down. Las-fire was beginning to spit down at them from gun positions higher up the dome slope. The Tanith were landing, as per instructions, on a wide balcony that ran entirely around the widest part of the dome's waist. Over the vox came a curt report announcing that both Corbec and Mkoll's squads were on the balcony too, about a hundred metres away.

Troopers Caober and Wersun were right behind Gaunt. He waved them wide to the right, to set up covering fire. He could see Sergeant Burone's drop-ship lining up ahead, hatches open as it came in over the balcony. Through the stiff, treated canvas of his hood, he could feel the air resonate with its whining thrusters.

'Hot contact!' the message buzzed over the vox. It was Sergeant Varl, somewhere behind him. A lattice of laser fire lit up the night maybe two hundred metres east, flickering along the balcony.

Gaunt saw figures ahead of him, armed men rushing out onto the balcony shelf. They were shadows, but he knew they weren't his own.

His bolt pistol barked.

'Move up!' he yelled. 'Engage!'

VARL'S SQUAD HAD come down into the middle of a firefight. Kolea's unit was dropping to their right, and Obel's somewhere behind.

Varl scurried forward, popping off random shots with his rifle. The enemy was secured around one of the major hatchways leading off the balcony walk into the dome. They were in behind flakboard and sandbags.

The Tanith edged forward, using ornamental planters and windscreens as cover, pumping fire at the entrance. Varl saw Ifvan and Jajjo scrambling up onto a walkway and running to get good shooting positions.

He ducked in behind a potted fern that had long since been eaten away by acid rain, and fired a sustained burst at a section of flakboard. Five other troopers, also in cover, joined him and the emphatic fire they laid up between them smashed the blast fence down. Bodies fell behind it.

'A flamer! I need a flamer!' Varl voxed. 'Where the feth is Brostin?'

HALF A KILOMETRE east of Gaunt, Rawne's assault units were dropping into the worst resistance offered by the secondary dome. A dozen men were shot off the ropes before they'd even reached the deck. Drop 2P had its belly shot out by ground fire and limped away, dragging streamers of men behind it.

There were enemy forces out on the balcony itself, firing up at the troop ships as they came over. And there were at least four multi-barrel autocannon nests firing out of windows further up the dome's surface.

Rawne paused in the hatchway of his ship.

'Sir?' Feygor asked, behind him.

'No fething way are we going down into that,' Rawne said sharply. Vertical las-fire hissed past the hatch.

'Charges! Give me charges!' Rawne said, turning back inside.

Feygor moved down the waiting squad with an open musette bag, getting every man to toss in one of his tube charges. When it was satisfyingly full, it was passed back up the line to Rawne at the door.

'Pilot to squad leader! Why aren't you going out? We can't hold this station for ever!'

'Feth you can! Do it!' Rawne growled back into the vox.

'I've got ships backing up behind him, and we're sitting ducks!' the voice on the vox complained.

'My heart bleeds,' replied Rawne, stripping the det-tape off one last charge, dropping it into the bag and tossing it out. 'Don't make me come up front and make your heart bleed too, you craven sack of crap.'

The satchel landed right in the midst of the ground troopers firing up from the balcony. Rawne could see it clearly. When it went off, it spewed out a doughnut shaped fireball that ripped fifty metres in every direction.

Rawne locked his arrestor hook to the rope.

'Now we go,' he said.

DROP 2K HAD come in too eagerly behind the troop ships halted by Rawne's delay. The pilot realised the flotilla ahead had cut to hover mode too late, and had to yaw hard, breaking out of line. In the back of the drop, the waiting lines of Ghosts were sent sprawling sideways. Trooper Nehn, crouching at the open hatch as point man, was thrown out, but managed to hold on to the rope. He was slammed back hard against the hull like a pendulum but maintained his frantic grip though the breath had been smashed out of him.

2 K's pilot tried to avoid fouling the other ships and turned wide. Angry and confused, the men in the drop bay had only just regained their feet when the ship threw them over again.

They had dropped down into range of the dome defence, and taken two missiles in the flank.

The drop was ablaze. Domor, the commanding officer, yelled at the men to stay calm. Bonin and Milo were trying to drag Nehn back inside.

'We have to get down!' someone yelled.

'There's nowhere to put down!' Domor replied.

'We've fething well overshot!' bawled Haller, the commander of 2K's other squad.

Domor grabbed a leather roof strap and hung on, his heavy musette bag, cinched lasgun and arrestor hook banging and flapping against his body as the drop wallowed and pitched. Trooper Guthrie was on the deck, blood leaking down inside his hood from a scalp wound he'd received head-butting a seat restraint on the first wild jolt.

'Medic! Here!' Domor cried, and then clambered over the backs of several sprawled men to reach the port hatch. Milo and Bonin had just succeeded in dragging Nehn back inside.

Domor looked out. Their drop, spewing sheets of flame from somewhere near the ventral line, was limping slowly forward up over the patched, greasy roof plates of the secondary dome itself. They were already a good three hundred metres past the DZ. Looking back, Domor saw the waves of Tanith ships coming in, roping out into a spasming fuzz of light. Domor's vox-set was awash with radio traffic from the assaulting forces. He recognised voices, coded deployments, call-signs. But it all sounded like it was coming from men who were fading away into a distance, like a party he was leaving too soon. The curve of the dome was chopping the transmissions.

They had missed. They'd had their chance and they'd fethed it. There was no going back, no reversing back through the deploying lines. They were overshooting up and across the target city-dome itself.

Under such circumstances, standing orders applied and they were clear: abort and pull out along 1:03:04 magnetic, and return to the base drogue. That's it, boys. Nice try, but no thanks. Go home and better luck next time.

But abort wasn't an option. Domor craned out. They'd clearly damaged a fuel-line, and that was on fire. And from the sway of the old, heavy drop, the pilot had lost a good proportion of his attitude control.

They'd never make it back to the drogue. Not in a million years.

Even if there was a chance, and Domor was fething sure there wasn't, a pull-out at this height and crawl rate would glide them right over the dome's lip-guns as a nice, slow, fat, fire-marked target.

They were dead.

VARL DUCKED. CHUNKS of stone and scabs of plasteel spattered from the archway above his head. Down the hall, someone was the proud owner of a heavy autocannon.

They'd broken the rim defence and forced access into one of the main hatches leading off the secondary dome's balcony. His squad was the first one inside, though from the sound of the vox-traffic, Rawne was making headway further around the dome edge.

The hatch they'd fought their way in through gave onto a wide lobby dressed with polished ashlar and set with angular, cosmetic pillars. The floor was littered with brick chips and dust, and the bodies of the enemy dead.

Varl knew he was facing the troops of the notorious Blood Pact. He'd paid special attention in the briefings. The Blood Pact weren't enflamed zealots. They were professional military, soldiers sworn to the badges of Chaos. He could tell from the tight, well-orchestrated resistance alone that he was dealing with trained warriors.

They were holding the lobby with textbook authority: light support weapons blocking the main throughway, peppering the hatch opening with measured, tight bursts.

Varl ran to the next pillar, and watched in dismay as gunfire chewed away a good chunk of its stone facing.

Stone splinters sprayed from the damage. He pulled himself in.

'Brostin!' he voxed. The flamer had got them through the opening. If they could move Brostin further forward into the lobby's throat, they might take the next mark.

Las-fire and solid rounds spat past him. Varl could see Brostin in cover three pillars away.

Varl peered out, and took a hit to his shoulder that toppled him back. He writhed back into cover, patting out the smouldering hole in his uniform. His augmetic shoulder, heavy and metallic, had absorbed the shot.

'Nine, six!'

'Six, nine!' Kolea voxed back.

'Where are you, nine?' Damn these gas-hoods! Varl couldn't see a fething thing.

'Behind you, on the other side,' Kolea returned. Crouching around, Varl could see the big Verghastite, ducked down behind a pillar on the right, with two other men from his squad.

Cannonfire pounded down the hallway, filling the air with dust and flying chips. Despite his hood, Varl could hear the clinking rain of spent cases the enemy gun was spilling out onto the marble deck. Varl slid round onto his knees and started to prep a tube charge.

There was a sudden increase in resistance fire, and the flooring between the pillar rows was speckled with the ugly mini-craters of heavy fire. Varl looked up and saw, to his disbelief, that Kolea had successfully run forward into the maw of the enemy, and was now two pillars ahead of him on the other side. Kolea stood with his back to the chipped, punished pillar and lobbed a grenade out over his shoulder.

The blast welled flame down towards them. Varl sprang up and ran through the smoke, dropping down behind a pillar ahead of Kolea. Seeing him, Kolea swung out and drew level, then moved one ahead.

It was like some stupid fething competition, like the brainless games of devil-dare Varl had played as a teenager. There was no skill in this. No tactics, no battle-smarts. It was just sheer balls. Running into gunfire, damning the bullets, shaming the devil and taunting him. They were edging ahead simply by dint of bravado, simply through luck that neither of them had been hit.

Kolea looked back at Varl.

Devil-dare. Bullets whickered all around.

Varl ran out, sidestepped a tight burst and then pushed his already thread-thin luck further in order to dive behind the

next pillar up. He could feel it vibrate against his back as cannonfire punched into the far side.

Devil-dare. Devil-fething-dare. But enough was enough.
The Emperor, may he be ever vigilant, had smiled on them
this far, but that was it. Another step would be suicide. Varl
knew luck was a soldier's friend. It'd stick by you, but it was
fickle, and it hated being asked for favours.

'Nine, six. Stay in cover. I think I–'

Autocannon shots barked out and chewed the wall. Kolea
had just made a mad dash down the wall-side of the pillars
on his half of the lobby and slid in safe behind a pillar ten
metres further forward.

'Nine!'

'Six?'

'You're a mad fething fool!'

'It's working, isn't it?'

'But it shouldn't be working and it won't keep working if
we do it again!'

'Cold feet, Tanith?'

'Feth you, Kolea!'

Of all the Ghosts, Varl and Kolea epitomised the best
aspects of the Tanith/Verghastite rivalry. There were a good
few from both backgrounds who manifested the uglier
resentments, prejudices or simple racial enmities that made
up the worst. Sergeant Varl and Sergeant Kolea had been
friends from an early stage, but their friendship was catalysed
in rivalry. Each was a notable soldier, popular with the men.
Each enjoyed a good relationship with Gaunt. And each was
in charge of a section that was considered by all to be fine,
solid and second-string.

There was nothing formal about the distinction. It was just
a given that a handful of platoons formed the regimental
elite: Mkoll's scouts, Rawne's merciless band, Corbec's dedicated unit, Bray's tightly-drilled, tightly-disciplined squad
and the determined, courageous mob schooled by Soric.
They were the best, the 'front five' as they were often called.
Kolea and Varl both yearned to elevate their own squads into
that illustrious upper echelon. It was all fine and dandy to be
regarded as part of the solid, dependable backbone. But it
wasn't enough for either of them.

In combat, that competition came out. It didn't help that both had missed the epic battle for the Shrinehold on Hagia. They had formed the rearguard then, and done a fine job, but they had not been there to share the glory of the big fight. To prove their worth.

And so now it came down to devil-dare. Stupid, dumb-ass devil-dare games, urging fate and luck and all the other monsters of the cosmic firmament to make one a hero-winner and the other a loser-corpse.

Varl had come up from the ranks. He had fought for his stripes, and not just been given them due to his record as a scratch-company hero like Kolea.

But enough was enough.

'No more, nine! No more, you hear?'

'You're breaking up on me, six,' Kolea voxed back.

'We need to get a flamer up, Kolea–'

'Do what you like... I'm going ahead–'

'Nine!'

Varl looked out from cover, and saw a fountain spray of las-fire and tracers vomit down the hallway. He saw Kolea running forward, somehow, impossibly, alive in the midst of it. He saw thousands of individual impacts as soot and dust and mortar was smashed out of the bullet-holes in the floor, the roof and the walls.

Kolea ran on. He'd lost his wife at Vervunhive and, he had believed, his children too. Some cruel twitch of fate had allowed them to survive and to end up in the care of the female trooper Tona Criid and her devoted Tanith partner Caffran.

Cruel wasn't the word. It was too cruel. It was beyond cruel. He'd only discovered the fact on Hagia, and pain had sealed his mouth. Those kids – Dalin and Yoncy – had been through so much, believing their parents lost and gaining fine new ones in the form of Criid and Caffran, Kolea had decided never to disturb their world again.

He had avoided them. He had stayed away. No one had ever found out the truth, except for Surgeon Curth, in whom he had confided.

It was better that way. It freed him.

Freed him to fight and die and serve the Emperor.

Kolea ran on into a rain of fire. He was a big man who had served a long time in the mines of Verghast. Grim, largely humourless, powerful. He should have formed a huge target, but somehow the enemy fire missed him. Shots ripped the air around him, cast sparks from the pillars, blew stone chips from the floor.

He lived.

He thought about diving for cover, but he was so nearly there it didn't seem to matter.

Kolea came on the enemy position from the side, leapt over the horseshoe of sandbags and shot the two cannon gunners down.

A third lunged at him from the left and Kolea's bayonet tip punched through his forehead with a crack.

These brutes were Blood Pact. They wore old but well maintained suits of armour-plated canvas dyed a dark red, drapes of ammo-belts and munition pouches secured on black nylon webbing, and crimson steel bowl helmets with sneering, hook-nosed blast-visors. Chaos insignia glinted on their sleeves and chests.

More Blood Pact troops rushed out at Kolea, assuming they had been stormed by force. Their red-tunicked forms twisted away as Varl ran forward, firing his lasgun on auto, yelling the names of his sisters, his father, his mother and his homestead farm.

Raflon, Nour and Brostin were right behind him. Raflon made a stupendously good shot that burst the skull of a Blood Pact trooper who was turning out of cover from behind a doorpost.

Then Brostin washed the hallway beyond with a bright belch of promethium flame. Something exploded. Two Blood Pact troopers staggered into the main hall, their red uniforms ablaze, the armour plating falling out of the burning canvas of their sleeves.

Wordlessly, Varl and Kolea heaved the enemy autocannon around on its tripod and blitzed down into the corridor beyond: Varl firing, his hands clamped to the yoke, Kolea feeding the belts from the use-bruised panniers.

The big old cannon had huge power. Varl knew that. A minute before he'd been running into it.

Heavy support fire blasted from their left. Bragg was alongside them now, firing his autocannon from the hip, his feeder Caill fighting to keep up the supply of fresh drum mags.

'On! In!' Kolea barked. Nour and Bragg, Caill, Raflon, Hwlan, Brostin and Brehenden, Vril and Mkvan, a dozen more, ran past them into the inner hall, covering and firing.

Varl threw the emptied cannon aside and looked at Kolea.

'You're mad, Gol.'

'Mad? War's mad. We broke them, didn't we?'

'You broke them. You're mad. Crazy. Insane.'

'Whatever.'

They picked up their lasguns and moved on after the point men. 'When I tell Gaunt what you did–' Varl began.

'Don't. Please, don't.'

Kolea looked round, and Varl could see his eyes, dark and serious behind the misted plates of his gas-hood.

'Just don't.'

'WE ROPE OUT. Now.' said Domor. Drop 2K lurched again as cannon fire struck it.

'Rope out?' Sergeant Haller returned, horrified.

'Just shut up and do it or we're dead.'

'Onto the dome?'

'Yes, onto the dome!'

'But we've missed the DZ! We should–'

'Should what?' snapped Domor, turning to stare at Haller. 'Abort? Take your chances with that if you like, Verghast. I don't think so–'

'Air speed's dropping!' Milo cut in.

'Thrusters are failing. I can't get lift!' the pilot called back from the cockpit.

'Go!' said Domor. Haller was at one hatch, Bonin and Nehn at the other. The burning drop was wallowing over the dome, in darkness now, the curve of the dome eclipsing the flare of the main fight. They couldn't see a thing. They might as well be over the edge of the dome for all they could tell. The night was awash of black with no solid edges.

'We have to–' Domor said.

* * *

IT SEEMED TO Commander Bree Jagdea that the fight was happening a long way away, on another planet. Flares and flashes lit up the night sky to her right, but they were a long, long way away.

She lay on the curved metal surface of one of Cirenholm's habitat domes, the secondary one she guessed. It was cold and the crossing night wind bit deep. Her arm and several ribs were boken from the ejected landing. Her flight suit was torn.

Her blimp-chute had barely had time to deploy as she had fired up out of the seat of her dead fighter. Smack, the dome had come up to meet her hard.

And here, she presumed, she would stay until the midnight frosts made her a brittle part of the dome roof decoration.

When Jagdea saw the drop-ship, it was already on fire and coming in low over the dome towards her, spitting debris and flame, crawling crippled from the main fight.

She saw the hatches were open, saw figures in the hatches. Men about to rope out.

They were going long. They were going long, off the edge of the dome, into the Scald.

She didn't think. She pulled the toggle on the canister in her chute webbing and popped bright incandescent fire across the dome roof around her.

'Here!' she screamed, flailing her one good arm, like someone in need of rescue. 'Here!'

In truth, she was the one doing the rescuing.

'FETH! WE JUST got a DZ!' Bonin yelped.

'What?' Haller said, pulling at his hood to get a clear view.

'There, sergeant!' Bonin pointed.

'Steer us to port! To port!' Domor voxed the pilot.

Drop 2K yawed left, up and over the side of the secondary dome, a dark hemisphere below it. There was a splash of almost fluorescent light on the surface of the dome, a fizzle of flare just now beginning to sputter away.

The men roped out. Milo led the squad out of the port, his hook whizzing down the cable until he slammed into the curving roof and tumbled off. Domor was behind him, then Bonin, then Ezlan.

On the starboard side, Haller came out, followed by Vadim, Reggo and Nirriam.

The men thumped down onto the roof, scrabbling for handholds, desperate not to slide off into the night. Twenty men down, twenty-five. Thirty. Thirty-five.

The drop's engines failed. Clinging to the curve of the roofing panels on his belly, Domor heard the pilot scream. He looked back. The drop-ship simply fell out of the air and smashed into the roof, crushing a half-dozen of the roping men under it.

Then it began to slide.

Three

AN AWFUL CREAKING, screeching sound filled the air, metal on metal. There were still at least twenty men attached to the ropes, their arrestor hook locks biting the loose cables because of the sudden slackening. The men were tangled, and being dragged. Domor, Nehn and Milo struggled up and watched the blazing drop slowly sliding and shrieking away down the curve of the dome, hauling Guardsmen after it.

The pilot was still screaming.

'Cut the ropes! Cut the fething ropes!' Domor yelled.

Bonin cut the rope with his Tanith blade and fell free. He rolled, and managed to seize hold of an icy roof strut. Eight of Haller's men sawed their way clear of the snarling ropes too. Ezlan lost his knife, but managed to writhe himself out of his webbing.

The moment his blade severed it, the drop rope came whipping out of Dremmond's arrestor hook because it was under too much tension. The blow left him sprawled on the roof with a long, deep slash from the hawser across his collar.

Six more of Haller's men and nine more of Domor's managed to cut themselves free of the straining ropes and cling onto the roofing panels.

Then the drop went off over the side of the dome under its own massive weight, jerking threads of shrieking men after it.

Silence.

Milo got to his feet, unsteady. It was suddenly very dark and cold. The raked roof underfoot was slick with frost. The only light came from the burning tatters of debris outflung across the steeper pitches of the dome, and the sky glow of the battle they had become detached from. Despite the figures struggling up around him, he felt monstrously alone. They were, in effect, castaways on a mountaintop at night.

'Sound off!' Domor stammered over the vox. One by one, out of order, the survivors reeled off their call-signs. Fifteen of Domor's squad had survived. Haller had fourteen. The soldiers began to congregate on a flat decking area behind a vox-mast that protruded from the dome like a corroded thorn. Everyone was unsteady on their feet and there were some heart stopping slips.

Ezlan and Bonin joined the group, carrying an injured female aviator between them. Her name was Jagdea. Her Lightning had been brought down and she'd ejected onto the roof. She'd been the one who'd popped the flare and guided them in.

Her arm was broken and she was slipping into shock, so she barely heard the mumbled gratitude of the Guardsmen.

Milo glanced round sharply as he heard a thump. Dremmond, wounded and weighed down by his flamer, had risen only to lose his feet on the ice. He'd gone down hard and was starting to slide, slowly but definitely, down the dome's curve.

'Feth! Oh feth!' he burbled. His gloved hands scrabbled at the slippery metal and plasteel, frantic for purchase. 'Oh feth me!'

Milo moved. Dremmond had already slid right past two troopers either too stunned to move or too aware of their own tenuous footing. Dremmond's dangling arrestor hook and promethium tanks were squealing over the roof metal.

Milo slithered down towards him. He heard several voices yell at him. His feet went out and he landed on his backside, sliding down himself now. Unable to stop, he banged into Dremmond, who clutched at him, and they slid together. Faster. Faster.

The lip of the roof looked hideously close. Milo could see the burnt score marks where the weight of the drop-ship had gone over just moments before.

They jerked to a halt. Breathing hard, Milo realised his lasgun strap had fouled a rusty rivet standing proud of the plating. Dremmond clung to him. The canvas strap began to stretch and fray.

Something heavy bounced down the frosty roof beside them. It was a length of salvaged drop-rope, playing out from the darkness above.

'Grab it!' Milo heard a voice call from above. He got his hands around it. Looking up, he saw a trooper edging hand over hand down the rope towards them. It was the Verghastite, Vadim. A huddle of shadows further up the slope showed where Bonin, Haller, Domor and several of the others were anchoring the other end of the rope under the vox-mast.

Vadim reached them.

'Like this, like this,' he said, showing them how to coil the rope around their palms so that it wouldn't work loose. 'You all tight?'

'Yes,' said Milo.

'Hang on.'

To Milo's incredulity, Vadim continued on down the rope past them, making for the very edge of the roof lip. The air-exchanger on the back of his rebreather hood puffed clouds of steam and ice crystals out as he exerted himself.

Vadim reached the lip, wound the trailing end of the rope around his ankle like an aerialist, and then rolled onto his belly, so that he was hanging out over the abyss headfirst.

'What the feth is he doing?' Dremmond stuttered.

Milo shook his head – a futile response for a man in a gas-hood – but he was lost for words. They could only hold on and watch.

Vadim moved again, rolling upright and freeing his ankle only to lash the rope end around his waist, using his arrestor hook as a double lock. Then he reached into his webbing and dug out a roll of cable, a metal reinforced climbing line much narrower in gauge than the drop rope, a standard issue part of every Guardsman's kit. He fiddled with it a moment, securing it to the lifeline the men above were holding out, and then swung back over the side.

'Taking the weight, you hear me, sergeant?' Vadim suddenly voxed.

'Understood,' voxed Haller.

'Make sure you're gakking well anchored,' Vadim said.

'We're tied back to a goddamn mast here.'

'Good. Then smooth, hard pulls. Count off three between and do them together or we'll all end up down there somewhere.'

'Got it.'

'Go.'

The main rope jerked. Slowly, Milo realised they were sliding up the dome again, a few centimetres at a time. He clung on and felt Dremmond's hands tighten on him.

'Come on!' Vadim urged from below.

It seemed to take an age. Milo felt numb. Then hands were reaching for him and dragging him and Dremmond up amongst the cluster of bodies around the mast where the rope was tied off.

When he looked back down at Vadim, Milo was astonished to see he wasn't alone. He was dragging two more figures with him. Milo immediately added his own strength to the steady, regular heaves.

Vadim had found Seena and Arilla, the two Verghastite women from Haller's squad who crewed the autocannon. They'd been dragged off the dome by the drop-ship, but their section of rope had parted and snagged around a vent under the lip. They'd been left hanging in space. Vadim had heard their desperate calls on his way down to Milo and Dremmond.

The Ghosts pulled the trio to comparative safety. Vadim lay flat for a moment, exhausted. Fayner, the one surviving field medic, checked the girls over and then packed Dremmond's ugly wound, the exposed areas of which were beginning to blister.

The Ghosts began to light lamp packs and check over their weapons and equipment. Haller and Domor were consulting pocket compass and viewers, looking up the massive swell of the dome. Domor called Bonin over. He was one of the best scouts in the regiment, one of Mkoll's chosen.

'What are we going to do?' Nehn asked Milo.

'Find a way in?' Milo shrugged.

'How?' growled Lillo, one of the veteran Vervunhive troopers from Haller's squad.

Bonin heard him and looked round. He held up a flimsy fold of paper.

'The Emperor has blessed us. Or rather, Gaunt has. I have a map.'

THERE WAS NO ONE there.

Zhyte peered out of cover, but the corridor ahead, a wide access way, was empty. Singis voxed in a confirmation from the far side.

Zhyte edged forward. The Urdeshi main force had been on the ground in the primary dome for almost an hour now and they'd advanced barely three hundred metres from the DZ itself. True, they were inside the dome. But it had taken time and men. They'd lost so many to the enemy nightfighters on the run into the DZ, and then so many, many more in the brutal fight to storm the hatchways.

Now, it seemed as if the enemy had simply given up and vanished.

Zhyte crawled on his knees and elbows over to Singis, who was logging the situation on a data-slate as his vox-officer Gerrishon whispered information from the other units.

'Let me see,' Zhyte said, taking the slate anyway. His number two, Shenko, was still held fast in a hard fight along the promenade. Zhyte could hear the ragged fighting and weapon discharge from outside. Three forces, including his own, had penetrated the dome proper through main hatchways, meeting fierce resistance from squads of the Blood Pact scum, nightmarish in their red battledress and snarling, hook-nosed masks. There were status reports from Gaunt's mob at the secondary DZ and Fazalur's at the tertiary, and it seemed they had ground to a halt too, but Zhyte didn't much care. This was his baby. The primary dome was the main objective, and the Seventh Urdeshi had been given that honour. It was a matter of pride. They would take this blasted place.

But it had all gone so quiet. Ten minutes before, these access halls had been the scene of ferocious, almost hand-to hand-killing. The corpses and the battle damage all around testified to that.

And then, the Blood Pact had simply melted away.

'They may have fallen back. Perhaps to better defensive positions deeper in the dome,' Singis suggested.

Zhyte nodded but he didn't honestly give a little pebble crap for that idea. If the Blood Pact had wanted to hold them off, they'd been in a position to do it from the beginning. The Urdeshi had managed a few tricks, forced a few advantages, but it was nothing much. The enemy defence had been superb, and viable. It made no sense for them to have abandoned it for 'better positions'. Singis was talking out of his arse.

Zhyte tossed the slate back to his adjutant. Though it hurt his pride to think it, this had been a disaster all round. His entire force might by now be impact-splats down in the Scald levels if it hadn't been for the Phantine Lightnings that had driven the enemy nightfighters off. Not that he'd ever admit it to that sour bitch aviator Jagdea. Thanks to the air support, he'd got a good proportion of his men down. He'd lost hundreds rather than thousands.

And now this. Like his storm-troops were being toyed with.

He yanked the vox-mic from Gerrishon.

'Belthini? Rhintlemann? You hearing me?' The officers commanding the other two intruder forces voxed back affirmatives immediately.

'I don't know what the good crap is going on, but I'm not going to roll about here all night. Three minute count, on my mark from now. We're going to push ahead. Stir 'em up at least.'

They confirmed the order. Enough of this creeping around, Zhyte thought, exchanging his weapon's clip for a fresh one. He had a pack satisfyingly full of fresh ones.

'Go left,' he told Singis. 'Take groups three and four. Six and two advance with me. First port of call is that main hatch there. I want it secure and I want the support weapons up smart to set up along that colonnade.'

'Yes sir.'

'While we're at it… Kadakedenz?'

The recon-officer crouching to Singis's left looked up.

'Sir?'

'Hand pick six men and push in through that side hatch. They could be lying in wait, hoping to enfilade us.'

'Enfilade us, sir?'

'Shoot us sideways in the arse, Kadakedenz!'

'I don't think that's what enfilade means, sir. Not technically–'

'I don't know what "shut the crap up you sag-arsed tosser" means, Kadakedenz. Not technically. But I'm going to say that too. Can you whip up a side team and skidaddle it sideways to support my move, or are you too busy making inadvertent crap-streaks in your britches?'

'I can do it, sir, yes sir.'

Zhyte looked at his wrist-chrono. The beater hand was ticking towards the static marker needle he'd punched and set while giving Belthini and Rhintlemann the order mark.

'Let's move like we mean business.'

IN A SIDE HALL off the main access to the secondary dome, gun smoke drifting in the cool air, Trooper Wersun was loading his last clip. 'Last chance box?' asked Gaunt, moving up next to him. Wersun reacted in surprise.

'Yes, sir. Last clip, sir.'

'Use it sparingly.' Gaunt huddled down next to him and slid a fresh sickle pattern magazine for his bolt pistol out of his ammo web. He'd sheathed his power sword for the moment.

As far as Gaunt knew, most of his men were now, like Wersun, down to their last. If he ever got out of this, he'd use the power blade of Heironymo Sondar to put on a novelty ventriloquist show for the Ghosts, using the Munitorium chief at Hessenville as the screaming puppet.

Gaunt's blood was up. This should have been easier. The Blood Pact were damn good. He'd been through a fight in the outer hatches that had been as hard and nasty as anything in his notable career.

'Caober?'

'Sir,' replied the Tanith scout, huddled up against a fallen pile of ceiling girders.

'Anything?'

'No, sir. Not a fething sign. Where did they go?'

Gaunt sat back against a block of bullet-chipped masonry. Where indeed? He was overheating in the hood now, and sweat was dribbling down his spine.

Beltayn, his vox-man, was nearby. Gaunt waved him over.

'Mic, sir?'

'No, plug me in.'

Beltayn wound a small cable from his heavy, high-gain vox-pack and pushed the jack into a socket on the side of Gaunt's hood. Gaunt's headset micro-bead now had the added power of Beltayn's unit.

'One, two?'

'Two, one.'

'Colm? Tell me you see bad guys.'

'Not so much as a murmur, boss,' Corbec replied over the link. His force was advancing slowly down the access halls parallel to Gaunt's.

'Keep me advised. One, three?'

'Three,' responded Rawne.

'Any good news where you are?'

'Negative. We're at the mouth of an access tunnel. Five zero five if you've got your map handy. Where did they go?'

'I'm open to offers.'

'Four, one.'

'Go ahead, Mkoll.'

'We've got the promenade clear. Bray, Tarnash and Burone are holding the west end, Soric and Maroy the east. I think Kolea, Obel and Varl got their squads in through a hatch west of you.'

'I'll check. Any movement?'

'It all went quiet about ten minutes ago, sir.'

'Stay on top of them, Mkoll.'

'Understood.'

'Nine? Six? Twelve?'

Kolea, Varl and Obel responded almost simultaneously.

'We've still got contact here, sir!' Varl said urgently. 'We-feth!'

'Six? Six, this is one?'

'Six, one! Sorry. It's hot here. Got us a firefight in an antechamber, heavy fire, heavy cover.'

'One, six, report position. Six?'

'Twelve, one,' Obel cut in. 'Varl's under fire. Kolea's boys are moving in support. We're through to access 588.'

Gaunt waved a hand and Beltayn passed him the chart slate.

Five eight eight. Bless Varl, Obel and Kolea. They were hard in, deeper than any Ghost unit. And from the look of Beltayn's log, deeper than any Imperial force. They were almost into the main habs inside the secondary dome. Excluding casualties, Gaunt had perhaps seventy-five men almost a kilometre inside the city.

'Right,' said Gaunt. 'They've set the pace. Let's close it up.'

IT WAS THE small, dead hours of the night, and a hard crust of frost had formed over the outer surface of Cirenholm's secondary dome. The air was black-cold, and polluted snow crystals twinkled down.

The survivors of drop 2K moved slowly up the bowl of the vast superstructure, their progress hampered by the treacherous conditions and by the injured: Commander Jagdea, who had to be carried: Dremmond with his lacerated shoulder; Guthrie with his head wound; Arilla, who had dislocated an elbow when the drop went down.

Bonin moved ahead, at point. The whole, vast roof was creaking as the temperature contracted the metal. On occasions, their rubber soled boots stuck fast if they stood in one place too long.

The light wash in the sky from the main assault behind the curve of the dome seemed to have died down. Had they lost? Won? All Bonin could see were the bars of smoke drifting up from the domes and the fathomless night punctuated by stars.

His mother, God-Emperor rest and protect her, had always said he had been born under a lucky star. She said this, he was sure, because his life had not been easy from the start.

His had been a difficult birth, during a cold spring in County Cuhulic, marked by inauspicious signs and portents. Berries out late, haw-twist turning to white flowers without seeding, the larisel hibernating until Watchfrost. While still a babe in arms, he had been blighted by illness. Then, while he was still in the cradle, forest fires had taken their home in the summer of 745. The whole county had suffered then, and the Bonin family, fruiters by trade, had suffered with the best. It had taken two hard years of living in tents while his father and uncles rebuilt the homestead.

Until the age of eight, Bonin had been known as Mach by all the family. His mother had always had this thing about Lord Solar Macharius, especially since a copy of his *Life* had been the only thing she had been able to save from the family home during the fire. An often bewildered and contradictory devotee of the fates, his mother had considered this another of her signs.

At eight, as was the custom with most old Tanith families, Bonin had been baptised and given his true names. It was considered that a child grew into the names he or she would need, and formally naming a child at birth was premature. The custom wasn't observed much now.

Bonin stopped his reverie and gazed up at the cold night sky. The custom wasn't observed at all now, he corrected himself. All those billions of lights up there, and not one of them was Tanith.

He remembered the day of his baptism. Coming down to the river on a chilly spring afternoon, the sky over the nalwoods a sullen white. Shivering in his baptismal smock, his older sisters hugging him to keep him warm and stop his tears.

The village minister at the waterside.

His mother, in her best dress, so proud.

Dunked in freezing, rapid river water and coming up crying, he had been given the name Simen Urvin Macharius Bonin. Simen, after his father. Urvin after a charismatic uncle who had helped rebuild their home.

Bonin remembered his mother, soft, warm and excited, drying him off after the baptism in the private shrine of their house, under the painted nalwood panels.

'You've been through so much, you're lucky. Lucky. Born under a lucky star.'

Which one, Bonin wondered now, halting and looking up at the curve of the dome as the ice gleamed.

Not Tanith, that was certain.

But the luck had never left him. He was sure his mother had rubbed raw luck into him that day with the rough folds of the towel.

He had survived the fall of Tanith. On Menazoid Epsilon, he had walked away without a scratch when a concussion round vapourised the three men in the fox-hole with him. On Monthax, he had seen a las-bolt pass so close to his face he could taste its acrid wake. On Verghast, he had been part of Gaunt's and Kolea's team in the assault on the Heritor's Spike. During the boarding, he had lost his grip and fallen off. He should have died. Even Gaunt, who'd seen him fall, presumed him lost, and was stunned to find out he had survived.

There were sixteen vertebrae in his back made of composite steel, and an augmetic socket on his pelvis. But he was alive. Lucky. Fated. Just like his mother had always told him. A sign.

Born under a lucky star.

But, he often wondered, how long would it burn?

The deck under his boots was glossy wet, not caked in frost.

Bonin knelt down and felt the roof plating. Even through his glove, he could feel the warmth.

Ahead, a quarter of a kilometre away, rose the stacks and smoking flues of Cirenholm's vapour mill. The drizzle of wet heat was keeping this part of the roof thawed.

Bonin consulted the map Gaunt had given him. The mill superstructure was the only thing that penetrated the roof of the secondary dome. There were inspection hatches up here, ventilator pipes.

A way inside.

Whatever the star was, it was still watching over him.

THE ACCESS TUNNEL marked on the map as 505 gave out into what had once been an ordered little park. High overhead, in the girders of the dome roof, sunlamps and environment processors hung in bolted cages, but they had long since been deactivated and the trimmed fruit trees and arbors had died off. Leaf litter, grey and dry, covered the mosaic paths and the areas of dead grass. Brittle-branched grey-trunked trees filled the beds, grim as gravestones.

Rawne moved his squad out into the park, using the trees as cover. Feygor swung to the left at the head of a fireteam. ready to lay down protective fire on the main force. Leyr, the platoon's scout, edged forward. The air was cold and dry.

Tona Criid, on the right hand edge of the formation, suddenly started and turned, her weapon rising.

'Movement, four o'clock,' she whispered briefly into her micro-bead.

Rawne held his hand out, palm down, and everyone dropped low. Then he pointed to Criid, Caffran and Wheln, circled his hand and pointed ahead with a trident of three fingers.

Immediately, the three troopers rose and ran forward, fanning out, keeping their heads low. Criid dropped behind a rusty bench, and Caffran tucked down behind the plinth of a stone centaur whose rearing forelimbs had been shot off. Wheln got in behind a brake of dead trees.

Rawne glanced to his left and saw Neskon crawling forward with the hose of his flamer ready. Leclan was covering him. To Rawne's right, Banda had her long-las resting on the elbow of a low branch. Like Criid, Jessi Banda was one of the Verghastite females who had joined the Ghosts. They seemed to have a particular expertise for marksmanship, and sniper was the one regimental speciality where there were as many Verghastites as Tanith. And as many women as men.

Rawne's opposition to women in the regiment was so old now it was gathering dust and everyone was tired of hearing it. He'd never questioned their fighting ability. He just didn't like the added stress of sexual tension it put on the ranks.

Jessi Banda was a good example. Cheerful, sharp tongue, playful, she was a good-looking girl with short, curly brown hair and curves that the matt-black battledress couldn't hide. She'd been a loom-worker in Vervunhive, and then a member of Kolea's scratch company guerillas. Now she was a specialist sniper in the Imperial Guard, and a damn good one. The death of one of the Tanith snipers had forced her rotation into Rawne's platoon.

He found her distracting. He found Criid, the surly ex-gang girl, distracting. Both of them were very easy on the eye. He tried not to think about Nessa, the sniper in Kolea's unit. She was downright beautiful...

'Sir?' whispered Banda, cocking her head at Rawne. Through the lenses of her gas-hood, Rawne could see a smile in her eyes.

Feth! I'm doing it again! Rawne cursed himself. Maybe it wasn't them. Maybe it was him...

'Anything?' he asked.

She shook her head.

'Movement!' Wheln hissed over the vox.

Rawne saw them for a brief moment. Four, maybe five enemy troopers in muddy red, moving hurriedly down the walkway on the far right hand edge of the park.

Wheln's lasrifle cracked, and Caffran and Criid quickly opened up too.

One of the figures buckled and dropped and las-shots splintered against the wall of the park. Two of the others turned and started to fire into the park. Rawne saw their iron-masked faces, sneering above the flashing muzzles of their weapons.

There was a loud report from his right. Banda had fired, loosing one of the sniper-variant long-las's overpowered 'hot shot' rounds. One of the firing enemy was thrown back against the wall as if he'd been struck by a wrecking ball.

A flurry of fire whipped back and forth through the park edge now. There must have been more than five of them, Rawne decided. He couldn't see. He ran forward, dodging between tree trunks. A sapling just behind him ruptured at head height and swished back and forth from the recoil like a metronome arm.

'Seven one, three!'

'Seven one, sir!' Caffran responded. Rawne could hear the background fire echoed and distorted over the vox-link.

'Sit-rep!'

'I count eight. Five in the bushes at my ten, three back in the doorway. We've splashed another four.'

'I can't eyeball! Call it!' Rawne ordered.

From behind the statue's plinth, Caffran glanced around. Whatever faults you could lay at Major Rawne's door – and heartlessness, lack of humour, deceit and cruelty would be amongst them – he was a damn fine troop leader. Here, with no view of his own, he was devolving command to Caffran without hesitation, allowing the young private to order the deployment. Rawne trusted Caffran. He trusted them all. That was enough to make him a far greater leader than many of the so-called 'good guys' Caffran had seen in his Guard career.

'Wheln! Criid! Tight and right. Hit the door. Leclan! Osket! Melwid! Concentrate on those bushes! Neskon, up and forward!'

There was a crackle of barely verbal acknowledgements. The las-fire coming out of the park's tree-line into the path-edge bushes increased in intensity.

Caffran got off a few more shots, but something heavy like a stubber was bracketing his position, chipping shards of stone off the plinth and gouging divots out of the dead grass. He threw himself back as one rebounding shell scarred his boot and another pinged hard off his warknife's blade, leaving an ugly notch in the fine-honed edge.

'Banda! See the panels on the end wall?'

'Got 'em, Caff.'

'Fifth one in from the left, middle rivet. Aim on that, but drop the shot about five metres.'

'Uh huh…'

There was another sharp whine-crack and part of the straggled bushes blew apart as the hot-shot went through it. The stub fire ceased. If she hadn't actually killed him, Banda had certainly discouraged the bastard.

'Got one!' whooped Melwid meanwhile.

Criid fired from behind the bench until a trio of close shots splintered the seat-back. She got down onto her belly in time to see two of the enemy running from the doorway towards another clump of bushes near the end of the path. She flicked her toggle to full-auto and raked them from her prone position. One of them dropped a stick grenade he had been about to toss, and the blast threw fine grit and dry clumps of dirt into the park.

Rawne had moved in close now, into the stands of dead trees by the edge of the fighting. Leyr was nearby. With a coughing rush, flames spewed out across the line of bushes as Neskon finally got range. Rawne heard harsh, short screams and the firecracker blitz of ammunition cooking off.

'Breakers!' Leyr shouted.

Rawne turned, and caught a glimpse of two red-tunicked figures sprinting from the path into the trees, moving past them into the park. He jumped up and ran, leaping fallen boughs and kicking up stones and dead leaves.

'Left! Left!' he shouted to Leyr who was running too.

Rawne ran on. Breathing came hard when you exerted yourself in a rebreather. Running jarred the hood so that visibility was impaired.

He caught a glimpse of red, and fired once, but the shot simply skinned the bark of a tree. Leyr fired too, off to his left.

Rawne came round the side of a particularly large tree and slammed into the Blood Pact trooper who had been dodging the other way. They went sprawling.

Swearing, Rawne grappled with the man. The enemy trooper was hefty and strong. His arms and body seemed hard, as if packed with augmetic systems. His big, filthy hands were bare and showed the scar tissue of deep, old wounds across the palms, made during his ritual pledge of allegiance to the obscenity Urlock Gaur.

He fought back, kicking Rawne hard and spitting out a string of curses in a language Rawne didn't know and had no intention of looking up later.

They rolled in the dirt. Rawne's weapon, clamped between them, fired wildly. All Rawne could see was the front of the foe's tunic: old, frayed, stained a dull red the colour of dried blood. It occurred to Rawne that it probably *was* dried blood.

Rawne got an arm free and threw a short but brutal punch that lurched the growling brute off him. For a moment, he saw the man's face: the battered iron grotesque fashioned in the shape of a hook-nosed, leering fright mask, hinged in place under a worn bowl helmet covered in flaking crimson paint and finger-daubed runes of obscenity.

Then the Blood Pact trooper head-butted him.

Rawne heard a crack, and felt the stunning impact and a stab of white-hot pain in his left eye. He reeled away. The hooked nose of the iron grotesque had punched in through the left lens of Rawne's gas-hood like a blunt hatchet, breaking the plastic and digging deep. His head was swimming. He couldn't see out of his left eye and he could feel blood running down inside his hood.

Raging, Rawne threw a hooking punch that hit the enemy in the side of the neck. His assailant fell sideways, choking.

Rawne drew his silver Tanith knife, grabbed the man around the left elbow to yank his arm up against the side of his head, and stabbed the blade up to the hilt in the man's armpit.

The soldier of Chaos went into violent spasms. Rawne rolled back onto his knees.

Leyr came out of the bushes nearby. 'The other one's dead. Ran straight into Feygor. I–feth! Medic!'

Leclan was the platoon's corpsman, one of the troopers trained in the rudiments of field aid by Dorden and Curth. As soon as he saw Rawne, he checked the brass air-tester sewn into the side of his kit.

'Air's clean. Stale but clean. Get that hood off.'

Leyr pulled Rawne's gas-hood off and Leclan took a look at the face wound.

'Feth!' Leyr murmured.

'Shut up. Go and do something useful,' Rawne told him. 'How is it?'

'Looks a right mess, sir, but I think it's superficial.' Leclan took out some tweezers and started removing slivers of lens plastic from Rawne's face. 'You've got blood in your eye from the cuts, and your eyelid is torn. Hang on, this'll smart.'

Leclan sprayed counterseptic from a puffer bottle and then taped a gauze pad over Rawne's eye.

'I haven't lost the eye then.'

'No, sir. But Dorden needs to look at it.'

Rawne got up and tucked his gas-hood away in his belt. He'd had enough of it anyway. He went over to the corpse and pulled out his knife, twisting the grip to break the suction and free the blade.

Feygor was moving the platoon up. The fight on the path was over.

'We got them all,' Caffran reported.

'Any casualties?'

'Only you,' said Feygor.

'You can all lose the hoods if you want,' said Rawne. He walked down to the path. Criid, Wheln, Neskon and Melwid were examining the bodies.

'Made a mess of this,' said Neskon, indicating the charred bush and the three blackened corpses behind it. 'I think they were carrying something.' Rawne knelt down and took a look, ignoring the reek of promethium and the spicy stink of seared meat. It was some kind of equipment box, scorched with soot and burned out. Rawne could see melted cables and broken valves inside.

'Sir,' said Feygor quietly. The platoon had tensed at movement from the south door, but it was more Ghosts. Captain Daur's squad, supported by Corporal Meryn's which had brought Commissar Hark along with it.

'This park area's secure,' Rawne told them. Hark nodded.

'Does that hurt?' asked Daur.

'You ask some damn fool questions sometimes, Verghast,' Rawne snapped, though he knew full well that the young, handsome captain was exercising his trademark ironic wit.

'Your men are unhooded,' observed Hark, holstering his plasma pistol.

'A necessity with me. But the air's clean.'

Hark almost ripped his own hood off. 'Damn well glad to get rid of that,' he said, trying to hand-comb his thick, dark hair before putting his cap on. He smiled at Rawne. 'We've been so busy I hadn't even checked the gauge.'

'Me neither,' said Rawne. 'Come and take a look at this. I could use a–'

'Good eye?' Daur finished for him. Rawne heard Banda and Criid snigger.

'Get the men to unhood, captain, if you please,' Hark told Daur. Daur nodded and walked away, smiling.

'Insufferable feth,' Rawne growled as he walked the commissar over to the path.

'In the God-Emperor's illustrious brotherhood of warriors, we are all kindred, major,' returned Hark smoothly.

'A little boost from the holy primers?'

'No idea. I'm getting so good at this I can make lines like that up off the cuff.'

They both laughed. Rawne liked Hark, probably about as much as he disliked Daur. Daur, good-looking, popular, efficient, had entered the regiment's upper command like a virus, dumped there on an equal footing to Rawne himself, thanks to Gaunt's generous efforts to integrate the Verghastites. Hark, on the other hand, had come in against Gaunt's will, indeed his original task had been to turn Gaunt out of rank. Everyone had hated him at first. But he'd proved

himself in combat and also proved himself remarkably loyal
to the spirit of the Tanith First. Rawne had been pleased when
Gaunt had invited Hark to stay on as regimental commissar
in support of Gaunt's own split role.

Rawne welcomed Hark's presence in the Ghosts because he
was a hard man, but a fair one. He respected him because
they'd risked their lives for each other in the final battle for
the Shrinehold on Hagia.

And he liked him because, if only technically, he was a
thorn in Ibram Gaunt's side.

'You really don't like the Verghastites, do you, Rawne?' said
Hark.

'Not my place to like or dislike, sir. But this is the Tanith
First,' Rawne replied, stressing the word 'Tanith'. 'Besides, I've
only seen a handful of them that can fight as hard or as well
as the Tanith.'

Hark nodded slyly over at Banda and Criid. 'I see you keep
the decorative ones in your platoon though.'

Now it was Hark's turn to joke at Rawne's expense, but
somehow it didn't matter. Rawne would have floored Daur
for a quip like that.

Hark crouched down and looked at the half-melted box.

'Why do we care what this is?' he asked.

'They were moving it through the park. That way,' Rawne
added, indicating the direction the Imperials had been
advancing. 'Must have been important because they were
breaking cover to move it.'

Hark drew his blade. It was a standard issue, broad-bladed
dress dagger, a pugio with a gold aquila crest. He was the only
man in the regiment who didn't have a silver Tanith warknife.
He picked at the edge of the box-seal with the pugio's top.

'Vox set?'

'Don't think so, sir,' said Rerval, the vox-officer in Rawne's
squad.

'It's a generator cell for a void shield.'

They looked round. Daur had rejoined them.

'Are you sure, captain?' asked Hark dubiously.

Daur nodded. 'I was a garrison officer on the Hass West
Fort, sir. Part of my daily duty was to test start the voids on
the battery nests.'

Smug know-all bastard, Rawne thought.

'So what were they doing w–'

'Sir!' Caffran called down the pathway. He was with Feygor's fireteam at the end hatch.

They hurried down to join him. Meryn and Daur deployed their troops out across the park to cover all the access points.

The hatch was open and its arch was dim. Beyond it, Rawne could see a corridor with a grilled floor leading deeper into the dome structure.

'Cables, there, inside the jamb,' said Feygor, pointing out what they'd all missed. Feygor had notoriously sharp eyes. He had been able to spot a larisel at night at a hundred metres back home in the Great West Nals. And kill it with a dirty look. Feygor should have been in the scout section, but Rawne had worked determinedly not to lose his lean, murderous ally to Mkoll's bunch. And it was just as likely Mkoll didn't want Feygor anyway.

'Booby trap,' Caffran said, speaking what they were all thinking. A quick vox-check confirmed that all the accessways off the northside of the park showed similar signs of tampering.

Daur called Criid over. 'Permission to risk my health recklessly,' he asked Hark lightly.

'Don't wait on my account,' Rawne muttered.

'You have an idea, captain?' Hark asked.

'Get everyone to fall back from the doorways,' Daur said. He borrowed Criid's lasrifle and the small, polished brooch mount she kept in her pocket. It was her little trademark, and Daur requisitioned it now, sending her back into cover.

Daur fixed the mount to the bayonet lug of the rifle as he had seen Criid do and then gingerly extended the gun out at arm's length.

'Pray to the Golden Throne…' Hark whispered to Rawne, down in cover.

'Oh, I am,' said Rawne.

The brooch-mount had been polished to a mirror, and it was a canny tool for seeing round corners without risking a headshot. Rawne knew that several Ghosts had copied Criid's idea, realising how useful such a thing was for room to room clearance. Scout Caober used a shaving mirror.

Daur peered in via the little mirror for a few seconds and then ran back to the line.

'Thanks, Tona,' he said, handing the brooch and the weapon back to Criid.

'The door's rigged with a void shield,' Daur told them. 'It's not active yet, but it's charged.'

'You know because?'

'Smell of ozone.'

'So they're intending to block our advance in this section with shields. We better get in there and disable them,' Feygor said.

'Unless they're waiting for us to try,' said Daur.

'Might explain why they've fallen back so suddenly,' said Hark. 'Bringing us forward, luring us, so they can cut us off.'

'Or in two,' said Daur.

'What?' asked Rawne.

'You ever been standing in a void field when it was activated, major?'

'No.'

'It was a rhetorical question. The field edge would cut you in half.'

Rawne looked at Hark. 'I say we run it. Get as many through as we can.'

'So that those who get through can be cut down with nowhere to run because there's a void at their backs?' Daur asked sourly.

'You got a better idea, Verghast?'

Daur smiled at him without warmth and tapped the pips on his coat. 'Address me as "captain", major. It's a small courtesy, but I think even you should be capable of it.'

Hark held up his hand. 'Enough. Get me the vox-officer.'

FREE OF THE damn gas-hood at last, Gaunt set his cap on his head, brim first. He glanced at his watch, took a sip of water from his flask, and looked down the hallway.

Two storeys high, it was ornate with gilt and floral work, and the floor was a chequerboard of red and white pouskin tiles. Crystal chandeliers hung every ten metres, blazing out twinkly yellow light that shone from the huge wall mirrors.

Gaunt glanced back. His platoon was in cover down the length of the hall, using the architraves and pillars for shelter. Wersun and Arcuda were guarding a side door which led into a section of staterooms that had already been swept. There was a scent in the air. Fading perfume.

Cirenholm had been a rich place once, before Gaur's Blood Pact had overrun it. Here in the palatial halls of the secondary dome, the elegance lingered, melancholy and cold.

Caober reappeared, coming back down the hall, hugging the shadows. He dropped down next to Gaunt.

'Shield?'

Caober nodded. 'Looks like what Commissar Hark described. It's wired into the end doorway, and to the pair adjoining. There was a staircase, but I didn't fancy checking that without a fireteam.'

'Good work,' said Gaunt and took the mic Beltayn held out.

'One, four?'

'Four, one,' Mkoll replied. 'All exits north of 651 are wired for shields.'

'Understood. Stay where you are.' Gaunt looked at his chart, and ran a finger around a line that connected the sites his men had reported as covered by shields. They'd all found them: Corbec, Burone, Bray, Soric. Sergeant Theiss's squad had actually passed one, and then fallen back rapidly once Gaunt had alerted them. Only the spearhead formed by Obel, Kolea and Varl had gone beyond, too far beyond to call back now.

'What are they up to, d'you think, sir?' asked Beltayn. 'Something's awry.'

'Yes it is, Beltayn.' Gaunt smiled at the vox-officer's use of his favourite understatement. He looked at the chart again. His company – with the exception of the spearhead – had penetrated about two-thirds of a kilometre into the dome and had all come up against prepared shield emplacements, no matter what level they were on. Soric's mob were six levels lower thanks to a firefight and the chance discovery of a cargo lift. It was as if the enemy had given up the outer rim of the dome to lure them in against this trap.

But what kind of trap? Was it meant to stop them dead? Cut their force in half? Pull them on and trap them without hope of retreat?

Gaunt took the mic again. 'Boost it. I want Zhyte and Fazalur,' he told the vox-man.

'1A, 3A… this is 2A. Respond. Repeat, 1A, 3A, this is 2A.'

White noise. Then a burp of audio.

'… A… repeat this is 3A. Gaunt?'

'Confirmed, Fazalur. What's your situation?'

'Advancing through the tertiary dome. Low resistance.'

'We've found shields here, Fazalur. Void shields laid across our path. Any sign there?'

'Active shields?'

'Negative.'

'We've seen nothing.'

'Watch for them and stay in contact.'

'Agreed, 2A, I stand advised. Out.'

'1A this is 2A, respond. 1A respond this channel. 2A to 1A, respond…'

'I've got Commissar Gaunt on the primary channel, sir,' Gerrishon called.

'Tell him I'm busy,' snorted Zhyte, waving the next squad forward. His unit was now a kilometre into Cirenholm's primary dome, exploring the marble vaults and suspiciously derelict chambers of the sky-city's commercial district. Ten minutes before, he had linked up with Belthini's group, and together they'd begun sectioning the outer dome. There was still no sign of the enemy. No sign of anyone, in fact, apart from his own puzzle-camoed troops. His skin was starting to crawl.

'He's quite insistent, sir. Says something about shields.'

'Tell him I'm busy,' Zhyte repeated. His men were executing bounding cover as they played out down the wide hallway, passing under vast holo-portraits of Phantine's great and good.

'Busy with what, sir?'

Zhyte stopped with a heavy sigh and turned to look at his suddenly pale vox-officer. 'Inform the stubborn little pool of canid-piss that I'm taking a masterful dump down the neck of Sagittar Slaith and I'll call him back when I've finished the paperwork.'

'I, sir–'

'Oh, give me that, you limpoid!' Zhyte spat and snatched the mic, cuffing Gerrishon for good measure.

'This had better be good, Gaunt,' he snarled.

'Zhyte?'

'Yes!'

'We've found shields, Zhyte, dug into doorways along marker 48:00 which would correlate to 32:00 on your map–'

'Do you have a point or are you calling for advice?'

'I'm calling to warn you, colonel. Secondary dome is wired for shields and tertiary may be too. Watch for them. Slaith, Emperor rot him, is no fool, and neither are the Blood Pact. They're planning something, and–'

'Do you know the name of my regiment, Gaunt?'

'Say again?'

'Do you know the name of my unit?'

'Of course. The Urdeshi Seventh Storm-troop. I don't see w–'

'The Urdeshi Seventh Storm-troop. Yes, sir. Our name is woven in silver thread on an honour pennant that hangs amongst the thousand flags beside the Golden Throne on Terra. We have been an active and victorious unit for a thousand and seventy-three glorious years. Is the Tanith First marked on an honour pennant, Gaunt?'

'I don't believe it is–'

'I know for a damn fact it isn't! You were only born yesterday and you're nothing! Nothing! There's only a bloody handful of you anyway! Don't you dare presume to tell me my business, you piece of shit! Warning me? Warning me? We are taking this bastard city piece by piece, hall by hall, with our blood and our sweat, and the last thing I want to hear is you whining about something that's making you soil your britches because you're too scared to do a soldier's job and get on with it!

'You hear me, Gaunt? Gaunt?'

GAUNT CALMLY HANDED the mic back to Beltayn.

'You get him, sir?'

'No. I got some fething idiot who's about to die,' said Gaunt.

ZHYTE CURSED AND threw the mic back at his vox-officer. The handset hit Gerrishon in the face and he fell down suddenly.

'Get up, you pile of crap! Gerrishon! On your feet!'

Zhyte paused abruptly. There was a widening pool of blood spreading out across the floor under Gerrishon's head. The vox-man's face was tranquil, as if he was sleeping. But there was a blackened hole in his forehead.

'God-Emperor!' Zhyte howled and turned. A las-round hit him in the shoulder and slammed him to the floor.

Everything, every last damn bloody thing, was exploding around him. He could hear screams and weapons fire. Laser shots spluttered along the walls, shattering ancient holoplate portraits out of their frames.

Zhyte crawled round. He saw three of his advance guard topple as they ran. Mists of blood sprayed out of them. One was hit so hard his left leg burst and came spinning off.

His men were firing. Some were screaming. All were yelling. A grenade went off.

Zhyte got up and ran back down the hallway, firing his weapon behind him. He ducked behind a pillar and looked back to see Blood Pact troopers spilling into the hall from all sides. They were bayoneting the Urdeshi men in cover, and firing wild but effective bursts at those trying to retreat.

'Regroup! Regroup!' Zhyte yelled into his micro-bead. 'Hatch 342! Now!' Three four two. There was a gun nest there. Support fire.

He turned and fell over a corpse. It was Kadekadenz, his recon man. His carcass had been messily eviscerated by sidelong las-fire, and ropes of steaming entrails spilled out of it like the tentacles of some beached cephalopod.

'Singis! Belthini! Group the men!' Group them, for g–'

A blow to the shoulder slammed him over. Zhyte rolled, and saw the iron mask of a Blood Pact trooper gurning at him as he plunged his bayonet down.

The rusty blade stabbed through the flesh of Zhyte's thigh and made him shriek. He fired twice and blew the Chaos soldier off him, then tore the blade from his leg. Blood was squirting from a major artery.

Zhyte got up, and then fell over, his boots slipping in his own blood. He grasped the Blood Pact soldier's fallen rifle, the smeared bayonet still attached, and rolled over, firing.

He hit one, then another, then a third, swiping each one off his feet with the satisfying punch of a solid las-hit.

Singis grabbed him and began to half-drag, half-carry him back towards the hatch. There were corpses all around. Down the hall, Zhyte could see nothing but a mob of charging Blood Pact troopers, chanting and howling as they came on, firing, guns at belly height.

He saw his men, littering the marble floor of the hallway. Zofer, on his back, jaw-less. Vocane, doubled-up and hugging the belly wound that had killed him. Reyuri, his legs in tatters, groping at the air. Gofforallo, just upper body and thighs attached by a smouldering spine. Hedrien, stapled to the wall by a broken bayonet blade through the chest. Jeorjul, without a face or a left foot, his gun still firing in spasming hands. He saw a man he couldn't recognise because his head had been vapourised. Another that was just pieces of meat and bone wrapped in burning shreds of puzzle-camo.

Zhyte screamed and fired. He heard heavy weapon fire, and laughed like a maniac as tracers whinnied down the hall and tore through the front ranks of the advancing Blood Pact.

'Shut up! Shut up!' Singis yelled at him. 'Get on your feet and help me!'

Zhyte fell dumb, like a stunned drunk, shock setting in. His trousers were soaked red with his blood. Dyed red. Like the Blood Pact.

They were in the doorway. Three four two. Belthini was dragging him through. He couldn't see Singis, but he fell sidelong across the hatch opening, and saw Bothris and Manahide manning the .50 cal cannon, raking the enemy with tracer fire. Three four two. His support weapon pitch.

'Give the bastards hell!' he said. At least he thought he said it. He couldn't hear his own voice and they didn't seem to hear him.

There was blood welling up in his throat.

Everything went quiet. Zhyte could see the furious flashes of the .50's barrel. The lancing tracers. The las impacts all around. He could see men's mouths moving, yelling. Manahide. Bothris. Belthini, in the doorway, over him, a look on his face that seemed touchingly concerned.

Between Belthini's legs, Zhyte saw the Blood Pact. They had Rhintlemann. They were hacking him apart with their bayonets. He was vomiting gore and screaming.

Zhyte couldn't hear him.

He could hear nothing but his own pounding heart.

He sagged. Belthini stooped over him. Belthini said something.

Zhyte suddenly realised he could smell something. Something sharp, pungent.

Ozone.

It was ozone.

His head fell sideways. His skull bumped against the floor, and glanced off the sill of the hatch.

He saw the little box in the hatch frame, wired to the power sockets in the wall. There was a light flickering inside it.

Ozone.

He crawled. Crawled forward. He was sure he said something important, but Belthini was looking over at the gun team and didn't hear him.

There was a flash.

Just a bright flash, as if light had suddenly become solid, as if the air had suddenly become hard. He tasted smoke and heat.

Zhyte looked back in time to see the void shield engage across the doorway, chopping Manahide and Bothris in two, along with their .50, which exploded. It was quite amazing. A boiling fog of blood and atomised metal. Men falling apart, torsos and skulls cut vertically like scientific cross-sections. He saw smoothly severed white bone, sectioned brains, light coming in through Manahide's open mouth as the front of his face and body spilled forward on the other side of the shield.

Two sliced portions of human meat slumped back next to him, their edges curled and sizzling from the void field.

Zhyte looked up and saw Belthini trapped on the other side of the shield, his image distorted and blurred by the energy. He was shouting, desperate, hammering his fists. No sound came through.

Belthini was hit from behind by about six or seven las-rounds. Blood sprayed up the shield and he fell against it, sliding down like a man sliding down a pane of glass.

'Oh shit,' said Zhyte, hearing himself for the first time.

He realised the pain in his leg was gone.

And then he realised that was because his legs were still on the other side of the shield.

Four

HE WAS THE only one in the group who could see the stars.

They were hidden behind the black on black cloud cover that roiled across the heavens above the secondary dome, but he, and only he, could detect their light spill.

Sergeant Dohon Domor was known affectionately as Shoggy Domor by the men of the regiment. He'd been blinded in action back on Menazoid, years ago now as it seemed to him. He'd become quite used to the bulbous augmetic optics that crudely replaced his eyes.

Shoggy Domor. A shoggy was a little amphibian with bulging eyes found in the woodland pools on Tanith. He corrected himself: an *extinct* amphibian. The nickname had stuck.

Domor tried his micro-bead one last time, but there was nothing but static fizzle. They were out of range, and their main gain vox-sets, both of them, had gone down with the drop, still attached to vox-officers Liglis and Gohho.

He walked with careful steps up the dome's treacherous curve to rejoin the team. His augmetic eyes whirred and adjusted to reduce the light glare from the mill stacks ahead. The tips of the chimneys showed as flaring yellow, the stacks themselves as orange. The figures of the men were red shadows and beyond them the night cooled into shapes of blue, purple and black.

'Anything?' asked Sergeant Haller.

'No,' Domor replied. His limbs were beginning to ache from the cold and he could feel the throb of raw bruises. All their uniforms and the canvas of their gas-hoods were beginning to stiffen with hoarfrost.

With Bonin leading the way, flanked by Vadim, the survivors of drop 2K climbed cautiously into the scaffolding superstructure surrounding Cirenholm's vapour mill. Steamy gusts of hot, wet air exhaled over them, thawing their ice-stiff clothes and making them sweat suddenly. They could feel the thunder of massive turbines underfoot, shaking the roof housing. Meltwater and condensation drooled off every surface.

The beams of their lamp packs twitched nervously back and forth. It seemed more than a little likely that the enemy would have positioned sentries around the roof access here.

Commander Jagdea was back on her feet. Fayner, the corpsman, had given her a shot of dexahedrene and bound her broken right arm up across her chest in a tight brace. She carried her snub-snouted automatic pistol in her left hand.

They moved in under a dripping stanchion onto a massive grilled exhaust vent that steamed away in the cold of the night. Amber heat glowed far below down the shaft. Domor's energy sensitive vision adjusted again.

'Ah, feth!' Nehn shuddered.

The edges of the vent and all the girders around were thick with glistening, writhing molluscs, each one the size of an ork's finger. They turned towards the lights, fleshy mouthparts twitching and weeping viscous slime. They were everywhere, thousands of them. Arilla brushed one from her sleeve and it left a streak of ooze that hardened quickly like glue. The fat slug made a disgusting, meaty sound as it bounced off the roof.

'Thermovores,' said Jagdea, her breathing shallow and rapid. 'Vermin. They cluster around the heat exchangers feeding off the bacteria in the steam.'

'Charming,' said Milo, crushing one underfoot and really wishing he hadn't.

'They're harmless, trooper,' said the aviator. 'Just watch for skinwings.'

'Skinwings?'

'The next link of the food chain. Pollution mutants. They feed on the slugs.'

Milo thought about this. 'And what feeds on the skinwings?'

'Scald-sharks. But we should be all right. They don't usually come in close to the cities. They're deep sky hunters.'

Milo wasn't sure what a shark was. Indeed, he wasn't really sure what the Scald was either, but he was conscious of the stress Jagdea put on each word.

Bonin had stopped to consult the map, conferring with the sergeants and with Corporal Mkeller, the Tanith scout assigned to Haller's squad.

'That way,' Bonin said, and Mkeller concurred. The troop followed the scouts under a series of dripping derricks that rose up from the skin of the dome into the freezing night. Navigation lights winked on the mast tops, and on the fatter, higher columns of the chimneys. The slugs squirmed around them, following their lights, dribbling slime and forming glittering snot-bubbles around their snouts.

Bonin stopped by a raised vent and used his knife blade to scrape off the clusters of thermovores. Together with Mkeller, he managed to break the vent grille away and toss it aside.

Bonin peered in. 'It's tight, but we can make it. Break out ropes.'

'No,' said Vadim.

'What?'

'Let me look at that map,' Vadim said. He turned the thin paper sheet Bonin offered him in his gloved hands.

'That's a hot gas out-flue.'

'So?'

'So, we'll be dead if we go down there.'

'How do you reckon that?' asked Mkeller.

Vadim looked up so that Bonin and Mkeller could see his eyes behind the lenses of the hood. 'It's a fifty metre vertical climb. With our numbers and our impediments–' he glanced over at Jagdea, 'it'd take us upwards of two hours to get down there.'

'So?'

'I don't know how often this thing vents, but none of us want to be halfway down it when the hot gas comes up. It'd broil us. Clothes, armour, skin, flesh… all cooked off the bones.'

'How the feth do you know so much?' asked Mkeller.

'He was a roofer, back at Vervunhive,' Milo said quickly. 'He knows about this kind of thing.'

'I did some work on the heating systems. Vox-masts and sensor blooms mostly, but heating too. Look at the way the grille you pulled off is made. The louvres curl up... out. It's an out-flue.'

Bonin seemed genuinely impressed. 'You know this stuff, then? Good. You call it.'

Vadim looked at the map again, pausing to wipe condensing vapour from the eye plates of his hood. 'Here... here. The big intakes. Intake shafts for the cooler coils. It's a longer climb, and we'll have to be wary of duct fans and inrush–'

'What's inrush?' asked Domor.

'If they cycle up the fans for extra cooling, we could be caught in a wind tunnel effect. I'm not saying it's safe, but it's safer.'

There was a sudden bang and a howl of heat. The flue Bonin and Mkeller had been contemplating suddenly voided a thick cloud of superheated gas-flame and soot. It seemed, comically, to underscore the validity of Vadim's advice.

Bonin watched the donut of expelled gas-flame wobble up into the sky.

'I'm convinced,' he said. 'Let's go with Vadim's plan.'

ALL ACROSS THE secondary dome, the shields were lit, blocking them in and penning them in the outer limits of the dome. An anxious vox-signal from Fazalur in the tertiary dome confirmed that it was happening there too.

And then the signal cut off abruptly.

There was nothing from the Urdeshi at primary except a strangled mess of incoherent panic.

'Form up and move in!' Gaunt ordered, swinging his squad around. He voxed ahead to Corbec and Bray, instructing them to sweep laterally along the edge of the shield block and converge on him.

'Can't raise the spearhead,' Beltayn said.

Gaunt wasn't surprised. The shield effects distorted vox-links badly. The platoons led by Varl, Kolea and Obel were cut off from the main force, deep in the heart of the enemy-held dome.

As he moved his men around, down a wide stairwell and across a series of ransacked aerodrome hangars, Gaunt tried to work out the enemy tactics. Part of it seemed blindingly obvious: allow the Imperial forces a foothold in the perimeter of the dome, and then deprive them of advance. The question was... what next?

He didn't have to wait long to find out.

The Blood Pact had been waiting. They hadn't withdrawn at all. They'd concealed themselves in false floors and behind wall panels.

Now the Imperial invaders were penned in, they sprung their ambush, coming out in the midst of the confused guard units.

Guard units who no longer had any room to manoeuvre.

THE TROOPER NEXT to Colonel Colm Corbec turned to speak and then fell silent forever as a tracer round blew his head off. A brittle rain of las-fire peppered down onto Corbec's squad from balcony positions all along the mezzanine floor he was moving across.

'Down! Down and cover! Return fire!' Corbec yelled.

He saw three troopers drop, and watched in horror as the metal-tiled flooring all around ruptured and punctured in a thousand places under the cascade of enemy shots.

Corbec crawled behind an overturned baggage cart that shook and bucked as rounds struck it. He tugged out his las-pistol and blasted through the mesh at indistinct figures on the gallery above.

Trooper Orrin was beside him, firing selective rounds from his lasrifle.

'Orrin?'

'Last chance box, sir,' Orrin answered.

Corbec fired another few shots with his pistol and tugged his remaining clip from his ammo-web, handing it to Orrin.

'Use it well, lad,' he said.

Corbec was pretty sure none of his men had any more than a single clip of size three left after the initial assault. Loaded, they might do this. They might hold.

But running empty... it would be a matter of minutes until they were totally overwhelmed.

Already, he could see two or three of the best men in his
squad – Cisky, Bewl, Roskil, Uculir – crouching in cover,
heads down, their ability to resist gone.

They were out of ammo.

Corbec prayed with all his heart that someone, someone in
authority… Ornoff, Van Voytz, maybe even Macaroth himself, would punish the simpletons in the Munitorium who,
for want of a signed docket, had hung them all out to dry.

Corbec crawled forward to the end of the cart. Someone
was crying out for a medic, and Corpsman Munne was darting through the rain of fire to reach him, aid bag in his hand.

Corbec fired his las-pistol up at the gallery. He had six clips
– size twos – left for the handgun and that was his only arm
now he'd given his last rifle pack to Orrin. There had been a
plentiful supply of size two/pistol format in the drogue's
stores. But few of the regular men carried pistols.

He saw Uclir firing a solid-ammo revolver at the enemy. A
trophy gun, taken on some past battlefield. A lot of Ghosts
cherished captured weapons. He hoped Uclir wasn't the only
man in his squad to have kept his trophy with him and in
working order.

There was a blast of serious firepower from his left. Surch
and Loell had managed to get the light support .30 onto its
brass stand and were firing. Their peals of tracers chased
along the upper levels and several dismembered red figures
tumbled down into the air shaft along with sections of
stonework.

Told of the shortage of standard rifle packs before lift-off,
Corbec had wisely assigned troopers Cown and Irvinn to
hump extra boxes of .30 shells for the support weapon. At
least his land-hammer had some life in it yet.

Lancing beams of terrible force, bright white and apoca-
lyptic, shafted down from the massing enemy. A
tripod-mounted plasma weapon was Corbec's best guess. He
saw two of his men blown into flakes of ash by it.

Corbec fired his pistol twice more and then ran, braving
the torrent of indiscriminate fire, back to a marble portico
where Muril crouched with the platoon scout Mkvenner.

'Up there!' Corbec yelled as he skidded in beside them.

'Where?' Muril asked, swinging her long-las.

Muril, a female Vervunhiver with a heroic track record from the Zoican War, was Corbec's chosen sniper. Rawne had once asked Corbec why he'd personally selected Muril for the second platoon – Rawne seemed to have an unseemly interest in the female soldiers these days – and Corbec had laughed and told him it was because Muril had a deliciously dirty laugh and red hair that reminded him of a girl he'd been a fething fool to leave behind in County Pryze.

Both facts were true, but the real reason was that Corbec believed Muril to have a shooter's eye second only to Mad Larkin, and that given a well-maintained lasrifle and a generous crosswind, she could pick off anything, anywhere, clean and true.

'Get the fething heavy weapon!' Corbec urged her.

'I see it… gak!' She took the weapon off her shoulder.

'What?' asked Corbec.

'The gakking discharge from it… so bright… just about blinding me through the scope every time it fires. Screwing the scope's photoreceptors…'

Corbec watched in horror as Muril calmly uncoupled the bulky power-scope from her weapon and aimed it again, by naked eye, down the barrel to the foreplate.

'You'll never make it…' he whispered.

'As you Tanith would say, fething watch me–'

Muril fired.

Corbec saw a spray of dust and stone chips burst from the gallery overhead.

'Yeah, yeah, okay–' Muril growled. 'I was just getting my eye in.'

The plasma weapon fired again, blowing a hole out of the lower gallery and sending Trooper Litz into the hereafter, incinerated.

'I see you,' said Muril, and fired again.

The hot-shot round blew the head off one of the Blood Pact gunners and he dropped out of sight. Another iron-masked warrior ran over to recrew the gun as the loader yelled out, but Muril had already used her first hit as a yardstick and she was firing again. Once, twice…

The third round hit the weapon's bulky power box and a whole section of the upper gallery exploded in a cone of

energy. The floor level blew out, and thirty or more Blood
Pact warriors tumbled to their deaths in an avalanche of blistered stone.

'I could kiss you,' Corbec murmured.

'Later,' Muril replied, adding a 'sir' that was lost in her dirty,
triumphant laughter.

Leaving her to refit her scope, Corbec and Mkvenner ran
towards the stairhead, where the team with the .30 autocannon was doing its level best to stem the tide of the Blood Pact
stormers charging down at them. The stairs were littered with
bodies, body parts and gore.

Loell was winged and knocked down by a stray round, but
Cown leapt up to take over the ammo feed.

The .30 was chattering, its air-cooled barrel glowing red-
hot.

Then it jammed.

'Oh feth–' stammered Corbec.

The Blood Pact were all over them.

'Straight silver! Straight silver!' Corbec ordered, and shot
the nearest enemy soldier with his pistol as he drew his
warknife. The troops in his squad pressed forward, those that
had power left firing, those that didn't using their lasrifles like
spears, their warknives locked to the bayonet lugs.

There was a brief, brutal struggle at the stairs. Corbec
stabbed and fired, at one point ending up with a Blood Pact
trooper's iron mask caught around his knife, the blade
through the eye-slit.

He saw Cisky drop, trying to hold in his ripped guts. He
saw Mkvenner halfway up the stairs, firing his last few rounds
and killing an enemy with each one. He saw Uclir clubbing
the brains out of a Chaos trooper with his solid-ammo
revolver, his last few bullets used up.

A spear of flame ripped up the staircase, consuming the
tide of enemy troops descending on them. Furrian, Corbec's
flamer-man, advanced into the press, blitzing his drizzles of
fire across the screaming foe, driving them back.

'Go, Furrian! Go, boy!' Corbec bellowed.

Furrian had grown up in the same wood-town as Brostin,
and shared his unhealthy enthusiasm for naked flames. The
tanks on his back coughed and spat liquid promethium that

the burner head in his hands ignited into blossoms of incandescent fire.

Now we're turning this, thought Corbec, now we're fething turning this.

A las-round hit Furrian in the head. He twisted and fell, the flamer spurting weak dribbles of fire across the floor.

Then another las-round hit the tanks on Furrian's back.

The blast-wash of fire knocked Corbec down. Uclir screamed as his clothes caught fire and he pitched off the staircase, a blazing comet of struggling limbs. Orrin lost his face to the flames, but not his life. He rolled on the floor, shrieking and squealing through a lip-less mouth, choking on the melted fat of his own skin.

The Blood Pact poured in. They were met by Mkvenner, Cown and Surch, the only men still standing at the stairhead after the blast. Corbec struggled up, gasping, and saw something that would remain in his mind until his dying day: the most heroic display of last stand fighting he would ever witness.

Mkvenner was by then out of ammo, and Cown had nothing but his Tanith blade.

Surch was firing a laspistol, and had attached his warknife to a short pole.

Mkvenner swung his lasgun and decapitated the first enemy on him with the bayonet, las-rounds passing either side of him. He spun the weapon and smashed a Chaos soldier down with the butt-end before ramming the blade into the belly of another.

Cown opened the torso of a Blood Pact trooper with a downward slash, and then punched his knife through the eye-slit of the iron grotesque that followed. There were enemy troopers surging all round them.

Surch shot two, then pistol-whipped another when his handgun ran dry. He drove an iron mask back into the face behind it with the dumb end of his makeshift spear shaft and then sliced it round to cut the right hand off another of their visored foes.

The warknife flew out of Cown's hand as a Blood Pact trooper with a short sword all but tore his arm off. Cown fell down, cursing, and then grabbed a drum magazine from

beside the .30. He used it to beat the swordsman to death
before passing out across him.

Surch killed four more and wounded a fifth before a las-
shot hit him in the knee, dropped him and exposed him to
the butt of an enemy gun.

Mkvenner... Mkvenner was terrifying. He was using his
lasrifle as a quarter staff, spinning it and doing equal damage with the stock end as with the blade. Urlock Gaur's
chosen finest tumbled away from him on either side, cut,
clubbed or smashed over by his heavy boots. Lanky and
long, Mkvenner kicked like a mule and moved like a dancer.
Mkoll had once told Corbec that Mkvenner had been trained
in the martial tradition of cwlwhl, the allegedly lost fighting
art of the Tanith wood-warriors. Corbec hadn't believed it.
The wood-warriors were a myth, even by Tanith's misty standards.

But as he gazed at Mkvenner then, Corbec could believe it.
Mkvenner was so fast, so steady, so direct. Every hit counted.
Every swing, every strike, every counter-spin, every stab. The
wood-warriors of ancient Tanith lore had fought in the old
feudal days, using only spear-staves tipped with single edged
silver blades. They had united Tanith and overthrown the
Huhlhwch Dynasty, paving the way for the modern democ-
ratic Tanith city-states.

Mkvenner seemed to Corbec like a figure from the fireside
tales of his childhood. The Nalsheen, the wood-warriors, the
fighters of legend, masters of cwlwhl.

No wonder Mkoll had such a special admiration for
Mkvenner.

But even he, even a Nalsheen, couldn't withstand the
assault forever.

Corbec stumbled to join him, firing wildly with his laspistol.

He fell, halfway up the steps.

Then light and dazzling streams of las-fire sliced into the
pouring foe from the top of the stairs.

Sergeant Bray's platoon had found them, moving along a
higher level to fall on the Blood Pact from the rear. Twenty-
five strong, Bray's squad quickly slaughtered the enemy and
wiped the upper gallery clear.

Bray himself hurried down the steps, pausing only to finish off a couple of wheezing, twitching Blood Pact fallen, and joined Corbec.

'Just in time, I think,' Bray smiled.

'Yeah,' panted Corbec. The colonel clambered up the stairs and helped the exhausted, gasping Mkvenner to his feet.

'Brave lad,' Corbec told him. 'Brave, brave lad…'

Mkvenner was too breathless to reply.

Supporting Mkvenner, Corbec looked back at Bray.

'Get ready,' he said. He could hear snare drums now, and the ritual hollering of the enemy as they regrouped in the galleries and halls around them. 'Get your platoon into position. Scare up as many working weapons and viable ammo as you can from the enemy dead. This is just beginning.'

'D'YOU EVER consider,' murmured Varl, taking a lho-stick out of a little wooden pocketcase and putting it between his lips, 'that we might have been too good?'

Kolea shrugged. 'What do you mean?'

Varl pursed his lips around the lho-stick, but he didn't light it. He wasn't that stupid. It was just a comfort thing, trying to block out just how much he really wanted a smoke right then. 'Well, we sure pushed ahead, didn't we? Right into the heart of them, leading the way. And look where it's got us.'

Kolea knew what the Tanith-born sergeant meant. They were, it seemed, cut off from the main force now. The last few transmissions received from Gaunt had spoken about shields or something. Now there was nothing but ominous vox-hiss. The three platoons under Varl, Kolea and Obel, numbering some seventy men, were deep in the secondary dome and utterly without support.

They had moved, cautiously, through block after block of deserted worker habitats, places that had presumably been looted and abandoned when the Blood Pact had first taken Cirenholm. Little, tragic pieces of evidence were all that showed this had once been an Imperial town: a votive aquila from a household shrine tossed out and smashed in the street; two empty ale bottles perched on a low wall; a child's toy lasgun, carved from monofibre; clothes hanging on a washing line between habs that had been left so long they were dirty again.

On the end wall of one hab-terrace was a large metal noticeboard that had once proudly displayed the workforce's monthly production figures, along with the names of the star workers. The words 'Cirenholm South Mill Second Shift' were painted in gold leaf along the top, and under that the Phantine flag and the motto, 'Our value to the beloved Emperor'. Someone had taken a lasgun to the sign, holing it repeatedly, before resorting to a flamer to burn off most of the paint.

Kolea looked at it sadly. Both it, and the hab area they were in, reminded him of the low-rent hab-home he had lived in with his family in Vervunhive. He'd worked Number Seventeen Deep Working for over a decade. Sometimes, at night, he'd dream of the smell of the ore-face, the rumble of the drills. Sometimes, he'd dream of the faces of his workmates, Trug Vereas, Lor Dinda. There'd been a proudly maintained production notice in their hab-block too. Kolea's name had appeared on it more than once.

The workers who had lived here had been employed by Cirenholm's vapour mill. Kolea wondered where they had gone, how many of them were still alive. Had the Blood Pact slaughtered the population of Cirenholm's domes, or were the poor devils penned up somewhere?

He looked back down the street block. It was broken and ruined, and made all the more dingy by the dirty yellow light shining down from the girdered roof. At least when his exhausting shifts down Number Seventeen Deep Working had been done, he'd risen to daylight and open air, to the sun rising or setting behind the artificial mountain of Vervunhive.

The Ghosts were prowling down the streets, checking the habs on either side. Varl had insisted on room-to-room checking, and it made sense. They hadn't seen an enemy since they'd first broken into the inner dome areas. The Blood Pact could be dug in anywhere. This hadn't turned into the straight fight they had been expecting. Not at gakking all.

Obel stood with a fireteam at the head of the street, looking out into a small market yard that had served the worker habs. Shops and businesses were boarded up or ransacked.

'Look at this,' Obel said, as Kolea approached. He led him into a broken down store that had once been the paymaster's office.

Munitorium crests were painted on the walls. Kolea scowled when he saw them. His opinion of the Imperial Munitorium was miserably low. He didn't know a man in their section of the company who had more than one las-cell remaining now.

Obel opened a drawer in the paymaster's brass desk, a raised mechanical lectern, with cable-sockets that showed it had once needed a cybernetic link to an authorised official in order to operate. The clamps had been broken and the drawer now rolled free and loose. Kolea was amazed to see the slots were still full of coins.

'They ransacked the city and they didn't loot the money?' Kolea wondered.

Obel picked a coin out of the tray and held it up. It was defaced. Someone with a makeshift tool, formidable strength and an obsessive amount of time on their hands, had crushed the coin and obliterated the Emperor's head. In its place was a crudely embossed rune. It made him queasy just to look at it.

Obel tossed the coin back. 'I guess that says something for the discipline of these bastards. They're more interested in leaving the mark of their maker everywhere than getting rich.'

Kolea shuddered. Every coin in the tray was the same. It was a strangely little thing, but somehow more horrifying than the sights of destruction and desecration he'd seen in his time. The arch-enemy wanted to take the Imperium and reshape every last little piece of it in his own image.

Outside, Kolea saw the hand-daubed words that the Blood Pact had painted on the walls. Words he didn't understand, made of letters he didn't know, mostly, but some were written in Low Gothic. Names. 'Gaur' and 'Slaith'.

Urlock Gaur, he knew, was the warlord controlling the main enemy strengths in this sector of the war, a fiend who commanded the loyalty of the Blood Pact. Gaunt had spoken of him with a mixture of revulsion and respect. From the recent turn of fortune the Crusade had experienced, it was clear this Urlock Gaur was a capable commander.

'Slaith' he wasn't too sure about. The commanding officers had mentioned several of Gaur's field commanders, and Kolea was pretty certain Slaith had been one of them. Perhaps he was the devil behind the war here on Phantine.

Varl wandered up and joined the both of them. 'What d'you think, eh?' he asked them. Obel shrugged.

'We've got to be closing on the vapour mill,' Kolea replied. 'I say we push on and take that.'

'Why?'

'Because we're on our own, and there doesn't seem a way back. If we're going to go down, I say we go down doing something that matters.'

'The mill?' asked Varl.

'Yes, the mill. Think how bad it could be. We could be the only ones left, and if we are, that means we'll not be getting out of here in one piece. Let's hurt them with what we have left. Let's take out their main power supply.'

On the far side of the marketplace, Larkin scooted in through the doorway of another smashed shop, taking care not to kick up the broken glass on the floor. He held his longlas ready. Baen and Hwlan, the scouts from Varl and Kolea's squads, had moved forward with fireteams to clear the west side of the market, and they'd taken the snipers with them.

Larkin looked round and saw Bragg behind him in the doorway, covering the line of open street with his heavy cannon. Caill was close by, shouldering the ammo hoppers for Bragg's support weapon.

'Anything, Larks?' Bragg hissed.

Larkin shook his head. He stepped back out onto the street. Fenix, Garond and Unkin hurried past, covering each other as they went into the next tumbled set of premises. Larkin could see Rilke and Nessa, his fellow snipers, positioned in good cover behind a stack of rotting crates, guarding the northern approach to the market hub.

Larkin moved on, slightly more comfortable with the idea of Bragg and his firepower flanking him. His sharp eyes suddenly caught something moving in a shop that Ifvan and Nour had supposedly already cleared.

'With me, Try,' Larkin hissed. As a rule, Mad Larkin didn't do brave. He preferred to lie back, pick his targets and leave the hero stuff to the likes of Varl and Kolea. But he was getting edgy. He wanted something to shoot at before he snapped, or before the tension dredged up another of his killer headaches from the dark sludge at the bottom of his brain.

He licked his lips, looked over at Bragg, who nodded reassuringly over the heavy barrel of his .50, and kicked in the old wooden door.

Larkin swept his long-las from side to side, peering into the gloom.

Dust swirled up in the sickly light that shafted in through the door and the holes in the shutters.

'Gak you, Tanith. You nearly gave me a cardiac.'

'Cuu?'

Trooper Cuu loomed out of the shadows at the back of the shop, his feline eyes appearing first.

'What the feth are you doing back there?'

'Minding my own business. Why aren't you minding yours, Tanith?'

Larkin lowered his weapon. 'This is my business,' he said, trying to sound tough, though there was something about Lijah fething Cuu that made him feel anything but.

Cuu laughed. The grimace put a nasty twist in the scar that ran down his face. 'Okay, there's enough to share.'

'Enough what?'

Cuu gestured to a small iron strong box that lay open on the shop counter. 'I can't believe these brain-donors left all this behind, can you?'

Larkin looked into the box. It was half full of coins. Cuu began pocketing some more and tossed a handful down the dirty counter to Larkin.

Larkin picked one up. It seemed like an Imperial coin, but the faces had been messed up. Cut, reworked, with a clumsy sign he didn't like.

'Take some,' said Cuu.

'I don't want any.'

Cuu looked round at him, a nasty sneer on his face. 'Don't you go trying to cut in on my action and then get high and mighty about it,' he hissed.

'I'm not–' Larkin began.

'Looting is contrary to regimental standing orders,' Bragg said softly. He was looking in through the doorway behind Larkin.

'Gak me, it's big dumbo too.'

'Shut up, Cuu,' Bragg said.

'What's the matter, big dumbo? You going all holy on me like Larkin?'

'Put the coins back,' Bragg said.

'Or what? You and Mad Larks don't got nothing that can threaten me, sure as sure.'

'Just put them back,' Bragg said.

Cuu didn't. He pushed past Larkin, and then stepped past Bragg into the street. As he did so, he paused, grinning up at the massive support gunner. 'Let's hope we don't meet up on some exercise again any time soon, eh, big dumbo?'

'What does that mean?' asked Bragg.

'Don't want to cut you with my paint stick again,' said Cuu.

Bragg and Larkin watched him walk away. 'What was that about?' asked Caill, striding up. Bragg shook his head.

'That guy's a–' Larkin paused. 'Someone needs to teach him a lesson,' he finished. 'That's all I'm saying.'

Five

AN INVISIBLE PLUME of hard, cold air was tearing at him. Somewhere far below in the amber darkness, he could here a steady, dreadful 'whup! whup! whup!', the sound of beating fan blades.

Milo's fingers were going stiff. The climbing cable cut into his palms, even though he was sure he was holding it the way Vadim had shown him.

'Left!' hissed a voice. 'Milo! Left! Move your feet left!'

Milo floundered around, trying not to kick the hollow metal walls of the great vent, but still making what seemed to him was the sound of heavy sacks of root vegetables bouncing down a tin chute.

'Left! For gak's sake! There's a rim right there!'

Milo's left foot found the rim and he eased his right over on to it.

'Vadim?' he gasped.

'You're there. Now let go of the cable with your left hand.'

'But–'

'Gakking do it! Let go and reach out. There's a bulkhead right beside you.'

Milo was perspiring so hard now he felt like his whole skin might just slip off. He couldn't see anything except the darkness, couldn't feel anything except the cable biting into his hands and the sill under his toes, and couldn't hear anything except his own frantic breathing and the threatening 'whup! whup! whup!' from below.

That, and the persistent voice. 'Milo! Now!'

He reached out, and his fingers found reassuringly solid metal.

'Now slide round. Slide round to me… that's it.'

Milo tried, but his balance was shot. He lunged as he started to fall. 'Feth!'

Strong hands grabbed him and dragged him over the edge of a hard metal frame.

'Got you! I got you! You're down!'

Milo rolled on his back, panting, and saw Vadim looking down at him in the sub-light. The Verghastite was smiling.

'Good job, Milo.'

'Feth… really?'

Vadim helped him up. 'That's no easy climb. I wouldn't have wished it on many of the guys I used to roof with. Damn sight more sheer than I was expecting, and gakking few grab-holds. Not to mention that in-rush. You feel it?'

Milo nodded. He looked back through the inspection plate Vadim had hauled him in through. Below, far below, now he had a better angle, he could see the massive turning blades of the fan. Whup! Whup! Whup!

'Feth–' he breathed. He looked back. 'Where's Bonin?'

'Here,' said the scout, emerging from the shadows. Bonin and Vadim had gone down first. 'Wasn't easy, was it?' Bonin asked, as if it had been a walk in the fields.

Vadim nudged Milo aside and reached into the vent again, pulling out Lillo, whose face was pink and sweaty with fear and exertion.

'Never again…' Lillo murmured, crouching down to rest and wiping his brow.

'I don't think we should bring anyone else down,' Vadim said to Bonin. 'It's taking too long.'

Bonin nodded and activated his micro-bead.

'You hear me, Shoggy?'

'Go ahead. Are you down?'

'Yeah, all four of us. Rest of you stay put for now. It's no easy ride. We'll scope around and see if we can't find a proper roof access to let you in by.'

'Understood. Don't take too long.'

The four Ghosts checked their lasrifles and unwrapped their camo-cloaks. They were inside Cirenholm's vapour mill now, moving along the gantries and catwalks like shadows. The thunderous purring of the main turbines covered the slight sounds they made as they spread out.

Bonin gestured them into cover, then waved Vadim and Milo forward. They had reached a main deck area suspended over the primary drums of the turbines. The air was damp and smelled of oil and burned dust.

Lillo crossed the other way at Bonin's signal. When he was in place, Bonin started forward again.

He spotted a skeletal stairwell that looked promising. Roof access, perhaps.

Bonin got in cover behind a bulkhead and signalled the others forward. Lillo drew up to flank the scout, and Vadim and Milo hurried past, making for the end of the deck walkway.

Milo dropped again, but Vadim moved on. Milo cursed silently. The Verghastite had moved too far and broken rhythm of the smooth, bounding cover they were setting.

'Vadim!' he hissed over his link.

Vadim heard him and stopped, realising he had gone too far. He looked for good cover and hurried round into the mouth of an airlock.

The airlock hatch suddenly opened.

Light flooded out.

Vadim turned and found himself face to face with six Blood Pact warriors.

IN THE GLOOM, Milo saw the abruptly spreading patch of light shine out from the airlock where Vadim had gone to ground.

A moment later, Vadim flew into view, diving frantically headlong, firing his lasrifle behind him with one hand.

A burst of answering las-fire exploded out after him. Milo saw the gleaming red bolts sizzling in the air, spanking off the grille deck and a hoist assembly, and snapping the handrail of the deck. He wasn't sure where Vadim had ended up, or if he'd been hit.

'Vadim? Vadim?'

Several figures moved out of the airlock onto the deck, fast and proficient, in a combat spread. Milo glimpsed red battle-dress, gleaming crimson helmets, the glint of black ammo-webbing, and dark faces that looked like they had been twisted into tortured expressions of pain. Two of them fired from the hatchway, down the length of the deck, providing protective fire for the others who ran out into the open.

Milo raised his weapon, but Bonin's terse voice came over the micro-link. 'Milo! Hold fire and stay low! Lillo… open up from where you are!'

Milo looked behind him. Lillo was further back down the deck than either himself or Bonin. The Verghastite started firing on semi-auto, squirting quick bursts of fire at the figures emerging from the airlock. The shots streamed down the deckway past Milo at hip height.

The enemy troops immediately focused their attention on Lillo, firing at him and moving down the deck towards him, hugging cover. Milo could see Bonin's simple but inspired tactic at once. Lillo was drawing the enemy out, stringing them between Milo and Bonin's firing positions.

'Wait… Wait…' Bonin murmured.

The enemy were closer now. Milo could see their faces were in fact metal masks, cruel and rapacious. He could smell the stink of their sweat and unwashed clothes. These have to be Blood Pact, he thought.

'Wait…'

Milo was crouched so low his legs were beginning to cramp. His skin crawled. He tightened his grip on his lasrifle. Laser bolts criss-crossed the air around him – blue-white from Lillo's Imperial weapon, flame-red from the Chaos guns.

'Now!'

Milo swept round and fired. His ripple of shots punched into a bulkhead, missing the Blood Pact trooper who hunched against it. The masked warrior whipped around at the now close source of opposition and Milo corrected his hasty aim, putting two rounds into the enemy's face.

Bonin had opened up too, deftly cutting down two of the Blood Pact as they were crossing for better cover and a better angle on Lillo.

A sudden silence. By Milo's reckoning, there were still three of them left. He could hear one creeping slowly towards the row of fuel drums concealing Bonin, but his own cover blocked his view. Milo got down and slowly pulled himself round on his belly. He could almost see his target. A shadow on the deck showed that the trooper was almost on top of Bonin.

Milo lunged out of cover, firing twice. He hit the Blood Pact trooper and sent him tumbling over, wildly firing the full-auto burst he had been saving for Bonin.

There was a fierce cry. Milo looked round to see another of the Blood Pact charging him, shooting. Las-rounds exploded off the plating behind him, nicking the stock of Milo's weapon and burning through his left sleeve.

Bonin appeared out of nowhere, leaping off the barrels full length. He smashed into the charging foe, the impact carrying them both over hard into the deck's handrail. The scout threw a savage uppercut, and his silver warknife was clenched in his punching fist. Screaming, the enemy clutched his neck and face and fell backwards off the deck.

A single las-shot rang out. The last Blood Pact trooper had been running back for the airlock. Lillo had cut him down with one, well-judged round.

Lillo hurried forward. 'Check the airlock,' Bonin told him, wiping his blade clean before sheathing it.

'Thanks,' said Milo. 'I thought he'd got me.'

'Forget it,' smiled Bonin. 'I'd never have got that one sneaking up on me.'

They joined Lillo at the airlock. 'Think we got them all. This one's an officer, I think.' He kicked the body of the one he had brought down in flight.

'Where's Vadim?' Milo asked.

They looked round. Desperate for cover, Vadim had thrown himself out of the airlock hatchway. It seemed to all three of them that in his panic, Vadim had gone clean off the edge of the deck into space.

'Hey!'

Milo got down and looked over the rail. Vadim was swinging by one hand from one of the deck's support members about five metres down.

'Feth!' said Milo. 'Get a rope!'

BONIN SEARCHED THE bodies of the dead Blood Pact, and found a ring of digital keys in the pocket of the officer's coat.

'Sorry,' Vadim said to everyone, now back on the deck. 'Got a bit ahead of myself.'

Bonin said nothing. He didn't have to. Vadim knew his mistake.

They approached the massive metal staircase and followed it up into the roof space. The captured keys let them through locked cage doors one by one. It would have taken them hours to cut or blow their way through.

At the top of the stairwell there was a greasy metal platform with a ladder up to a ceiling hatch. Bonin climbed up and tried the keys until he found one that disengaged the blast-proof lock on the hatch. 'Hoods,' he advised, and all four of them struggled back into their rebreathers before he opened the hatch. Orange hazard lights began spinning and flashing around the platform as the hatch opened to the night and freezing air billowed in.

'Someone's going to notice this,' Lillo said.

There was no helping it. Time was against them. The team they'd taken out would be missed soon anyway.

Bonin climbed out onto the roof and voxed to Domor and the main force. It took about fifteen minutes for them to struggle up through the mill's superstructure and get into the hatch. Bonin sent the first few troopers to arrive down the stairwell with Milo and Lillo to secure the base and the access to the deck. As soon as the last man was inside, Bonin closed and relocked the hatch. The hazard flashers shut down.

Down on the deck, those troopers – like Seena and Arilla – who had come through the drop crash minus weapons helped themselves to the battered, old-pattern lascarbines belonging to the Blood Pact. Avoiding the airlock, they continued on down the stairwell until they reached the main floor of the turbine chamber. It was dark and oily, with a low-level smog of exhaust smoke, but the darkness and the noise swallowed them up. Mkeller and Bonin, working from the map, snaked them through the sump levels of the mill, between the turbine frames, under walkframes, over coils of pressurised pipes. Moisture dripped down, and unwholesome insect vermin scuttled in the corners.

Somewhere high above them, light shone out. The Ghosts froze. Light from an opened hatch or airlock spread out across one of the upper catwalks, and they saw a line of figures hurrying along the walk onto a raised deck level. A moment later, and more light appeared. Another group, more soldiers, lamps bobbing as they crossed an even higher walkway, moving to support the first.

Bonin and Milo had dumped the Blood Pact dead off the deck into the darkness of the sump, but there had been no disguising the las-damage to the deck area.

Once it seemed safe to move again, they filed along the narrow companionways of the sump, and reached an inner hatch that opened with a turn of the digital keys.

In fireteam formations now, Jagdea protected in one of the middle groups, they went through into a main service corridor, round in cross-section with heavy girder ribs. Dull blue lights glowed out of mesh boxes along the backbone of the roof.

The corridor wound away, passing junctions, crossways, stairwells and elevator hatches. Haller grew increasingly uncomfortable, and he could see it in the faces of the Verghastites too. It was a maze. They'd turned so many times, he wasn't even sure of basic compass orientation anymore. But the Tanith seemed confident. Corbec had once told Haller that the Tanith couldn't get lost. It wasn't in their genes, he reckoned. Something to do with the perpetually mystifying pathways of that homeworld forest they were forever banging on about.

Now he believed it. Bonin, who like all the Tanith scouts had a grim-set face that never seemed to find much to be cheerful about, didn't even consult the map any more. He paused occasionally to check stencilled wall signs, and once backed them up and rerouted them up a level via a stairwell. But his confidence never wavered.

They came at last to a small side hall that seemed particularly dingy and long out of use. They were, by Haller's estimation, in the very basement levels of the city dome, lower even than the mill sump levels. Racks of old, cobwebbed work coveralls and crates of surplus industrial equipment had been stacked there out of the way. Most of the rooflights had gone. There was a door at the far end. A metal hatch, painted blue with a flaking white serial stencil.

Bonin paused, and looked over at Mkeller. The other scout, an older man with greying hair shaved in close to the sides of his head, returned the look with a nod.

'What is this?' whispered Haller.

'Rear service access to the mill's main control chamber.'

'Are you sure?'

'I don't need to open the door to prove it's the rear service access to the mill's main control chamber, if that's what you mean, sir.'

'Okay, okay...' Haller glanced at Domor. 'What do you think?'

'I think it's the closest thing to a target that we're going to get. Unless you'd care to hide in these sub-basements until, oh, I don't know... the end of time?'

Haller smiled. 'Point taken. And as our beloved colonel-commissar is so fond of saying... do you want to live forever?'

THE BLAST RIPPED down the length of the stateroom, shredding the painted wood panelling, dashing up the polished floor tiles and tearing one of the crystal chandeliers off the roof. The chandelier crashed and rolled like a felled, crystal tree. Its twin wilted and swayed from the ceiling.

The wispy blue smoke began to clear.

Gaunt blinked away the tears that the smoke had welled up, and coughed to clear his throat. He looked around.

Though some were brushing litter off themselves, the Ghosts in his squad seemed to have weathered the powerful explosion.

'Form and point, by threes. Let's go!' Gaunt growled over his micro-bead. 'Soric, watch our behinds.'

'Read you, sir,' crackled Soric's reply. His squad, along with those of Theiss, Ewler and Skerral, were dug in at their heels, holding off the mounting assaults of the Blood Pact.

Drawing his sword and powering it up, Gaunt ran forward with Derin and Beltayn, following the lead team of Caober, Wersun and Starck. Debris crunched underfoot. Gaunt's boot caught a crystal twig of chandelier and it went tinkling away across the dust.

Before he'd even reached the grand doorway at the end, he heard Caober's snarl of frustration and knew what it meant. The shield was still intact. They'd brought down the entire frontice of the doorway, frame and all, with the combined tube charges and det-sticks of the entire platoon and still the energy screen fizzled at them, untroubled.

'Sir?' asked Beltayn.

Gaunt thought fast. There had been a protocol for retiring – Tactician Biota had coded it 'Action Blue Magus' – but there was no point giving that signal. They were penned into the outer levels of the secondary dome by the shield wall to one side and the Blood Pact to the other. There was nowhere to retire to, and no hope of calling up an evac. Even if the drop fleet had returned to the drogue and refuelled, as they were supposed to do, the enemy held the DZ now, the only viable landing zone.

Biota had expected them to win, Gaunt thought. Dammit, he had expected them to win. Cirenholm should have been tough, but not this fething tough. They had seriously underestimated the resolve and strategic strength of the Blood Pact.

Gaunt took the mic from Beltayn.

'One to close units, by mark 6903. Shield is not breached. Repeat, not breached. Stand by.'

He consulted his data-slate chart, as Beltayn hurried to import updated troop positions from his vox-linked auspex. It was tight. Too tight. The Ghosts were entirely hemmed in by the enemy, and they were slowly being squeezed to death against the shield line.

With virtually no room to play with, Gaunt knew he had to make the best of what defensive positions he had.

'This is one,' Gaunt continued. 'Soric, Theiss, Skerral, hold your line. Ewler, angle west. The chart shows a service well two hundred metres to your right. I want it blocked and covered. Maroy, hold and provide protective fire for Ewler's move. Confirm.'

They did so in a rapid stutter of overlapped responses.

'One, further… Burone, you hear me?'

'Sir!'

'What's it like there?'

'Low intensity at present, sir. I think they're trying to flank us.'

'Understood. Try not to lose any more ground. Fall back no further than junction hall 462.'

'Four six two, confirmed.'

'Tarnash, Mkfin, Mkoll. Try to spread south to the vestibule at 717. There's a series of chambers there that look like they could be held.'

'Understood, sir,' replied Mkfin.

'Read you, one,' said Mkoll.

'Tarnash? This is one. Confirm.'

Crackling noise.

'Tarnash?'

Gaunt looked at Beltayn, who was adjusting the tuning dial. The harried vox-officer shook his head.

'One, twenty?'

'Go ahead, one.'

'Soric, Tarnash may be down, which means there may be a dangerous hole in your left flank.'

'We stand advised, sir.'

'Mkendrick, Adare… press your gain to the right. Soric needs the cover.'

'Understood, sir. It's fething hot this way,' Adare responded.

'Do your best. Wix, you still holding that loading dock?'

'Down to our last dregs of ammo, sir. We can give you ten minutes' resistance at best before it comes down to fists and blades.'

'Selective five, Wix. Use your damn tube charges, if you have to.'

A transmission cut across abruptly. 'Ten-fifty, one!'

'Go ahead, Indrimmo.'

The Verghastite's voice was frantic. Gaunt could hear rattling autofire over the link. 'We're out! My squad is out! Count zero on all las! Gak! They're on all sides now, we–'

'Indrimmo! Indrimmo! One, ten-fifty!'

'Channel's dead, sir,' murmured Beltayn.

Gaunt looked desperately back at the shield, the real enemy. It was denying him every possibility of constructing a workable defence. For a moment, he considered striking at the cursed shield with his power sword, but he knew that was no way to finish the life of Heironymo Sondar's noble weapon.

'Ideas?' he asked Caober.

The scout shook his head. 'All I figure is this shield system must be running off the city power supply. It must be sucking up a feth of a lot of juice to stay this coherent.'

Gaunt had worked that much out. If only he could reach the spearhead, Varl, Obel and Kolea... if they were still alive. Maybe they could hit in as far as the vapour mill and...

No. That was just wishful thinking. If the three squads of the spearhead were still alive, they'd be fighting for their lives now, alone in the heart of the enemy-held dome. Even if the shields hadn't been blocking their vox-broadcasts and he could talk to them, hoping they could storm the mill was futile.

Gaunt snapped round from his reverie, as what seemed like a grenade blast ruptured in across the stateroom from the left. Before the smoke had even cleared, he saw red-clad figures moving through the breach in the shattered wall.

The Imperial maps of Cirenholm were good, but the Blood Pact owned the turf, and knew every last vent chute and subbasement. They'd got into the stateroom wall space somehow, behind the rearguard of Soric and the rest.

And they were storming out into the middle of his strungout platoon.

He didn't have to issue instructions. His men reacted instinctively, even as some of them were cut down by the initial firing. Wersun ran forward, clipped twice by las-rounds, firing tight bursts that knocked at least three of the Blood Pact infantry off their feet. Caober and Derin went in head to head, stabbing with fixed blades and loosing random shots.

Vanette, Myska, Lyse and Neith leapt up and chattered their shots into the wall-breach. Myska was hit in the left forearm and fell over but was back on his feet again almost at once, using a soot-streaked jardiniere as a rest for his weapon now he was firing one-handed.

Starck fell, hit in the throat. Lossa was caught in the forehead by a las-round, stumbled blindly holding his head, and then had his legs shot out from under him by two Blood Pact at close range.

Those enemy soldiers both died quickly as successive rounds from Gaunt's bolt pistol burst their torsos.

Gaunt leapt over Wersun, who was now lying in a pool of blood, panting, and sliced his sword at the next black metal grotesque he saw.

The blue-glow of the blade glimmered in the air and was followed by a sharp stench of burnt blood. There was another to his left, raising a lascarbine that was quickly cut in half, along with the forearms clutching it.

Gaunt recoiled, the power-blade deflecting a las-round, and ran at the next group of enemies. Three of them, stumbling through the smoke-filled gap in the wall. One doubled over, hit by Derin's shots. Gaunt impaled another on his blade and slammed bodily into the third. That one tried to fire, but Gaunt dragged the sword and the heavy corpse draped on it absorbed the shots at point blank range. Gaunt punched the muzzle of his bolt pistol into the black visor and fired.

It was feral confusion now. Many of his Ghosts were dry. They fell into the mob of Blood Pact pressing through the breach with blades, fists or lasrifles swung like clubs.

A shot crisped through the sleeve of his jacket. Gaunt fired again, blowing a figure back into his comrades so they all fell like bowling pins. He fired again, but there was nothing now except a dull clack.

He was out. There was no time to change bolt clips.

He scythed with the power sword, severing bayonets, gun-muzzles and wrists. Two of the Chaos filth jumped on him, trying to bring him down. One got too near to his sword and tumbled off, eviscerated.

The other went limp suddenly, and Caober pulled him away, his straight silver in his hand.

Gaunt rose. Almost immediately, Beltayn cannoned into him and dragged him down again.

There was the chugging roar of a .30, and then the whoosh of a flamer. Bool and Mkan, manning the support weapon, and Nitorri, the squad's flame-trooper, had at last been able to move up from their positions at the end of the stateroom and address the assault. Gaunt crawled back to cover as the heavy cannon and the flames drove the enemy back into the wall.

Nitorri's left shoulder sprayed blood as a parting shot struck him. He slumped over. Lyse, one of the female Verghastites, a veteran of the Vervunhive Civil Defence Cadre, ran forward, knelt by Nitorri's shuddering body, and scooped up the flamer's hose. She swept it back and forth across the breach, igniting the panelwork and combusting the last two Blood Pact troopers who had dared to linger.

Gaunt wished he had a few more tube charges left.

'Cover that hole!' he yelled at the crew of the .30. 'You too, Trooper Lyse. Good work.'

'Sir! Commissar Gaunt sir!'

'Beltayn?'

The vox-officer held out his headset urgently.

'Sir,' he said. 'It's Scout Trooper Bonin.'

'SAY AGAIN, SIR! I can barely hear you!' Bonin kept the headset pressed to his ear and looked over with a desperate shrug to Nirriam, who was trying to adjust the big vox-unit.

There was another brief snatch of Gaunt's voice.

'Stand by, sir. We'll try and raise you on another channel.'

Bonin cut the link. 'Can you boost it?' he asked Nirriam. Nirriam raised his eyebrows, like a man who'd just been asked to inflate a drogue with lung-power.

'I dunno,' said the Verghastite. A basic infantryman, Nirriam had once done a secondary skills course in vox use, which meant he was the best qualified operator Haller and

Domor's sections could rustle up. And that wasn't saying much.

Nirriam pulled up a metal-framed operator's chair and perched on it as he tried to familiarise himself with the vox unit. It was the mill control's main communication desk, so old it was almost obsolete. Time and use had worn all the switch and dial labels blank. It was like some fiendish, inscrutable puzzle.

Bonin waited impatiently, and glanced around the room. The chamber was a fan vault, two storeys high, and provided workstation positions for the mill's thirty tech-priests. Everything was finished in brass, with shiny cream enamel coating the extensive pipework running up and down the walls. The floor was paved in grubby green ceramic tiles. It had a faded air of elegance, a relic of a more sophisticated industrial age.

There were four exit points: a hatch on the upper gallery overlooking the main chamber and three on the ground floor, including the old service access they had come in through. Domor had spread the squads out to cover them all. Lillo, Ezlan and Milo were dragging the corpses into a corner.

There had been five adepts on duty, along with two Blood Pact sentries and an officer with a silver grotesque and shabby gold frogging down his tunic front. Bonin and Mkeller hadn't been in the mood for subtlety. Most of the shooting was done by the time the main body of the party got into the chamber.

Commander Jagdea was looking dubiously at the dead and the blood decorating the tiles. Milo had taken it to be disgust at first, but she was a warrior too, and had undoubtedly seen her fair share of death.

Her face pale with pain from her injury, she had looked at Bonin angrily. 'We could have questioned them.'

'We could.'

'But you killed them.'

'It was safer.' Bonin had left it at that and moved away.

Now the wisdom of her remarks was chafing at him. If they'd kept the adepts alive – adepts, indeed, who may have been loyal Imperial citizens working under duress – one of them might have been able to operate the control room's vox-unit.

No point regretting that now, Bonin thought. He silently prayed his lucky star was still with him.

'Nirriam?'

'Give me a chance, Bonin.'

'Come on–'

'Gakking do it yourself!' the Verghastite complained, now down under the desk unplugging the switch cables one by one to blow on them.

Domor came over, pausing to check on Dremmond, Guthrie and Arilla who sat on the floor leaning against the wall, resting. Fayner was checking their wounds.

'Anything?' Domor asked.

Bonin made an off-hand gesture in the direction of Nirriam. 'He's working on it,' he said.

'Try it now!' Nirriam snorted. Bonin was certain the sentence had actually finished with a silent 'gak-face'.

Bonin put the headset back on and keyed the mic.

'Thirty-two, one. Thirty-two, one, do you read?'

Nirriam leaned past him and gently turned a dial, as if it might actually do some good.

Bonin was surprised to find it did.

'-irty-two. One, thirty-two. You're faint but audible. Do you read?'

'Thirty-two, one. We hear you. Messy channel, but it's the best we can do.'

'There's serious void shield activity in the dome, and it's blocking the signals. Micro-beads are down. Are you getting through on your main vox?'

'Negative. We're using a captured system. Must have enough power to beat the interference.'

As if to prove it wasn't, there was a sudden yowl of trash noise before Gaunt's voice continued.

'…were dead. Report location.'

'Say again, one.'

'We thought you were dead. I was told your drop had gone down in the run. What's your situation and location?'

'Long story, one. Our drop did go in, but Haller and Domor got clear with about thirty bodies. Minimal casualties on the survivors. We're inside the–' Bonin paused. He had suddenly realised that the channel might not be anything like secure.

'One, thirty-two. Repeat last.'

Bonin took out his crumpled map. 'Thirty-two, one. We're... around about 6355.'

There was a long pause. The vox-speakers whined and hissed.

'One, thirty-two. Standby.'

GAUNT SPREAD HIS map out on the top of a damaged side table. His gloves were bloody, and left brown smears on the thin paper where he flattened it.

Six three five five. 6355. There was no fething 6355 on the chart. But Bonin had said 'around about'...

Gaunt reversed the sequence. 5536. Which meant...

The mill. The main control room of the vapour mill.

Feth!

Gaunt looked round at Beltayn and took the mic from him.

'One, thirty-two. We're blocked in by an enemy shield wall ignited along marker 48:00. It's sourcing power from the main city supply. We need that supply cut, and fast if we're going to survive much past the next quarter hour. Do you understand?'

'Thirty-two, one. Very clear, sir. I'll see what we can do. Standby.'

Gaunt could feel his pulse racing. Had the Ghosts just been cut the luckiest fething break in Imperial combat history? He realised he had become so resigned to defeat and death in the last few minutes that the idea they could still turn this around genuinely shook him.

He could suddenly taste victory. He could see its shadow, feel its heat.

He suddenly remembered the things that made the burden of command and the grind of service in the Emperor's devoted Guard worthwhile.

There was a chance. Could he trust it? Making best use of it would require him to trust it, but if that trust was misplaced, his men would be slaughtered even more swiftly and efficiently than before.

And then he remembered Zweil. The old ayatani, stopping him outside the drogue *Nimbus's* Blessing Chapel.

Let me look in your eyes, tell you to kill or be killed, and make the sign of the aquila at least.

Gaunt felt a sudden gnawing in his gut. He realised it was fear. Fear of the unknown and the unknowable. Fear of the supernature that lurked beyond the galaxy he was familiar with.

Zweil had said *trust Bonin*.

How could he have known? How could he have seen…

But the old priest's words echoed in his head, rising from holy depths to make themselves heard above the aftershock of the hours of combat that had flooded his conscious mind.

The saint herself, the beati, told me… you must trust Bonin.

He'd dismissed it at the time. He had barely remembered it as they approached the DZ, tense and busting fit to scream. It had gone from his head during the rush of the drop and the ever thicker combat that had followed.

But now it was there. Zweil. In his head. Advising him. Giving him the key to victory.

He had to trust it.

Gaunt grabbed the vox-mic from his waiting com-officer and began to order a series of retreats, across the board, to all the squads he could reach. Dismayed complaints came in from many units, especially from Corbec, Hark and Soric. Gaunt shouted them down, aware that Beltayn was staring at him as if he was mad.

He checked the chart, surveying the spaces and chambers currently inaccessible behind the shield wall. He ordered all his men to pull back against the shield, with nowhere to run, and gave them quick instructions of how to deploy once they were able to move again.

Something in his tone and his confidence shut them up. They listened.

Upwards of a hundred squad officers, suddenly seeing a chance to live and to win.

'Fall back, hold on, and pray. When I give the word, follow your deployment orders immediately.'

The sound of explosions rocked down the length of the stateroom. Sensing a change in the dispersal of the Ghosts, the Blood Pact had renewed their assaults, bringing up heavy support weapons and seeding grenades.

Gaunt shouted orders to his squad. All we have to do is hold them, he thought.

And all I have to do is trust Bonin.

Six

'IDEAS?' BONIN ASKED. He was answered by sighs and shaken heads.

'They might have known,' Jagdea said quietly, looking over at the heap of corpses in the corner.

Fething woman! Bonin thought he might strike her. He detested an 'I told you so'. He looked around the control room, trying to perceive the mysteries of the vast mechanism. He felt like a child. It was hopeless. Dial needles quivered mysteriously, gauges glowed inscrutibly, levers and switches seemed to be set 'just so'. He was a soldier, not a fething tech-priest. He had no idea how to shut down a vapour mill.

'If we had tube charges, we could blow it,' said Ezlan.

'If we had tube charges,' Lillo echoed.

'Then what?' Haller groaned. He strode over to the nearest workstation and pulled a brass lever. There was absolutely no perceptible change in anything. He shrugged.

'If–' Milo began.

'If what?' said about ten people at once.

'If the Blood Pact rigged their shields into the main supply, it would be non-standard. I mean, cut in, intrusive. You know, like when we hike a breaker cable in to wire a door release.'

Domor nodded.

'I hear Milo,' said Vadim. 'If they hooked it in, it would look jury-rigged. We might be able to recognise it.'

Bonin had been considering a desperate ploy of connecting all the power cells they had and forcing an overload. In the light of Milo's more subtle idea, he put the notion of an improvised bomb to the back of his mind.

'Let's try then, shall we?' he asked. Then he paused. Haller and Domor, sergeants both, were actually in charge here. He had overstepped the line. He glanced at them, embarrassed.

'Hey, I'm with Bonin,' Domor said.

'He's got my vote,' said Haller.

'Then... go!' Bonin exclaimed.

The Ghost survivors of drop 2K scurried off in every direction as if they'd all been simultaneously slapped on the behinds. Inspection panels were prised off, service hatches pulled out, lamp packs shone up under workstations.

The only ones not searching were the sentries: Seena at the upper door, Mkeller and Lwlyn at the lower main doors and Caes, with Dremmond's flamer, at the service hatch.

Bonin came out from under a work console and turned his attention to a wall plate. The wing nuts were stiff, and he had to use the pommel of his warknife like a mallet to move them.

Beside him, Vadim was investigating the guts of a relay position, up to his wrists in bunches of wires.

'Of course,' Vadim said cheerfully, 'we could just turn every dial and switch to zero.'

'I thought of that. I also thought we could simply shoot the living feth out of everything in sight.'

'Might work,' Vadim sighed.

'Can I just say–' said a voice behind them. Bonin glanced round. It was Jagdea, her slung arm looking more uncomfortable than ever.

'What, commander?'

'I'm an aviator so I don't know much about vapour mills, but I think I know a little more than you, having lived on Phantine all my life. The mill is a gas generator. It produces billions of litres of gas energy under extreme pressure. The priesthood that maintains the Phantine mills are privy to thousands of years of lore and knowledge as to their governance.'

'And your point... because I'm sure you have one somewhere,' said Bonin, finally forcing the wall plate off.

'It's an ancient system, working under millions... I don't know... billions of tonnes of pressure. Blow it up, shoot it up, shut it down... whatever... it's likely that the system will simply explode without expert control. And if this vapour mill explodes... well, I don't think there'll be a Cirenholm left for the taking.'

'Okay,' said Bonin, with false sweetness, 'Thanks for that.' He turned to resume his work. Damn woman was going to get his knife in her back if she didn't shut up. He knew she didn't like him. Damn woman.

Damn woman had a point. They were playing around, fiddling in ignorance, with a power system that kept an entire city alive. That was real power. Jagdea was right. If they got this wrong, there wouldn't be anything left of Cirenholm except a smouldering mountain peak.

'Feth!' Bonin cursed at the thought.

'What?' said Jagdea from behind him.

'Nothing. Nothing.'

'Of course,' Jagdea continued, 'if that boy was correct–'

'Milo.'

'What?'

'Trooper Brin Milo.'

'Okay. If Milo was correct, and the enemy has wired their shields into the mill systems, isn't it likely they did it at source in the main turbine halls rather than down here in the control room?'

Bonin dropped the wall plate wth a clang and rose, turning to face her. 'Yes. Yes it is. Very likely. But we're here and we're trying our damnedest. We can't go back now, because the foe is everywhere. So we work with what we have. Have you any other comments to make, because, if you haven't, quite frankly I'd love it if you shut up now and helped us look. You're really pissing me off.'

She looked startled.

'Oh. Well. All right. What would you like me to do?'

Bonin glanced about. 'Over there. Between Nirriam and Guthrie. Take a look at that desk, if you'd be so kind.'

'Of course,' she said, and hurried over to it.

'Way to go with the lady, Bonin,' laughed Vadim.

'Shut the feth up,' said Bonin.

'Sarge! Sarge!' They all heard Seena sing out.

'What?' replied Haller, looking up from a maintenance vent he had been buried to his shoulders in.

Seena was up on the gallery, watching the upper doorway.

'We've got company.' Her voice was sweetly sing-song.

What it meant was anything but.

* * *

'COME ON! COME ON!' Corbec was yelling, standing up and waving his arms despite the enemy crossfire splashing all around. The Ghosts in his squad, along with Bray's troops, dashed back through the hatchway, a rain of fire dropping around them.

Irvinn stumbled, and Corbec dragged him through the hatch by the scruff of his neck.

'Is the shield down, chief?' he babbled.

'Not yet, son.'

'But Commissar Gaunt said it would be! He said it would be!'

'I know.'

'If the shield isn't down, we're backing ourselves into a trap, chief, we–'

Corbec cuffed the young trooper around the side of the head. 'Gaunt'll come through. That's what he does. He'll come through and we'll live! Now get in there and take your position!'

Irvinn scrambled on.

Corbec looked back in time to see two more Ghosts fall on their way to the hatch. One was Widden, whose body was struck so hard by .50 fire it was deformed completely. The other was Muril. She was hit and thrown in a cartwheel that ended with her lying on her face.

'No!' Corbec roared.

'Colm! Wait!' Sergeant Bray yelled.

'Get them back in, Bray, get them back in!' Corbec howled, running out from the hatchway towards Muril. Las-fire ripped up the deck around him, filling the air with a fog of atomised tiles.

Somehow, he reached Muril. He rolled her over. Her face was white with dust and dotted with blood that soaked into the dust like ink into clean blotting paper. Her eyelids flickered.

'Come on, girl! We're going!' he shouted.

'C-colonel–'

He looked her over, and saw the wound in her upper thigh. Bad, but survivable. He hoisted her onto his shoulders.

One of his legs gave way suddenly and they both fell over into the dust, kicking up a serene cloud of white mist.

Everything seemed to slow down. Everything seemed to go quiet.

Corbec saw the enemy las-rounds swirling through the dust in what seemed like slow motion; crackling barbs of red light, eddying wakes behind them in the dust; the oozingly slow on-off flashes of explosions; the strobe of tracers; the drops of bright red blood falling from Muril onto the floor, making soft craters in the dust.

He lifted her up again, and ran, but it was hard work. His leg didn't want to move.

There was a sudden pain in his back, and then another really biting lance of agony through his left shin.

He toppled in through the hatchway, into Bray's arms. Merrt and Bewl ran forward, mouths open, managing to catch Muril before she hit the ground.

'Medic! Medic!' Bray was yelling.

Corbec realised he couldn't move. Everything felt strangely warm and soft. He lay on his back, looking at the panelled roof.

It seemed to slide up and away from him.

The last thing he heard was Bray still screaming for a medic.

VIKTOR HARK FIRED his plasma pistol into the knots of foe around the doorway. The combined squads of Rawne, Daur and Meryn were spread out and dropping back through the dead park. There was nothing behind them except shield-blocked hatches.

They'd given up valuable ground on Gaunt's orders. There had been nothing in return.

Hark fired again. They were going to be killed. One by one, with the shield at their backs.

SERGEANT AGUN SORIC, hero of Vervunhive, sat back against the wall. The wound in his chest was sucking badly, and bloody foam was bubbling around the seared entry hole. Slowly, he raised his lasgun in one hand, but the weight of it was too much.

Men in red with metal grotesques were prowling forward towards him through the smoke.

Sergeant Theiss knelt beside him, coming out of nowhere. He fired at the enemy, forcing them into cover.

'Pull him up!' Soric heard Theiss yell.

Soric felt himself being lifted. Doyl and Mallor were under him, and Lanasa had his feet.

Theiss, with Kazel, Venar and Mtane, laid down backing fire.

'Are we through?' gurgled Soric. 'The shield…?'

'No,' said Doyl.

'Well…' said Soric, his eyes fading. 'It's been a good run, while it lasted…'

'Soric!' Doyl yelled. 'Soric!'

THE FIRST OF the Blood Pact hit the vapour mill control chamber along the upper passage.

Seena returned their fire until Ezlan and Nehn joined her. Her gunfire was punctuated with curses about the .30 she should have been firing.

It was a narrow hall, and the three Ghost guns could hold it… unless the enemy brought up something more punishing.

Three minutes after the upper hatch was assaulted, the lower main door guarded by Mkeller came under fire. He saw a grenade slung his way in time to slam the heavy iron hatch shut. The blast shook the door. Haller ran up and helped Mkeller throw the lock bolts on the corners of the hatch.

'That won't hold them long,' said Mkeller, and as if to prove it, the thump of beating fists and gun-stocks began against the door.

Lwlyn, stationed in the other main floor doorway, suddenly fell back on his backside with a curse. Blood soaked out across his battledress from his left shoulder.

'I'm hit,' he said, then fainted.

Ferocious las-fire ripped in through his hatchway. Two bolts struck Lwlyn's unconscious form sprawled in the open and made sure he would never wake up.

Guthrie reached the door and yanked it shut as las-fire hammered on the outside.

'If we're going to do something, we'd better do it now!' Guthrie yelled.

Bonin glanced at Domor. Domor shrugged. The chamber was a mess, with spools of wires draped out of every corner.

'For what it's worth, soldier,' said Jagdea, sitting down against the wall, 'I think you did your best.' She slid her short-bladed survival knife from her boot-top and slit open the cuff of her pressure suit. Bonin saw her tumble two white tablets out of the hollow cuff and tip them into her palm. She raised them to her mouth.

Bonin leapt forward and slapped them aside.

'What the feth are you doing?'

'Get off me!'

'What the feth are you doing?'

'Taking the honourable route out, soldier. We're dead. Worse than dead. Fighter Command give us those tablets in case we have to ditch behind enemy lines. The Blood Pact don't take prisoners, you know.'

'You were going to kill yourself?'

'Skinwing venom, concentrated. It's quite painless, so I'm told.'

Bonin slowly shook his head. Upon the gallery, Seena, Ezlan and Nehn were blasting away.

'Suicide, Commander Jagdea? Isn't that the coward's way out?'

'Screw you, soldier. How much clearer do you need it? We're dead. Dee-ee-ay-dee. I'd rather die without pain than greet the death they're bringing.'

Bonin dropped down in a crouch in front of her and scooped up the poison pills. He rolled them in his palm.

'Colonel-Commissar Gaunt taught me that death was something to be fought every last step of the way. Not welcomed. Not invited. Death comes when it comes and only a fool would bring it early.'

'Are you calling me a fool, Bonin?'

'I'm only saying that all is not yet lost.'

'Really?'

'Really. It may only be a soldier's ignorant philosophy, but in the Guard, we keep fighting to the end. If we die, we die. But suicide is never an option.'

Jagdea stared up at him.

'Give me the pills.'

'No.'

'I think I outrank you.'

'I hardly care.' Bonin dropped the tablets onto the floor and crushed them with his heel.

'Damn you, Bonin.'

'Yes, commander.'

'Do you really think something's going to change here? That we might be miraculously rescued?'

'Anything's possible, as long as you allow for it. My mother told me I was born under a lucky star. That luck's never left me. There have been times I should have died. At Vervunhive. I can show you the scars.'

'Spare me.' Her voice was thin and frail now.

'I believe in my luck, Jagdea. Tanith luck.'

'Screw you, we're all dead. Listen to that.'

Bonin heard the furious hammering at the doors, the frantic resistance of the trio on the gallery.

'Maybe. If we are, I promise you won't suffer.'

'You'll do me yourself? How gallant.'

Bonin ignored the sarcasm. 'Tanith First-and-Only, ma'am. We look after our own.'

ON THE GALLERY, Nehn flinched back, winged. Seena saw a Blood Pact trooper charging them… only to fall. In all the worlds, it looked to her like he had been hit in the back of the head by a hot-shot.

The assault lapsed.

Her micro-bead chirped. 'Who's down there?'

It was the Imperial Guard channel.

'Twenty-fourteen, come back?' she whispered.

'Nine, twenty fourteen. That you, Seena?'

'Sarge?'

'Large as life and twice as ugly, girl.'

'It's Kolea! It's Kolea!' Seena sang out to the chamber.

THE COMBINED SQUADS of Obel, Kolea and Varl moved in through the upper gallery and joined up with Haller and Domor's units. It was all very calm, matter of fact. There were a few handshakes and greetings. No whooping, no cheering, nothing to betray the elation they all felt. Nothing to acknowledge the dazzling fortune that had just turned their way.

By then, nearly psychotic levels of Blood Pact opposition were thrashing in at the main ground floor hatchways. Varl sent the flamers to subdue it.

'Of course,' Kolea was saying.

'Really?' asked Haller, who'd been his second in the Vervunhive scratch units.

'You don't work mines and power plants all your life and not know how the generator flow-systems work.'

Kolea walked over to what seemed like a side console and threw a nondescript lever.

The lights dimmed. The gauges dropped. The thundering pant of the turbines pitched away.

He turned from the console and saw the dumbstruck faces all around.

'What? What?'

THE SHIELDS WENT down.

THERE WAS AN electrical crackle and a sudden, violent rush of air as the shield at the end of the stateroom vanished and pressure equalised.

'Now,' yelled Ibram Gaunt. 'Now, now, now! Men of Tanith, Men of Verghast! The tables turn!'

'Show me what the Imperial Guard can do!'

A REAPPRAISAL OF COMBAT POLICY
CIRENHOLM CITY OCCUPATION,
PHANTINE
214 to 222.771, M41

*'Cirenholm was taken after seven hours of determined assault.
A handsome victory for the Imperial Guard. That's what the
textbooks will say. However, the crucial gains that enabled the
victory were achieved not by mass assault, but by the stealthy
application of highly trained, highly disciplined individuals who
were sensibly trusted with an unusual degree of command auton-
omy, and who used their polished covert skills to disable the
enemy defences more completely than ten thousand slogging
infantry units could ever have managed.
It's just a shame we didn't plan it that way.'*

– Antonid Biota, Chief Imperial Tactician,
Phantine Theatre

One

SWOLLEN PLUMES OF brown fire-smoke drifted up from the
south-facing edges of Cirenholm's trio of domes, and diluted
into yellow smog in the hard morning sunlight.

From the upper observation deck of the primary dome, it
was difficult to believe Phantine was a toxic world. The bright

135

sun made the high altitude sky powder-blue and, down below the sculptural curves of the domes, great oceans of knotted white cloud spread out as far as the eye could see. Only occasionally was there a dark stain or a ruddy surge of flame visible beneath the clouds as the inferno of the Scald underlit them.

Like a pod of great sea mammals, the drogues were coming in. Eight of them, each a kilometre long from nose-ram to tail fins, coasting along on the morning wind, their taut silver and white skins gleaming. Pairs of tiny, fast moving Lightnings crossed between them, making repeated low passes over the city. Gunships, weapon-mounted variants of the drops that had brought them to Cirenholm, slunk along beside the vast drogues in escort.

It was cold up on the observation deck. The city's heating systems were still off-line. It was taking a long time to get the vapour mill running back to optimum after the sudden shutdown.

Gaunt pulled his long storm coat tight. Ice crystals were forming on the glass of the observation port, and he wiped them off with a gloved hand. There was something infinitely relaxing about watching the drogues approach. He could just hear the distant chop of their massive prop banks. Every now and then, the glass vibrated as a Lightning burned low overhead.

'Ibram?'

Gaunt turned. Hark had entered the observation gallery, cradling two beakers of steaming caffeine.

'Viktor, thank you,' Gaunt said, taking one.

'Quite a sight,' noted Hark, blowing the steam off his caffeine as he sipped it.

'Indeed.'

A pilot tug had just fluttered out to anchor the nose of the lead drogue and drag it into the hangar decks under the lip of the primary dome. Gaunt watched the letters painted on the drogue's nose – ZEPHYR – slowly disappear one by one as it passed into the deep shadow under the lip.

Gaunt drank his hot caffeine gingerly. 'What's the latest?' He'd remained on station with Beltayn for six hours, supervising the comm-traffic, before catching a few, restless hours of sleep in an unaired room off the grand states in secondary. Since he'd risen, he'd tried to stay away from the babbling voxes. He needed calm.

'Some fighting still in the northern sectors. Rawne's pretty much cleared the last of secondary. Tertiary is clean, and Fazalur's moving his forces up into primary to bolster the Urdeshi. Heaviest resistance is up in the north block of primary. Some bad stuff, but it's just a matter of time. We found the citizens, though. Kept in mass pens in the tertiary dome. Fazalur liberated them. We're beginning rehousing and repopulation.'

Gaunt nodded.

'What?' asked Hark.

'What what?'

Hark smiled. It was a rare expression for him. 'That look in your eyes. Sadness.'

'Oh, that. I was just pitying the Urdeshi. They had the worst of it, all told. What's the count now?'

'Twelve hundred dead, another nine hundred wounded.'

'And us?'

'Twenty-eight dead. Two hundred wounded.'

'How's Corbec?'

Hark sighed. 'It's not looking good. I'm sorry, Ibram.'

'Why? You didn't shoot him. What about Agun Soric?'

'They've crash resuscitated him twice already. He should have died on the spot, the wound he took.'

'Agun's a tough old feth. He'll go when he wants to.'

'Let's hope it's not yet, then. I don't know which we'd miss most.'

Gaunt frowned. 'What do you mean?'

Hark shrugged. 'Corbec's the heart of the Tanith First. Everyone loves him. We lose him, it'd be a body blow to all. But Soric is cut from the same cloth. He means a lot to the Verghastites. If he dies, I think it'll knock the stuffing out of the Verghast sections of the regiment. And we don't want that.'

'They have other leaders: Daur, Kolea.'

'And they're respected. But not like Soric. He's their father figure, like the Tanith have Corbec. Kolea could make more of himself, but I don't think he wants to be a totem. I honestly think Kolea would be happier as a basic trooper.'

'I think so too, sometimes.' Gaunt watched the next drogue, the *Boreas*, as it was tugged in under the hangar housing.

'Daur's a good man too,' Hark continued. 'I like him, but he's... I don't know. Perky. Eager. The Verghastites don't like that very much. He's not grounded like Soric. And the Tanith positively despise him.'

'Daur? They despise Daur?' Gaunt was shocked.

'Some of them,' said Hark, thinking of Rawne. 'Most of the Tanith genuinely appreciate the Verghast new blood, but none of them can really shake the notion of intrusion. Intrusion into their regiment. Daur landed authority equal to Major Rawne. To many, he exemplifies the invasion of the First-and-Only by the Vervunhivers.'

'To Rawne, you mean?'

Hark grinned. 'Yes, him especially. But not just him. It's an honour thing. Surely you've noticed it?'

Gaunt nodded without replying. He was well aware of the way Hark was testing him. Hark was a loyal man, and had begun to perform his duties as regimental commissar impeccably. But he was always testing boundaries. It pleased Hark to think he was more in tune with the First's spirit than Gaunt.

'I know we've got a good way to go before the Tanith and Verghastite elements of this regiment reach comfortable equilibrium,' said Gaunt after a long pause. 'The Tanith men feel proprietorial about the regiment. Even the most broad-minded of them see the Verghastites as outsiders. It's their name on the standard and the cap badge, after all. And it's got nothing to do with ability. I don't think any Tanith would question the fighting spirit of the Vervunhivers. It's just a matter of... pride. This is and always was the Tanith regiment. The new blood we brought from Verghast is not Tanith blood.'

'And, in reverse, the same goes for the Verghastites,' agreed Hark. 'This isn't their regiment. They've got their own insignia, but they'll never get their name on the standard placard. They feel the resentment of the Tanith... they feel it because it's real. And they understand it, which makes things worse. They want to make a mark for themselves. I'm actually surprised the divide hasn't been more... difficult.'

Gaunt sipped the last of his drink. 'The Verghastites have made their mark. They've helped our sniper strength grow enormously.'

'Yes, but who's given them that edge? The women, for the most part. Don't mistake me, the girl snipers are a god-damned blessing to this combat force. But male Verghast pride is dented because the women are the best they can offer. They've made no scouts. And that's where the true honour lies. That's what the First is famous for. The Tanith scouts are the elite, and have the Verghasts produced even one trooper good enough to make that cut? No.'

'They've come close. Cuu.'

'That bastard.'

Gaunt chuckled. 'Oh, I agree. Lijah Cuu is a fething menace. But he's got all the qualities of a first-rate scout.'

Hark set his beaker down on the windowsill and wiped his lips. 'So... have you given any thought as to how we can improve the regimental divide?'

You're testing again, Gaunt thought. 'I'd welcome ideas,' he told Hark diplomatically.

'A few promotions. I'd make Harjeon up to squad rank. And LaSalle. Lillo too, maybe Cisky or Fonetta. We'll need a few fresh sergeants now Indrimmo and Tarnash are gone.'

'Cisky's dead. More's the pity. But I agree in principle. Not Harjeon. An ex-pen pusher. The men don't have any respect for him. Lillo's a good choice. So's Fonetta. LaSalle, maybe. My money would be on Arcuda. He's a good man. Or Criid.'

'Okay. Arcuda. Makes sense. I don't know about Criid. A female sergeant? That might cause more problems than it solves. But I think we should fast-track two or three into the scout corps.'

'Viktor, we can't do that if there isn't the talent. I'm not going to field point men who haven't got the chops for the job.'

'Of course. But Cuu, like you said. There are others. Muril.'

'Isn't she wounded?'

'Getting a brand new steel hip, but she'll make it. Also Jajjo, Livara and Moullu.'

Gaunt frowned. 'They're possibles. Some of them. Muril's got potential, and Livara. But I've never known a man as clumsy as Moullu, for all that he's light on his feet. And Jajjo? I'd have to think about that. Besides, the cut's not down to me. It's Mkoll's call. Always has been.'

'You could order him t–'

'Viktor, enough. Don't push it. The scout elite has always been Mkoll's area. I happily bow down to his expertise, I always have. If he thinks any of that list can make the grade, he'll take them. But if he doesn't, I'm not going to force them on him.'

'That's fine. Mkoll knows his stuff.'

'He does. Look, I'll keep my eyes open. I'll do everything I can to balance out the Verghastite/Tanith mix. Positive discrimination if necessary. But I won't risk damaging the combat core by advancing those who aren't ready or good enough.'

Hark seemed satisfied with this, but then he surprised Gaunt with a final comment. 'The Verghast need to know you value them as much as the Tanith, Ibram. Really, they do. What will destroy them is the idea they're latecomers who can't make the grade. They feel like second-class elements of this regiment. That's not good.'

Gaunt was about to reply, taken aback by the remark, but the deck's inner door slid open and a vox-officer dressed in the fur-trimmed uniform of the Phantine Skyborne entered and saluted.

'Lord General Barthol Van Voytz is coming aboard, Colonel-Commissar Gaunt. He requests your company.'

THE DROGUE NIMBUS was already edging in towards the vast hangar bay under the primary dome, a little tug-launch revving its over-powered thrusters as it heaved the vessel home. The drogue's immense aluminium propeller spars were making deep, whispering chops as they slowed to a halt.

Van Voytz had flown ahead. Escorted by two Lightnings that veered away sharply once it had reached the hangar mouth, his chequer-painted tri-motor purred in under the shadow. It was a stocky transport plane with a bulbous glass nose, and it made a heavy but clean landing on the deck way, its powerful double-screwed props chattering into reverse as soon as its tail hook caught the catch-line.

Gaunt stood waiting in the gloom of the hangar, a hangar which already accommodated the massive bulk of the drogue *Aeolus* without seeming full.

The tri-motor's engines were still roaring as the footwell slapped down from the hull and Van Voytz emerged.

'Guard, attention!' Gaunt barked and the honour detail of Ghosts – Milo, Guheen, Cocoer, Derin, Lillo and Garond, under the supervision of Sergeant Theiss – smacked their heels together and shouldered arms smartly. Theiss held the company standard.

The lord general bent low under the downwash of the props and hurried forward up the ramp, flanked by his aide, Tactician Biota and four splendid bodyguard troopers with blue-black tunics, hellguns and gold braid around the brims of their shakos.

'Gaunt!'

'Lord general.'

Van Voytz shook his hand. 'Damn fine job, soldier.'

'Thank you, sir. But it wasn't me. I have a list of commendations.'

'They'll all be approved, Gaunt. Mark my words. Damn fine job.' Van Voytz gazed up around him as if he'd never seen a hangar deck before. 'Cirenholm. Cirenholm, eh? One step forward.'

'One step back for the Urdeshi, with respect.'

'Ah, quite. I'll be having words with Zhyte once he's out of surgery. He screwed up, didn't he? Man's a blow-hard menace. But you, Gaunt... you and your Ghosts. You turned this fiasco on its head.'

'We did what we could, lord.'

'You did the Guard proud, colonel-commissar.'

'Thank you, sir.'

'You quite pulled a fast one, didn't you?'

'Sir?'

'You and your covert experts. He quite pulled a fast one, didn't he, Biota?'

'He seems to have done, lord general,' Biota replied mildly.

'Making us do a rethink, Gaunt. A radical rethink. Ouranberg awaits, Gaunt, and your work here has prompted us to make a hasty reappraisal of combat policy. Hasn't it, Biota?'

'It has, lord general.'

'It has indeed. What do you think of that, Gaunt?'

Ibram Gaunt didn't know quite what to think.

ONTI FLYTE REGARDED herself as a true Imperial citizen, and had raised her three children in that manner. When the arch-enemy had come to Cirenholm, and overrun it so fast, she'd felt like the sky had fallen in. Her husband, a worker in the mill, had been killed by the Pact in the initial invasion. Onti, her children and her neighbours, had been herded out of their habs by the masked brutess and shut up in a pen in the bowels of tertiary.

It had been hellish. Precious little food or water, no sanitation. The place had stunk like a drain by the end of the first day.

After that there had been disease and dirt, and the stench had become so high she could no longer smell it.

Now, as the Imperial Guard escorted them back to their habs, she could smell the stink. It was in her clothes and in her hair. She knew the street-block shower would have queues, and the laundry would be full to bursting, but she wanted her kids clean and dressed in fresh clothes. That meant getting the outhouse tub full, and hard work with the press.

A nice young Guardsman in black called Caffran had seen her and the kids back to their hab. Onti had kept apologising for the way they smelled. The boy, Caffran, had been so polite and kind.

It was only when she was back in her place, in the little parlour of her terraced hab, that she'd cried. She realised how much she missed her husband, and she was haunted by what the arch-enemy had undoubtedly done to him.

Her children were running around. She wanted them to quiet down. She was beside herself. The nice soldier – Caffran – looked in on her as the streets outside swarmed with people returning to their homes under escort.

'Do you need anything?' he asked.

'Just a handsome husband,' Onti had joked, painfully, but trying hard.

'Sorry,' the nice soldier said. 'I'm spoken for.'

Onti had put her head in her hands when he was gone and sobbed over the parlour table.

Her eldest, Beggi, had run in to tell her that the tub was almost full. He'd put the soap crystals in, the special ones, and all the kids said they wanted their mam to have the first bath.

She kissed them all in turn, and asked Erini to warm up a pot of beans for them all.

Onti went out into the yard and saw the steam wallowing from the outhouse where the tub sat. She could smell the peppermint vapours of the soap crystals.

On the other side of the yard fence, her neighbour, an old pensioner called Mr Absolom, was sweeping out his back step.

'The mess they made, Ma'am Flyte,' he cried.

'I know, Mr Absolom! Such a mess!'

Onti Flyte went into the outhouse and dragged off her filthy clothes.

Naked and wrapped in a threadbare towel, she was testing the water with her hand when she heard the creak.

She looked up and froze, realising someone was crouching in the back of the outhouse.

She felt vulnerable. She felt open. For a terrifying moment, she thought it was one of the arch-enemy, gone to ground. One of the foul, masked Blood Pact.

But it wasn't.

The figure stepped out of the shadows.

It was a fine young Guardsman. Just like the lovely young man who had escorted her and the kids back to her hab.

'Well, you shouldn't be in here, sir,' she said. 'You know what people say about a fine soldier boy...'

She sniggered.

The soldier didn't.

Onti Flyte suddenly realised that she was in trouble. Really bad trouble. She opened her mouth, but nothing came out.

The soldier stepped forward. He was very distinctive looking.

He had a knife. A long, straight silver knife that shone against the black fabric of his battledress.

She felt a scream building inside her. This wasn't right. This wasn't how it worked.

'Don't,' he said.

She screamed anyway. For a very short time.

Doc Dorden held the chipwood tongue depressor in the same confident way Neskon held his flamer. 'Say "Aaargh",' he said.

'Sgloot–' Milo managed.

'No, boy. "Aaargh"… "AAARGH"… like you've been stuck with an ork bayonet.'

'Aaargh!'

'Better,' smiled Dorden, taking the stick out of Milo's mouth and tossing it into a waste sack taped to the side of his medikit. He grabbed Milo by the head with both hands and examined his eyes, dragging the lids aside with firm fingertips.

'Any nausea?'

'Only now.'

'Ha ha… any cramps? Blood in your spittle or stools? Headaches?'

'No.'

Dorden released his head. 'You'll live.'

'Is that a promise?'

Dorden smiled. 'Not one in my power to give, I'm afraid. I wish–'

The old Tanith doctor added something else, but his words were lost in the background hubbub of the billet hall. Milo didn't ask him to repeat it. He was sure from the doc's sad eyes it had had something to do with his son, Mikal Dorden, Ghost, dead on Verghast.

It was the third day after the raid. The Tanith First had been assigned billets in a joined series of packing plants in the secondary dome. Hundreds of wood bales had been laid down in rows for cots and the Munitorium distribution crews had dropped a pair of thin blankets on each one. Most Ghosts had supplemented this meagre bedding with their camo-cloaks, bedrolls and musette bags stuffed with spare clothing.

The noise in the chamber was huge. In Milo's alone there were nine hundred men, and the wash of their voices and their activities filled the air and echoed off the high roof. The men were relaxing, cleaning kit, field stripping weapons, smoking, dicing, arm-wrestling, talking, comparing trophies, comparing wounds, comparing deeds...

Dorden, Curth and the other medics were moving through the billets, chamber by chamber, doing the routine post combat fitness checks.

'It's amazing how many troopers hide injuries,' Dorden was saying as he collected his kit together. 'I've seen five flesh wounds already that men didn't think were worth bothering me with.'

'Honour scars,' said Milo. 'Marks of valour. Lesp's such a good needleman, they're afraid they'll not have the marks to show and brag about.'

'More fool them, Brin,' said Dorden. 'Nour had a las-burn that was going septic.'

'Ah, there, you see?' replied Milo. 'Verghast. They want the scars most of all, to match our Tanith tattoos.'

Dorden made a sour face, the sort of sour face he always made when confronted by naive soldier ways. He handed Milo two pill capsules of different colours and a paper twist of powder.

'Take these. Basic vitamins and minerals, plus a hefty antibiotic boost. New air, new germ pool. And sealed and recirculated, which is worse. We don't want you all coming down with some native flu that your systems have no defence against. And we don't know what the scum brought here with them either.'

'The powder?'

'Dust your clothes and your boots. The Blood Pact had lice and now they're gone, the lice are looking for new lodgings. The poor Phantine found their billets in tertiary were infested.'

Milo swigged the pills down with a gulp from his canteen and then set about obediently sprinkling his kit with the powder. He'd been halfway through stripping his lasrifle when the doc reached his cot in the line, and he wanted to get back to it. Troops were being pulled out every few hours to assist in Major Rawne's final sweep of the primary dome. Milo was sure he would be called soon.

Dorden nodded to Milo and moved on to Ezlan at the next cot.

Milo looked across the busy activity of the cot rows. Two lines away, Surgeon Curth was checking a trooper's scalp wound. Milo sighed. He liked Doc Dorden a lot, but he wished Curth had reached his row first. He would have enjoyed being examined by her.

He pushed his half-stripped las to one side and lay back on his cot with his hands behind his head, staring at the roof and trying to blot out the noise. Try as he might, over these last few months, he had been unable to stop thinking about Esholi Sanian, the young scholar who had guided them to the Shrinehold on Hagia, their last battlefield. He'd liked her a lot. And he had been sure the feeling was mutual. The fact that he would never, ever see her again didn't seem to matter to Milo. She wouldn't leave his mind and she certainly wouldn't leave his dreams.

He'd never spoken about it to anyone. Most of the Tanith had lost wives or sweethearts on the home world, and most of the Verghastites had left their loves and lives behind. There were females in the regiment now, of course, and every last one of them was the object of at least one trooper's affection. There were some romances too. His friend Caffran's was the best. His first love Laria had perished with Tanith, and he'd been as forlorn as the rest for a long time. Then on Verghast, right in the thick of the hive-war, he'd met Tona Criid. Tona Criid... ganger, hab-girl, scratch fighter, mother of two young kids. Neither Caffran nor Criid, both of whom Milo now counted amongst his closest friends, had ever described it as love at first sight. But Milo had seen the way they looked at each other.

When the Act of Consolation had been announced, Criid had joined the Ghosts as standard infantry. Her kids came along, cared for during times of action by the Ghosts' straggling entourage of cooks, armourers, quartermasters, barbers, cobblers, musicians, traders, camp followers and other children. Every Guard regiment had its baggage train of non-combatants, and the Ghosts' now numbered over three hundred. Regiments accreted non-combatant hangers-on like an equine collected flies.

Now Caff and Criid were together. It was the Ghosts' one, sweet love story. The troops might smile at the couple, but they respected the union. No one had ever dared get in between them.

Milo sighed to himself sadly. He wished that Sanian had been able to come along with him that way.

He thought for a moment about going down to the hangar deck where the entourage was encamped. He could get a meal from the cook-stoves, and maybe visit one of the overly-painted women who followed the regiment and saw to the men's needs.

He rejected the idea. He'd never done that and it didn't really appeal except at the most basic level.

Anyway, they weren't Sanian. And it wasn't sex he was after. Sanian was inside his head, like it mattered she should be there. He didn't want to do anything that might eclipse her memory.

And he couldn't for the life of him explain why the memory of her refused to fade. Except… the prophecy. The one the old ayatani priests of Hagia had made. That Milo would find some way, some purpose, in years to come.

Milo hoped that had something to do with Sanian. He hoped that was why she remained bright in his mind. Maybe, somehow, she was his way.

Probably not. But it made him feel better to think of it like that.

'Now that looks like trouble,' he heard Doc Dorden say from the next cot along.

Milo sat up and looked. Far away, at the entrance to the billet hall, he could see Captain Daur talking seriously with a pair of Imperial commissars Milo had never seen before. The commissars were flanked by eight armed Phantine troopers.

'ON WHOSE AUTHORITY?' Daur snapped.

'Imperial Taskforce Commissariate, captain, Commissar Del Mar. This is an internal security matter.'

'Does Colonel-Commissar Gaunt know about this?'

The two commissars looked at each other.

'He doesn't, does he?' smiled Daur. 'What about Commissar Hark?'

'You are delaying us, captain,' said the shorter of the two commissars. His name, he had told Daur, was Fultingo, and he was attached to Admiral Ornoff's staff. The other one, taller and gawkier, and wearing the pins of a cadet-commissar, had fresh Urdeshi insignia sewn onto his coat.

'Yes, I am. I want to know what this is about,' said Daur. 'You can't just march in here and start questioning my troops.'

'Actually, sir, we can,' said Fultingo.

'This is Gaunt's regiment, these are Gaunt's men…' Daur said quietly. 'Ibram Gaunt, the only commissar I know of to hold a command rank. Don't you think simple courtesy would have you approve it via him?'

'The God-Emperor's exalted Commissariate has little time for courtesy, captain.' Daur turned and saw Hark strolling up behind him. 'Unfortunately. However, as assigned Tanith First commissar, I intend to make sure that courtesy is extended.'

'They want to search the billet,' Daur said.

'Do they? Why?' Hark asked.

'A matter of internal security,' said Fultingo's cadet quickly.

Hark raised his eyebrows. 'Really… why?'

'Commissar Hark, are you refusing to cooperate?' asked Fultingo.

Hark turned. He took off his cap and tucked it under his arm. He fixed Fultingo with a poisonous stare.

'You know me?'

'We were briefed.'

'Yet I don't know you, or your… junior.' Hark waved his cap at the cadet.

'I am Commissar Fultingo, from the admiral's general staff. This is Cadet Goosen, who was serving under the Urdeshi Commissar Frant.'

'And Frant couldn't be bothered to attend?'

'Commissar Frant was killed in the assault,' said Goosen nervously, adjusting his collar.

'Oh, thrust into the limelight, eh, cadet?' smiled Hark.

'Not in any way I would have wished,' said Goosen. Daur thought that was a particularly brave response from the junior officer. Hark was in the process of bringing his full, withering persona to bear.

'So… Fultingo… what's this all about?' asked Hark softly.

'Something to do with that child, I should think,' said Curth. She'd joined them from the billet rows, her brow knotted. She pushed past the officers and the escort and knelt beside a small, grubby boy who was holding onto the last trooper's coat tails and trying not to cry.

'My name's Ana. What's your name?' she whispered.

'Beggi…' he said.

'Did you know that?' she asked Fultingo caustically.

Fultingo consulted his data-slate. 'Yes. Beggi Flyte. Eldest son of Onti Flyte, Cirenholm mill-wife.'

The boy was shuddering with tears now.

'He's deeply traumatised!' Curth spat, holding the child. 'Why did you see fit to drag him around these billets and–'

'He's deeply traumatised, ma'am,' said Fultingo, 'because his mother is dead. Murdered. By one of the Ghosts.

'Now… can we proceed?'

THE ENTOURAGE CAMP was a heady, smoky place half filling a cargo hangar. Cooks were roasting poultry and boiling up stews along a row of chemical stoves, and their assistants were dicing vegetables and herbs on chopping stands nearby. There was music playing, pipes, mandolins and hand-drums, and behind that there was the steady chink-chink of the armourers in their work-tents. Ghosts milled about, eating, drinking, getting their weapons sharpened, dancing and laughing, chatting conspiratorially to the painted women.

Kolea moved through the press. A fire-eater retched flame into the air and people clapped. The sounds reminded Gol of flamers in battle.

Someone offered him a smoked chicken portion for a credit but he waved them aside. Another, dressed in gaudy robes and sporting augmetic fingers, tried to interest him in a round of 'find the lady'.

'No thanks,' said Gol Kolea, pushing past.

A bladesmith was sharpening knives on a pedal-turned whetstone. Sparks flew up. Kolea saw Trooper Unkin waiting in line behind Trooper Cuu for his straight silver to be edged. Cuu's blade had already been rubbed in oil and was now set at the grinder, sparking.

He moved on. Black marketeers offered him size three clips.

'Where the gak were you?' he snarled, sending them away with a cuff.

Others had candy, porn-slates, exotic weapons, booze.

'Real sacra! Real, ghosty-man! Try it!'

'Can't stand the stuff,' growled Kolea, shouldering through.

A one-legged hawker showed off talismans of the Emperor, Tanith badges and aquila crests. Another, his face sewn together, produced chronometers, nightscopes and contraband micro-beads.

Yet another, limbless and moving thanks to a spider-armed augmetic chassis, displayed lho-sticks, cigars and several stronger narcotics.

A juggler tumbled past. A mime artist, her face yellow and stark, performed the death of Solan to an appreciative crowd. A small boy ran through the crowd, running a hoop with a stick. Two little girls, neither of them more than five years old, were playing hop-square.

'Going my way, handsome?'

Kolea stopped in his tracks. His Livy had always called him 'handsome'. He looked round. It wasn't Livy.

The camp-girl was actually pretty, though far too heavily made-up. Her dark-lashed eyes were bright and vivid. A beauty spot sat on her powdered cheek. She smiled at Kolea, her long skirt bunched up either side of her hips in her lace-gloved hands as she posed coquettishly. Her large, round breasts might as well have been bared given the flimsiness of the satin band that restrained them.

'Going my way?'

Her perfume was intoxicatingly strong.

'No,' said Kolea. 'Sorry.'

'Ball-less gak,' she hissed after him.

He tried to ignore her. He tried to ignore everything.

Aleksa was waiting for him in her silk tent.

'Gol,' she smiled. She was a big woman, fast approaching the end of her working days. No amount of powder, paint or perfume could really sweeten her rotund bulk. Her petticoats were old and threadbare, and her lace and holiathi gown was faded. She cradled a cut-crystal glass of amasec against her colossally exposed bosom with a wrinkled, ringed hand.

'Aleksa,' he said, closing the hems of her tent behind him.

She wriggled around on her pile of silk cushions. 'The usual?' she asked.

Gol Kolea nodded. He took the coins from his safe-belt, counted them again and offered them to her.

'On the nightstand, please. I don't like to get my gloves dirty.'

Kolea heaped the coins on the side table.

'Okay then… off you go,' she said.

He climbed on to the heap of cushions, and crawled across past Aleksa. She lay back, watching him.

Kolea reached the wall of the tent and parted the silk around the slit Aleksa had made for him.

'Where are they?'

'Right there, Gol.'

He angled his head. Outside, across the walkway, two children were playing a nameless game in a gutter puddle. A small boy and a toddler, laughing together.

'They've been okay?'

'They've been fine, Gol,' said Aleksa. 'You pay me to look after them so I do. Yoncy had a cough last week, but it's cleared up.'

'Dalin… he's getting so big.'

'He's a feisty one, no doubt. Takes a lot of watching.'

Kolea smiled. 'Which is all I do.'

He sat back on the cushions. She leaned forward and rubbed his shoulders with her hands.

'We've been through this, Gol. You should say something. You really should. It's not right.'

'Caff and Tona… they're doing right by them?'

'Yes, yes! Believe me, they're… I was going to say they were the best parents those kids could get… but you know what I mean.'

'Yeah.'

'Oh, Gol, come on.'

He looked round at her. 'They're mine, Aleksa.'

She grinned. 'Yes, they are. So go out there and claim them.'

'No. Not now. I won't gak up their lives any more. Their daddy's dead. It has to stay that way.'

'Gol… it's not my place to say this–'

'Say it.'

Aleksa grinned encouragingly. 'Just do it. Criid will understand. Caffran too.'

'No!'

'Criid's a good woman. I've got to know her, the time she spends here. She'd understand. She'd be… oh, I don't know. Grateful?'

Kolea took one last look through the slit. Dalin had made a paper boat for Yoncy and they were sailing it down the murky gutter.

'Too late,' breathed Kolea. 'For their sakes, and for mine, too late.'

THE PARTY REACHED the end of the last Ghost billet hall. Off-duty troopers watched them curiously as they passed by the cots. The boy had done little except stare and occasionally shake his head.

'Nothing?' asked Hark.

'No one he recognises,' said Fultingo.

'Satisfied, then?' snapped Curth.

'Not at all.' Fultingo dropped his voice. 'That boy's mother was killed in a frenzied knife attack. The wounds match exactly the pattern and dimensions of a Tanith warknife.'

'Knives can be stolen. Or lost in battle. Or taken from the dead. Some of the Ghosts may be missing their blades…' Hark said confidently. Daur knew it was for show. A warknife was a Ghost's most treasured possession. They didn't lose them. And they made sure their dead always went to the grave with their straight silver.

Fultingo wasn't put off anyway. 'Several witnesses saw a man in Tanith First battledress leaving the area of the habs. A man in a hurry.'

'Large? Small? Bearded? Clean-shaven? Tanith colouring or Verghast? Distinguishing marks? Rank pins?' Hark demanded.

'Lean, compact. Clean-shaven,' Goosen read from his notes. 'No one got a clear look. Except the boy. He's the best witness.'

Hark looked round at Daur and Curth. 'I deplore this crime, commissar,' he said to Fultingo. 'But this witch hunt's gone far enough. The boy's been through the halls and he hasn't recognised anyone. There's been a mistake. Your killer isn't a Ghost.'

Hark led them out into the corridor away from the men. It was cold, and condensation dribbled from the heating pipes that ran along the wall.

'I suggest you check with other regiments and explore other avenues of enquiry.'

Fultingo was about to reply, but they had to move aside as a platoon of weary Ghosts thumped down the corridor, dirty and smelling of smoke. A clearance squad returning from the fighting in the primary dome. Some were wounded or at least blood-stained.

'We haven't seen all of the men,' said Fultingo as they clomped past. 'There's still a number in the active zone and–'

'What is it? Beggi?' Curth said suddenly, crouching by the boy. He was pointing. 'What did you see?'

The boy didn't speak, but his finger's aim was an inexorable as a long-las.

'Detachment, halt!' Hark shouted, and the returning platoon came up sharp, turning in fatigued confusion.

'Is there a problem, commissar, sir?' asked Corporal Meryn, moving back from the head of the line.

'Is that him, Beggi?' asked Curth, warily.

'Is that the man?' echoed Hark. 'Son, is it?'

Beggi Flyte nodded slowly.

'Trooper! Come over here,' Hark growled.

'Me?' asked Caffran. 'Why?'

Two

THE GREAT BELLS of the Phantine Basilica pealed out into the morning across a municipal square at the heart of primary dome, and the sound of them raised cheering from the great gathering of Cirenholmers. The bells had been cast seventeen centuries before to serve the original Basilica some five kilometres below at a time when Phantine culture had occupied the surface of the planet. Since then, the cities had been serially abandoned and rebuilt on higher and ever higher ground to escape the rising blanket of pollution, and each time, the

bells had been removed and transported up to the newly con-
secrated church.

Now they rang for joy. And they rang to signal the end of
the service of deliverance that had been held to formally
mark the liberation of Cirenholm. The night before, the last
of the Blood Pact dug into the northern edges of the primary
dome had been slaughtered or captured. Cirenholm was
free.

Ecclesiarchs from Hessenville had conducted the service as
all the Imperial priests in Cirenholm had been butchered
during the invasion. The worthies of the city attended, some
still sick and weak from their suffering during the occupation. So many citizens had come, the majority had been
forced to congregate outside in the square and listen to the
service via brass tannoys.

Hundreds of Imperial officers from the liberation force had
also attended as a gesture of respect. Van Voytz, dignified in
his dress uniform, had risen to say a few words. Diplomatically, his speech mentioned the efforts of the Tanith,
Phantine and Urdeshi without differentiation. This was not a
time for rebukes.

When the service was over and the bells were ringing,
Gaunt rose from his pew and followed the crowds outside
into the square. He paused briefly to speak to Major Fazalur,
the stoic Phantine troop leader, and to a young officer called
Shenko who was now, apparently, acting commander of the
Urdeshi.

'How's Zhyte?' Gaunt asked.

'His fighting days are over, sir,' Shenko replied, with obvious awkwardness. 'He's to be shipped off-world to a veterans'
hospice on Fortis Binary.'

'I hope his time there is happier than mine was,' said Gaunt
with a reflective smile.

'Sir, I–' Shenko fumbled for the words.

'I don't bite, despite what you may have heard.'

Shenko grinned nervously. 'I just wanted to say… Zhyte
was a good commander. A damn good commander. He saw
us through hell several times. He always had a temper and his
pride, well… I know he made a mistake here, sir. But I just
wanted to say–'

'Enough, Shenko. I have no animosity towards the Urdeshi. I've actually admired their fortitude since Balhaut—'

'You saw action on Balhaut?' asked Shenko, his eyes wide.

'I did. I was with the Hyrkans then.' Gaunt smiled. Was he so old his past actions had a ring of history in the ears of younger men?

'Ask one of your veterans to tell you about Hill 67 sometime. The Hyrkans to the west of the ridge, the Urdeshi to the east. I don't bear a grudge, and I'm certainly not going to damn a whole regiment because of the attitude and actions of one man. Zhyte should have... ah, never mind. Your boys paid for his mistake here. Feth, Zhyte paid too, come to think of it. Just do me a favour.'

'Sir?'

'Be what he wasn't. We're going into the next theatre together soon. I'd like to think the Urdeshi will be allies, not rivals.'

'You have my hand on it, colonel-commissar.'

Gaunt walked away down the steps, through the throngs of people, stiff in his braided dress uniform.

Confetti streamed in the wind, and citizens pushed forward to hang paper garlands around the necks of their liberators and kiss their hands. Real flowers had vanished from Phantine eight centuries before, except for a few precious blooms raised in specialist hortivatae. But the paper mills still functioned.

With a garland of paper lilies around his neck, Gaunt made his way slowly through the crush on the square, shaking the hands thrust at him. He caught sight of a particularly striking officer dutifully shaking hands. It was Rawne. Gaunt smiled. He so seldom saw Rawne in full ceremonial regalia, it was a shock.

He moved over to him.

'Nice pansies,' he whispered mockingly in Rawne's ear as he shook the eager hands.

'Speak for yourself,' returned Rawne, glancing from his own garland to Gaunt's. The suturing around his blood-shot eye made his glare even angrier than usual.

'Let's get out of here,' said Gaunt, still smiling outwardly at the crowd.

'Good idea! Where to?' said Ayatani Zweil, appearing out of the press of reaching hands. Zweil had a half dozen garlands round his neck.

THEY PUSHED TO the edge of the crowd and, with hands aching, made off down a side street. Even then they were stopped several times to be kissed, hugged or thanked.

'If this is the upside of a soldier's life, no wonder you like it,' said Zweil. 'I haven't been worshipped this much since I was a missionary on Lurkan, walking the beati's path. Of course, at that time, I was much better looking, and it helped that the locals were expecting the return of a messiah named Zweil.'

Gaunt chuckled, but Rawne wasn't amused. He tore off his garland and tossed it into the gutter.

'The mawkish praise of sweaty hab-folk isn't why I signed up,' he sneered. 'That rabble probably thanked the Blood Pact just as effusively when they arrived. It always pays to be nice to the armed men controlling the place you live in.'

'You truly are the most cynical devil I've ever met, major,' Zweil remarked.

'Life sucks, holy father. Wake up and smell the flowers.'

Zweil toyed wistfully with the paper blooms around his neck. 'If only I could.'

'If you didn't sign up to enjoy the adulation of the Imperial common folk, Rawne,' Gaunt said, 'what did you do it for?'

Rawne thought for a moment.

'Feth you,' was all he could come up with.

Gaunt nodded. 'My thoughts exactly.' He stopped. 'This will do,' he told them.

IT WAS A tavern. Built into the basement of a shabby records bureau, there was a steep set of steps running down from street level to the door. It had been closed since the Blood Pact occupation, and Gaunt had to pay the nervous owner well to get them in.

The place was dismal and littered with smashed glasses and broken furniture. The heathens had caroused their nights away, breaking everything they were finished with. Two girls, the owner's teenage daughters, were sweeping up debris. They'd already filled several sacks. The owner's brother was furiously scrubbing the walls with a bristle-brush dipped in caustic soda, trying to obliterate the obscenities that had been daubed on the plastered walls.

Gaunt, Rawne and Zweil took seats on a high bench beside the bar.

'I shouldn't be open,' the owner said. 'But for the saviours of Cirenholm, I'll gladly make an exception.'

'A double exception, I hope,' said Zweil.

'What will you have?'

'You have any sacra?' Gaunt asked.

'Uhh… no, sir. Not sure what that is.'

'No matter. Amasec?'

'I used to,' the owner said ruefully. 'Let me see if there's any left.'

'What are we doing here?' Rawne growled.

'Our duty,' Gaunt told him.

The bar owner returned with a pathetically dented tray on which sat three shot glasses of different sizes and a bottle of amasec.

He set the glasses down in front of the trio. 'My apologies. These are the only glasses I could find that haven't been broken.'

'In that case,' Gaunt assured him, 'they will be perfect.'

The owner nodded, and filled each glass up with the strong liquor.

'Leave the bottle,' Zweil advised him.

Rawne turned his glass slowly, eyeing the serious measure of alcohol. 'What are we drinking to?' he asked.

'The glorious liberation of Cirenholm in the name of the God-Emperor!' Zweil declared, smacking his lips and raising his shot.

Gaunt arrested his rising arm with a hand. 'No, we're not. Well, not really. At battle's end, Colm Corbec would have sniffed out the nearest bar and done just that. Today, he can't. So we're going to do it for him.'

Gaunt took up his glass and studied it dubiously, like it was venom.

'Colm Corbec. First-and-Only. Would that he was here now.'

He knocked back the shot in a single gulp.

'Colm Corbec,' Rawne and Zweil echoed and sank their shots.

'How is he?' Rawne asked. 'I've been at the front until now... not had a chance to... you know...'

'I went by the infirmary on my way here,' Gaunt said, playing with his empty glass. 'No change. He's probably going to die. The medics are amazed he's lasted this long.'

'Won't be the same without him...' Rawne muttered.

Gaunt looked round at him. 'Did I just hear that from Major fething Rawne?'

Rawne scowled. 'There's no shame in admitting we'll be poorer without Corbec. Now, if it was you that was at death's door, I'd be buying drinks for the whole fething regiment.'

Gaunt laughed.

'Speaking of which,' Zweil said, refilling their glasses.

Gaunt held his glass but didn't drink. 'I made a point of seeing Raglon earlier. Gave him brevet command of second platoon. He's got the chops for it, and as Corbec's adjutant, he's the obvious choice.'

Rawne nodded.

'And, on the record for a moment, I hereby give you second command, major. Until further notice.'

'Not Daur?' asked Zweil.

'Feth Daur!' Rawne spat, knocking back his drink.

'No, ayatani. Not Daur,' said Gaunt. 'Any reason it should be?'

Zweil sipped his drink and shrugged. 'The divide, I suppose.'

'The what?' asked Rawne, refreshing his own glass.

'The divide between the Tanith and the Verghastites,' Zweil explained. 'The Vervunhive mob feel like they're always in second place. In terms of morale, raising Daur to second would have pleased them.'

Rawne snorted. 'Fething Verghasts.'

Gaunt looked round at Zweil. The priest's remarks had reminded him forcefully of Hark's comments on the observation deck a few days before. Had Hark and Zweil been talking? 'Look, ayatani-father... I admire you and trust you, I use your advice and seek your council... spiritually. But when it comes to regiment protocol, I trust myself. Thank you for your opinion though.'

'Hey, I was just saying–' said Zweil.

'The Tanith First is the Tanith First,' said Gaunt. 'I want to make sure there's a balance, but when it comes to second officer, it has to be a Tanith in the role. Elevating Daur would give the wrong message to the men.'

'Well, you know what you're doing, Ibram. Be careful of that balance, though. Don't lose the Verghasts. They already feel they're second-class Ghosts.'

'They are,' said Rawne.

'Enough, Rawne. I expect you to use the Verghastites as well as you use the Tanith.'

'Whatever.'

'How's Soric?' Zweil asked.

Gaunt raised his drink. 'Dying, like Corbec. Faster, perhaps.'

'Here's to the soul of the Verghasts, then,' said Zweil. 'Agun Soric.'

They toasted and drained their shots.

Rawne made to top up their glasses from the bottle. 'And a toast to the next action, God-Emperor save us. Ouranberg. May it be half of Cirenholm.'

'It won't be,' said Gaunt. He covered his empty glass to stop Rawne filling it. One for Colm, one for Soric. That would do. 'It will be hell. The lord general's struck with some idea involving the Ghosts that he won't explain. I have a bad feeling about it. And it's been confirmed that Sagittar Slaith is in personal command of Ouranberg.'

'Slaith himself?' muttered Rawne. 'Feth.'

'There is some good news,' Gaunt said. 'A drogue arrived from Hessenville this morning with twenty thousand size three clips in its hold.'

'Praise be!' said Rawne humourlessly.

'Praise be indeed,' Gaunt said. 'The invasion drop is imminent and I'm just glad the Ghosts will be going in well supplied.'

'I just hope the business with Caffran is done by then,' said Rawne.

'What business?' Gaunt asked.

'Oh, the murder thing?' said Zweil. 'That was just ghastly.'

'What "business"? What "murder thing"?' Gaunt growled.

'Oh dear,' teased Rawne. 'Did I say too much? Has Hark been keeping it from you?'

'Keeping what?'

'The First-and-Only's dirty laundry,' said Rawne. 'I'm surprised at Caffran, actually. Didn't think he had it in him. Son of a bitch has plentiful grazing in that Criid woman without looking elsewhere. And murder? He has to be really fethed up to do that sort of shit. Heyyy!'

Gaunt had pushed Rawne off the end of the bench to get past him.

'Gaunt? Gaunt?' Zweil cried. But the colonel-commissar was running up the steps into the street and gone.

VIKTOR HARK BACKED across the room, bumped into a filing cabinet and realised there was nowhere left to retreat to.

'When were you intending to tell me, Viktor?' asked Gaunt.

Hark rose slowly. 'You were busy. With the lord general. And politically, I thought you could do with being distanced from it.'

'I brought you into this unit to serve as a political officer I could trust. Play all the spin you like, Viktor. But don't you ever dare keep me out of the loop again.'

Hark straightened his jacket and looked at Gaunt. 'You don't want this, Ibram,' he said softly.

'Feth that! I am the Ghosts! All the Ghosts! If it affects any one of them, it affects me.'

Hark shook his head. 'How did you ever get this far being so naive?'

'How did I ever think to trust you that you don't know that?' said Gaunt.

Hark shook his head sadly. He reached to the desk and handed Gaunt a data-slate. 'A hab-wife called Onti Flyte was butchered three nights ago. Stabbed with a Tanith knife. Witnesses saw a Ghost running from the premises. The victim's son positively identified Caffran. Case closed. I didn't bother you with it because it was just a minor incident. That's what I'm here for, sir. Taking care of the crap while you focus on the bigger picture.'

'Is that so? What will happen to Caffran?'

'Commissar Del Mar has ordered his execution by las-squad at dawn tomorrow.'

'And it didn't occur to you that I'd question the loss of a trooper as valuable as Caffran?'

'Given his crime, no sir.'

'And what does Caff say?'

'He denies it, of course.'

'Of course... he'll deny it particularly if he was innocent. I take it at least a routine investigation is being carried out? Witnesses can sometimes be mistaken.'

'Del Mar's staff is running the case. A Commissar Fultingo is lea–'

'You've just washed your hands of it?'

Hark fell silent.

'Local, civil law enforcement and the task force Commissariate have jurisdiction, of course. But this is also squarely a regimental matter. A matter for us. If there's a chance Caffran is innocent, I'm not going to let it go. Leave me the slate and get out of here,' Gaunt said.

Hark tossed the data-slate onto the table and walked out. 'Sir?' he asked, pausing in the doorway. 'I know Caffran's been with you from the start. I know he's well-liked and that he's a good soldier. But this is open and shut. The Tanith First are a remarkably well-behaved group of soldiers, you know. Sure, we get to deal with brawling and drinking, a few feuds and thefts, but nothing compared to some units I've served with. Summary execution for capital offences is almost routine in other regiments. Murder, manslaughter, rape. The Guard is full of killers and many of them can't help themselves. Dammit, you know that! Strict, rapid discipline is the only way to maintain control. I repeat, this is just a minor incident. It is nothing compared with the vital nature of the holy war we're undertaking. You shouldn't be wasting your time on this.'

'I'm wasting my time, Hark, precisely because it is so uncommon in this regiment. Now get the feth out of my sight for a while.'

* * *

VARL FOUND HIS way to the infirmary by following the scent of disinfectant. It was confusing at first, because almost every hallway and access in the secondary dome smelled of the stuff. There were Munitorium and civil work gangs all over the city hosing down floors and scrubbing away the reek and filth of the enemy.

But the infirmary had a stink of its own. Disinfectant. Blood.

The taskforce medicae had occupied an apprentices' college on one of the mid-level floors, close by the dome skin. The walls and roofs of some of the larger rooms demonstrated the gentle curve of the city's shape. Flakboard and shielding raised by the enemy had been stripped away from the windows to let in the cool light. Outside, through thick, discoloured armourglas, the pearly cloudscape spread away as far as the eye could see.

The place was busy. Varl edged his way in between weary nurses and arguing orderlies, bustling corpsmen resupplying their field kits from a dispensary, cleaning crews, walking wounded. Every chamber he passed was full of casualties, mainly Urdeshi, supported in crude but functional conditions. The worst cases were screened off in side wards.

The smell of pain was inescapable, and so was the low, background murmur of groans.

Varl slid his back to a wall to allow two medicae orderlies hurrying along with a resuscitrex cart to pass, and then entered the gloom of an intensive ward. The lighting was low-level, and trained around the individual beds. There was a steady, arrhythmic bleep of vitalators and the asthmatic wheeze and thump of the automatic respirator bellows.

Corbec lay on a rumpled cot, half-tangled in khaki sheets, like a shroud-wrapped pieta in an Imperial hero shrine. His limbs were sprawled, knotted in the fabric, as if he had turned restlessly in his dreams. Drips and monitor cables were variously anchored into his massive arms and chest, and his mouth and nose were plugged with larger, thicker tubes. It looked as if they were choking him. Corbec's eyes were sealed with surgical tape. Through his thick, black body hair it was possible to see the yellowing bruises and the hundreds of little, scabby cuts that marked his skin.

Varl stood looking at him for a long time and realised he couldn't think of anything to say or do. He wasn't even sure why he'd come.

He was halfway down the corridor on his way out when Dorden called out to him.

'Looking in on the chief, Varl?' the old doctor asked, coming over, his attention half on a data-slate he was reviewing.

Varl shrugged. 'Yeah, I–'

'You're not the first. Been Tanith in here all morning. In ones or twos. A few Verghastites too. Paying their respects.'

Varl breathed out deeply and stuck his hands in his pockets of his black combat pants. 'I don't know about respects,' he said. 'I don't mean that nasty, doc. I mean I… I think I just came to see.'

'To see Colm?'

'To see if it was true. Corbec's dying, they say. But I couldn't picture it. Couldn't see it in my head to believe it.'

'And now?' asked Dorden, handing the slate to a passing nurse.

'Still can't.' Varl grinned. 'He's not going to die, is he?'

'Well, we should all keep hoping and praying–'

'No, doc. I wasn't looking for no reassurance. If he's going to die, I hope you'd tell me. I just don't feel it. Standing there, I just don't. It doesn't feel like his time. Like he's not ready and he's fething well not going to let go.'

It was Dorden's turn to smile. 'You saw that too, huh? I haven't said that to anyone because I didn't want to get hopes up unfairly. But I feel it that way as well.'

'Doesn't seem hardly fair, does it?' said Varl. 'Corbec takes some punishment. He almost missed the show on Hagia and I know those injuries have only just healed. Now this.'

'Colm Corbec is a brave man and he takes risks. Too many risks, in my opinion. Mainly because, like all good officers, he leads by example. You know he got messed up this way saving Muril's life?'

'I heard.'

'Take risks, Varl, and sooner or later you get hurt. In Corbec's case sooner and later.'

Varl nodded, threw a half-salute, and turned to go. Then he hesitated.

'Doc?'

'Yes, sergeant?'

'About taking risks. I, uh… look, if I tell you something, it's just between us, right?'

'I can offer standard medicae confidentiality, Varl, providing it doesn't conflict with Guard security issues. And… I'm your friend.'

'Right, good.' Varl drew Dorden to one side, off the main corridor, into the entrance to one of the critical wards. He dropped his voice.

'Kolea.'

'Shoot.'

'He's a fine soldier. One of the best.'

'Agreed.'

'Good leader too.'

'No arguments.'

'We'd never have pushed the assault as far as we did if it hadn't been for him. He really… he did a real Corbec, if you know what I mean.'

'I do. You men pulled off a great victory. Getting in as far as the mill to support Domor and Haller's squads. Lucky break for us all. I hear Gaunt's going to commend a bunch of you. Don't tell him I told you.'

'It's just, well… Kolea was taking risks. Big risks. Crazy risks. Like he didn't care if he lived or died. I mean, he was insane. Running into enemy fire. It was a miracle he wasn't hit.'

'Some men deal with battle that way, Varl. I refer you to our previous conversation about Corbec.'

'I know, I know.' Varl struggled for the words. 'But this wasn't brave. This was… mad. Really fethed up. So mad, I said something to him, said I'd tell Gaunt what a crazy stunt he'd pulled. And he swore me not to. Begged me not to.'

'He's modest–'

'Doc, Gol lost his wife and his kids on Verghast. I think… I think he doesn't care any more. Doesn't care about his own life. I think he's looking for the reunion round.'

'Really?'

'I'm sure of it. And if I'm right, he's not only going to get himself dead, he's going to become a risk to the men.'

'It's good you told me this, Varl. Leave it with me for now. I'll be discreet. Let me know if you catch any more behaviour like it from him.'

Varl nodded and made his way out.

The canvas curtain behind Dorden slid back and Curth came through, peeling off bloody surgical gloves and tossing them into a waste canister.

'I didn't know you were there,' Dorden said.

'Assume I wasn't.'

'That was a confidential chat, Ana.'

'I know. It'll stay that way. I'm bound by the same oaths as you.'

'Good.'

'One thing,' she said, moving across to a trolley rack and sorting through data-slates. 'What's a reunion round?'

Dorden shook his head with a sigh. He scratched the grey stubble of his chin.

'Guard slang. It means… it means Kolea doesn't want to live without his lost loved ones. His dead wife, kids. He wants to be with them again. And so he's throwing himself into every fight that comes along without heed for his own safety, doing whatever he can do, until he finally catches that reunion round he's praying to find. The one that will kill him and reunite him with his family.'

'Ah,' said Curth. 'I had a nasty feeling that's what it was.'

'What did you do?'

Caffran slowly rose to his feet, mystified. The shackles linking his wrists clanked and drew tight where they ran down to his ankle-hobble. He'd been stripped down to his black vest and fatigue pants. His boot laces and belt had been removed.

'What do you mean?' he asked. His voice was dry and thin. The air in the dingy cell was damp and the light bad. A hunted look on Caffran's face showed that he was still dealing with the shock of the accusations.

'I mean what did you do? Tell me.'

'I didn't do anything. I swear.'

'You swear?'

'I swear! Nothing! Why… why have you come here, asking me that?'

Kolea stared at him. The shadows made it impossible for Caffran to read his expression.

Kolea was just a furious, threatening presence in the little cell.

'Because I want to know.'

'Why?'

Kolea took a menacing step forward. 'If I find out you're lying… if you hurt that woman–'

'Sergeant, please… I didn't do anything!'

'Sergeant Kolea!'

Kolea stopped a few paces from Caffran. He turned slowly. Silhouetted, Gaunt stood in the cell doorway.

'What are you doing here, Kolea?' Gaunt asked, stepping into the cell.

'I–' Kolea fell silent.

'I asked you a question, sergeant.'

'The men in my troop were… concerned… about what Caffran had done… I–'

Gaunt held up a hand. 'That's enough. You're out of line being here, Kolea. You should know that. Get out. Tell your men I'll talk to them.'

'Sir,' Kolea murmured and left.

Gaunt took off his cap and swung round to look at Caffran. 'Any idea what that was about, trooper?'

'No, sir.'

Gaunt nodded. 'Sit down, Caffran. You know why I'm here.'

'To ask the same questions Kolea did, probably.'

'And?'

Caffran slowly sat down on the cell's ceramic bench. He cleared his throat and then looked up, meeting Gaunt's gaze.

'I didn't do it, sir.'

There was a long silence. Gaunt nodded. 'All I needed to hear, Caff.'

He walked back to the door and put his cap back on.

'Keep your spirits up, Caff. If it's in my power to get you out of this, I will.'

'Thank you, sir.'

Gaunt stepped out into the brig hall. The Commissariate guards closed the heavy door, threw the bolts and ignited the shield. They saluted Gaunt, but he ignored them as he strode away.

IN THE RAIN, the mill-habs looked especially dismal. It wasn't real rain, naturally. Every two days, each section of the hab-district was sluiced with water from the dome's ceiling pipes. The idea was to maintain hygiene and keep the streets washed down.

It simply made everything glisten with wet and smell like a stale toilet stall.

The Flyte household had been boarded, and aquila seals stamped to the doors. The kids had been sent to stay with neighbours.

He jumped over the back fence into the rear yard and looked about, his cloak pulled up over his head against the downpour. If the outhouse was well roofed, then there might be some traces left to find. If it wasn't, the rain would have rinsed everything of value away.

He looked around, peering in through the cracked rear windows of the hab. All sorts of litter and broken debris was scattered in the weed-rife yard.

He went into the outhouse, breaking the aquila seal and ignoring the stencilled Commissariate warning notice. Inside, it smelled of rotting fibreboard and mineral waste. There was no light. It wasn't particularly watertight, but he could still see the dark stains on the wall, the floor, and the rim of the old, battered tub. One was a handprint. A perfect handprint. A woman's.

He looked around. The rafters were low, and there was a gash in one of them right above the bath. He took out a lamp pack and shone it up, probing the cut with the tip of his Tanith knife, and carefully teased out a tiny sliver of metal that he put in his hip pouch.

He sniffed the air. He sniffed the fibreboard wall. He got down on his hands and knees and shone the lamp-pack under the tub.

Something glinted.

He reached for it.

'Don't move! Not a bloody centimetre!'

Torchlight shone in at him.

'Out, slowly!'

He obeyed, keeping his hands in the open.

The young cadet commissar in the doorway looked very scared, an automatic pistol aimed at him. But credit where credit was due. He'd come up fething quietly.

'Who are you?' the cadet said.

'Sergeant Mkoll, Tanith First,' Mkoll replied quietly.

'Goosen? What's going on in there?' shouted a voice outside.

An older man, another commissar in a long, dripping storm coat, appeared behind the twitchy cadet. He almost took a step back in surprise when he saw Mkoll.

'Who the hell are you?'

'One of the neighbours reported an intruder, sir,' said Goosen. 'Said he thought it was the killer come back.'

'Cuff him,' said the older man bluntly. 'He's coming with us.'

'May I?' Mkoll said, gesturing to his battledress pocket.

Goosen covered him carefully as Mkoll reached into the pocket and drew out a folded document. He held it out to the older man.

'Signed authorisation from Colonel-Commissar Gaunt, my unit commander. His instructions for me to conduct an evidential search of the scene, pursuant to the case.'

The commissar looked it over. He didn't seem convinced. 'This is irregular.'

'But it's a fact. Can I lower my hands now?'

Goosen looked at the commissar. The older man shrugged. 'Let him be.'

The commissars looked round. Captain Ban Daur stood at the yard's back gate. He had no weapon drawn but, despite the rain, his coat was pulled back for easy access to his holstered laspistol.

Daur sauntered in, put his hand on Goosen's weapon and slowly pointed it down.

'Put it away,' he advised.

'Are you with him?' the commissar asked, indicating Mkoll.

'Yes, I am, Fultingo. Gaunt's rostered a team of us to carry out a regimental inspection of the case.'

'There's no time. The execution is—'

'Postponed. Gaunt obtained a delay order from Commissar Del Mar's office an hour ago. We have a grace period to assess all the evidence.'

Fultingo sneered at Mkoll. 'You sent a trooper into a crime scene?'

'Mkoll's unit chief of the Tanith scouts. Sharpest eyes in the Imperium. If there's something to find, he'll find it.'

'Who's in charge of your investigation?' asked Fultingo. He looked angry, thwarted. 'I'm going to lodge a formal complaint. You, captain? No… Hark, I'll bet.'

'Gaunt has taken personal charge of the case,' said Daur. Mkoll had lowered his hands and was inspecting the outside of the shed.

'Gaunt?' queried Fultingo. 'Gaunt himself? Why is he bothering with this?'

'Because it matters,' said Mkoll without looking round.

Fultingo stared at Daur, the dome-water dripping off his nose and cap-brim. 'This is a criminal waste of resources. You haven't heard the last of it.'

'Tell someone who cares,' hissed Daur.

Fultingo turned on his jackbooted heel and marched out of the yard, Goosen scurrying after him, kicking up wet gravel.

'Thanks,' said Mkoll.

'You were handling it.'

Mkoll shrugged. 'Any progress?'

'Hark's done what Gaunt asked him to do. Everything's so tied up with red tape, Caff's safe for a few days. Dorden's examining the victim's body this evening. Hark's now circulating a questionnaire to the Ghosts just to see if anything flags up.'

Mkoll nodded. Daur shivered and looked about. The artificial rain was trickling to a stop, but the air was still filmy and damp. Steam rose from heating vents and badly insulated roofing. Water stood in great, black mirrors along the uneven street and in the ruts of the yard-back lane. Daur could smell stove fires and the faint, unwholesome aroma of ration meals cooking. Somewhere, children squealed and laughed as they played.

Although he couldn't see them, Daur could feel the eyes in all the back windows of the hab-street, eyes peering out from behind threadbare drapes and broken shutters, watching them.

'Gakking miserable place,' Daur remarked.

Mkoll nodded again and looked up. 'The worst kind. No sky.'

That made Daur smile. 'Mkoll,' he said. 'Since we're out here, off the record, as it were, you think Caffran did it?'

Mkoll turned his penetrating gaze round and directed it at the taller Verghastite officer. Daur had always admired and liked the chief scout. But for a moment, he was terrified.

'Caffran? Do you even have to ask?' said Mkoll.

'Yeah, right. Sorry.'

Mkoll wiped his wet face with a fold of his camo-cloak. 'I'm done here, sir.'

'Right. We can go back then. Did you turn up anything?'

'The prosecutors did a lousy job... unless someone's been in there since. They could have taken prints off the blood marks. Too late now, the damp's got in. But they missed... or ignored... a knife scar in the beams. I dug out a shard of metal.'

'From the knife?'

'I think so. The frames of all these buildings are made of surplus ceramite sheathed in paper pulp. The core's hard enough to nick a blade. Whoever did it was in a frenzy. And has a notch in his knife.'

'Well, gak! That's a start!'

'I know,' agreed Mkoll. 'More interestingly, I found this. Right under the tub.'

He held out his hand, palm up, and showed what he had found to Daur.

A gold coin.

'An Imperial crown?'

Mkoll smiled. 'A defaced Imperial crown,' he said.

Three

LORD GENERAL VAN VOYTZ had chosen a generous High Gothic style manse in the upper levels of Cirenholm's primary dome for a command headquarters. Painted eggshell green, and supported by some of the integral pillars that rose up into the dome's roof structure, the manse was one of forty that over-looked a vast, landscaped reservoir complete with lawns and woodlands of aug-cultivated trees.

This lakeland habitat, complete with pleasure yachts rocking in coves at the timber jetties, had been the playground of Cirenholm's wealthiest and most influential citizens before the Blood Pact's arrival. Two planetary senators, a retired lord general, a worthy hierarch, six mill tycoons and the city governor had all owned homes around the shore.

All of them were dead now. There was no one left to object to Van Voytz's occupation. Not that any of them would have. The liberating lord general had power and, more crucially, influence, over them all.

An Imperial transport speeder still wearing its invasion camouflage skimmed Gaunt over the lake. Evening had fallen, and lights from the shoreline twinkled out over the dark water. Despite the gloom, Gaunt could see the burnt-out ruins of some of the properties, grim as skulls. He could also see the silhouettes of crosses dotted along the shore. No one had found the time yet to take down the murdered worthies of Cirenholm.

The speeder slowed and ran up the little beach in front of the manse in a wash of spray. Shielding their eyes from the drizzle, Urdeshi sentries waved the vehicle in. The speeder crossed a lawn and some low box hedges and settled on the arc of mica-shingled driveway outside the manse.

Gaunt stepped out into the night air, pulling on his storm coat. He could smell the water and the fading ozone reek of the cooling engines. Two staff limos were pulling away from the front steps, and speeder bikes and other Imperial transports sat parked under wet trees.

There were more sentries on the steps. Two of them, and Van Voytz's junior aide, hurried down to meet him.

'The lord general is waiting for you in the library, colonel-commissar. Go through. Have you eaten?'

'Yes, with the men.'

'A drink then?'

'I'm fine.'

Gaunt walked into the light of the hall. It was a stunning interior of polished rethuric panels, gold-laced shaniffes and

displays of antique porcelain. He wondered how the hell any
of this had survived unbroken.

The trompe l'oeil ceiling showed him vistas of the
Empyrean, complete with dogged starships. The hall floor
was piled with Guard-issue locker crates and roll-bags full of
clothes.

'Through here,' the aide said.

Gaunt passed a side room which was bare apart from an
enormous ormulu fireplace and a single escritoire lit by a
floating glow-globe.

The tactician, Biota, sat working at the desk, veiled by holo
displays and charts. He didn't look up.

Two Urdeshi storm-troops hurried past in full kit. They
broke step only to salute.

The aide stopped outside a towering pair of gordian-wood
doors. He knocked briefly and listened to his micro-bead.

'Colonel-Commissar Gaunt,' the aide said into his vox-mic.
A pause. 'Yes, sir.'

The aide opened the doors and ushered Gaunt inside.

As libraries went, this one was contrary. The huge, arched
roof, three storeys high, encased a wide room lined with
shelves, with wrought iron stairwells and walkways allowing
a browser access to the upper stacks.

But the shelves were empty.

The only books were piled on top of a heap of army crates
in the centre of the parquet floor.

Gaunt took off his cap and wandered in. Lamps glowed
from wall-brackets and autonomous glow-globes circled and
hovered around him like fire-flies. At the end of the room,
under the big windows, was a recently unpacked tactical
desk. Its power cables snaked off and were plugged into floor
sockets. A half-dozen library chairs were drawn up around it.

An open bottle of claret and several glasses, one half full,
sat on a salver on a side table.

There was no sign of Van Voytz.

Gaunt looked around.

'A tragedy, isn't it?' said Van Voytz, invisible.

'Sir?'

'This house belonged to Air Marshal Fazalur, the father of
our friend Major Fazalur. A splendid soldier, well decorated,

one of the planet's heroes. An even more splendid biblio-
phile.'

Van Voytz suddenly appeared from under the wide tactical
desk. Just his head and shoulders. He grinned at Gaunt and
then disappeared again.

'Dead now, of course. Found his corpse on the beach. Most
of his corpse, anyway.' Van Voytz's voice was partially muffled
by the table.

'He had the most amazing collection of books, charts, data-
slates and first editions. A wealth of knowledge and a real
treasure. You can tell by all the empty shelves what size his
collection was.'

'Extensive,' Gaunt said.

'They burned them all. The Blood Pact. Took all the slates,
all the books, ferried them out into the woodland behind the
manse, doused them with promethium, and burned them.
There's a huge ring of ash out there still. Ash, melted plastic,
twists of metal. It's still hot and smoking.'

'A crime, sir.'

Van Voytz appeared again.

'Damn right a crime, Gaunt!' He reached over, took a swig
of wine from the glass, and then dropped out of sight once
more.

Gaunt wandered over to the pile of books and lifted one.
'*The Spheres of Longing*... Ravenor's greatest work. Feth, this is
a first edition!'

'You've read Ravenor, Gaunt?'

'A personal favourite. They spared some things then? This
volume alone is priceless.'

'It's mine. I couldn't bear the place looking so empty so I
had some of my own library freighted up from Hessenville.'

Gaunt put the book down carefully, shaking his head. He
couldn't imagine the sort of power that could order the Imperial Munitorium to fast ship a person's private book
collection to him in a war zone. Come to that, he couldn't
imagine the sort of power that would enable one to own a
first edition of *The Spheres of Longing*.

He glanced at some of the other books. *The Life of Sabbat*,
in its folio print. *The Considerations of Solon*, mint. Garbo
Mojaro's *The Chime of Eons*. A perfect copy of *Liber Doctrina*

Historicas. The complete sermons of Thor, cased. *Breaching the Darkness* by Sejanus. An early quarto of the *Tactica Imperium*, with foil stamps and plates complete. A limited issue of Slaydo's treatise on Balhaut, on the original data-slate.

'You like books, Gaunt?'

'I like these books, sir.'

Van Voytz emerged from under the desk and gave the display machine's cold flank a slap.

'Bloody thing!' He was clad in dress-uniform breeches and boots, but stripped down to an undershirt. Gaunt saw the lord general's tunic was hung over the back of one of the chairs.

'They shipped this thing in,' said Von Voytz, sweeping up his glass and sipping it as he flapped an arm at the tactical desk. 'They shipped it in and left it here. Did they plug it in and test start it? No. Can I get the holo-display to work? No. I tried. You saw me under there.'

'It's really a tech-magos's job, sir.'

Van Voytz grinned. 'I'm a lord general, Gaunt. I can do anything!'

They both laughed.

'Where are my manners?' said the general. He sloshed some of the contents of the bottle into one of the empty glasses. Gaunt took it. He realised he was still holding the copy of the *Tactica Imperium*.

'Cheers,' said Van Voytz.

'Your health, sir. The Emperor protects.'

'You like that one?' Van Voytz asked, pointing at the book Gaunt was holding.

'It's beautiful–'

'Keep it. It's yours.'

'I couldn't. It's priceless.'

'I insist. It's mine to give. Besides, you deserve it. A gift to recognise your efforts here on Phantine so far. I'm serious. Keep it.'

'I… thank you, sir.'

Van Voytz waved a hand. 'Enough of that. Damn desk.' He took a sip of claret and kicked the offending piece of furniture. 'I had holo graphics of Ouranberg to show you. The whole assault plan.'

'I could come back tomorrow, sir.'

'Don't be silly, Gaunt. You've got your hands full. I'll speak. You'll listen. You'll get the gist. It'll be like it was back in the days of Sejanus and Ponthi. You're Ponthi.'

'An honour, s–'

'I'm kidding, Ibram. Just kidding. I asked you here to talk about the Ouranberg assault. Biota's been totting things up, and he says I'm crazy. But I have an idea. And it involves your mob.'

'So you said, sir.'

'Don't look so… constipated, Ibram. You'll like this. I had the idea when I was reviewing your attack report. Damn fine men you've got there.'

'Thank you.'

'Good at stealth work. Smart. Capable. If we're going to take Slaith down, we'll need all of that.'

Gaunt put the book back on the pile and gulped his drink. 'It is Slaith then, sir?'

'Oh, you betcha. Probably with loxatl mercenaries. Ouranberg's going to be a real party.'

Van Voytz refilled his glass. 'Before we get into the planning, I hear there's a problem in your regiment.'

'A problem?'

'A fellow up on capital charges.'

'Yes sir. I'm dealing with it.'

'I know you are. And you shouldn't have to. It's a company level matter. Just let him hang.'

'I can't, sir. I won't.'

The lord general swigged his wine again and sat down on one of the chairs. 'You're a regimental officer now, Gaunt. Trust your staff to deal with it.'

'This matters to me, sir. One of my men has been falsely accused. I have to clear him.'

'I know all about it. I spoke with Commissar Del Mar this afternoon. I'm afraid you're wasting your time, Ibram.'

'Caffran's innocent, sir, I sw–'

'This man… Caffran is it? He's a dog soldier. A common trooper. The case against him is las-proof.

'You have more important things to be devoting your time to.'

'With respect, lord, I haven't. I stand where I stand today because of the common dog soldiers. I would not be me without their efforts. And so I make sure I look after every last one of them.'

Van Voytz frowned. 'Well, shame on me–'

'Sir, I didn't mean–'

Van Voytz waved his hand. 'I'm hardly offended, Gaunt. Actually, it's refreshing to hear an officer remember the basics of good command. The Imperial Guard is nothing without the Imperial Guardsmen. No one should get so high and mighty they forget that. Your personal code of honour is unusually robust. I just hope…'

'Sir?'

Van Voytz rose and started to put his jacket back on. 'I was going to say I hope it doesn't get you killed. But, you know, it assuredly will. Eventually, I mean. That's the curse of a code of honour as resolute as yours, colonel-commissar. Stick by it, and you'll end up dying for it.'

Gaunt shrugged. 'I always supposed that was the point, sir.'

'Well said,' Van Voytz replied, fiddling with the buttons of his frogging. 'Your dual role is a problem, though. Say the word and I'll transfer you out of the Commissariate. You'll be Brigadier Gaunt… no, let's not mess around, shall we? You'll be Lieutenant-General Gaunt, sectioned to me, Guard and Guard alone. A full Imperial Guard officer with commissars at your beck and call.'

Gaunt was mildly stunned.

'The uniform would suit you, Gaunt. Lieutenant-General, Tanith First-and-Only. No more fussing over discipline matters. No more wasting command time.'

Gaunt sat down. 'I'm flattered, sir. But no. I'm happy where I am.'

Van Voytz shrugged. He didn't seem put out. 'If you say so. But don't dwell on this man Caffran, please. I won't have it. Now… let me tell you my ideas about Ouranberg…'

FOR ALL DORDEN's efforts with the powder, the lice had taken hold. While fumigation crews filled the billets with noxious chemical clouds, the Ghosts reported en masse to a grand municipal bathhouse in primary. Kit was stripped off for steam-cleaning, and the troops, shivering in their shorts and vests, lined up in the cold stone atrium to have their heads shaved. The buzz of three dozen clippers filled the air above the chatter. Servitors shunted back and forth, sweeping up the hair for incineration.

Once shaved, the troops were sent through into the steaming shower blocks armed with cakes of tar-soap, their boots slung by the laces around their necks. On the far side of the shower blocks were halls lined with rush mats where stiffly-old but clean towels were stacked. Munitorium aides stood by at trestle tables piled with clean reserve kit that stank of yet more powder.

Gaunt and Daur walked into the drying halls and there was a general fuss and shuffling as naked or half-dressed troops tried to come to attention.

'As you were,' Gaunt called out, and they relaxed back to their ablutions. Gaunt nodded to Daur and the captain consulted a data-slate.

'Listen up,' Daur called out. 'If you hear your name, get dressed and assemble at the exit. I'll only call this once…'

Still toweling off their newly bald heads, the troops paid attention.

'Mkvenner! Doyl! Bonin! Larkin! Rilke! Nessa! Banda! Meryn! Milo! Varl! Cocoer! Kuren! Adare! Vadim! Nour! That's it! Fast as you like!'

Larkin was tugging a clean black vest over his bony torso and scowled at Bragg as he heard his name called. 'Oh, what now?' he grumbled. Larkin looked mean and cadaverous with his hair cropped.

'What have you done, Larks?' Bragg chuckled.

'Fething nothing!' snapped Larkin, struggling to pull on starch-stiff fatigue pants. Buckling his belt, he shuffled over to join the others in unlaced boots.

'That's everyone,' said Daur to Gaunt and the colonel-commissar nodded. Painfully aware of the shaven heads around him, Gaunt pointed to his own hair. 'Don't worry, it's my turn next,' he said. 'Lice have no respect for rank.' The Ghosts smiled. They all looked like raw recruits again, their scalps unhealthy white. Gaunt felt especially sorry for the women.

'Very well,' he said. 'Imperial Command has assigned an operation to us. Details later, for now it's enough for you to know the lord general conceived it himself and considers it a critical mission. Its successful execution has priority over all other Imperial operations at this point.'

A few eyes widened. Larkin made a soft, disheartened moan. Banda elbowed him.

'I've personally selected you all for this operation, for reasons that will become obvious to each of you. The operational name is Larisel. You will not speak about it in general or specific terms to anyone, even other Ghosts outside this group. I want you all assembled at sub-hangar 117 by 18.30 with full kit, gear and personal effects. I mean everything, prepped for transport. You won't be going back to the billet.'

'Is that because this is a... one-way mission?' asked Varl euphemistically.

'I won't lie, sergeant. Larisel will be ultra-high risk. But the reason you won't be going back to the regimental billet is that I'm moving you all to secondary billet for speciality training and mission-specific instruction. Okay?'

There were mumbles and nods.

'Any questions? No? Okay, good. I have supreme confidence in you all: your abilities and your characters. I'll say it again before you get underway, but good fortune to you all. The Emperor protects.'

Gaunt glanced round at Daur. 'Anything you want to add at this stage, captain?'

'Just one thing, sir.' Daur stepped to the front, reaching one hand into the patch pocket of his black tunic jacket. 'Regarding Trooper Caffran. As you know, we've been doing the rounds, asking questions, collecting data. I fully expect some valuable information to come out that way. Word of mouth, trooper to trooper. But from here in, you're going to be effectively separated from the regimental main force, so there's going to be much less opportunity to keep you in the loop as far as the ongoing investigation is concerned. Therefore, for now... I want to inspect everyone's warknife. I want to hear from any of you who has noticed notching or damage to the warknives of any other trooper. And has anyone seen one of these before?'

He took a small waxed envelope from his pocket, opened it and held up a gold coin.

'Imperial crown, local issue... purposely defaced on both head and reverse. Does anyone have one like it? Does anyone know anything about its origin? Does anyone know of another trooper who has one? If you're uncomfortable about speaking out now, see me, or the colonel-commissar, or Commissar Hark, in confidence. That's all.'

'Dismissed,' Gaunt said.

The group broke up, muttering to one another. Daur and Gaunt turned together and walked off down the outer hall.

'I've got hopes about the coin,' confided Daur. 'We already know from a dozen Ghosts, including Obel and Kolea, that there were more of the same in the business premises of the adjacent mill sector. But all of them swear they left the coins well alone because of the markings.'

'We'll see. If anyone did get greedy, he'll not want to admit it. They know how strict I am about looting. Did you check Caffran's blade?'

Daur sighed. 'It's notched. He said it happened during the firefight in the park at 505, but we've only got his word. Del Mar's staff will be all over that like a bad rash if it gets out.'

'Then don't let it out,' said Gaunt. 'They've got all the rope they need as it is. Don't give them any more.'

'WHAT DO WE do?' Larkin whispered anxiously to Bragg as he finished lacing up his boots. Bragg leaned beside him, pulling on his vest.

'We tell Gaunt,' Bragg answered simply.

'We can't!'

'Why not?' Bragg asked.

'Because we don't betray our own. I've never been a rat in my life, and I don't intend to start now.'

'I don't think that's the reason, Larks,' Bragg said. He smiled. 'We'd rat if it got Caffran off. No, I think you're scared of him.'

'I am not!'

'I think you are. I know I am.'

Larkin's eyes widened. 'You're scared of Cuu?'

'All right, not scared exactly. But wary. He's a mean piece of work.'

Larkin sighed. 'I'm scared of him. He's a maniac. If we report him, and he gets off later, he'll come for us. He'll fething come for us. It's not worth it.'

'It's worth it to Caff.'

'I'm not crossing Cuu. Not for anything. There's something about him. Something sick. He could go to the firing squad and then come back and haunt me.'

Bragg laughed.

'You think I'm joking.'

Bragg shook his head. 'Cuu's a fething maniac, Larks. If anyone in this mob is capable of that killing, it's him. If he's guilty, we don't have to worry about it. If he's innocent, well, then he gets off. And honestly, what would he do then? Kill us? Get off a murder charge and then commit a double murder?'

'I'm not doing it,' Larkin hissed firmly.

Bragg fingered the new, pink skin healing on the gash in his shoulder. 'Then I might,' he said. 'He's no friend of mine.'

THE BILLET HALL was fairly quiet except for the occasional cough or sneeze. The stink of the recent fumigation still clung to the air.

Milo expertly stowed the last of his kit in his backpack, lashed it shut and then secured the tightly rolled tubes of his bed-roll and camo-cloak to it.

Vadim, already packed and ready to go, wandered over to him. 'You ever been picked for special ops before, Milo?'

'Some. Not quite like this.' Milo pulled on his tunic, checking the contents of the pockets, and then strapped on his webbing. 'Sounds… high profile,' he added, hooking his gloves to his webbing before rolling his beret and tucking it through the epaulette of his tunic. He hoisted up his backpack, shook the weight onto his shoulders and then did up the harness.

'Sounds suicidal to me,' Vadim muttered darkly. He rubbed his sandpaper scalp. The lack of hair had altered the proportion of his head and made his strong nose seem almost beak-like. He looked like a dejected crow.

'We'll see, won't we?' Milo said, cinching the sling of his lasrifle before shouldering it. He inspected his makeshift cot one last time to make sure he hadn't left anything. 'I tend not to worry until I know I've got something to worry about.'

Fully prepped and weighed down with kit, Nour and Kuren moved across the billet to join them. They shook hands and exchanged banter with other Ghosts as they crossed the hall. None of them had explained where they were going and no one had asked, but it was clear they were shipping out for some special duty and that prompted numerous farewells and wishes of luck.

Kuren had put on his drop-issue balaclava, rolled up into a tight woollen hat. 'Fething lice,' he grumbled, 'my fething head's cold.'

'Set?' Milo asked the three of them. They nodded. It was just after 18.00 and time to leave.

Milo looked across to Larkin's cot. The master sniper was finishing up his almost obsessive prep on his gun, packing up the cleaning kit and sliding the long foul-weather cover over the weapon. 'Larks? You ready?'

'Be right there, Milo.'

Bragg sat down on the cot next door. 'You... you have a good time now, Larks.'

'Oh, funny.'

'Just... come back again, okay?'

Larkin noticed the look in Bragg's eyes.

'Oh, I fething well intend to, believe me.'

Bragg grinned and held out a big paw. 'First and Only.'

Larkin nodded and slapped Bragg's palm. 'See you later.'

He walked over to the others. Trooper Cuu, who had been lying on his back gazing at the roof, sat up suddenly and grinned at Larkin as he went by.

'What?' asked Larkin, stopping sharply.

Still grinning, Cuu shook his head. 'Nothing, Tanith. Not a thing, sure as sure.'

'Come on, Larkin!' Nour called.

Larkin scowled at Cuu and pushed past him.

'Trooper Cuu!'

The sudden shout made the five troopers stop and turn. Hark had entered the billet with Sergeant Burone and two other Ghosts. All three troopers carried weapons. They marched down the aisle towards Cuu's bunk.

'What's this?' Vadim whispered. There was a general murmur of interest all around.

'Oh feth,' Larkin mumbled.

Cuu got up, staring at the approaching detail, confused.

'Kit inspection,' Hark told him.

'But I–'

'Stand aside, trooper. Burone, search his pack and bed-roll.'

'What is this?' Cuu blurted.

'Stand to attention, trooper!' Hark snarled and Cuu obeyed. His eyes flicked back and forth as he stood there rigidly. 'Pat him down,' Hark told one of the men with him.

'This is out of order,' Cuu stammered.

'Silence, Cuu. Give me his knife.' The trooper frisking Cuu unbuckled Cuu's warknife from his sheath and passed it to the commissar. Hark inspected the blade.

'Nothing, sir,' Burone reported. Cuu's entire kit was spread out across his cot, wherever possible taken apart. Burone was checking the lining of Cuu's backpack and musette bag.

'The blade's clean,' Hark said, as if disappointed.

'He had it ground and sharpened the other day.'

Hark glanced round. Kolea stood prominently in the group of Ghosts who had gathered to watch. 'I saw him, sir,' Kolea said. 'You can check with the knife grinder.'

Hark looked back at Cuu. 'True?'

'So fething what? It's a crime to keep your blade sharp these days?'

'That insolence is pissing me off, trooper–'

'Sir…' the trooper frisking Cuu called. He yanked up the top of Cuu's left pant leg. A tight cloth bag was taped to his shin above the top of the boot.

Hark bent down and pulled the tape off. Coins, heavy and gold, spilled out into his hand.

Turning the coins over, Hark rose again. He looked at Cuu. 'Anything to say?'

'They were just… no.'

'Take him in,' Hark told his detail.

Burone's men grabbed Cuu. He began to struggle.

'This is unfair! This is not right! Get off me!'

'Behave! Now! Or things will get even messier!' Hark warned him.

Cuu stopped thrashing and the men frog-marched him forward. Hark and Burone fell in behind. As they swept past Milo's group, Cuu's cat-eyes found Larkin. 'You? Was it you, you gak?' Larkin shuddered and looked away.

Then Cuu was being taken past Bragg. Bragg was smiling.

'You? You gak! You filthy gak! Big dumbo's set me up! He's set me up!'

'Shut up!' Hark roared and they swept him out of the hall.

Bragg looked across at Larkin and shrugged. Larkin shook his head unhappily.

'Well that was interesting,' Vadim said.

'Yeah,' said Milo. He checked his watch. 'Let's go.'

SUB-HANGAR 117 WAS low down on the west skirts of Cirenholm secondary, close to one of the dome's main recirculator plants. There was background throb in the air, and a constant vibration. Extractor vents moved warm, linty air down the access corridor and across the entrance apron.

By the time Varl arrived with Cocoer, it was almost 18.30 and most of the others were already there. Banda and Nessa stood talking to the Tanith sniper Rilke, and Corporal Meryn and Sergeant Adare sat on their kit-packs with their backs to the wall, smoking lho-sticks and chatting. Doyl, Mkvenner and Bonin, the three scouts, lounged over near the other wall in a huddle, conversing privately about something. Secret scout lore no doubt, Varl thought.

'Boys,' he nodded to them and they returned his greeting.

'Hey, Rilke, girls,' he said approaching the snipers. He threw a brief wave over at Adare and Meryn.

'We're a few short, aren't we?' said Cocoer, setting down his pack.

'Not for long,' Rilke said. Milo, Larkin and the others were approaching along the rust-streaked tunnel.

'Well, what do we think, eh?' asked Varl. 'Think Gaunt has arranged a nice day out and a picnic for us?'

Banda snorted. Nessa, who had been deafened on Verghast, had to lip-read and so smiled gently a heartbeat after Banda's derisive noise.

'Let's see... three scouts, four snipers, and eight dog standards like me and Cocoer,' Varl said, looking around. 'What
does that sound like to you?'

'It sounds like an infiltrate and sanction detail,' said a voice
from behind him. Mkoll strode purposefully up onto the
apron, his field boots ringing on the metal plating. 'And it's
four scouts, actually. I'm in this too.' Like all of them, Mkoll
wore full matt-black fatigues and high-laced boots, and
heavy-pouched webbing, with a full field kit and weapons on
his back. The sleeves of his tunic were neatly rolled up past
the elbows. He did a quick head count and then consulted
his wristwatch. 'Everyone here and it's bang on 18.30. We got
the first part right then.'

They followed him through the hatch into the hangar. It
was cold and dim in the echoey interior, and they could see
little except for the area just inside the hatch which was illu-
minated by a bank of overhead spots. Four men were waiting
for them in the patch of light.

They were all big, powerful young men wearing cream-
coloured quilted jackets and baggy, pale canvas pants
bloused into the tops of high jump-boots. The sides of their
heads were brutally shaved, leaving just a strip on their
crowns. Not as a result of lice treatment, Varl thought. These
men kept their hair that way. They were Phantine troopers.
Skyborne specialists.

Mkoll greeted them and the four Phantines snapped back
smart salutes.

'Major Fazalur sends his compliments, sir,' said one with a
silver bar on his sleeve under the Phantine regimental patch.
'He asked us to wait for you here.'

'Fine. Why don't you introduce yourselves?' Mkoll suggested.

'Lieutenant Goseph Kersherin, 81st Phantine Skyborne,' the
large trooper replied. He indicated his men in turn. 'Corporal Innis Unterrio, Private first class Arye Babbist, Private first
class Lex Cardinale.'

'Okay. I'm Mkoll. Tanith First. You boys'll get the hang of
the others soon enough.' Mkoll swung round and faced the
waiting Ghosts. 'Drop your packs for now and loosen off.
Let's get you into groups. Four teams. Sergeant Varl, you're

heading first team. Sergeant Adare, third team. Second team
is yours, Corporal Meryn. Fourth team is mine. Now the rest
of you... Doyl, Nessa, Milo, you're with Adare. Mkvenner,
Larkin, Kuren... Meryn. Varl gets Banda, Vadim and Bonin.
Which leaves Rilke, Cocoer and Nour for me. Let's group up
so we get used to it. Come on. Good. Now, as you will have
spotted, each team contains a leader, a trooper, a sniper and
a scout. The bare minimum for light movement, stealth and
insertion. None of us will enjoy the back-up of a support
weapons section or a flamer on this. Sorry.'

There were a few groans, the loudest from Larkin.

'So,' said Mkoll with what seemed like relish. 'Let's get onto
the fun bit. Lieutenant?'

Kersherin nodded and walked over to a dangling control
box that hung down from the roof on a long, rubber-sleeved
cable. He thumbed several switches. There were a series of
loud bangs as the overhead light rigs came on one after
another, quickly illuminating the entire, vast space of the
hangar with cold, unfriendly light.

On the far side, rising some thirty-five metres above a floor
layered with foam cushion mats, stood a large scaffolding
tower strung with riser cables and pulleys.

'You see?' said Larkin to the Ghosts around him. 'Now I do
not like the look of that.'

Four

THE EXECUTION YARD was an unprepossessing acre of broken
cement, walled in on three sides by high curtains of pock-
marked rockcrete, and by the Chamber of Justice on the
fourth.

The Chamber of Justice, Cirenholm's central law court and
arbites headquarters, had suffered badly during the Blood
Pact occupation. The uppermost floors of the tall, Gothic
revival building were burnt out, and the west end had been
heavily shelled. Most of the office and file rooms were ransacked. An immense chrome aquila, which had once hung
suspended on the facade over the heavy portico, had been
shot away by determined stubber fire, and lay crumpled and
flightless on the main steps. On one side of the entry court

sat a chilling heap of dented arbites riot helmets, a trophy mound raised by the Blood Pact after their defeat of the lightly armed justice officers who had staunchly held out to the last to defend this sector of the city.

Despite all that, the prison block below ground was still functioning and it was the only true high security wing that Cirenholm could offer, and so the taskforce Commissariate had been forced to occupy the Chamber as best it could.

From a window at the rear of the first floor, Gaunt looked down onto the execution yard. The six-man firing squad, hooded and dressed in plain grey fatigues that lacked patches, insignia or pins, took absolution from the waiting Ecclesiarch official with routine gestures, and then lined up and took aim.

There was no fuss or ceremony. The hawkish commissar in charge, a black silk cloth draped over his balding pate, raised a sabre and gave the command in a tired voice.

The prisoner hadn't even been blindfolded or tied up. He just cowered against the back wall with nowhere to run.

Six las-shots, in a simultaneous flurry, spat across the yard and the prisoner toppled, rolling back to slide clumsily down the wall. The presiding commissar yelled out something else, and was already sheathing his sabre and taking off his black cloth as the squad filed off and servitors rolled a cart out to collect the body.

Gaunt let the scorched brocade curtain fall back against the broken window and turned away. Daur and Hark, who had been watching from the neighbouring window, exchanged a few words and went to look for something to sit on. Half-broken furniture was piled up along one wall of the battered stateroom.

The tall, ten-panelled door opened and Commissar Del Mar strode in. He was a lean man of advanced years, white-haired and reliant on augmetic limb reinforcements, but he was still striking and imposing. A good hand-span taller than Gaunt, he wore black dress uniform with a purple sash and a long cloak lined with red satin. His cap and gloves were arctic white.

'Gentlemen,' he said immediately, 'sorry to keep you waiting. Today is full of punishment details and each one requires my authority and seal. You're Gaunt.'

'Sir,' Gaunt saluted and then accepted Del Mar's handshake. He could feel the rigid armature of Del Mar's artificial hand through the glove.

'We've met, I believe?' said Del Mar.

'On Khulen, the best part of a decade ago. I was with the Hyrkans then. Had the pleasure of hearing you address the Council of Commissars.'

'Yes, yes,' Del Mar replied. 'And also on Canemara, after the liberation. Very briefly, at the state dinner with the incoming governors.'

'I'm impressed you remember that, sir. It was… fleeting.'

'Oktar, God-Emperor rest his soul, had nothing but praise for you, Gaunt. I've kept my eye out. And your achievements in this campaign have brought you recognition, let's face it.'

'You're very kind, sir. May I introduce my political officer, Viktor Hark, and Captain Ban Daur, acting third officer of my regiment.'

'Hark I know, welcome. Good to know you, captain. Now, shall we? We've a busy morning of what might be described as testimonial sifting to get through. Tactician Biota is here, along with a whole herd of staff officers, and Inquisitor Gabel is ready to present his working party's findings.'

'One extra matter I'd like to deal with before we get down to business,' said Gaunt. 'The case of Trooper Caffran.'

'Ah, that. Gaunt, I'm surprised that–' Del Mar stopped. He glanced round at Hark and Daur. 'Gentlemen, perhaps you'd give us a moment? Fultingo?'

Commissar Fultingo appeared in the doorway. 'Show the commissar and the captain here to the session hall, if you would.'

Commissar Del Mar waited until they were alone. 'Now then, this Trooper Caffran business. I'll be blunt, it's beneath you, Gaunt. I know I'm not the first person on the senior staff to caution you about this. Commissar or not, you're an acting field commander, and you should not be occupying your time or thoughts with this. It is a minor matter, and should be left to the summary judgement of your commissar.'

'I have Hark's support. I'm not going to back down. Caffran is a valuable soldier and he's innocent. I want him back in my regiment.'

'Do you know how many individuals I've had shot since we arrived, Gaunt?'

'A half-dozen. That would be the average for a taskforce this size.'

'Thirty-four. True, twenty of those were enemy prisoners who we were done with interrogating. But I've been forced to put to death seven deserters, four rapists and three murderers. Most of them Urdeshi, but a few Phantine too. I expect that kind of statistic. We command killers, Gaunt – violent, dangerous men who have been trained to kill. Some snap and desert, some attempt to slake their violent appetites on the civilian population, and some just snap. Let me tell you about the murderers. One, a Phantine private, wounded, went berserk and killed two orderlies and a nurse in the tertiary hospital. With a gurney. I can't begin to imagine how you kill someone with a gurney, but I guess it took a great deal of rage. The second, an Urdeshi flame-trooper, decided to ignite a public dining house in secondary and toasted four members of Cirenholm's citizenry who had every right to believe the danger was now past. The other, another Urdeshi, shot a fellow trooper during an argument over a bed-roll. My justice was swift and certain, as the honourable tradition of the Commissariate dictates and Imperial law demands. Summary execution. I'm not a callous man, Gaunt.'

'I didn't presume you were, commissar. Neither am I. As a sworn agent of the Commissariate, I do not hesitate to dispense justice as it is needed.'

Del Mar nodded. 'And you do a fine job, clearly. The Tanith First have a nearly spotless record. Now one of them steps out of line, one bad apple. It happens. You deal with it and move on. You forget about it and put it down as a lesson to the rest of the men. You don't tie up my office with demands for grace periods and the constant, deliberate interference of Commissar Hark.'

'Hark plagued you on my instruction, sir. And I'm glad he did. Caffran is innocent. We managed to buy enough time to identify the real killer.'

Del Mar sighed. 'Did you now?'

'He was arrested last night, sir. Trooper Cuu, another of my regiment. A Verghastite.'

'I see.'

'Those Tanith that are alive today, sir, are alive because I plucked them from their home world before it died. I consider them a precious resource. I will not give up any of them unless I know for sure it's right. This isn't right. Caffran's blameless. Cuu's the killer.'

'So... what are you asking me, Gaunt?'

'Release Caffran.'

'On your word?'

'On my recognisance. Try Cuu for the crime. The evidence against him is far more damning.'

Del Mar gazed out of the window. 'Well, now... it's not that simple any more, Gaunt,' he said. 'It's not that simple because you've made an issue of this. One crime, one suspect, that's routine. One crime, two suspects... that's an inquiry. A formal one. You've forced this, Gaunt. You must have realised.'

'I had hoped we might skip the formalities. Proceed to Cuu's court-martial and have done.'

'Well, we can't. We now have to depose this Caffran first and clear him and then try the other one. And given the impending attack on Ouranberg, I don't think you can afford the time.'

'I'll do whatever it takes,' Gaunt said, 'for victory at Ouranberg... and for my men.'

GAUNT ESCORTED COMMISSAR Del Mar to the session hall where Inquisitor Gabel's briefing was set to begin. Gabel had been interrogating the captured Blood Pact since the first day of occupation and was now ready to present his findings so that the Taskforce's senior officers and the strategic advisors could deliberate how the data might impact the plans for the assault on Ouranberg.

The session hall was a badly ventilated room packed with bodies, smoke and bad odours, but it was the only room in the Chamber of Justice large enough to contain the officers and support a large grade tactical holo-display.

Gesturing through the press of bodies, Gaunt brought Hark over to him.

'You're excused this. I'll stay and record the findings.'

'Why?' Hark asked.

'Because Del Mar's not going for it. He's insisting we clear Caff formally before they commit Cuu. I need you out there, working up the case on my behalf.'

'Ibram–'

'Dammit, Viktor, I can't not be here now. They keep telling me I should depend on my staff. Feth, you keep telling me. So go do it and do it well. I want to expend no more than a morning on Caffran's deposition. I can't afford any more. Van Voytz's been talking about going on Ouranberg in less than a week. Make a watertight case for Caff so we can get it done with quickly and I can turn my full attention to the invasion.'

'What about Cuu?'

'Cuu can go to hell, and I wash my hands. Caffran's my only concern. Now get along and do it.'

Hark paused. There was a strange expression on his face that Gaunt had never seen before. It was strangely sympathetic, yet baffled.

'What?'

'Nothing,' said Hark. 'They're starting. I'll go. Trust me, Ibram.'

'I do, Viktor.'

'No, I mean trust me to do this. Don't change your mind later.'

'Of course.'

'Okay. Okay, then.' Hark saluted and pushed his way out of the room.

Gaunt shouldered his way over to Daur.

'Everything okay, sir?'

'I believe so.'

A hush fell as Inquisitor Gabel, a cadaverous monster in matt-rose powered plate armour, stalked to the centre of the room and activated the tactical desk with his bionic digits. A hololithic display of Ouranberg city flickered into life.

'Soldiers of the Emperor,' Gabel rasped through his vox-enhancer, 'this is Ouranberg, the primary vapour mill city on this world, a vital target which we must recapture intact. It is held by a minimum of five thousand Blood Pact warriors under the personal command of the brute Slaith. We believe at least three packs of loxatl mercenaries support him. Now, here is what we have learned from the interrogated enemy prisoners...'

VARL WAS FALLING to his death.

He yowled out in terror, tried to address his fall and snagged so that he ended up dropping side on. Two metres from the ground, the counterweight pulley began to squeal as it rode the cable and bounced him to a halt, upside down, with his head mere centimetres from the mat.

Lieutenant Kersherin walked over to him and knelt down in front of him.

'Know what that was, sergeant?'

'Uh… exhilarating?'

'No. Hopeless,' Kersherin rose and gestured to the waiting Unterrio to clear Varl from the harness. Then he looked up at the figures perched on the top of the tower.

'Next one in sixty seconds!'

Thirty-five metres up, Milo stood on the tower's unnecessarily narrow and flimsy stage, holding on to the rail with one hand. He was next. Banda, Mkvenner and Kuren were waiting on the back of the stage behind him for their turns.

The Phantine trooper with him, Cardinale, beckoned Milo over as the pulleys were reset and the counterweight balanced.

He checked Milo's harness and tightened one of the straps.

'Don't look so worried. You've done this three times already. Why so unhappy?'

'Because it's not getting any better. And because I only own three pairs of undershorts and we're going for a fourth try.'

Cardinale laughed and hooked Milo up to the running line. 'Remember, face down, limbs out, even if that mat looks like it's coming up really fast. Then curl in and roll as you land. Come on, show that loudmouth Varl how it's done.'

Milo nodded and swallowed. Holding on to the riser wires, he set first one foot and then the other at the lip of the stage. What had they called it, back in drop instruction? The plank? That had been bad enough, and those practice towers had only been half the height. This tower was five metres higher than the longest possible rope drop they could have made. Also, this wasn't roping. This was jumping. Jumping out into space, hands empty. No one, not Mkoll, not Kersherin, had said anything to them yet about what Operation Larisel was specifically about, but they were clearly training for more than a long rope. The wires and cables and pulleys involved in this training were simply there to provide the simulation. Where they were going, it would be rope free.

And that, not the mats thirty-five metres underneath his toes, was the truly alarming prospect.

Babbist, a dot below them, flashed a green bat-board.

'Go!' Cardinale said.

Milo tensed.

'Go! The Emperor protects!'

'I–'

Cardinale helpfully shoved him off the plank.

'Better,' noted Kersherin, watching Milo's drop from a distance below. Beside him, Mkoll nodded.

'Milo's picking it up. Some of the others too. Nessa. Bonin. Vadim.'

'That Vadim's a natural,' Kersherin agreed.

'He has a head for heights. Apparently used to work the top spires of Vervunhive. That's why Gaunt picked him for this. Meryn and Cocoer aren't too shabby either. And to my complete surprise, Larkin's getting it too.'

'Self preservation, I think. Fear is a wonderful concentrator.'

'That much is certain.'

Milo was picking himself up and taking a jokey bow to the scattered applause of his comrades. Banda had taken her place up on the plank.

'The weakest?' Mkoll asked.

'Oh, Varl and Adare, by a long way. Doyl is too stiff. Banda tries way too hard and it throws her out. You could do with pulling your knees up.'

Mkoll grinned. 'Duly noted. Can we get them ready in time?'

'Tall, tall order. Skyborne training was six months. We've got barely as many days. We'll do what we can. No sense in cutting any out now in the hope of nosing out better candidates. We'd be starting over with them.'

'Here she goes,' Mkoll said, pointing.

They watched as Banda leapt off the tower and whizzed down on the tension of the pulleys. It was cleaner, though she bounced hard on landing.

'That's a lot better,' Kersherin remarked. 'She'll get there.'

A LITTLE LATER, once Mkvenner and Kuren had also made their fourth drops, Kersherin gathered them round and sat them down on the mats in a semi-circle. Water bottles and ration wraps were passed out. There was a lot of chatting and joking as adrenalin fizzed its way out of them.

'Listen up!' Kersherin said. 'Theory time. Private Babbist?'

Babbist came forward to the front of the semi circle, and Unterrio hurried in to deposit a field-kit sized crate in front of him before backing out.

Babbist opened the crate and lifted something out for them all to see. It was a compact but heavy metal backpack with a fearsome harness that included thigh loops, and a hinged arm with a moulded handgrip on the left side. The backpack sprouted two blunt, antler-like horns from the shoulders that ended in fist-sized metal balls. It was painted matt-green.

'What we have here, friends and neighbours,' said Babbist, patting the old, worn unit, 'is a classic type five infantry jump pack. Accept no imitations. Formal spec, for those that need it, is Type Five Icarus-Pattern Personal Descent Unit with dual M12 gravity nullers and a variable-vent compressor fan for attitude control. Which, I gather, many of you need.'

There were some laughs, but the Ghosts' attention was fixed on the device.

'Manufactured on Lucius forge world,' Babbist continued, 'it's the standard Guard variant of the assault jump pack. Smaller and lighter, not to mention more compact, than the heavy jobs used by the Adeptus Astartes. The Marines, Emperor bless 'em, need heavier duty babies to hold them in the air. Besides which, we're not gods. We wouldn't be able to stand up with one of the Astartes packs yoked to us.'

Babbist leant the pack against his knees and opened his hands to his audience. 'Remember how in Fundamental and Preparatory they told you your las was your best friend? Look after it and it'd look after you? Right, forget that. This is your new best friend. Get to know him intimately or you'll end up a stain on the landscape. If your old friend the las complains, remind him that without your new friend here, he's not going to see any action.'

Larkin slowly raised a hand.

Babbist frowned, surprised, and glanced at Mkoll.

'Out with it, Larks,' Mkoll said.

'Uh… is this just an interesting little lecture to occupy our minds during snack break… or should we conclude that at some point in our approaching yet ever fething shortening future, we're going to be strapped to one of those things and thrown into the sky? Just asking. I mean, would we be right off the mark in connecting the… thrilling wire jumps we've been making off that lovely tower with a situation that combines one of those with a lot of screaming and looseness of bowel?'

There was a well-judged pause. 'No,' said Mkoll directly, and everyone, even Larkin, laughed despite the spears of anxiety that suddenly stabbed through them.

'I see Trooper Larkin has sussed out what Operation Larisel has in store for you all,' said Babbist. 'As a prize, he can come up here and help me demonstrate this baby.'

Urged on by the Ghosts around him, Larkin got to his feet. 'I'm not jumping out of anything,' he said as he walked over to Babbist.

'Legs in the yokes, one step, two step…' Babbist said, directing Larkin's hesitant motions. 'And up we go… good. Forestraps over your shoulders as you take the weight.'

'Feth!' baulked Larkin.

'Hold it while I do up the waist cinch… okay, now feed those forestraps over to me.' Babbist snapped the metal tongues of the shoulder strap buckles into the spring-loaded lock that now rested against Larkin's chest. 'Then the leg straps up like so…' These too clunked into the chest lock. 'Right. Just pull the yokes in a bit. That's it. How does it feel?'

'Like Bragg is sitting on me,' Larkin said, staggering with the weight.

More laughing.

'The type five weighs about sixty kilos,' Babbist said.

'I'm dying here,' Larkin moaned, shifting uncomfortably.

'That's sixty kilos dormant,' Babbist added. He reached over and pulled down the pack's hinged control arm. It now stuck out at waist height on Larkin's left side, the joystick handgrip extending vertically in exactly the right place for his left hand to grasp it comfortably. The handgrip was a finger-moulded black sleeve of rubber set on a collar of milled metal with a fat red button sticking from its top.

'Let's try it active,' said Babbist. He lifted a small plate marked with a purity seal on the right flank of the pack and threw two rocker switches. Immediately the pack began to whine and throb, as if turbine power was building up inside it. Babbist closed the plate again.

'Feth me!' Larkin said, alarmed.

'Relax,' said Babbist. 'That's just the fan rising to speed.' Babbist had a gentle grip on the handstick. He softly depressed the red button.

'How's that?'

'Holy–' Larkin stammered. 'The weight's gone. I can't feel it any more.'

'That's because the antigrav units–' Babbist indicated the two metal balls that projected out above Larkin's shoulders on their blunt antlers, 'are taking the weight. The red button determines grav lift, people. I'm just touching it and it's taking the weight of the pack. A tad more–'

'Feth!' Larkin gurgled to more laughter. He had risen twenty centimetres off the ground and hung there, feet dangling.

Babbist kept hold of the handgrip. 'It's touch sensitive. Depressing it just a little, like this, gives Larkin hover. If he was, say, dropping at terminal velocity, he'd probably need to depress it by two thirds for the same effect.'

'So he could jump from a drop, press that red button, and hover?' Milo asked.

'Yes. And pushing the button all the way gives lift,' said Babbist. He squeezed the button and Larkin rose again.

'It's a subtle thing. You'll get the hang of how much thumb pressure works… deceleration, hover, lift. There'll be time to practise. The other aspect of the pack is direction. There's a powerful compressor fan inside there.' Babbist swung the floating Larkin around so they could see the pack on his

back. 'Here,' he said, 'and here, here, here, here, and here.' He
indicated louvres on the top, bottom and four corners of the
pack. 'Whether you're pressing the red button or not, angling
the handgrip will direct the internal fan via these ducts. In
other words, you point the handgrip, like a joystick,
whichever way you want to go and the compressor fan will
give you the appropriate thrust.'

Babbist yanked on the grip slightly and Larkin gusted sideways slightly. He yelped.

'The combination of controls means that you can jump
from a ship, control your rate of descent and manoeuvre
yourself onto the target. Questions so far?'

'How often do they fail?' Banda asked.

'Virtually never,' said Babbist.

'Call me Miss Virtually,' said Banda to a round of sniggering.

'What about crosswinds?' asked Mkvenner.

'With enough practice, you'll know how to compensate for
windshear with a balance of lift and directional thrust.'

'When do we get to have a go?' asked Vadim gleefully.

VIKTOR HARK SET down his stylus and sat back in his chair. It
was late, the dome lights had dimmed, and his office, a
makeshift corner of a machine shop near the regiment billets,
was getting cold.

Hark pushed aside the reams of notepaper and documents
he had managed to accumulate, and picked up a data-slate.
His thumb on the speed-scroll button, he surveyed the data.
Caffran, Cuu, the evidence and witnesses for and against each
of them. He sighed and tossed the slate aside. 'You haven't
thought about Cuu, Gaunt,' he murmured to himself. 'You're
so damn keen to get Caffran freed, you haven't thought about
the consequences.'

Hark got to his feet, pulled on his leather storm coat and
looked about for his cap. Unable to locate it, he decided he'd
do without it. He walked to the door, went out, locked it carefully behind him, and made off in the direction of the stairs.
No going back now.

'Gaunt?'

He halted in his tracks and looked down.

'No, father, he's not here.'

Zweil appeared below, moving up the staircase. 'Oh, Viktor. I'm sorry. I thought you were Ibram.'

'He's out still, with Daur and Rawne. The second day of tactical briefings.'

'A soldier's lot is never done,' Zweil sighed. He had drawn level with Hark and now sat down on the steps.

Hark paused. He hadn't got time for this.

He'd have to make time. He sat down on the gritty stairs next to Zweil.

'How're things?' Zweil asked.

'Bad. Next big show is coming up and we're still tied down to the stuff with Caffran and Cuu.'

'Caffran didn't do it, you know,' Zweil said.

'You have evidence?'

'Only the best kind,' Zweil tapped his forehead. 'He told me. I believe him.'

'That's what we're working on.' Hark said. 'What about Cuu? Is he clean?'

Zweil seemed to sulk.

'Father ayatani?'

'Cuu I don't know,' Zweil said. 'I've never met a man like him. I can't read him.'

'So he could be hiding something?'

'He could also be a difficult person to read. Everyone seems convinced that Cuu is the guilty one.'

'He is,' said Hark.

'Maybe, Viktor.'

Hark tried to control his anxious breathing. 'Father... how far would you go?'

'On a date? I'm a man of the cloth! Although, it has to be said that in my youth–'

'Forget your youth. Ayatani Zweil... you say you're with us to answer the spiritual needs of the men. In clerical confidence, I believe? Answer this–'

'Off you go.'

'A man is blameless, palpably so, but you've been instructed to prove that innocence. And there is no solid proof you can find. How far do you go?'

'Is this about Caffran?'

'Let's keep it hypothetical, father.'

'Well... if I knew an innocent man was going to be punished for something he didn't do, I'd fight it. Down to the wire.'

'With no proof?'

'Proof denies faith, Viktor, and without faith the God-Emperor is nothing.'

'So if you were convinced you were in the right, you'd fight to correct that injustice however you could?'

'Yes, I would.' Zweil was quiet for a while, studying the profile of Hark's face. 'Is this about Caffran?' he repeated.

'No, father.' Hark got up from the steps and walked away.

'Viktor? Where are you going?'

'Nowhere that needs to concern you.'

Five

THE COURT CHAMBER was nothing special. A square room hung with black drapes. A raised stage in the centre of the room, with seats and long desks on three sides for the opposing councils and the presiding officials. No banners, no standards, no decoration. It was depressingly banal and plain, depressingly rudimentary.

Gaunt took his seat on the defence side with his adjutant Beltayn and Captain Daur. There were four chairs, but no one had seen Hark since the previous night. The prosecution council – Fultingo and two aides – arranged themselves opposite Gaunt. A Commissariate clerk was laying out papers on the court table while another adjusted and set the vox/pict drone that hovered at the edge of the platform to document the proceedings.

'All rise and show respect!' one of the clerks announced, and chairs scraped back as Commissar Del Mar and two senior commissars strode in and took their places behind the centre table.

'Be seated,' said Del Mar curtly. He flicked through the papers laid out in front of him and handed a data-slate to one of the clerks.

'I have a time of 09.01 Imperial, 221.771 M41. Mark that. Court is now in session. Clerk of the court, please announce the first case on the docket. Let the accused be brought in.'

'Imperial Phantine Taskforce, courts martial hearing number 57, docket number 433.' The clerk read from the slate in a loud, nasal voice. 'Trooper Dermon Caffran, 3rd Section, Tanith First Light Infantry, to answer a charge of murder, first degree.'

As he was speaking, armed Urdeshi soldiers walked Caffran into the hall and stood him in the middle of the open side of the stage facing Del Mar. His wrists were manacled, but he had been allowed to shave and put on his number one uniform. He looked pale but determined. In fact, his face looked strangely expressionless. Lad's scared stiff, Gaunt thought. And no wonder. He nodded to Caffran and the young man made a very brief, nervous response, a little tilt of his chin.

There was something odd about Caffran, and it took a moment for Gaunt to realise it was the fact that the boy still had thick hair. Locked away, he'd missed the shearing and fumigation. Gaunt smiled to himself wryly, feeling the itch of his own fresh-shaved scalp.

'Where's Hark?' he whispered aside to Daur.

'Damned if I know, sir.'

Del Mar cleared his throat. 'A word to both councils before we get into this. I don't wish to appear as if I'm diminishing the gravity of the crime, but this case has become unnecessarily protracted. I want it finished. Speedily. That means no delaying antics, and a minimum of witnesses.' Del Mar made a light gesture in the direction of the papers in front of him, one of which was the call-list of witnesses Gaunt had submitted to the clerk. 'No character witnesses. Expert and eye witnesses only. Is that clear, colonel-commissar?'

'Yes, sir.' It was clear. Gaunt didn't like it but it was clear. Bang went the majority of names on his list.

'And you, Fultingo,' said Del Mar. 'I expect decent procedure from you too. Don't start in on anything that will provoke the defence council into… digressions.'

'Yes, sir.'

'Read the particulars, please.'

The clerk rose again. 'Be it known to the courts martial that on the night of 214 last, citizen Onti Flyte, resident of the Cirenholm South Mill second shift workforce housing, was assaulted and stabbed to death in her place of habitation.'

'Commissar Fultingo?'

Fultingo rose to his feet, and took a data-slate from his aide. ''Onti Flyte was a widow and a mother of three. Like all the residents of that district, she had just been rehoused by the liberation forces, following detention under the enemy occupation. The resident families were brought back to the South Mill habitat under escort during the course of that evening. Only a short while after returning to her home – we judge somewhere between 21.50 and 23.00 – she was attacked and murdered in her outhouse. The murder was committed using a long, straight knife, matching in all particulars the distinctive warknife carried by all Tanith infantry. An individual fitting the description of a Tanith trooper was seen leaving the vicinage at that time. The victim's eldest son, Beggi Flyte, later positively identified Trooper Caffran as the assailant. Deployment logs for the night show that Trooper Caffran was one of the escort detail assigned to South Mill.'

Fultingo looked up from the slate. 'In short, lord commissar, there seems to be little room for doubt. We have the right man. I urge you to rule so that punishment may be carried out.'

He sat down. Caffran hadn't moved. 'Gaunt?' Del Mar invited.

Gaunt got up. 'Lord, no one, not even Caffran himself, denies that he was present in the area that night. Futhermore, Caffran admits seeing and speaking with the victim and her family. He remembers escorting her to her home and making sure she was settled. The prosecution depends squarely on the identification made by the victim's son. The boy is very young. Given the terrible stress suffered by all Cirenholmers during the occupation, and adding to that the ghastly death of his mother, he is deeply, pitifully traumatised. He may easily have identified the wrong man. He had seen Caffran close up during the rehousing. When asked to pick out a Tanith trooper, he chose Caffran because he was the only one whose face he clearly recognised. I move we drop the charge and release Trooper Caffran. The real killer is yet to be prosecuted.'

Fultingo was back on his feet before Gaunt had even sat down. 'There we have the whole meat and drink of it, lord commissar. Gaunt expects us to believe this bright, intelligent boy would forget the face of his mother's killer, and simply recall the face of a soldier who helped them briefly earlier the same night. We really are wasting time. A mass of circumstantial evidence points to Trooper Caffran, and the positive ID clinches it. The defence can offer nothing, I repeat, nothing substantial in the way of evidence to contradict the prosecution's case. Just this whimsical theory of trauma-related mistaken identity. Please, sir, may we not simply end this now?'

Del Mar waved Fultingo back into his seat and looked at Gaunt. 'I am tempted to agree, Gaunt. Your point has some merit, but it's hardly an ironclad defence. The soldier admits that he was "helping out in the area until about midnight". Many saw him, but not so positively or for so long that he could not have found the time to carry out this heinous act. If you've nothing else to add, I will close the session.'

Gaunt stood up again. 'There is one piece of evidence,' he said. 'Caffran couldn't have done it. With respect to your comments about character, I have to insist on stating the fact that Caffran is a sound, moral individual with a spotless record. He is simply not capable of such a crime.'

'Objection,' growled Fultingo. 'You've already said character has no relevance, lord.'

'I am aware of what I said, commissar,' Del Mar replied. 'Seeing as Gaunt has chosen to ignore my instruction, may I remind him that for all his spotless character, Caffran is a soldier. He is a killer. Killing is not beyond him.'

'Caffran serves the Emperor as we all do. But he understands the difference between killing on a battlefield and predatory murder. He could not do it.'

'Gaunt!'

'Lord, would you send a basic infantryman to crew a mortar or a missile rack? No. He wouldn't have the ability. Why then would you maintain so staunchly that Caffran had done something he simply doesn't have the moral or emotional ability to undertake?'

'That's enough, Gaunt!'

The door at the back of the room opened suddenly and Hark hurried in. As quietly as possible, he took his seat next to Gaunt.

'My apologies,' he said to the court.

'You might as well have not bothered showing up at all, Hark. We're done here.'

Hark rose and handed a slip of paper to the clerk, who brought it round to Del Mar.

'Craving your patience, lord commissar, I submit the name of one last witness to be appended to the list.'

Gaunt looked surprised.

'Objection!' snapped Fultingo.

'Overruled, Fultingo,' said Del Mar reading the slip. 'It's late and it's annoying, but it's not against the rules. Very well, Hark, with Colonel-Commissar Gaunt's permission, let's see what you've got.'

IT WAS COLD out in the gloomy hall outside the courtroom. Tona Criid sat on a side bench under an oil painting of a particularly ugly Chief of Arbites and fidgeted. She'd come to give Caff her support, maybe even speak up for him if she was allowed, although Daur had advised her that character witnesses were unlikely to be heard.

But she hadn't even been permitted to observe.

Dorden was with her. He'd come to read his statement on the examination of the body if that proved relevant. And Kolea was there too. He was sitting right down at the end of the hall on his own. She wasn't sure why. Caff's section leader was Major Rawne. She supposed that with Rawne busy running the regiment up to speed, Kolea had been sent in his stead as a serving officer to bear witness to Caff's good character.

'It'll be fine,' said Dorden, sitting down next to her. 'Really,' he added.

'I know.'

'Who's that man, do you think, doc?' she added after a moment, whispering.

A hunched, elderly civilian sat on the benches opposite them.

He'd arrived a few minutes before with Commissar Hark, who'd set him on the seat and hurried into the court chamber.

'I don't know,' said Dorden.

The court door opened and Criid and Dorden looked up expectantly. A clerk looked out. 'Calling Cornelis Absolom. Cornelis Absolom. Is he present?'

The old man got up and followed the clerk into the court.

'STATE YOUR NAME for the record.'

'Cornelis – ahm! – Cornelis Absolom, sir.'

'Occupation?'

'I am retired, sir. These last three years. Before that I worked for seventeen years as a night watchman at the vapour mill gas holders.'

'And how did you get that post, Mr Absolom?'

'They were looking for a man with military training. I served nine years in the Planetary Defence Force, Ninth Phantine Recon, but I was injured during the Ambross Uprising, and left the service.'

'So it's fair to say you are an observant man, Mr Absolom? As a night watchman and before that, in the recon corps?'

'My eyes are sound, sir.'

Commissar Hark nodded and walked a few paces down the stage thoughtfully.

'Could you describe to the lord commissar and the court your relationship with the deceased, Mr Absolom?'

'Ma'am Flyte was my next door neighbour.'

'When was the last time you saw the deceased?'

The old man, who had been given a chair to sit on because of his unsteady legs, cleared his throat.

'On the night of her murder, Commissar Hark.'

'Could you describe that?'

'We had just returned to the habs. The place was a mess, a terrible mess. I wanted to sleep, but I had to sweep out my parlour first. The smell… I was in my backyard and I saw her over the fence. She was going to the outhouse. We exchanged a few words.'

'About what, Mr Absolom?'

'The mess, sir.'

'And you didn't see her again?'

'No, sir. Not alive.'

'Can you tell the court what happened later that night, Mr Absolom?'

'It wasn't much afterwards. I'd filled a sack with rubbish, mostly food that had rotted in my pantry. I went out into the yard to dump it down by the back fence.

'I heard a sound from Ma'am Flyte's outhouse. A thump. Followed by another.

'I was worried, so I called out.'

'And then?'

'A man came out of the outhouse. He saw me at the fence, and ran off down the back lane.'

'Can you describe the man?'

'He was wearing what I know now to be the uniform of the Tanith First, sir. I had seen them earlier that night. They escorted us back to our homes.'

'Did you see the man's face?'

Absolom nodded.

'Please voice your answer for the vox-recorder, Mr Absolom,' Del Mar prompted softly.

'I'm sorry, lord. Yes, I did. I did see him. Not clearly, but well enough to know him.'

'Mr Absolom, was it the accused, Trooper Caffran?'

The old man shuffled round to take a look at Caffran.

'No sir. The man was a little taller, leaner. And older.'

Hark looked back at Commissar Del Mar. 'No further questions, lord.'

Fultingo got up at once. 'Mr Absolom. Why did you not come forward with this information earlier? You raised the alarm and alerted the authorities about the death. You were questioned, by me and my assistant, and claimed not to have seen any suspect.'

Absolom looked down the stage to the commissar. 'May I be honest, lord?'

'This court expects no less, sir,' said Del Mar.

'I was scared. We'd been through weeks of hell at the hands of those heathens. Ma'am Flyte didn't deserve what happened to her, no sir, but I didn't want to get involved. The tough questions of the commissars, the searches... and I didn't want to risk the man coming back.'

'To silence you?'

'Yes, lord. I was terribly afraid. Then I heard a man had been arrested and I thought, that's an end to it.'

Del Mar had been scribbling a few notes. He put the holo-quill back in its power-well. 'Your answers have a ring of truth to them, Mr Absolom. Except for one thing. Why did you come forward now?'

'Because Commissar Hark came to see me. He said he thought they might have the wrong man. When he showed me this lad's picture, I knew he was right. You hadn't caught the killer at all. I came forward today so that justice would not let this young man down. And because I was afraid again. Afraid that the real killer was still at large.'

'Thank you, Mr Absolom,' Del Mar said. 'Thank you for your time and effort. You are excused.'

'Lord, I—' Fultingo began.

Del Mar held up a hand. 'No, Fultingo. In the name of the God-Emperor of Terra, whose grace and majesty is everlasting, and by the power invested in me by the Imperial Commissariate, I hereby declare this case concluded and the accused cleared of all charges.'

FROM THE COURT doorway, Gaunt watched Criid hugging Caffran, and Dorden shaking the young man's hand. He turned to Daur and Beltayn.

'Thanks for your efforts, both of you. Beltayn, take Caffran back to the billet and see he has a good meal and a tot of sacra. Give him and Criid twelve-hour liberty passes too. He'll want to see his kids.'

'Yes, sir.'

'Ban, escort Mr Absolom back to his home and repeat my thanks.'

'I'd like that duty, Ibram,' Hark said. 'I promised the old man a bottle of beer and the chance to tell me his war stories.'

'Very well.' Gaunt faced Hark. 'You pulled it off.'

'I did what was asked of me, Ibram.'

'I won't forget this. Caffran owes his life to you.'

Hark saluted and made his way over to the old man.

'The clerk tells me Cuu's trial has been set for tomorrow morning, sir,' said Daur. 'They want that cleared away too. Shall I prepare the defence notes?'

'I won't be defending.'

Daur frowned. 'Sir?'

'Cuu's guilty. His crimes nearly cost us Caffran. The Commissariate can deal with him. I'll have Hark cover the formalities.'

'I see,' said Daur stiffly.

Gaunt caught his arm as he began to move away. 'You have a problem, captain?'

'No, sir. Cuu's probably guilty, as you say. I just thought–'

'Ban, I regard you as a friend, and I also expect all my officers to be open with me on all matters. What's on your mind?'

Daur shrugged. 'You just seem to be dismissing Cuu. Leaving him to his fate.'

'Cuu's a killer.'

'Most likely.'

'He'll get justice. The justice he deserves. Just like Caffran did.'

'Yeah,' said Daur. 'I guess he will.'

Down at the end of the hallway, Kolea watched the people spilling out of the court. He saw Caffran embracing Criid and the smiles on the faces of Daur and Gaunt.

He sighed deeply and went back to the billet.

GAUNT PUSHED OPEN the hatch to sub-hangar 117 and went inside. The cargo servitor escorting him followed, carrying the munition crate. The servitor wore the painted insignia of the Munitorium on its torso casing.

It was cold inside the hangar, and for a moment, Gaunt thought he had come to the wrong place. There were a few equipment packs and lasrifles heaped up along one wall, but no sign of anybody.

Then he looked up.

Twenty human figures were floating and bobbing up in the rafters of the hangar.

One saw him, turned and swooped down. As he approached, Gaunt heard the rising whine of a compressor fan. The man executed a decent turn and landed neatly on his feet, taking a few scurrying steps forward to slow himself. Gaunt recognised him as Lieutenant Kersherin.

Keeping his left hand on the jump-pack's control arm, the Skyborne specialist threw a neat salute.

'Colonel-commissar!'

'Stand easy, lieutenant. You seem to be making progress.'

'At a variable rate. But yes, I'd say so, sir.'

'I'd like to talk to them. If they're not too busy.'

Kersherin said a few words into his micro-bead and the floating figures began to descend. The three other Phantines made perfect, experienced landings. The Ghosts mostly made hesitant groundfalls, though Vadim, Nessa and Bonin reached the ground like experts. Varl and Adare thumped down hard and clumsily and made Gaunt wince.

They helped each other off with their jump packs, and the Skyborne trainers went round to double-check all the circuits had been shut down properly.

'Gather in,' said Gaunt. He slid a chart out of his pocket and began to unfold it. They grouped around in a half-moon.

'First of all, I thought you'd like to know that Caffran was cleared of all charges this morning.'

There were appreciative claps and cheers from the Ghosts.

'Next thing. More important to you. The time's come to tell you a little more about Operation Larisel. You've worked out by now that it's going to involve a grav-drop. And I'm sure you've guessed the target.'

Gaunt opened out the chart and laid it on the floor.

'Ouranberg, the primary target here on Phantine. A city five times larger than Cirenholm. Well defended. Strongly garrisoned. Not an easy target, but that's why they give us shiny medals.'

The Ghosts peered in to get a look at the chart of Ouranberg's sprawling, multi-domed plan.

'You'll get copies of this soon, and the chance to get decent familiarisation on a holo-simulation. For now, this is the target. Or rather, where the target can be found. Operation Larisel, as the name doubtless suggests to the Tanith amongst you, is a hunting mission. A grav drop, a stealth insertion and then a hunt.'

'What for?' asked Varl.

'In about a week, the taskforce will begin its assault on Ouranberg. The strength of resistance will depend on the morale and spirit of the Blood Pact and their allied units. At the moment, that's very high. Unbreakably high, perhaps.

The rumours you may have heard are true. The enemy forces at Ouranberg are personally commanded by the Chaos General Sagittar Slaith, one of Warlord Urlock Gaur's most trusted lieutenants. His foul charismatic brand of leadership inspires almost invincible devotion and loyalty from his troops. If we move against a dug-in force under his command, the cost will be high, punishing. Even if the assault is successful, it will be a bloodbath. But if Slaith is removed from the equation, we face a much more vulnerable foe.' Gaunt paused. 'The purpose of Operation Larisel is to locate Slaith and eliminate him in advance of the invasion. To decapitate the enemy forces and break their spirit right at the start of the main military advance.'

No one said anything. Gaunt looked at their faces, but they were all taking this in and their expressions gave nothing away.

'Briefings on how to locate and identify Slaith will follow in the next day or so. We have a lot of data that we think will be invaluable to you. Operation Larisel will take the form of four teams – I believe you're already divided up – that will deploy to different insertion points in the city. Four mission teams, coming in from four different angles. Four times the chance of success.'

Gaunt turned to the crate that the waiting servitor was carrying and popped open the lid. 'One last thing for now, something to factor in to your training. It's been confirmed, I'm sorry to say, that loxatl mercenaries are active under Slaith's command at Ouranberg. Tac reports and battlefield intelligence have shown that these alien scum are particularly resistant to las-fire.'

Gaunt lifted a bulky weapon from the crate. It was an autorifle, almost a small cannon, with a heavy gauge barrel and a folding skeleton stock. He slapped a fat drum magazine into the slot behind the gnurled metal of the foregrip.

'This is a U90 assault cannon. Old, but powerful. Fires .45 calibre solid rounds at semi and full auto. Kicks like a bastard. The drum-pattern clip holds forty rounds. I've borrowed these four from the Urdeshi. They're manufactured on their home world. Not a terribly good weapon and prone to fouling, but with plenty of stopping power and the best trade-off of power against weight we could manage. Each team should assign one member to carry one in place of his or her standard las. The drums marked with a yellow cross carry standard shells.' He took another out of the crate and held it up. 'The ones with the red cross are drummed with explosive AP shells. We think these old solid-slug chuckers, firing armour piercing, will be your best chance against the loxatl. Designated troopers should get practice with them as soon as possible.'

Gaunt put the weapon and the spare drum back in the crate.

'I'll be back to continue briefing tomorrow. We'll deal with DZ specifics then, and begin a survey of the target landscape. Until then... keep up the good work.'

'Oh feth,' Larkin said, 'this keeps getting better and better.'

FOR THREE DAYS, supply barges from Hessenville had been arriving to dock in the hangars along Cirenholm's skirts. Those that arrived under escort on the morning of the 221st were accompanied by the drogue *Skyro*, carrying two Urdeshi and one Krassian regiment to bolster the invasion forces.

Many of the barges had been lugging aerial ordnance and parts to strengthen the taskforce's air wing, along with some eighteen Marauders and twenty-seven Lightnings. Since the afternoon of the 215th, the strike wings had been flying sorties north of Cirenholm to wrest air superiority from the Ouranberg squadrons, and now long-range night raids had begun on the city itself. Admiral Ornoff's intention was to soften the city's defences and neutralise as much of the enemy's air power as possible prior to the main assault, 'O-Day' as it was called.

The effect of the bombing raids was difficult to judge. In three nights of missions over three hundred thousand tonnes of explosives were dropped on Ouranberg at a cost of four Marauders.

The fighter sorties were somewhat easier to evaluate. Unless scrambled to meet a detected raid, which were few and far between, the Lightnings went up in four-ship patrols, hunting enemy traffic as directed by Sky Command Cirenholm's modar, astrotachographic and long range auspex arrays. Twenty-nine enemy planes of varying types were claimed as kills during the first five days, for a loss of two Lightnings. On the afternoon of the 220th, four wings of Phantine Lightnings were rushed up to intercept a mass raid by fifty enemy dive bombers and escort fighters. Eight more Lightnings and six Marauders were fast-tracked up to join them as the battle commenced. The northern perimeter guns of Cirenholm blistered the cloud cover with flak.

The engagement lasted forty-eight minutes and was punishingly hard-fought. The enemy was utterly routed before they could land a single item of munitions on Cirenholm. They lost a confirmed tally of thirty-three planes. The Phantine lost six, including the decorated ace Erwell Costary. Flight Lieutenant Larice Asch personally shot down four enemy aircraft, raising her career score to make her one of the few female Phantine aces, and Pilot Officer Febos Nicarde succeeded in notching up seven kills. Ornoff awarded him the Silver Aquila. It took hours for the twisted contrails and exhaust plumes created by the vast air battle to dissipate.

Inside the Cirenholm hangars, Munitorium workers, Imperial Guardsmen and volunteer citizens alike toiled in shifts to unload, process and store the vast influx of material. Some of the Hessenville barges also brought food and medicae supplies for the wounded population.

Mid-afternoon on the 221st, just about the time Caffran was being discharged, five platoons of Ghosts under the supervision of the Munitorium were off-loading crates from a barge's cargo hold and wheeling them on trolleys through to a sub-hangar.

Rawne had put his adjutant Feygor in charge, partly to ensure that the Ghosts got the pick of the inventory for their support weapons and rocket launchers. The air was a racket of clattering carts, raised voices, whirring hoists and rattling machine tools. The Ghosts were stripped to their vests, sweating hard to heft the laden trolleys up through the arch of the sub-hangar and then riding them back down the ramp empty with whoops and laughs. The sub-hangar was beginning to look like a mad warlord's pipe dream. Across the wide floor, rows of ammo crates and munition pods alternated with rows of carefully lined-up rockets. Along one wall, rack-carts with thick, meaty tyres carried fresh-painted bombs and missiles destined for underwing mounting. Some of the men had not been able to resist the temptation of chalking their names on the warheads, or writing such taunts as 'One from the Ghosts' or 'Goodbye fethhead' or 'If you can read this, scream'. Others had drawn on fanged mouths, turning the missiles into snarling predators. Others, touchingly, had dedicated the bombs as gifts to the enemy from fallen comrades.

'Running out of floor space,' Brostin told Feygor, mopping the perspiration from his brow.

Feygor nodded. 'Don't break your rhythm. I'll see to it.' He went in search of a Munitorium official, who agreed to open up the next sub-hangar along.

Feygor took Brostin with him to open up the sliding metal partition into the next sub-space. They passed Troopers Pollo and Derin wheeling a cart of grenade boxes out into the back corridor.

'Where the feth are you going with that?' Feygor asked.

'The hall,' Pollo replied as if it was a daft question. 'We're getting too full in here…'

Feygor looked out into the gloomy access hall behind the hangar. Already, work crews had lined up nine carts of munitions along one wall.

'Oh, feth… this isn't right,' Feygor growled. 'Take them back inside. All of them.'

The two men groaned.

'Rustle up some others to help you. We're going through into that sub-hangar there,' Feygor said, pointing. 'I have no idea why you thought this was a good place to dump stuff.'

'We were just following the others,' Derin said.

'What?'

'The guys ahead of us. There was a Munitorium fether with them, and they seemed to know what they were doing.'

'Go and get that guy over there,' snapped Feygor, indicating the Munitorium chief he'd spoken to. Derin hurried off.

Fifty metres down the back corridor from them, another hatch opened off the sub-hangar. As Feygor waited for the clerk to arrive, he saw three Ghosts wheeling another cart through, accompanied by a Munitorium aide.

'Ah, feth…' Feygor said. He was about to shout out when Pollo said 'They must be hot.'

There was something about Pollo's tone that made Feygor look again. The three Ghosts were wearing full kit, including tunics and wool hats.

'With me,' Feygor said to Brostin and Pollo, and moved forward at a jog. 'Hey, hey you there!'

The Ghosts seemed to ignore him. They were intent on getting their cart of missiles into a service elevator.

'Hey!'

Two of them turned. Feygor didn't recognise either of them. And Feygor prided himself on knowing every face in the regiment.

'What the feth…?' he began.

One of the 'Ghosts' suddenly pulled a laspistol and fired on them.

Feygor cried out and pulled Brostin into the wall as the shots blistered past them.

Pollo had been a nobleman's bodyguard back on Verghast, a trained warrior of House Anko. Expensive neural implants, paid for by his lord, gave him a reaction time significantly shorter than that of unaugmented humans. With a graceful sweep that combined instinct and immaculate training, he drew an autopistol from his thigh pocket and returned fire, placing his body without thinking between the assailants and his comrades.

He dropped the shooter with a headshot. The others fled.

'After the bastards!' Feygor bellowed. He was on his feet, his laspistol ripped from its holster. Brostin had wrenched a fire-axe from a wall bracket.

The interlopers pounded away down a side hall and into a stairwell. As he ran, Feygor keyed his headset. 'Alert! Security alert! Hangar 45! Intruders heading down-block to level thirty!' The sub-hangar behind them erupted in commotion.

They burst into the stairwell and heard feet clattering on the steps below. Feygor took the stairs three at a time, with Pollo close on his heels and Brostin lumbering after.

Feygor threw himself against the banister and fired down the airspace. Two hard-round shots ricocheted back up at him. They heard a door crash open.

The lower door led into a service area, a wide machine shop that seemed menacingly quiet and dark, and which glistened with oil. Feygor charged through the door and was almost killed by the gunman who had ducked back to lie in wait behind the hatch. Two bullets hissed past the back of his head and made him stumble. A moment later, Brostin came out of the door and pinned the gunman to the wall with one splintered whack of the fire-axe.

Shots rattled back across the machine shop. Feygor spotted one muzzle flash in the semi-gloom, dropped on one knee and fired his laspistol from a double-handed brace. The target lurched back against a workbench and fell on his face.

There was no sign of the third one. Pollo and Feygor prowled forward. Both swung around as they heard a door squeak. For a moment, a figure was framed against the light outside. Pollo's handgun roared and the figure flew out of sight as if yanked by a rope.

Brostin found the machine shop lights.

Pollo checked that the man he'd hit at the door was dead, and returned to find Feygor rolling his kill over on the oily floor. There was no mistaking the man's grizzled face, or his hands, thick with old scars. The Ghost uniform didn't even fit him particularly well. But it was a Ghost uniform. Right down to the straight silver warknife in his belt case.

'Feth!' said Feygor.

'Look at that,' said Pollo. He knelt down. Near to the bloody hole Feygor had put through the corpse, the black Tanith tunic had another rent, a scorched puncture that had been hastily sewn up with back thread.

'This isn't the first time this tunic's been worn by a dead man,' he said.

Six

HALF-DECENT FOOD was an understandable rarity on Cirenholm, but the late lunch placed in front of Gaunt and Zweil looked surprisingly inviting.

'You've excelled yourself, Beltayn,' Gaunt told his adjutant.

'It's not much, sir,' said Beltayn, though he was obviously pleased by the compliment. 'If an adj-officer can't rustle up some proper meat and a little fresh bread for his chief, what good is he?'

'Well, I hope you saved some for yourself too,' said Gaunt, tucking in. Beltayn blushed.

'If an adj-officer can't fill his own stomach, what good is he to his chief?' Gaunt reassured him.

'Yes sir.' Beltayn paused, and then produced a bottle of claret. 'Don't ask where I got this,' he said.

'My dear Beltayn,' said Zweil, pouring himself a glass. 'This act alone will get you into heaven.'

Beltayn smiled, saluted and left.

Zweil offered the bottle to Gaunt, who shook his head. They were sitting at a table in the stateroom of the merchant's house Gaunt had co-opted for his officers. It was a little cold and damp, but well appointed. Zweil smacked his lips and ate with gusto.

'You're pleased about Caffran?' he said.

'A weight off my mind, father. He says to thank you for the spiritual support you've offered.'

'Least I could do.'

'You'll be busy the next few days,' Gaunt said. 'The invasion hour approaches, and men will be looking for blessing and counsel.'

'They've already started coming. Every time I go to the chapel, there are Ghosts waiting for me.'

'What's the feeling?'

'Good, good... confident. The men are ready, if that's what you want to hear.'

'I want to hear the truth, father.'

'You know the mood. How's Operation Larisel shaping up?'

Gaunt put down his cutlery. 'You're not meant to know about that.'

'Oh, I know. No one is. But in the last two days Varl, Kuren, Meryn, Milo, Cocoer and Nour have all come to say penance and receive benediction. I couldn't really not know.'

'It'll be fine. I have every confidence.'

There was a knock at the door and Daur came in. He looked excited.

'Captain. Pull up a chair and pour yourself a drink. I can call Beltayn back, if you're hungry.'

'I've eaten,' said Daur, sitting with them.

'Then report.'

'A little disturbance on the hangar decks earlier. Feygor rumbled some interlopers trying to steal munitions.'

'Indeed?'

'They were Blood Pact, sir.'

Gaunt pushed away his plate and looked at the Verghast officer. 'Seriously?'

Daur nodded. 'Three of them dressed as Ghosts and another disguised as a Munitorium clerk. They're all dead. A bit of a firefight, I hear.'

'Feth! We should–'

Daur raised a hand. 'Already done, sir. We scoured the vicinity with fireteams and smoked out a cell of them hiding in the basement levels. They must have been there since the liberation, lying low. They didn't go without a fight. We found they had sneaked about three tonnes of explosive munitions down there. Probably intended to cause merry hell when they were up to strength.'

Gaunt sat back. 'Have you alerted the other commanders?'

Daur nodded. 'We're coordinating a fresh sweep of the entire city to check for any others that may have slipped the net the first time. No traces yet, so we may be clean. It may have been an isolated group. We have, however, already identified six locals who were assisting them.'

'By the throne!'

'I think the Blood Pact had threatened them, but they'd also paid them well for their troubles. In defaced gold coins.'

Gaunt pushed his unfinished meal aside. 'This has all been handed on to Del Mar?'

'I believe the interrogations and executions are already underway.'

'Extraordinary...' Zweil mused. 'We free them from these monsters, and still the taint persists.'

'Sir,' said Daur, choosing his words carefully, 'the Blood Pact were using disguises. Stolen clothes and equipment. They had obtained at least nine full sets of Tanith uniform.'

'Where from?'

'The morgue, sir. When we checked, nine bodybags had been opened and the corpses stripped.'

'The fething heathens…'

'Sir, they had everything. Ghost fatigues, webbing, even warknives.'

Gaunt realised where this was heading. The realisation stunned him. He looked at Daur.

'You're talking about Cuu, aren't you?'

Daur sighed. 'Yes sir, I am. A man dressed in Tanith uniform, wielding a warknife, carrying defaced coin. It's no longer so simple.'

'Oh feth,' Gaunt murmured and poured himself a glass of wine. 'It is. Cuu's a stone killer. We've got him.'

'With respect,' said Daur. 'Maybe we haven't. I don't like Cuu, but he maintains that all he is guilty of is looting the coins. What if he's innocent? There's now a reasonable doubt.'

'Yes, but–'

'Colonel-commissar, you went to the wire for Caffran on the basis of reasonable doubt. Doesn't Cuu deserve that kind of loyalty too? He's a Ghost, just like Caffran.'

'But–'

'But what? He's a Verghastite? Is that it?' Daur rose angrily.

'Sit down, Daur! That's not what I meant.'

'Really? Tell that to all the Verghastites in this regiment tomorrow when Cuu goes to the wall.'

He marched out and slammed the door.

'What?' Gaunt growled at Zweil.

The old father shrugged. 'Man's got a point. Cuu's a Ghost. He should expect the great and honourable Ibram Gaunt to fight his corner just as much as he did for Caffran.'

'Cuu's a killer,' Gaunt echoed.

'Maybe. If you're expecting me to confirm or deny that on the basis of confession, forget it. I am a sponge for secrets, for the good of men's souls, but I do not leak. Otherwise men would not trust me. Only the God-Emperor hears what I hear.'

'The Emperor protects,' said Gaunt.

'Are you biased?' Zweil asked impertinently.

'What?'

'Biased? Towards the Tanith? It's often thought you are. You favour the Tanith over the Verghastites.'

'I do not!'

Zweil shrugged. 'It's just the way it seems sometimes. To the Vervunhivers especially. You value them, appreciate them, even like some of them, men like Daur. But you always look to the Tanith first.'

'They've been with me longer.'

'No excuse. Are the Verghastite second-class members of this regiment?'

'No!' Gaunt slammed down his glass and got up. 'No, they're not.'

'Then stop making it seem as if they are. Quickly, before the Tanith First comes apart at the seams and splits down the middle.'

Gaunt was silent. He gazed out of the window.

'How many times in the last week have you mentioned Corbec in your addresses to the men? Keeping them updated on his progress? And how many times have you mentioned Soric? Two chief officers, both beloved of the men, both ostensibly valued by you... both dying. But Corbec is in every rousing speech you make. Soric? Forgive me, Ibram, but I can't remember the last time you even mentioned him.'

Gaunt turned round slowly. 'I refuse to accept that I'm as biased as you say. I have done everything to induct the Verghastites properly and fairly. I damn well know there is rivalry... I–'

'What, Ibram?'

'If you can even think this is true... and if Daur thinks it too, as he most obviously does, I will do what I have to. I will show the regiment that there is no division. I will demonstrate it so there is no doubt. I will not have anyone believing that I somehow favour the Tanith. The Ghosts are the Ghosts. Always and forever, first and only. It doesn't matter where they come from.'

Zweil toasted Gaunt and drained his glass. 'I take it you know how to do that?'

'Yes, though it goes against my ethical judgment and sticks in my throat, I do. I have to fight for Cuu's life.'

THEY NOTCHED UP twenty kilometres doing circuits of the secondary dome's promenade and then picked up the pace and took the thirty flight central dome stairwell at a sprint.

By the time Kolea's section arrived back in the withered park ground set aside for exercise, they were panting and drenched with sweat.

'Fall out,' Kolea said, his own breaths coming in gasps. He leaned over against his knees so that his dog-tags swung from his neck, and spat on the ground.

The men flopped down in the dust or shambled off to find water. Across the grey, dead grass, Skerral and Ewler's sections were doing callisthenics, directed by Sergeant Skerral's booming voice.

Hwlan tossed Kolea a water bottle and the sergeant nodded his thanks before taking a big gulp.

The section felt light, and he didn't like it. There had been a few casualties during the assault, but Rawne had promised to rotate some men up from lower platoons to make up the balance.

What Kolea particularly noticed was the gaping hole left by the three who had disappeared since their arrival on Phantine. Nessa and Nour, sidelined for special ops by Gaunt. And Cuu.

Kolea didn't know what to think about that.

'We should maybe visit Cuu tonight, if we get the passes,' Lubba said as if somehow tuned to Kolea's thoughts. It was likely the subject was on every mind in the section.

'What do you mean?' Kolea said.

'Go see him. Wish him well. That'd be okay, wouldn't it, sarge?'

'Yeah, of course.'

Lubba, the squad's flamer operator, was a short, thick-set man covered in underhive tattoos. He leaned back against the fence. 'Well, we won't be seeing the poor gak again, will we?'

'What?'

'He'll be dead by this time tomorrow. Against the wall,' Jajjo said.

'Only if he's guilty–' Kolea began. 'I can't believe Cuu, even Cuu, would do a thing like that.'

'Doesn't matter though, does it?' said Lubba sitting up again. 'Old Gaunt put his balls on the block to get Caff released. He won't bother this time. Fact is, I reckon Cuu was the trade-off. Cuu in exchange for Caff.'

Kolea shook his head. 'Gaunt wouldn't do that–'
Several Verghastites laughed.
'He wouldn't!'
'Caff's Tanith, ain't he? Much more valuable.'
Kolea got up. 'It doesn't work like that, Lubba. We're all Ghosts.'
'Yeah, right.' Lubba sat back and closed his eyes.
There was a stillness for a moment, broken only by Skerral's distant yells. For the first time, Kolea felt the mood. The feeling that gnawed at the Verghastites. The feeling they were second-class. He'd never sensed it before. He'd always got nothing but respect from Gaunt. But now…
'Come on!' he said, clapping his hands. 'Up and into the shower block! Go! Mess-call's in twenty minutes!'
There were moans and the men got despondently onto their feet. Kolea trailed them back towards the park hatch.
Ana Curth, dressed in old combat fatigues, was sitting on a rickety bench at the end of the path near the hatch. She was leaning back with her legs stretched out and crossed, reading a dog-eared old text.
'Good book?' Kolea asked, pausing by her.
She looked up. 'Gregorus of Okassis. The *Odes*. One of Dorden's recommendations. Either I'm very stupid or I'm just not getting it.'
'So,' Kolea said, turning to watch the men on the far side of the park doing star jumps. 'This is just a little down-time between shifts?'
'Yeah. I like the fresh air.' He looked round and saw the ironic smirk on her face.
'Actually. I was waiting for you. Obel said you'd be bringing your section back this way at the end of training.'
'Me?' Kolea said.
'You.'
'Why?'
'Because I felt like meddling where I wasn't wanted. Got a minute?'
He sat on the bench next to her.
'Remember what we talked about, back at Bhavnager? You confided in me.'
'I did. Who have you told?'

She slapped him playfully on the arm with her text. 'No one. But that's the point. You should.'

'Not this again.'

'Just answer me this, sergeant. Are you trying to get yourself killed?'

Kolea opened his mouth to reply and paused. He was taken aback. 'Of course I'm not. Unless you count enlistment in the Imperial Guard as a death wish.'

She shrugged. 'People are worried about you.'

'People?'

'Some people.'

'Which people?'

Curth smiled. He liked her smile. 'Come on, Gol,' she said. 'I'm not about to–'

'I let you into my confidence. Seems only fair you trust me as far.'

She put the text down and stretched her arms. 'Got me. Okay. Fair enough. One of the people would be Varl.'

'I ought to–'

'Not say anything to him,' she cut in, flippantly. 'Confidences, remember?'

'All right,' he growled.

'Varl... amongst others, I think... believes you're taking unnecessary risks. They think it's because you've lost your wife and kids, and that you're looking for a... what was it? A reuniting round.'

'Reunion round.'

'Uh-huh. That's it. That's what they think, anyway. But I know better, don't I?'

'So?' He picked up her text and began thumbing through the pages. Poems. Long, old poems like the kind he'd struggled through in Elementary Grade twenty-five years before.

'Well, are they right to be worried?'

'No.' He glanced at her quickly, and saw she was gazing at him intently. 'No. I'm not... not taking risks. I don't think I am. Not deliberately.'

'But?'

Kolea chewed his lip for a second. He looked down at the book with a little shake of the head. 'There was a moment. During the assault. I ran into the gunfire. I... didn't care.

Varl saw me. Even now, I can't imagine what I was thinking.'

'That you want to escape?'

He turned his head and met her eyes. There was no guile in them. Only care. The care that made her a great healer.

'What do you mean?'

'We all want escape. Escape from poverty, fear, death, pain. Escape from whatever we hate about life. And we all have our ways. The Ghosts who drink to drown the terrors of war. The ones who gamble. The ones who have a superstition for every thing they do.' As she was speaking, she slid a packet of lho-sticks out of her jacket pocket and lit one. 'Me, it's bad old poetry, a park bench in pretend sunlight, and these damn things.' She took a drag. She'd given up years before after her promotion to surgeon. The old habit had crept up on her again those last few months. 'And I like a glass of sacra now and then. Feth, I escape in all sorts of ways, don't I?'

He laughed, partly at her frank remark and partly at the way her Verghastite accent made the Tanith curse sound. She was one of the few from Vervunhive who had cheerfully borrowed that other world's oath.

'You, though,' she went on. 'Well, there's no escape, is there? Drink, narcotics… they must only make it worse. The hell of having your kids so near and yet so far away. For you, it must seem like there's only one escape. An escape from life itself.'

'You're a psychiatrist now, then?'

She blew a raspberry. 'There is another way, you know. Another escape.'

'I know.'

'Do you?'

'Yeah. I tell them. I tell Caff and Tona. I reveal myself to the kids. Don't think I haven't thought about it. Ana, it would hurt them all. Caffran and Criid… it would destroy them. It'd be like taking their children away. And Dalin and Yoncy. Gak, the trauma. They've survived losing me. Finding me again might be too much.'

'I think they'd survive. All of them. I think they'd benefit in many ways. I think it would matter to them. More than you know.'

He flicked the pages of the text. 'Maybe.'

'Not to mention the good it will do you. Will you think about it?'

'What if I don't?'

'Oooh… you've no idea how persistent I can be. Or how many unnecessary medical checks I can order for you.'

'I'll make you a deal,' said Kolea. 'The assault on Ouranberg is close. Real close. Let me get through that. Then I'll… I'll come clean. If you think it's for the best.'

'I do. I really do.'

'But not before Ouranberg. Caffran and Criid will need their heads together for that. I'll not drop a bombshell like this just before a big show.'

Curth nodded and exhaled a plume of smoke. It shone blue in the artificial light as it billowed away. 'Fair enough.'

Kolea fidgeted with the book again, flipping the pages one last time before handing it back.

He stopped. The text had fallen open on the title page. A yellowing certificate had been pasted onto the endpaper. It was a scholam prize, awarding Mikal Dorden a merit in elementary comprehension.

'Dorden lent you this text?'

'Yes,' she said, leaning over. 'Oh. I hadn't noticed that. It must have been his son's.'

For the first few years of the regiment's life, Mikal and Tolin Dorden had been unique amongst the Ghosts. Father and son. Doc Dorden and his trooper boy. The only blood relationship to survive the fall of Tanith.

Mikal had died in the battle for Vervunhive.

Kolea gave her back the ragged old book.

'Gol?'

'Yeah?'

'Don't leave it too long. Don't leave it until it's too late.'

'I promise you I won't,' he said.

Seven

AT 08.00 IMPERIAL on the morning of the 222nd, the Ghosts assigned to Operation Larisel met in an office annexe off the training sub-hangar. They had exercised, showered and eaten a good breakfast brought in from the billet kitchens. There was a tension in the air, but it was a fine-tuned, taut feeling of readiness and an eagerness to get on and do.

The annexe had been cleared so as to accommodate a tactical desk, and folding chairs had been arranged in a circle around it.

'Take your seats,' Kersherin told them as they filed in.

When Captain Daur arrived, everyone was surprised to see him.

He walked in casually and took off his cap and jacket. 'Morning,' he said.

'Where's the colonel-commissar?' asked Mkoll.

'He's asked me to convey his apologies and take his place. Something came up.'

Daur walked over to the tac-desk and loaded a data-spool into the slot. The unit hummed and information scrolled across its glass screens. Daur typed in the password that would let him access the confidential files.

'What something?' Adare called out. Daur ignored him.

'Let's talk about Ouranberg,' he said, getting their attention. The Phantine troopers took their seats amongst the Ghosts.

Daur keyed a stud on the desk and a large hololithic image of the target city rose majestically into being above the optical emitters. A three-dimensional landscape, covering the table top.

'There it is,' he said.

They all craned forward.

'Stand up, if you want to. You need to get to know this place. Let's begin with basics. Two linked domes, Alpha and Beta, primary habitation. Built against and between them to the north is the main vapour mill complex. Here, you see? Adjoining that and Beta dome is Gamma, a smaller habitat sector. Minor habitat domes cluster around the north edges of the mill. The main aerodrome is here, in the cleavage between Gamma and Beta, if we want to think in anatomical terms.'

'Hey, let's not,' said Banda. Several men laughed.

Daur held up an apologetic hand. 'Fine. Here… you see? Here at the southern face, the main porta is–'

'What's a porta?' asked Larkin.

'Gateway, Larks.'

'Just so's I know,' Larkin said, making careful notes in his jotter.

'The main porta, anyway. A sixty metre square vacuum hatch called Ourangate. In front of it, extending out on an apron of rock for about a kilometre, give or take, is Pavia Fields, a kind of ornamental platform.'

What are those? Nessa signed.

'Standing stones. Monolithic war memorials,' said Daur, catching her gestures easily and answering at once. 'It's called the Avenue of the Polyandrons and it marks the formal approach to Ourangate. Linked to the Pavia Fields platform by a causeway is the Imperial Phantine Landing Station, the main dock point for drogues. Especially if they're carrying Imperial nobility. Extending on another causeway from the north-east of the city is the secondary vapour mill complex, built on a neighbouring peak. The mountain top Ouranberg is constructed on actually rises up through the city, hence this... Ouranpeak.'

Daur indicated the fang of rock that jutted out of the top of the city model, between the Beta and Gamma domes.

'What are those extensions to the west and north?' Mkvenner asked.

'Stacks,' Daur said. 'Linked by supported pipelines to the main mill. They use them to flare off waste gases.'

He looked round the room. 'Okay so far? Let's talk about drop zones. Any questions up to this point?'

'Yeah,' said Varl. 'What did you say Gaunt was doing again?'

'You've STARTED?' Gaunt said.

'Yes we have,' Commissar Del Mar said wearily. 'Time is precious, so we moved the sessions up by half an hour.'

'I wasn't notified.'

'Gaunt, I understood you weren't bringing a challenge to this hearing.'

'I changed my mind,' said Gaunt. He stepped up onto the platform and walked to the empty row of seats on the defence side.

Cuu, hunched, shackled and defeated, stood where Caffran had been the morning before.

'Approach the bench,' said Del Mar. Gaunt walked over to him and lent down on the table.

'I just about tolerated your showboating with Caffran yesterday, Gaunt,' whispered Del Mar. 'I can't believe you've got the brass neck to turn up again today. This is the devil you put in the frame for the killing. It's a done thing. You said yourself he was the one.'

'I may have been wrong. A moment, please.'

Before Del Mar could protest, Gaunt walked back down the stage and faced Cuu.

'Did you do it?' he said simply.

'No, sir!' There was animal fear in Cuu's ugly, piercing eyes. 'I looted gold, enemy gold, for that I'll put my hand up. But I didn't do no killing. Sure as sure.'

Gaunt hesitated. Then he walked back to Del Mar, took a pack off his shoulder, and emptied the contents onto the desk in front of the commissar.

Ghost daggers, nine of them, each one wrapped in plastene.

'What is this?' asked Del Mar.

'Warknives. Straight silver, Tanith issue. Some are notched, as you can see. Any one of them might be the murder weapon.'

'And why should I believe that?'

'Because these were recovered from a Blood Pact cell operating in the undercity. They had acquired several sets of Tanith fatigues and these knives. They were using defaced coinage to bribe the locals. The evidence I sent you – the blade shard, the coin under the bath – it all points to Cuu there. Unless you take into account the notion that not everyone dressed as a Ghost that night was a Ghost.'

'You're truly pissing me off now, Gaunt,' said Del Mar. 'I won't stand for this.'

'I don't care. All I care about is my duty. There are reasonable grounds for the dismissal of charges against Trooper Cuu. As reasonable as the grounds you threw Caffran's case out on.'

'I'm warning you–'

'Don't even try. You know I'm right.'

Del Mar sat back, shaking his head. 'What about the old man? The witness?'

'I showed him a picture of Cuu and he didn't recognise him either.'

'I see. So the Ghost who was seen, the one who undoubtedly slew Onti Flyte...'

'...was very likely a Blood Pact trooper masquerading as a Ghost, yes.'

Del Mar sighed.

'Reasonable doubt,' said Gaunt.

'Damn you, Gaunt.'

'Sir, can we square this away so that I can get on with my real duties?' Gaunt said, sarcastically stressing the word 'real'.

'He admits looting?'

'Yes, sir.'

'Then he'll be flogged. Case dismissed.'

GAUNT DIDN'T STAY to see the sentence carried out. As he came down the steps of the Chamber of Justice, he met Hark hurrying in. The man looked tired, his eyes still puffy with sleep, and he was trying to smooth down his hair with his fingers.

Hark stopped in his tracks when he saw Gaunt.

'Sir?'

'It's done. Cuu has been cleared of the murder.'

Hark fell into step with him as they descended into the yard.

'I... I wish you had kept me informed, sir.'

'Informed, Viktor?'

'That you'd changed your mind about Cuu's guilt.'

Gaunt glanced at him. 'It was an eleventh hour decision. I thought you'd be pleased. Between the pair of you, you and ayatani Zweil have been on at me for days about being even-handed towards the Verghastites. And you were right. A popular Ghost gets into trouble, and I move heaven and earth to get him out of the mess. A less-popular Verghastite gets in trouble, and I cut him adrift. I dread to think what it would have done to Verghastite morale if I'd left Cuu to face the court alone this morning.'

'I am pleased, sir. For inevitable reasons, you do seem to have favoured the Tanith until now. Even if you didn't think that's what you were doing.'

'Captain Daur brought me up sharp, I'm glad to say.' He stopped walking and turned to Hark. 'You still seem… put out, Viktor.'

'Like I said, I wish you'd told me you had decided to go to bat for Cuu. I could have helped.'

'I managed fine.'

'Of course. But I could have done some leg work, organised evidence. That's what I'm here for.'

Gaunt raised a hand and the staff driver assigned to him started up the waiting car and drove it across the yard to collect him.

'I suppose you could have talked to witnesses. You probably would have preferred to do that yourself, rather than let me do it.'

'Sir?'

'I went to visit Mr Absolom, Hark. He'd seen the killer, after all. I had to make sure he didn't recognise Cuu. Mr Absolom's a fine old fellow. A service veteran, isn't he? He'd do anything for the Imperial Guard. Especially if a persuasive commissar came to see him and convinced him it was his duty.'

Hark's eyes darkened. 'You told me to guarantee Caffran's acquittal.'

'And a key witness would do that, wouldn't it? Absolom didn't recognise Cuu's picture, of course. But you knew that. He wouldn't recognise any picture. Because he didn't see the killer at all, did he, Viktor?'

Hark looked away. 'I suppose you'll want my resignation from the regiment?' he said bitterly.

'No. But I want you to learn from this. I will not break Imperial law. Better that Caffran had gone to execution innocent than lie to get him off. Commissars are often thought of as devious, Viktor. That reputation is justified. They are political animals who use all the tricks of politics to achieve their goals. That is not my way. And I will never sanction it in any man in my command. You could make an exemplary officer, Hark. My oh-so naive idea of an exemplary officer, anyway. Don't stoop to those methods again, or I will drum you out of this company and the Commissariate. Do we have an understanding?'

Hark nodded. Gaunt got into his car and was driven away out through the gate.

Hark watched him go. 'Naive. You said it.'

GAUNT STEPPED UP onto an empty ammo crate that Beltayn had lugged in. He raised his voice, and the sound of it silenced the men gathered round in the main billet.

'Men of Tanith, men of Verghast. Ghosts. The word has just been given. Weather permitting, we go for Ouranberg at dawn on the 226th. Make ready for the Emperor's work. That is all.'

As he got off the box and put his cap back on, Gaunt thought about the information he hadn't been at liberty to announce. By the time the invasion began, the squads of Operation Larisel would have been active in Ouranberg for over twenty-four hours.

God-Emperor willing.

THE DROP
OURANBERG, PHANTINE,
224.771, M41

'Never, ever, ever fething again.'

– Trooper Larkin, 2nd Team marksman,
Tanith First

JUST AFTER MIDNIGHT, in the first hour of the 224th, Scald-storms rose cyclonically in the cloud oceans north of Cirenholm. Jarring, superheated belts of fire, dozens of kilometres long, crackled up into the higher reaches of the sky, and the borealis flickered and roiled in queasy, phantom coils.

Air visibility and sensor ranges were cut to less than five kilometres. Plumes of rising ash blotted out the stars. The poisonous heart of Phantine raged against the night.

The storms had been predicted by the Navy's long-range auspex, and the twitching senses of the taskforce astropaths. This was what the tacticians had been waiting for.

The drogues *Zephyr* and *Trenchant* had reached their holding position several hours before midnight. Hugging a dense reef of altocumulus cloud forty kilometres across, they kept station in a shallow gulf of sky called the Leaward Races, almost in the dead centre of the great air desert known as the Western Continental Reaches.

On the flight deck of the *Zephyr*, Admiral Ornoff ordered the launch.

Ornoff had used the drogues judiciously to pursue his policy of nightly raids. By releasing the bomber shoals from carriers that varied their positions, he ensured that the defences of Ouranberg never knew from which direction to expect the next raid. Enemy hunter squadrons searched for the drogues by day, hoping to surprise them before they could unleash their armadas, but the Western Continental Reaches were vast, and Ornoff used the mammatocumulus of the regular Scald-storms as cover.

The night raid of the 224th would approach Ouranberg from the south-east, covering a distance to the target of about three hundred and forty kilometres. They would use the prevailing jet streams of the Reaches to maximise speed, hugging the ultra-violet void where the troposphere became the stratosphere.

Including the fighter escort of Imperial Navy Lightnings and Thunderbolts, the raiding force numbered some six hundred aircraft. Thirty matt-grey Marauders of the Phantine Air Corps took the role of the pathfinders, pressing ahead clear of the main formation to light up the target with illumination-mines and incendiary payloads. Six minutes behind them came a mass wave of over three hundred heavy bombers. Most of these were lumbering, six-engined Magogs, painted an unreflective black. The Magog was a prop-driven, atmospheric type that had been in service for centuries, but the wave also included two dozen Behemoths, the awesome and ancient giants of Phantine Bomber Command.

Following the first wave came a second pack of Marauders, from either Imperial Navy or Urdeshi regimental squadrons. The green mottle-camo of the former distinguished them from the silver-belly/beige-top two-tone of the latter. All seventy of them were laden with fuel-air explosive payloads.

The third wave numbered almost two hundred craft. More Magogs, as well as twenty Urdeshi Marauder Destroyers and thirty Phantine Shrikes. These destroyers, and the elderly hook-winged, single-engined Shrike jets, were specialist dive bombers that would finish the raid by carrying out pinpoint low-level runs into a target zone that, by then, should have been grievously punished.

Flying as part of the second wave were four void-blue Phantine Marauders that carried no bombs at all. Larisel 1, 2, 3 and 4.

KERSHERIN AND THE other Skyborne specialists checked the Ghosts over one by one, covering every detail down to boot laces and pocket studs with what would have seemed like obsessive fuss had the tension not been so high.

Each member of the Larisel teams wore a modified version of their standard Tanith uniform. In place of regulation underwear, they had been issued silk-lined, rubberised body-gloves that acted both as insulation against the extreme cold and a seal against the corrosive atmosphere. Over that went the black Tanith tunic, breeches and webbing, and over that a zip-up leather jump-smock that came down to the hips and was laced with chain-mail. Light equipment that would normally have been carried in a kit bag or backpack was distributed into the uniform pockets of the tunic and the webbing pouches and the smock closed up tightly over the top. Gloves and boots were then pulled on, and gaiters buckled around the wrists and boot-tops to form a tight seal.

By then, the Ghosts were already sweating in the hot and abnormally heavy gear. They raised their arms as light belts-and-braces of outer webbing were fitted. These had pouches at the hips for additional kit items, and secure loops for lamp packs, flares, a rope-coil, a short-nose laspistol, a saw-edged cutting knife and the Tanith blade. Their camo-cloaks were tightly wound with a scrim-net around a pack of tube charges and grenades, and stuffed into a musette bag that was lashed horizontally from the front of the outer webbing across the groin. Medi-packs, bag-rations and power-cells for the lasrifles and pistols were loaded into the troopers' thigh pouches.

Not everyone was carrying a lasrifle. Apart from the four snipers with their long-las variants carried in covers with slings, Milo, Cocoer, Meryn and Varl had the U90 cannons. The solid ammunition took up a lot more space, so while the four of them carried spare cells in their thigh pouches for the

other team members' guns, every member of the squad was
strung with a bandolier of drum magazines. For the drop, the
four U90's had slim, twenty-five round clips fitted and
wrapped into place with adhesive tape. The higher capacity
drum-mags they all carried in their bandoliers were too bulky
to jump with. The cannons, like the lasrifles, had their muzzles plugged with wax stoppers to prevent them fouling on
impact.

Camo paint was applied to their faces, and micro-beads fitted into their ears and tested. Then they pulled on their
woollen hats and did up their smock collars ready for the helmets. Varl kissed the silver aquila that hung on a chain
around his neck before dropping it down into his tunic and
buckling up the neck of the over-jacket.

The helmets were black steel with integral visors. Inside,
they had a leather liner-cap that buckled in place around the
chin. A canvas frill around the bottom of the helmet tucked
inside the smock collar and sealed with a zip. A pressurised
air-bottle, which hooked to the chest webbing, would feed
oxygen into the helmet cavity during the jump.

Finally, the jump-packs were lifted onto their backs,
strapped on, and the power engaged for a final check. Main
weapons were cinched tight across their chests. Safeties were
double-checked. Kersherin offered up a brief but heartfelt
prayer for them all.

They could see little, and hear even less, except the crackle
of the vox. It was hard to walk under the weight, and they
shuffled around, smacking hands with each other awkwardly
for good luck.

Once the four Phantine Skyborne were suited – an operation that took a great deal less time – they were all escorted
by ground crew across the *Trenchant's* number five flight deck
to the four Marauders and man-handled inside.

'Feth!' Milo heard Adare moan. 'I've had enough already.'

The Marauders they were using for the drop had been
stripped for the job, with all bombs and weapons except the
nose cannons removed. They normally required a crew of six
including gunners, but for this raid only two flight crew, a
pilot and a navigator, would take them up. The nose guns
were slaved to the pilot's control, and the navigator would

coordinate the drop with the Skyborne officer aboard. The flight crew was already in position in the cockpit above the cabin, completing final checks and blessings.

The squad members eased their overweight bulks down onto the bare cabin floor.

THE LAUNCH WENT smoothly. Ornoff took that to be a good sign. One Magog turned back almost at once, reporting bombs hung, and another aborted after about fifteen minutes, voxing in that it had suffered a critical instrument failure. The first landed safely on the *Zephyr's* runway deck. The other, presumably blind, missed the drogues completely and flew on east into the burning clouds. It was never seen again.

A raid launch with only two aborts. That was the best they'd managed since they'd begun bombing Ouranberg. On the bridge of the *Zephyr*, Ornoff felt a confidence rising within him. He summoned the drogue's chief ecclesiarch and ordered an impromptu service of deliverance.

THE PASSAGE WAS noisier, colder and more turbulent than anything the Ghosts had experienced riding the drops in over Cirenholm. They were much higher and travelling much faster. Not long after the violent take-off, with cabin temperature and pressure dropping away and skins of ice forming on the metal surfaces inside the cabin, they all began to appreciate the sweltering layers of clothing they were wearing.

There was a surprising amount to see, given that the cabin had limited ports and they were trussed up in helmets and visors. What had been the payload officer's pict-plate had been switched on in each of the Marauders, filling the darkness of each cabin with a chilly green glow, and displaying a detailed modar picture of the raid formation.

In Larisel 1, Varl eased forward, struggling with the weight on his body. He keyed his vox and gestured to the Phantine, Unterrio, who was tuning the pict-plate.

'That's the bomber waves?'

'Yeah,' answered Unterrio. Even using the vox, he had to raise his voice above the engine noise and the constant thunder of the wind. 'We're here in this belt.'

Varl looked closer, trying to focus through the visor's eye-plates. He realised each foggy band of modar returns was actually made up of hundreds of individual dots, each one accompanied by a graphic number.

'Every craft has an identifying transponder,' Unterrio explained. 'It helps us pick up bandits quicker. Time was, enemy cloud-hunters would slip in amongst the bomber shoals and bide their time, moving within the formation, choosing their kills. Now, if you don't display a code, you're fair game.'

'Gotcha,' said Varl. It made sense. He looked round at the cabin and saw that the other members of 1st Team – Banda, Vadim and Bonin – were listening in and looking with interest.

'Which ones are the other jump-craft?' voxed Vadim.

Unterrio raised a gloved paw and pointed to spots on the plate. 'That's Larisel 4, Sergeant Mkoll. That's Sergeant Adare's ship, Larisel 3. Here, just hidden by the graphic of that Navy Marauder… that's Larisel 2. Corporal Meryn's bird.'

It took a moment for Varl to make sense of the jumping, flickering display. It seemed that the four jump-craft were spread out thinly amongst the bomber wave.

The Marauder lurched, and the engines seemed to swoon and stutter.

'What was that?' Varl voxed, his voice sounding dry and hard over the link.

'Turbulence,' replied Unterrio.

IN LARISEL 3, Specialist Cardinale was conducting a similar explanation of the plate graphics for the benefit of Milo and Doyl. Nessa and Adare, perhaps resigned to being mercilessly insulated against the world, were playing blade, parchment, rock. Their giggles snickered over the vox-link as their heavy-gloved hands beat out the repetitive gestures of the game.

LARKIN WISHED THERE was a window to see out of, but there wasn't. He sat on the bare floor of Larisel 2's cabin and gazed at the others. Kersherin was studying the aiming-plate display. Kuren and Meryn were chatting. Mkvenner looked like he was asleep.

'How long?' Larkin asked Kersherin.

'Forty minutes,' replied the Phantine.

SCOUT SERGEANT MKOLL had not been designed to fly. But still he had not challenged Gaunt's decision to pick him for this operation. Mkoll didn't do things like that. And he knew that when the time came and he got onto the target, he would be the right man for the job.

But the flying. That was a fething nightmare. He'd never been higher than the top branches of a nalwood until Gaunt had taken the Tanith off-world. Space travel – which, like Colm Corbec, he reviled – at least didn't seem like flying.

This was much worse. The vibration, the elemental wrath beating at the craft. It was as if the air really didn't want you to forget you were eight kilometres up thanks only to its charitable physics.

And the waiting. That was the mind killer. Waiting for action. Waiting for the moment. It allowed fears to grow. It gave a man time to worry about the struggle ahead. Combat was hell, but at least it was against real enemies, people you could actually shoot. The enemies here were time and fear, imagination and turbulence... and cold.

Mkoll felt sick. He hated the waiting almost as much as he hated the weight they were forced to wear. He felt anchored to the metal deck. When the time came and the jump-call was given, he wasn't entirely convinced he would be able to get up.

He looked round Larisel 4's cabin. Babbist, the Phantine trooper, was fighting with the display plate. It kept rolling and flickering on him, showing nothing but green fuzz. Bad tubes, Mkoll decided. If Babbist didn't get it working, they would be going in blind.

Cocoer and Nour were sitting back as if sleep. Nour probably was. He switched off that way sometimes in the lag before combat. Twitchy and already running on adrenalin, Rilke the team sniper was stripping and reassembling the firing mechanism of his long-las, getting used to manipulating it with his heavy gloves. Mkoll wanted to grab him and tell him to stop, but he knew it was simply a coping strategy.

He keyed his vox and leant forward. 'Okay, Rilke?'

'Sure, yeah,' crackled the sniper, his hands repeating the process over and over again. 'Actually, I'm fething scared, sarge. I keep wanting to throw up, but I know I can't in this visor.'

'That would be horrible,' Mkoll agreed.

He heard Rilke laugh.

'I only do this to keep my mind off the nausea,' Rilke added, holding up the trigger plate briefly before speedily fitting it again. 'Feth, I feel sick. My stomach is doing flips. How do you cope, sarge?'

'I watch you,' said Mkoll.

THIRTY MINUTES FROM the target, an unidentified contact wavered on to the screens and ten of the fighter escorts broke south to hunt it out.

'Probably just a heavy scald-flare,' Unterrio told the Ghosts. 'We're fine.'

The Marauder lurched badly again, the fifth or sixth time it had done so during the flight. The others didn't seem to be noticing the jolts any more, but Bonin was convinced it wasn't turbulence. The acute wariness that Mkoll had trained into Bonin and all the Tanith scouts was ringing all sorts of alarms in his head.

He got up, slowly, heavily, and thumped forward to the short rungs that led up into the cockpit. Unterrio was hunched over the pict-plate with Varl and he looked up as Bonin shuffled past, unhappy that he was moving around but not about to stop him.

Bonin peered up at the flight crew. They seemed to be fighting with the controls.

'Problem?' he voxed.

'No,' said the pilot. 'None at all.'

Bonin thought he recognised the voice. 'You sure?'

'Yes!' the pilot snapped and looked back at him. There wasn't much to see of the face through the visor of the pressure mask, but Bonin recognised the eyes of Commander Jagdea.

'Hello,' he said.

'Scout Trooper Bonin,' she replied.

'I thought you were hurt?'

'The break was treated and fused and I'm all strapped up in a pressure sling. You can fly a Marauder one-handed anyway. Not like a Lightning.'

'Whatever. Just so long as you're okay. You volunteer for this?'

'They asked for volunteers, yes.'

'You must like us,' Bonin ventured. She didn't answer. 'The engines shouldn't be doing that, should they?'

She looked back at him again. 'No, all right? No, they shouldn't. We've got a misfire problem. But I'm not going to let it affect the mission. I'll get you there.'

'I'm sure you will,' said Bonin.

THE SHOAL'S LUCK lasted until they were almost in sight of Ouranberg. About ten kilometres out, the scald-storm suddenly collapsed and faded, sinking its fires into the lower stratum and leaving the air bare and empty.

The Ouranberg defences picked them up almost immediately. The fighters were on them about two minutes later.

The cloud-hunters went through the shoal on afterburner, crossing north/south. Two stricken Magogs, on fire, ploughed their way down on steep dives into the Scald. A Navy Marauder ceased to be in a blizzard of shrapnel and ignited gas.

As the enemy craft banked round for another pass, they met the Imperial fighter escort. Through the cabin's slit window, Milo could see streams of tracers and bright flashes flickering against the clouds.

A brilliant light suddenly shone back through the cockpit, shafting down into the cabin.

'What was that?' asked Adare.

'The pathfinders just lit up the target,' the pilot announced. 'Five minutes. Go to stand by.'

The Ghosts all struggled to their feet. Cardinale moved between them, tugging out the air hoses that had linked them to the ship's supply and cutting in their own air-bottles.

'You're running on internal now,' he voxed. They nodded their understanding.

Then he opened each jump pack back-plate in turn and threw the start-up rocker switches. Lift power, a blessed relief from the weight, kicked in. The outside roar was so great they couldn't even hear the turbines.

Cardinale unplugged and refitted his own air hose and then turned his back to Nessa so she could throw his pack switches. Doyl moved to the back hatch and put his hand on the release lever. They all watched the screen.

THE FIRST MAIN wave came over the vast bulk of Ouranberg, which was already lit up with flares and combustion bombs. Dragging slowly through the air, the Magogs began to spill bombs from their bellies. Air-cracking flashes slammed out from each hiss of fire.

Above and around the bomber shoal, the fighters danced with the enemy in a furious dog-fight guided mostly by modar. Already, the ground batteries had opened up in full force. Floral patterns of flak decorated the air. Rockets lashed upwards. Hydra batteries zippered the air with tracer rounds.

One of the Magogs blew apart, a single engine nacelle still spinning its prop as it dived downwards, on fire like a comet. Another was caught in the spotlights and hammered with flak until it fell apart. A Behemoth, hit in the wing-base by a rocket, dipped slowly towards the city, on fire, and struck the Beta dome edge, causing an explosion that sent flame out more than five hundred metres.

Another was hit as it was opening its bomb-bay. The explosion took out the craft either side of it.

ON A CUE FROM Babbist, Nour wrenched open the side hatch of Larisel 4. Typhoon-force wind galed in, rocking them all. Nour flinched back, seeing the Navy Marauder flying next to them in the formation suddenly ignite and veer towards them.

The stricken craft, bleeding flames from behind the cockpit, missed them by only a few metres and dropped away, its fire trail marking out a spiral as it accelerated to its doom.

All that Nour had seen in the split second before the Marauder had pitched away was the pilot and the fore-gunner, hammering at the perspex of their screens, trying to break out as fire sucked into the crew spaces they occupied.

'Ready for drop,' Mkoll cried.

Nour shook himself. He couldn't get the image of the burning, hammering pilot out of his head.

'Ready.'

Babbist ushered Cocoer and Rilke up to the hatch.

THE DZ'S FOR Larisel had been selected carefully. Larisel 1, Varl's mob, was to drop onto the main vapour mills, with Larisel 4, under Mkoll's command, dropping on the mill worker hab-domes to the north-west. Adare's unit, Larisel 3, was going after the secondary vapour mills, and Larisel 2, under Meryn's control, was jumping on Beta dome.

Flak whickered up at them from the city. The first wave of Magogs had hammered Beta dome. Patterns of throbbing fire pulsed below: pin-points or clusters. White-hot fires raged up into the night and secondary explosions rippled through the domes.

'Go! said Cardinale.

Milo leapt from the Marauder. He was instantly struck by a fierce sideways force, a hammerblow of slipstream that turned him over and over. He tumbled, stunned, and fell, gunning his pack. Nothing seemed to happen.

'Relax, relax into it…' Cardinale said over the link, barely audible over the raging wind.

Ouranberg was coming up very fast and very hard. Milo yanked at his thruster control. Training had been all well and good, but nothing could have prepared him for leaping into space in this kind of cross-wind. He was being swept clear of the DZ.

Milo saw Nessa and Adare dropping past him, spreadea-gled, trimming their thrusters. He slid in behind them, the wind tearing at his mask.

The vast, dull-grey dome of the secondary mill rose up in front of him, a small city in its own right.

He coasted in.

LARKIN PASSED OUT as he left the hatch. It was partly fear, and partly the sledgehammer thump of the wind. He came round, felt his entire body vibrating and saw nothing but oily blackness.

'Larkin! Larkin!'

He realised he was falling on his back. He fought to right himself, over-cueing the jump-pack controls so he shot up like a cork. The wind was a thundering, buffeting howl in his ears. There was no sign of Mkvenner, Kersherin, Kuren or Meryn. The wounded, battered shape of the Beta dome was twinkling with hundreds of fires. He tried to make sense of it, tried to match what he saw to the carefully memorised picture of the cityscape and the DZ in his head.

Then he saw Meryn, passing him twenty metres to his left, looking stiff and awkward but at least in control. Squeezing his handgrip, he propelled himself after the sergeant.

LARISEL I WAS two minutes short of its DZ, juddering through flak, when the engines finally failed. Jagdea yelled at them to go, fighting to keep the nose of the leaden craft up as long as she could. They bailed: Vadim, Unterrio, Banda, Varl. Bonin hesitated, and clambered back to the cockpit ladder. The Marauder was beginning to vibrate wildly.

'Come on!' he cried. 'Move it! You've both got chutes! Come on!'

Jagdea pushed him back. There was a bright burst right outside the cockpit dome and flak sent ribbons of metal and glass spearing in at them. Bonin didn't have to look to see that the co-pilot was dead.

'Jagdea!' he bellowed, grabbing at her.

Stalling out, the Marauder rolled over onto its back and entered a terminal swan dive. Bonin was upside down, pressed into the roof, the harness of his jump-pack half-choking him.

Fighting the mounting G-force, Jagdea pulled a lever that fired the explosive bolts in the cockpit canopy's frame, and the damaged canopy ripped away entirely. She unbuckled her restraint harness and pulled at Bonin hard, yanking him up into the cockpit. The force of the wind did the rest, sucking them both up and out of the diving craft and scattering them away into the sky.

'ARE WE ON the target?' asked Mkoll.

'I don't know!' said Babbist.

'Are we on the target?'

'The damn aimer is off-line!' Babbist yelled, struggling to get the flickering, rolling image to freeze.

'We're going to overshoot if we're not careful,' said Nour.

'We go, we go now!' Mkoll decided.

'But–' Babbist began.

'We go *now!*'

Mkoll moved to the hatch. 'Come on! Line up and out!'

There was an odd bump, like something had flicked at his inner ear. Mkoll swayed and looked round. There was a smouldering hole in the deck of the cabin where a large calibre tracer round had punched through, killing Babbist on its way up to the roof. Nour had been knocked down, and Rilke and Cocoer were trying to lift him.

'Come on!' Mkoll cried. A shower of sparks blinded him. More tracer was riddling the cabin, ripping through the hull-skin. He heard Rilke scream and Nour yelling, 'It's going! It's going! It's going!'

VARL LANDED A damn sight harder than he might have wished, and lay for a moment on a section of reinforced roof plating, winded and bruised. Unterrio appeared over him, grabbing him by the hands and pulling him up.

'Feth,' said Varl.

They were on a wide manufactory roof structure adjoining the main vapour mill, high up above Ouranberg with only the mill chimneys and the crag of Ouranpeak rising above them. The sky was a bright fury, but the raid now seemed far away.

Banda had made it down on a roof section adjacent to theirs, and as they went down to join her, using the lift of the packs to bounce themselves along as if on springs, they heard Vadim calling urgently over the vox.

Unterrio spotted the young Verghastite up on the inspection walkway of a chimney flue. He was pointing up at the sky.

'There! There!' he said.

Varl looked. He wasn't sure what he was looking for, then he saw what Vadim's sharp eyes had already detected. A Marauder, about a kilometre and half away, turning south in a loop. It had to be Mkoll's bird, Larisel 4, making its pass on the mining habs.

Then he realised it was on fire.

'Feth, they had better–' he began. The Marauder exploded in mid-air. A big sphere of white light expanded in the sky and then was gone.

Mkoll, Rilke, Nour, Cocoer… just gone. Vital men, friends…

A whole team finished before they'd even begun.

LARISEL AND THUNDERHEAD
THE ASSAULT ON OURANBERG, PHANTINE, 224 to 226.771, M41

'Right through the specialist training, we'd all had this feeling of confidence, like the beloved Emperor was with us in all things. Then we were on the ground, and Mkoll and the others were dead, and we started to realise we didn't stand a chance.'

– Brin Milo, 3rd Team trooper, Tanith First

One

THEY HAD TO get off the roof-space fast. Thick streams of black smoke from petrochemical fires and incendiary bursts were washing back across them and across the roof structures of the Ouranberg's secondary vapour mill.

The smoke was pouring from the main city, carried by the powerful high-altitude winds and, if the Emperor was with them, it would have concealed them in the last stages of their jump.

But from the moment he was down, Doyl had been surveying the area. There were six defence towers in the immediate vicinity, all of them with decent views of the roof where they had landed, smoke or no smoke.

The five members of Larisel 3 hurried into the cover of a ventilator stack and got down. No firing had come their way; indeed, two of the towers were still spitting tracer streams at Imperial aircraft peeling off the target.

'Did they see us?' Milo voxed.

'We're alive, aren't we?' replied Sergeant Adare. 'I think their attention is on the sky above.'

'Check in,' voxed Specialist Cardinale. 'Any injuries? Any equipment losses?' There were none apparently. Adare made a special point of signing to Nessa to make sure she was okay.

'Did you hear what they said?' muttered Doyl. 'Sergeant Varl, on the vox, as we were coming in?'

Milo had. A brief, incomplete, dreadful message-burst. Mkoll's craft had gone up short of its drop point.

'I can't believe it–' he murmured.

'Me neither,' said Adare. 'God-Emperor rest their souls. But there's nothing we can do about it. Except go on with this and get some fething pay-back.'

Adare raised his gloved hand and exchanged palm-slaps with Doyl, Milo and Nessa. Cardinale hesitated and then smacked his own hand against Adare's proffered gauntlet. Milo knew Adare was trying to make sure the Phantine felt like part of the team.

In truth, Milo had returned Adare's palm-slap with little conviction himself. The loss of Mkoll was a profound shock. The scout sergeant had always seemed invulnerable, one of those Ghosts who would never fall. Milo even felt a little envious of Nessa. She couldn't read their lips because of the visors and no one had signed her the news. He'd been worried about how she might cope with the mission given her disability, but now it seemed she was lucky to be spared the bad news. At least for a while.

Doyl led them down the length of the ventilator stack and then across a narrow open space to the cover of some galvanised pipework. They moved sluggishly and heavily, even though the grav-units of their jump-packs were still on to ease the burden.

Cardinale helped Doyl out of his jump pack and the scout hurried on alone, looking for an entry point while the others got rid of their packs. Adare and Cardinale stowed the heavy units in a stack under the pipework, lashed them in place with rope and concealed them with a scrim net. Milo doubted there would be many foot patrols up here in the toxic atmosphere outside the dome, but the last thing they wanted was for the enemy to find traces of a troop landing.

They were still weighed down with kit, helmets and the armoured smocks, but now they felt a thousand times lighter. Nessa had taken her long-las out of its cover and assembled it, though with her visor in place, there was no point aligning the scope. Milo peeled the adhesive tape off his U90's twenty-five round clip and replaced it with a drum magazine marked with a red cross – the special armour-piercing load. Adare collected in and pocketed the plastic muzzle stoppers. Then he gently tried his vox-link. They'd picked up Varl's strangled message whilst still in the air. Now they were down, the hard structures of Ouranberg were blocking anything but short-range transmission. As Daur had predicted in his last briefing, there was going to be no contact between teams once the mission was underway. A full-gain vox-caster would have weighed one of them down unnecessarily. Besides, it wasn't impossible that the enemy was scanning for vox-calls on the known Imperial wavelengths.

Milo hunched down so that he had a good firing position, covering the space all the way from the pipework to what looked like a row of short exhaust flues on the edge of the roof section. Despite the bitter cold, he was hot, and he could feel cold sweat running down his spine. It was getting harder to breath. They were probably reaching the limit of their air-bottles.

Doyl reappeared. He had unshipped his camo-cloak and shrouded himself with it.

'Got a possible entry point. Thirty metres that way. Looks like a maintenance hatch and it's locked, but we should be able to force it.'

They ran forward, low, in single file, after his lead. The hatch was thick with rust and lay in the side of a raised hump in the roof, under the lea of an exposed roof spar. Milo and Cardinale stood look-out to either side with weapons ready as Adare and Doyl examined the hatch.

'I don't think it's pressurised,' said Adare.

'Me neither. We get through this and maybe down inside to a sealed door.'

'Cut it,' Adare said.

Doyl took out a compact cutting torch, said the prayer of ignition, lit its small energy blade and sliced into the lock. There were a few sparks and a slight glow, but Adare held his camo-cloak out to screen the work.

Once the teeth of the lock were cut, Doyl used his knife to force the corroded hatch out of its frame.

Adare led the way in, a lamp pack locked to his lasrifle's bayonet lug. The chamber appeared to be a circulation space around the head of an elevator assembly. Heavy machinery, caked in grease, jutted up out of the floor. Even with his helmet on, Milo could hear the wind moaning through rust holes in the metal roof-cover.

Doyl located a floor hatch in the far corner and they struggled down a short ladder into dark attic spaces that filled the cavity between the mill's outer roof and inner pressurised hull. It was now getting very hard to breathe.

The floor beneath them was a skin of clean metal ribbed with tension members. Unwilling to find out if the inner hull skin was load-bearing, they edged along the ribbing. After about fifty metres, they came across a break in the inner roof where rockcrete support piles of staggering proportions rose through to buttress the main roof.

One had metal rungs fused into the side, and they descended again, carefully, hand over hand, weapons slung on their backs.

Twenty metres down, the way was blocked. A huge moulded collar of industrial plastene sheathed the descending piles and sealed them against the downward sloping rim of roof-skin. Adare believed they would have to go back, but Milo spotted an almost invisible inspection plate in the metal skin. With Adare supporting his weight, Doyl leaned out from the rungs and pressed against the plate until it fell into the cavity behind. Doyl swung over and clambered through. A moment later, he voxed them to follow.

They were in a crawl space under the inner skin, and there was barely room to stand. Doyl replaced the plate, which had rubberised edging and formed a seal by being held in place by the internal pressure. Milo could feel the rush of air going out past him until Doyl got the plate back in position.

Gratefully, they unplugged their air-tubes and slid their visors up. The air was thin and cold and had a rough taste in it that stung their throats. But they were now inside the pressurised section of the mill.

'Did we trip an alarm?' Cardinale asked.

'I don't think so,' replied Doyl, checking the frame of the plate for signs of leads or breakers. 'The atmosphere processors might have lost a tiny amount of pressure while the plate was open, but I doubt it was enough for them to have noticed.'

'In case they did, and they're able to pinpoint the source, let's get moving anyway,' said Adare.

They hunched their way down the crawl space. It opened out dramatically, stretching out further than the eye could see, but didn't get any deeper. Doyl scouted around, and found a hatch in the floor some forty metres off. It was heavy-duty, Imperial design, and electronically locked.

The scout worked fast. He taped one of the six miniature circuit-breakers he carried in his tool-roll to the hatch frame, and secured its leads to either side of the lock. He waited until the little green rune on its casing lit up, indicating that the hatch's alarm circuit was now looping via the breaker, and then cut through the lock-tongue with his cutting torch. Though there was no immediate scream of klaxons, it was impossible to tell if the alarm had been bypassed, so they dropped through the hatch quickly and pulled it shut behind them.

The hatch had let them down into a maintenance corridor, old and dingy, and poorly lit. Centuries of condensation had rusted the walls, rotted the mat-boards and encouraged thick, lurid mould growths along the ceiling. The corridor ran north/south.

'South,' said Adare confidently, and they moved off. South, the direction of the main city structure of Ouranberg.

And the creature they had come to kill.

It had taken Bonin a full ninety seconds to gain control of his jump-pack, and that had felt like an eternity: tumbling, wheeling, spinning, with no sense of up or down. Somehow, Jagdea had shown the good sense to cling on to him, despite the violence of their drop.

By the time he had squeezed enough lift out of the grav-units to pull them both up, and begun to compensate for their drift with the turbines, they were well out to the east of Ouranberg.

'Hold on!' he voxed.

'My chute's intact! I'll drop!' she replied.

'Where to?' he asked. Below their dangling feet there was nothing but the frothing, fire-lit expanse of the Scald.

'It doesn't matter–'

'No! Just hold on!' His voice over the link sounded tinny and dull. The night winds beat and tugged at them.

Cautiously, Bonin nudged them towards the gloomy city, using little squirts of turbine power to buoy them along like a leaf on a racing stream. The crosswinds seemed to be with them, but every now and then, the gale suddenly gusted against them, and the pair were turned or blown back.

'Your grip still good?'

'Yes.' She had her hands and forearms locked up under his chest harness. He realised he had his right arm protectively clutched around her left shoulder, gripping the top of her inflator-chute's shoulder webbing.

'We're going to need more lift,' he said, depressing the red stud on the handgrip. The grey, eastern slopes of what had to be Gamma dome were looming in front of them like a mountain range.

They almost didn't clear Gamma dome. Bonin had to fight to stop the crosswinds smashing them into the outer hull, and the jump pack seemed to be struggling to find enough lift. Vortices of wind created by the dome's angular surface eddied them like chaff. And though, by the altimeter, they were climbing fast, the dome seemed to go on forever.

Gamma dome seemed to have been virtually untouched by the raid, though great flickers of orange and white lit the sky and the clouds behind it where Beta dome was ablaze.

As they hugged the curve of the dome up towards the sum-mit, a different level of wind patterns took over and suddenly started to carry them up with increasing speed. The dome-hull flicked by underneath them, and Bonin had to pull hard to the left to avoid collision with a protruding mast.

Then they were over, passing the massive icy crag of Ouranpeak, and dropping towards the main vapour mill.

'Varl! Banda! Vadim! Respond!' Bonin voxed. Foolishly, he had imagined his biggest problem was going to be getting anywhere near the mill. Now, seeing the size of it, he realised that finding his team mates was going to be a much taller order.

He repeated his calls as often as he dared. They soared down past a scaffolding tower structure that suddenly lit up and roared with heavy anti-air fire.

They weren't the target. The tower was plugging away at a Shrike dive-bomber that had misjudged its run. But Bonin had been concentrating so hard on steering and guiding, he hadn't even thought about the defence points and towers Ouranberg bristled with.

It was a sudden, sobering thought. Perhaps it was that they presented such a tiny target, perhaps luck was with them, but it now seemed like a miracle that they hadn't been spotted, tracked and fired on by any of the gun emplacements on Gamma dome.

Luck, Bonin decided. He couldn't see it because of the high, covering cirrocumulus, but he was sure his lucky star was still up there somewhere.

However, it wouldn't be for long.

'Brace yourself, Jagdea,' he said

'What? Oh sh–'

They dipped onto a lattice-truss roof in the shadow of mill head, but the angle was bad, the deceleration a little premature, and the roof a good deal steeper than Bonin had judged.

They bounced once, denting the alloy siding hard, and rolled, flying apart. Jagdea bounced again, twice, cried out in pain as the impacts jarred her recently-knitted break, and slithered to the edge of the guttering.

Bonin tried to gun the turbine, but the first impact had buckled the control arm and he couldn't find it. He crashed over the gutter, slammed into the side of a storage tank, and blacked out.

'Nice landing,' he heard Jagdea say as he came round.

She was hunched over him, tugging loose the buckles of his harness.

'Anything broken?'

'I don't think so.'

He sat up. He had landed on a strip of roof between the tank and the raised section where they had first tried to set down. The strip was a tarnished sluice of metal matted with wet filth where the upper roof structures drained water away. Looking round he saw that if he had continued to roll or slide, he would have gone clean off a fifty metre drop into a derrick assembly.

Together, they scrambled up the strip and onto a slab roof behind the tanks. Bonin prepped his lasrifle and Jagdea took out a service issue Navy pistol. He tried the vox again, but there was still no signal from his team.

They hurried west, crossing a walkway over a storage vat full of oily water with a surface sheen like rainbows. Nearby, a cluster of bare metal flues breathed burning gases into the sky.

The vox crackled. Bonin thought it might be Varl and the others, and retuned to get a clearer signal. What he heard then was guttural and nothing like Low Gothic.

He pulled Jagdea into cover just as three Blood Pact troopers in full hostile environment armour appeared on their tail, running up to the far end of the walkway over the vat. Their bobbing crimson bowl-helms reflected brightly in the dark fluid.

One had already seen them, and squeezed off a burst from his lascarbine. The shots thumped into the ducting they were crouched behind.

Bonin took aim. He fired a snap shot that winged the first Blood Pact trooper and checked the advance of the others. They all started shooting, making the ducting ring with the rapid hits.

The trooper he had winged tried to sprint across the walkway as the others covered him. Bonin put a las-round through his shoulder and then another into his iron-masked face. The trooper fell off the walkway loose-limbed and splashed into the vat, throwing up a heavy surge in the viscous liquid.

Bonin grabbed the pilot by the hand and they ran back down the length of the roof towards a row of large heat-exchangers that sprouted from the galvanised panels like dove-cotes. Las-bolts licked through the air around them.

As soon as they were down behind one of the exchangers, Bonin fired again. Two more Blood Pact had appeared on an adjacent roof, firing down from a chain-fenced walkbridge. It wouldn't take long for the four Chaos soldiers to coordinate a crossfire.

Shots spanked into the metal housing of the exchanger. Bonin fired low and hit one of the troopers on the walkbridge in the chest. The man collapsed and hung where his webbing had caught on the chain rail.

Another flurry of rounds slammed into the exchanger, and the entire top casing, a dome of thin metal, was wrenched off. Jagdea fired her pistol, but her aim wasn't great.

A shot ripped past near to Bonin's shoulder. The second man on the walkbridge had moved up, and was close to having the drop on them. There was nowhere to run without risking the steady firing of the advancing pair on their level.

The Blood Pact trooper on the bridge suddenly lurched forward so hard his body snapped the chain rail and he tumbled into the void.

'What the feth…?' Bonin began.

The two on the roof glanced around for a second, puzzled, and in that time a single, fierce las-shot exploded the head of the nearest.

Bonin snatched up his las and fired a burst on auto at the remaining foe. The Blood Pact trooper ducked down again behind a stanchion and didn't reappear.

'Hold your fire, Bonin,' a voice said over the link.

Varl appeared from behind the stanchion, sheathing his warknife.

'We're clear. Banda?'

'Nothing from up here, sarge.'

'Vadim?'

'Clear.'

'Unterrio?'

'Clear also. No movement.'

Varl hurried across to Bonin and Jagdea.

'Gotta move. Come on. Thought we'd lost you.'

They ran after him, up a fire-stair onto an upper roof over-looking the walkbridge.

'How didn't you?' Bonin asked.

'We heard your calls, and followed the signal. The bastards have got men up on the roof. Not because of us, I don't think. They brought down a lot of planes in the raid, and they're checking for ditched air-crew.'

'You sure about that?'

'No,' said Varl.

Banda rose from cover on the upper roof as they clambered up. Bonin was sure her long-las had taken out two of the enemy. 'Nice shooting,' he said.

'S'what they give the shiny medals for,' she returned. She nodded at Jagdea. 'I see you brought a friend,' she remarked ironically.

'Jagdea got us here alive, Banda. Least I could do was return the favour.'

'Gak! Down boy! I was only saying.'

Vadim and Unterrio came up a side-ladder and joined them.

'Good,' said Varl. 'Maybe now we're all finally here, we can get on. Roofscape's crawling with bad guys. I suggest we get inside.'

'You found a way in?' asked Bonin.

Varl looked at him, his eyes staring sarcastically through his visor. 'No we haven't – a) because we were looking for your sorry arse, I don't recall why, and b) because isn't that your job, Mister Scout?'

'Point,' admitted Bonin.

'Can we do it soon?' said Banda. 'This air-bottle's choking me up.'

'Okay, follow Bonin's lead, fireteam cover!' Varl ordered.

Jagdea caught Varl by the sleeve. 'Sergeant. I know I'm… not meant to be here. I think it's best if I stay put and give myself up.'

'No!' said Bonin.

'Like Boney said, commander: no,' Varl agreed.

'I appreciate the loyalty, but I'm not infantry trained, and certainly not covert-skilled like you. I'm dead weight. You should ditch me now. I understood the importance of this mission when I volunteered. I don't want to compromise it.'

'You're coming with us. End of debate,' Varl said.

'I'll take my chances, sergeant–'

'No!' said Varl.

'Commander Jagdea has a point, sergeant,' said Unterrio. 'We will be quicker and safer without her. This operation is too vital to risk. And like me, the commander is a Phantine. We care about the liberation of this world more than we care about our own lives.'

'Listen to Unterrio, sergeant,' said Jagdea. 'You've just killed a search party up here. Leave me for the Blood Pact to find, and I'll tell them it was me. Just a downed pilot. All they're expecting. It'll cover your presence.'

Varl tightened the strap on his U90 thoughtfully. 'I said no, I meant no. For one thing, they'd know you didn't do it unless we leave you with a long-las and a warknife, which I'm not prepared to do, because it would make them ask even more questions. For another... I'm not taking you out of kindness. Have you any idea how savage their interrogations would be? You wouldn't last. None of us would. Your "downed pilot" story would collapse so fething quickly you'd be selling us and your planet and your family. No, commander. No. You're coming. For our sake, not yours.'

FOR LARISEL 2, entry was easy. Huge sections of Beta dome were left punctured and shattered by the raid, and significant parts of it were still on fire. Gathering near the mast array at the dome's apex, the five-member team crossed onto the western side, and roped down to a collapsed roof section that was still issuing flame and smoke.

With Larkin covering them, Mkvenner and Meryn clambered down into the gash and secured the interior space. It was a habitat chamber, totally scorched through. Mkvenner picked his way across toasted carpet and found a door melted into its frame by the heat of the detonation that had blown out the room.

Sergeant Meryn kicked his way through smouldering plyboard and opened a side room that had also been gutted by the blast. A bomb had splintered straight through the floor here and gone off in the level beneath. There was a jagged hole in the flooring next to the atomised remains of a bed or a couch.

'Move down and form up,' Meryn voxed.

Kersherin, Larkin and Kuren dropped down through the roof, and Mkvenner led them through to Meryn. They looked down through the floor hole. Distant sirens were wailing, set off by the multiple breaches to the dome's pressurised shell.

'Nothing for the next two floors,' Mkvenner commented. The bomb had indeed demolished everything beneath them for two floors, partly through its impact and partly through its blast. Larkin glanced up and saw a standard dining fork impaled through a wall beam. The blast had turned even everyday objects into lethal shrapnel.

'Let's rope it,' Meryn decided. Mkvenner secured one end of his line-loop and lowered himself through the smouldering hole in the floor.

They swung down one level. Larkin tried to look away from the two blackened corpses that the detonation had crushed into the wall. The surviving shreds of the floor supported half a bureau, a litter of debris, the scattered pages of a book, and a miraculously unbroken vase.

Another level down and there was a floor again. The surface had been stripped off by extreme heat, and they balanced on the joists. One half of the room, a bed chamber, was eerily untouched. There was a tethwood chair, a shelf with drinking glasses and ornaments, and a good quality carpet that ended suddenly in a singed line where the floor had burned out. Discarded clothes hung over the chair. The only sign of damage in that half of the room was a slight blistering of the paint on the walls.

Mkvenner crossed to the door and opened it a slit. There was a corridor outside, plunged into emergency lighting.

'Let's go!' he voxed, and they followed him out into the hall in a fireteam spread.

Larkin was shaking. It was partly the trauma of the drop, partly combat tension, but mostly the shock of the news that Mkoll hadn't made it. He felt one of his migraine headaches pumping horror into his skull. He'd had the foresight to bring his tablets. Daur, Gaunt and Meryn had all insisted.

But with his visor down and working off his air-bottle, he couldn't take one.

They'd got about ten metres down the hallway when a three man emergency crew appeared, dressed in flame retardant white overalls and rebreathers. They panicked at the sight of the troopers and turned to flee.

'Oh, feth. Take them.' Meryn's order was terse but necessary.

Kuren and Kersherin opened fire and cut down the trio. It didn't feel right, Kuren thought. It didn't feel right at all, but they had to preserve their secrecy. Another emergency worker appeared and started running towards the elevator at the end of the hall. He had abandoned a blast victim who lolled on a stretcher in the open doorway of a room.

Mkvenner fired and the worker slammed over against the wall, slid down, and lay for a moment drumming his feet against the deck before he died.

'Feth,' said Mkvenner with distaste.

'We have to blow this hall,' Meryn said. 'They find shot bodies, they'll know we're here as good as if we left these poor fethers to talk. Blow it, and it'll look like a delayed fuse bomb going off.'

Mkvenner nodded and pulled out a couple of tube charges from his musette. Larkin watched, still shaking. This ruthlessness was a side of Corporal Meryn he hadn't seen before. Meryn, one of the younger Ghosts, was an able and reliable soldier. His service record was excellent, but Gaunt had not yet advanced him. Rawne, however, had recently taken Meryn under his wing. Now, it seemed, he was aiming to prove himself, taking no chances that might vitiate successes for the mission. He was doing things the way his hard-arsed mentor Rawne would do them. It wasn't the Meryn Larkin knew. He didn't like it, even though he knew it was the smart way to go.

'Larkin! Come on! We're leaving!' said Meryn, and they hurried down into the stairwell next to the elevator as tube charge blasts blew the hall out of the side of the dome above them.

* * *

GAUNT TOOK THE data-slate from his adjutant Beltayn and looked it over.

'Is this confirmed?'

'The data came via Admiral Ornoff.'

As far as the admiral could report, two of the Larisel craft had been destroyed before they had reached the target. Larisel 2 and Larisel 3 had landed. Ornoff believed from pilot reports that some if not all of Larisel 1 had dropped before their Marauder had gone down.

That was something.

Larisel 4 had exploded outright well short of the city. No survivors. No chutes.

'Oh dear God-Emperor,' Gaunt sighed. 'Mkoll.'

Two

FIVE HUNDRED AIR-HORNS simultaneously rasped out a long, bleating note, and workers started to shuffle around Ouranberg's secondary vapour mill in their thousands. It was a shift change, but there would be no rest for the gangs coming off station. Grim tannoy announcements ordered them to collect meal pails from their designated canteens and then assemble at the main bascule. There they would be broken into work details and sent across the causeway to Ouranberg itself, to assist in the rebuild and recovery.

'Failure to report will result in reprisal punishment of all members of an individual's work gang,' the tannoy emphasised over and over. The voice, already distorted by the bass-heavy vox-repeater, had a thick, hard accent and spoke in a monotone as if reading the words without understanding them. 'Reprisal punishment will be immediate. No excuses. Report to the assembly yard of the main bascule in twenty minutes.'

The long, expressionless declaration repeated itself several times, the delays and echoes of the capacious turbine halls turning it into a tuneless canon of overlaps.

No one complained. No one dared. The workers trudged from their posts and filed silently into the wire-caged walks that led away from the mill, while others hobbled in the opposite direction down parallel cage-ways to take their places. The air was thick with dust, and smelled like it was rotting, a byproduct of the ozone and pollutants generated by the mill. Yellowish light glared from mesh-basket lamps, flickered by the turning rotors of the soot-heavy ceiling fans.

Blood Pact personnel, armed with pain-goads and synapse disrupters, walked above the cage-ways on grilled platforms. Some of them, stripped down to black leather bib-overalls and iron masks, restrained leashed packs of snarling cyber-mastiffs with sweat-slick, corded arms and shouted abuse at stragglers. These were brutes from Warlord Slaith's slaver force, a specialised unit of the Blood Pact which enforced the Chaos army's occupation. Their cruel, relentless methods ensured that the captured workforce maintained output and serviced the industries Slaith had conquered. On Gigar, the slavers had worked the captive locals, night and day, for eight weeks, setting their canines on twenty individuals every time one slackened or collapsed. At the end of eight weeks, the wells of Gigar had produced enough promethium to fuel sixty Blood Pact motorised regiments for a year. And the hate-dogs were fat.

The workers of Ouranberg had been reduced to an almost zombie-like state, deprived of sleep, of decent food, of enough fluids. Distinctions of sex and age had vanished. All were swaddled in overalls and rag bandages stiff with grey dust. Coarse canvas hoods or shawls, similarly grey, draped them like monks. They were hunched and submissive. Battered rebreathers and work gauntlets dangled beneath the edges of their shrouds. Raw, black-bandaged feet left limping trails of blood on the dusty floor.

Though Ornoff's persistent bombing campaign might have been hurting Slaith's forces, it was turning the lives of the slave workers from a living hell to something indescribably worse. Every waking hour had to be spent on repair and rebuild work.

Slaith knew an invasion was coming, and he intended to throw it back by making Ouranberg a fortress. It was believed that the slavers were lacing the workers' meagre rations with stimulants to force them into twenty-four hour activity. Already, many had died of convulsive fits, or gone berserk and thrown themselves at the Blood Pact guns.

The air-horns blared again. The tannoy repeated its monotone order. A work crew from the mill's ninth level channeled
down the narrow cage-way towards the stair flights that
would take them to the assembly yard.

Just inside the mouth of the caged walk, a worker stumbled
and fell against the chain-fence. A Blood Pact guard on the
overhead platform jabbed down with his pain-goad, but the
crumpled worker was out of reach. His fellow workers just
hurried past him, not wanting to get involved. The slavers
pushed their way into the cage, shoving aside the workers
who were too slow-moving. The hate-dogs bayed.

'Don't,' hissed Adare, squeezing Milo's arm as they shuffled
forward.

Screams echoed down the chamber. One of the Blood Pact
started shooting into the crowd.

'Just keep going, for feth's sake,' Adare whispered.

Milo fought back the urge to throw off his filthy shawl and
open fire with the U90 lashed tight under his right armpit.
The screams were unbearable.

'We're dead if you even think about it,' Adare mumbled.

The members of Larisel 3 moved on with the trudging
mob. All of them were shrouded with stolen rags, grey dust
rubbed liberally into their hands and kit. Doyl had swathed
their boots and lower legs with bandage wraps, and dirt had
been rubbed in there too. They walked with shoulders bent.

More shots rang out behind them.

Milo choked back his rage. Peering out from under his
hood, he saw a slaver standing just the other side of the chain
fence, watching them all file past. Milo was close enough to
smell the bastard's rancid body odour, and see the ritual scars
on his misshapen hands, the eight-pointed brand of Chaos
on his bare sternum. The slaver's iron grotesque seemed to be
staring right at him.

Milo tensed his hand around the heavy cannon's trigger
grip…

And then they were out, clanging down the metal stairs
towards the assembly yard.

The secondary vapour mill was built into a volcanic plug, a
sister peak to the main outcrop on which Ouranberg was constructed. It was linked to the main city by a two kilometre long

cantilever causeway suspended between the two peaks. From the vast, dirt-filmed windows of the assembly yard, they could see out across the majestic causeway to the monumental, domed bulk of the city. Through cloud-haze, a thousand lights pulsed on masts and stacks and a million more glowed from ribbon windows and observation decks.

The yard was thronging with slave workers. Larisel 3 laced in amongst them. Milo stuck close to Nessa in case she missed a signal from Adare.

'Worship Slaith!' boomed the tannoy suddenly. 'Worship him for he is the overlord!' The Blood Pact cheered throatily, and the workers dutifully raised a suitable moan. 'Worship Slaith, and through your toil and blood, embrace the truth of *Khorne!*'

The very name made some workers wail and sob. Someone screamed. Whips cracked into the crowd. Milo felt his gorge rise and gooseflesh quiver across his hands and arms. That word. That foul, foul word, that name of darkness, an animal cry from the warp. It reeked with evil, far more than the simple combination of letters and sounds could convey. It was like a noise, pitched on a certain frequency, that triggered involuntary fear and revulsion.

Milo had seldom heard the True Names of Chaos spoken aloud. They were forbidden sounds, utterances that human mouths should not make.

He tried to forget it. He was terrified he would remember the name and speak it, or have it burn into his memory. Gaunt had once taught him there were four great names of darkness, that might arise alone, or in combination. Milo had made it a point of personal honour not to know any of them.

'Praise the warp! The warp is the one true way! The names of the warp are a billion and one, and each name is the lament of mankind! Worship the warp! Praise be the warp! Through the power of the warp, the Lord of Change will transmute the galaxy! The warp will engulf all things in a tide of blood!'

Milo sensed Nessa was shaking, and realised with an unexpected pang of fear that she was responding to the sounds even though she couldn't hear the words. He pushed her on through the crowd. He prayed to the God-Emperor of

Mankind that the tannoy wouldn't utter that awful word again.

Cardinale had reached the gateway of the yard, where workers pressed in to approach the bascule. He tried to block out the sounds, his hand clamped so tight around his little silver aquila, the wingtips were puncturing his palm. He suddenly registered the pain, and flexed his hand.

Cardinale looked back, trying to find the other members of the team without raising his head. He spotted Adare, and Doyl. There was no sign of the boy or the female sniper.

The gate joined the causeway via the bascule, a massive ironwork drawbridge lowered on thick chains from the winch house overhanging the drop. As its great bulk dropped down with a shuddering crash, Blood Pact slavers started to whip the workers into line. They opened the gate's barred shutter.

An electro-lash caught the back of Cardinale's calf and he fell to one knee as his leg spasmed.

'Up! Up!' a nearby slaver roared, though his hoarse snarls were mainly directed at the workers who had been completely knocked down by the whip.

Cardinale felt a strong hand support his arm and he got to his feet. Doyl was right next to him.

'Your leg?' the scout whispered.

'It'll be fine. We have to get through this gate.'

'I know.' Doyl turned and saw Adare a few rows behind them.

'First fifty!' yelled a slaver, speaking, like the tannoy, in a language unfamiliar to him. 'First fifty to Beta dome!'

Whips cracked and they spilled through onto the bascule and the causeway beyond. The causeway was a rockcrete thoroughfare broad enough to take a cargo truck. It was roofed with pressurised, wire-reinforced glassite and lit by crude strip lamps buried in the walls.

'Are they with us?' Adare whispered.

'Yeah,' replied Doyl. 'Don't look round. Milo and Nessa are about twenty metres back. I saw them both.'

There was a hold-up. Slavers drove the work gangs against the causeway wall in single file to let a cargo transport speed through. Cardinale took the opportunity of the pause to stoop and rub his aching calf.

'Oh shit,' he said suddenly.

'What?'

Cardinale started to search his pockets and the folds of his clothing. The slender chain was still wrapped around his hand, but it was broken. The silver aquila was gone.

'Move! Move!' a slaver screamed now the transport had passed. The workers resumed their march over the causeway.

'It must have snapped off,' Cardinale said.

'Never mind that. It doesn't matter,' Adare said.

'What if they find it?' Cardinale said, rubbing at the wingtip punctures in his palm flesh.

'Shut up, all right? Let me worry about that.'

They were halfway across the causeway.

Okay? Milo signed surreptitiously to Nessa.

I'm fine. That was scary.

True.

They were coming up on the entry porta to Ouranberg, the cyclopean gate house that defended the causeway and the northern approaches. Blood Pact banners fluttered from the batteries.

Nearly there.

In the assembly yard, with the tannoy still screaming out its noxious sermon, one of the slavers yanked on his hate-dog's chain. It was worrying at the filthy flagstones.

It had found something.

The slaver hunched over and raked his scarred fingers through the greasy muck. Something silver glittered.

A tiny double-eagle. An aquila. An Imperial totem.

'Alarm!' he screamed, ejecting spittle from between his rotten teeth. 'Alarm! Alarm!'

SIRENS BEGAN TO whoop. The mass of slaves on the causeway looked round in panic as the strip lights in the wall started to flash amber. The porta into Ouranberg was so close.

'Keep going!' Adare said.

'What do we do?' Cardinale stammered.

'Keep going, like I said. We're nearly there! Keep going and lock and load!'

The trio elbowed their way through the milling workers, closing on the gateway.

Behind them, Blood Pact soldiers were surging out across the bascule onto the causeway, pushing aside mill workers, or simply gunning them down. There was a terrible howling. The hate-dogs had been unleashed.

'COME ON!' MILO urged Nessa, squeezing her arm.

She surprised him by pulling back.

'No!' she said aloud. She dragged him back against the causeway wall amongst the cowering workers, and pulled his hood down over his head.

Nessa had fought the Verghast hive war as a scratch company guerilla. She knew how to mingle in the ordinary, how to hide in plain sight. Though his gut instinct told him to run, Milo remembered that, and trusted her.

He bowed his head.

Blood Pact troopers and slavers rushed past them, kicking down anyone foolish enough to get in their way. The hate-dogs, trailing ropes of drool, bounded ahead of them, baying, making the air stink with their rancid pelts.

Two confused mill workers were gunned down right in front of Milo and Nessa by the Blood Pact. Their bodies lay crumpled in spreading lakes of blood, kicked and trampled by the Chaos troopers who rushed after.

INSIDE THE PORTA, alarms were also ringing. Enemy troops, their iron masks glaring, were corralling all the slaves who had crossed the causeway to one side of the entrance hall. They were shouting and gesturing with their weapons.

'Feth!' said Adare as they came through the gateway, setting foot on Ouranberg proper for the first time.

'Go with the flow,' Doyl urged. 'Get in line and don't draw attention to yourself.'

They could all hear the howling coming closer.

'The dogs! The damned dogs!' Cardinale whined. 'They've got my scent—'

'Forget it!' Doyl said as loudly as he dared.

'We have to go active,' Cardinale said, fear in his voice.

'You fething well won't until I say, Phantine!' Adare growled. 'Get over! Over to the side with the other workers!'

'But the dogs!'

The dogs were on them, bursting through the screaming workers in the gateway, surging in towards them.

'Holy Emperor!' Cardinale yelled. He pushed Adare aside.

'Oh feth! No! Don't! Don't!' Adare shouted. 'In the name of the Golden Throne, Cardinale–'

Cardinale threw back his cloak disguise and wheeled round, firing his lasrifle on full auto at the bounding hate-dogs.

He blew three of them apart, two in mid-air. The fourth, a two hundred pound cyber-mastiff, barrelled into him and smashed him to the floor. Its steel jaws tore into the left side of his face.

'Active!' Adare bellowed, all hope lost. 'Go active, Doyl! We've no fething choice!'

Sergeant Adare wrenched out his lasrifle and blasted the dog off Cardinale point-blank.

Doyl swept round and raked the nearby Blood Pact guards with his own rifle.

Cardinale was screaming. Blood was pouring out of his torn neck. Adare grabbed him, his hands becoming slick with the Phantine's gore.

'Go! Go!' Doyl yelled, shooting dead two more of the approaching dog-pack. A third hate-dog fled, howling, dragging a foreleg.

'Get him clear, sarge! Get him clear!' Doyl cried. He blasted his weapon in a wide arc that toppled two Blood Pact sentries out of an autocannon nest overlooking the porta's entrance hall.

The slaves were shrieking and running in panic. Adare dragged Cardinale to his feet and fired his lasrifle one-handed. Doyl started cutting a desperate path for them through the frenetic mob. If they could get clear and just find somewhere to hide…

Doyl recoiled as a las-round creased his forehead. Blood started to trickle into his eyes. Cursing, he pulled out a tube charge, ripped off the det-tape and hurled it to his left. The concussive blast hurled three Blood Pact infantrymen into the air and added to the wild confusion.

Firing indiscriminately at anything that looked like a Chaos trooper, Adare cut a swathe through the press towards the

north-west exit of the entrance hall. He was virtually carrying
Cardinale by then. Mill workers fled in terror before him.

'Doyl! This way! Out this way! Come on!' Adare shouted.

Doyl, half-blinded by his own blood, followed Adare's
voice. He had to push and kick slaves out of his way. Several
of them collided mindlessly with him.

'Adare!'

'Come on, Doyl!'

Autocannon fire chopped into the crowd, and felled a
dozen workers. Doyl could smell fycelene and the metallic
scent of blood. The cannon rattled again.

Wiping the back of his sleeve across his eyes, Doyl turned
back, dropped to one knee, and aimed at the source of the
heavy fire. Blood Pact troopers were shooting their way
through the pandemonium of slaves. One had a support cannon on a bipod, and a slaver ran beside him, feeding belts of
ammunition. The jagged muzzle flashes of the cannon illu-
minated the gun's brutal work like a strobe light. Each flare
froze a snapshot of lurching figures, slaves falling, knocked
off their feet, crashing into one another

Doyl managed to shoot the gunner through the throat
before his wound blinded him again. Adare had reached the
north-east exit, and stumbled into the doorway, spilling Cardinale over. He scrambled up and lobbed a grenade high over
Doyl's head into the mob of enemy troopers.

'Come on!' Adare screamed at Doyl over the crump-
whoosh of the grenade. 'We can still do this! First and Only!
First and fething Only!'

Doyl ran towards Adare's cry.

Together, they broke out into a wide stone tunnel leading
off from the entrance hall. Smoke from the main hall was
blowing in and pooling under the arched roof. Slaves were
staggering, stunned, everywhere.

'We're clear!' Adare said to Doyl. 'Help me with him!'

They each seized one of Cardinale's wrists and started to
drag him. Doyl tried not to look at the Phantine's ruined face.

'Which way?' Adare asked.

'Left,' said Doyl.

They had only gone a few metres when a las-round caught
Adare in the knee and knocked him over. Blood Pact squads

were clattering into the tunnel from a side passage ahead of them.

'Feth!' Doyl despaired. He let go of Cardinale and fired from the hip and scored two hits. There were so many Blood Pact and so little cover they weren't hard to hit.

Neither am I, Doyl thought.

The enemy squads were firing as they charged. Hard rounds and las-bolts cracked and whined around the three Imperials. Doyl felt one pass through his cape and another kiss painfully across his thigh. Stone chips peppered his face from a ricochet off the tunnel wall.

Adare started shooting from a prone position, and the sergeant's efforts were suddenly bolstered by Cardinale. Soaked in his own blood, ignoring his wounds, the Phantine had struggled to his feet. He stood, swaying slightly, at Doyl's side, mowing down the cult warriors with haphazard bursts.

'Brace for det!' Doyl cried, and tossed another tube charge down the tunnel into the charge. The fireball collapsed part of the roof and buried the Blood Pact squads in masonry. A crimson bowl-helmet came spinning out of the blast and bounced off the tunnel wall.

'Cardinale! You hear me? You hear me? We can still make this!' Adare urged, trying to rise.

Cardinale nodded, unsteady on his feet.

'Back that way,' Adare ordered. 'Back down the tunnel!'

'Okay,' said Doyl. 'Okay, but we need to go to ground. We can't survive out in the open like this.'

'Agreed!' said Adare. He turned, his next words drowned by a buzzing roar.

Adare's chest exploded and he was slammed back against the wall with enough force to splinter bone. Hundreds of tiny, secondary impacts simultaneously peppered the stonework.

Doyl staggered backwards, trying to shield Cardinale. The Phantine had collapsed again. Doyl was sure Cardinale was dead. The scout could suddenly smell an odour of rancid milk mixed with mint.

The beast was moving so fast the Tanith scout could barely follow it. Using its dewclaws to grip the stones, it skittered along the tunnel roof, upside down. An armature frame of augmetic servo-limbs clamped around its torso automatically racked the xenos-pattern flechette blaster it had used to slay Adare. A crude leather bandolier dangled from its gleaming, mottled body. It gazed down its wattled snout at Doyl, doubled han lids flickering across its milky eyes protectively.

Doyl raked it with las-fire.

It barely flinched.

Doyl screamed and fired again. He emptied his size three clip into the beast until the power was gone.

It grabbed him by the throat with one of its powerful forelimbs and lifted him up. He gagged.

'The Emperor protects,' Doyl choked just before the loxatl pushed the muzzle of its flechette blaster into his eye and fired.

'MOVE THROUGH! MOVE through!' the slavers raged, making free use of their goads and lashes. Rounded up again, the slave details filed through into the entrance hall. The place was littered with debris and blood. Heretic troopers were dragging corpses away.

Are they…? Nessa signed.

Don't think about it, Milo replied. *It's down to us now.*

Following the crowd, heads down, the two survivors of Larisel 3 shuffled into the city.

VARL'S TEAM PROGRESSED steadily down through Ouranberg's main vapour mill complex, following back stairs and sub-corridors. Several times, they had to conceal themselves to avoid roaming patrols or hurrying work-gangs.

Bonin led the way. They'd ditched their extra jump kit, helmets and mail smocks, and the Ghosts had put on their stealth-cloaks. Varl had draped scrim-nets over Unterrio and Jagdea and smeared a little camo-paint on the pilot's face.

From all directions, the mill rang with the sounds of heavy labour. Drills chattered. Hoists whirred. Turbines rumbled and shook.

The tactical briefing had presumed Slaith to be secure somewhere in Alpha dome. Varl considered it a priority to obtain more specific information. Twice they stopped while Unterrio tried patching his data-slate into a city-system terminal, but it was futile. Slaith's forces had corrupted the Imperial database and flooded it with incompatible, unreadable sequences.

They crossed a series of storage halls, and skirted the edge of an air-wharf. Here, they had to wait in hiding for almost fifteen minutes while servitors loaded a cargo carrier. Only when the carrier lifted off the pad and flew off in the direction of the Alpha dome did the wharf clear, allowing them to continue. Banda paused to check a roster board hanging from one of the wharf's roof supports.

'Regular shipments to the Alpha dome,' she said. 'Every couple of hours.'

Varl nodded. He glanced at Jagdea. 'Could you handle one of those bulk carriers?'

'Yes,' she said.

They pressed on, but the way was blocked. Work-gangs under armed guard were clearing bomb damage from the next manufactory space. Bonin doubled them back, only to hear more escorted gangs tramping down the access tunnel in their direction.

'Feth!' Varl said. They were boxed in.

'Here! In here!' Bonin hissed. He'd forced the lock on a side door. They hurried through and he closed it behind them. They were in a small storeroom for machine parts. It stank of oil-based lubricant. Varl and Bonin flanked the door, weapons ready, listening to the feet marching past outside.

They could hear rough voices, and a series of vox-exchanges. Several individuals had stopped to converse just outside the door.

Vadim pushed to the back of the store. He quietly cleared some plyboard boxes from a grubby bench and hoisted himself up to reach a small fan-light window high in the wall. The window was crazed with dirt, and he had to use his pry-bar to move the latch.

Looks promising, he signed. Varl and the other Ghosts nodded. Jagdea and Unterrio, unfamiliar with gestures, frowned.

You first, I'll cover. Get those three through and Vadim after them, Varl's hands wrote in the air deftly. Bonin gave him a thumbs-up and went to the back of the room, taking Vadim's place on the bench. He squinted through the fanlight and felt cool air on his face. The little window looked out onto a circulation space between mill houses. He wedged the window open as wide as it would go with his warknife, and slithered through head first.

At the door, Varl watched Bonin's boots disappear. The voices outside were still arguing, but seemed to be moving away.

Bonin's face reappeared at the window and he reached an arm down. Banda got up, pushed her long-las through the gap and hauled herself after it. Vadim boosted her feet to help her on her way.

He turned and waved Jagdea up.

With Vadim pushing her feet, she was nimble enough, but the scrim-net Varl had insisted she wear snagged on the edge of the window frame.

She struggled, pinned. Vadim got up on the bench next to her and tried to unhook the netting. His efforts shook the old bench and wobbled the tall, spares-laden shelving next to it.

Varl kept glancing back. *Hurry the feth up!* he mouthed at Vadim. He was sure the harsh voices outside were getting closer again. He flexed his augmetic shoulder and adjusted his grip on the heavy U90.

Vadim drew his warknife and slit through the net, freeing Jagdea. She slithered out through the window, but the sudden motion of her release shook the bench again. Vadim swayed, and the shelf rocked.

A tin canister full of rivets dropped off the top shelf.

Varl saw it fall as if in slow motion. He closed his eyes, waiting for the inevitable.

There was no sound. He looked again. Unterrio had caught the canister a few centimetres from the rockcrete floor. The look of heart-stopped relief on the faces of Vadim and Unterrio almost made Varl burst out laughing.

Unterrio exited next. In the light of Jagdea's difficulties, he had the sense to take off his scrim-net and bundle it through the window ahead of him.

Vadim, crouching on the bench, looked back at Varl and beckoned him.

You go, Varl mouthed. He looked back at the door and then pressed his ear to it. The voices were right outside now. Right out fething side.

Bonin had broken the door lock to get them in, but Varl noticed a bolt, which he gingerly drew into place. He backed slowly from the door, keeping his gun aimed at it.

Vadim was through the window. He leaned back in to pull Varl up. Keeping his gun on the door, Varl sat on the bench and slowly drew his feet up. His left boot brushed the edge of the shelf.

Two litre-capacity flasks of lamp oil toppled and smashed on the storeroom floor.

Varl couldn't believe he'd been so stupid.

He could hear the voices, and saw the latch being waggled furiously.

'Come on!' Vadim hissed.

There was a hammering on the door now. Kicking. Shouting.

Then shots. The metal of the door around the latch deformed and burst under the impact of several las-rounds. The bolt still held.

Whoever was on the outside now opened fire directly at the door, punching six molten holes. Penetrating the door metal had robbed the las-rounds of most of their power, but they still had enough force to wind Varl and smash him off the bench.

'Varl!' Vadim shouted. Multiple holes now riddled the door and sparking las-shots rained into the storeroom.

'Feth!' said Varl. He was badly bruised on his shoulders and the backs of his legs from the hits. He got up, aimed his U90 at the door and opened fire, bracing against the recoil.

His weapon was loaded with a clip of standard .45 calibre rounds. Striking the metal door, they dented its surface wildly, but few penetrated. An answering storm of fire punished the door from the other side.

Varl popped the yellow-tagged drum out of his weapon, replaced it with a red, racked back the bolt, and blitzed the door with explosive armour piercing rounds. They went through the door like it was made of wet paper. The surrounding wall too. The explosive bullets blew bricks and metal shreds out into the corridor.

Varl turned, tossed the gun up to Vadim, and threw himself up through the fan-light.

An alarm was ringing. It was quickly answered by another. Larisel 1 dashed across the circulation space and towards a gulley that formed the waste-gutter for a small foundry.

'Not that way!' Bonin ordered, already spotting two guard towers on the far side of the foundry. 'Down here!' Another gulley, but it was piled with precast tiles for roofing repairs.

'Good one, Boney. There's no way through,' Banda said.

'Yes, there is,' Vadim announced and got up on the nearest pile of slabs without breaking stride. His sure-footed climbing skills exceeded theirs, but they followed, making it up to the top of a wall, and from there onto the pitched roof of a walkway cloister.

They hid under the tarpaulin covers of a barrel stack in the next workyard.

'I think we had better lie low for a while,' Bonin said.

'Yeah,' panted Varl, 'and then I think we go back to that wharf.'

MERYN'S TEAM, LARISEL 2, was the first to see the face of Sagittar Slaith. Every street and plaza in Beta dome had its public address screens and pict-plates tuned to a mesmerisingly grim live feed of various Blood Pact preachers gibbering blasphemies and extolling the virtues of their daemonic faith. The broadcasts were constant and relentless, captured by a fuzzy, handheld viewer that regularly went out of focus trying to remain trained on the capering, lunging hierarchs. They were painted, pierced devils, ranting in a mix of their own warp-twisted language and bastardised Low Gothic. Some would preach for hours at a time, twitching and spasming as if they were thrashing through narcotic highs. Others would scream hysterically for a few short minutes before disappearing. The pict image would then jump and flicker as it cut to the next preacher.

The members of Larisel 2 tried to ignore the broadcasts, but they were pretty much inescapable. They echoed and rang around every street and access tunnel.

Of the team, Larkin was the most disturbed by the transmissions. On the way down through the bombed sections of the upper habs, they had ditched their jump kit and, freed of the visored helmet, Larkin had at last been able to take some of his powerful anticonvulsants. He felt better for a while, but the migraine itself merely subsided. It kept rumbling around the edges of his brain like a storm that refused to break.

Once they got into the primary sector levels, there was a pict-address plate on every other corner. Larisel 2 hugged back streets, sub-walkways and deserted yards, but there was no respite from the blaring voices and jerking pictures. Larkin felt his stress levels soaring, and the migraine began to boil up again.

The comprehensible, Low Gothic parts of the sermons were bad. The speech used, the concepts, the ideas, were all hard to take and often shocking. But the gabbled warp-words were much worse, as far as Larkin was concerned. His mind knotted as it imagined the meanings.

Worst of all, what really chilled Larkin, was the sight of Ouranberg citizens, ragged, often weeping, watching the broadcasts. They seemed to be under no duress. They simply stood at street corners, in squares and wide commercial parades, gazing at the screens, their minds gradually corroding under the poisonous bombardment of warp-lies.

Mkvenner steered them well. He had an unerring instinct for avoiding foot patrols, and swept them into cover each time a speeder went over. They stayed out of sight of crowds, and only once had to silence an individual who spotted them. A middle-aged man had simply walked out into a yard as they were sprinting across it. He had stared at them without saying a word and then just turned and wandered back into his hab.

Meryn had broken from the group and followed the man into the building. A few minutes later, he re-emerged and they moved on.

No one asked Meryn what he'd done. Everyone knew. Everyone knew it was absolutely paramount to maintain the mission's secrecy for as long as possible. It was a necessary evil. Just like shooting the rescue crews. A necessary evil.

Larkin didn't like it much at all. 'Necessary evil' seemed to him to be one of those too-clever phrases men used to excuse wrongs. And there was quite enough unnecessary evil in the fething galaxy without deliberately adding to it.

On balance, what he really didn't like was the fact that Meryn showed no emotion. He remained calm, unexpressive. Probably a quality Rawne, maybe even Gaunt, would admire as utterly professional devotion to duty. But Larkin thought that he might feel easier about stuff if Meryn showed just one ounce of regret or upset.

Just before dawn on the 224th, they stopped for a rest break, taking shelter on the first floor of an abandoned weaver's. Once the day cycle started, movement would be restricted, and they needed to get some bag-rations inside them and catch some sleep. The weaver's premises, which had been looted and then boarded up, overlooked a small municipal square full of burned-out vehicles and litters of debris. A public-address screen on the opposite side of the square boomed out the latest tirade of Slaith's preachers. Citizens stood around oil can fires gazing at the broadcast.

They ate, then Kuren took the first watch.

He woke them all after about two hours. It was still dark outside. The lamps that should have cut in automatically at the start of the day cycle had been shot out. Ouranberg seemed to be locked into a permanent twilight, which Mkvenner realised would help their progress immensely.

Kuren had woken them because of the broadcasts.

The preachers had shut up, and a good fifteen minutes had gone by with nothing on the screen but white noise.

Then Sagittar Slaith had appeared.

He was utterly terrifying.

They had been shown a few blurry longshots of a being believed to be Slaith during the pre-mission briefings, vague suggestions of someone tall and heavy-set, but nothing that could be called a likeness.

The face on the screen was entirely hairless: bald, shaven, lacking even eyebrows and lashes. His ears were grossly distended by the weight and number of the studs and rings that pierced them. They looked like a lizard's frill. Slaith's teeth were chrome triangles, like the tips of daggers. Three huge and old diagonal scars marked each cheek, ritual cuts made to seal his pact with Urlock Gaur. He wore a white fur cloak over a spiked suit of maroon power-armour. His eyes were pupil-less white slits.

His voice was the soft, muffled throb of a nightmare that had woken the sleeper in terror with no clear memory of why he was afraid.

He spoke to them. Directly to them. He used Low Gothic haltingly.

'Imperial soldiers. I know you are here. I know you are here in my city uninvited. Creeping like vermin in the shadows. I can smell you.'

'Feth!' stammered Larkin. Meryn shushed him.

'You will die,' Slaith continued. His eyes never blinked. 'You will die soon. You are beginning to die already. A hundred thousand agonies will carry you to your graves. Your death-screams will shake the Golden Throne and wake that rancid old puppet you claim to serve. I will cut your flesh and make you swear the Blood Pact. I will burn your hearts on the altar of Chaos. I will send your souls to the warp where my lord, the Blood God, mighty Korne, will remake you in his image. His alchemy will reforge your souls in the beauty of eternal darkness, where His Pain will be yours forever.'

At the mention of the forbidden name, Larkin felt his senses sway. He grew feverishly hot. He saw that the others had all gone pale. Kersherin was gulping hard, trying not to vomit.

'Give up your futile mission now, and I will grant you the mercy of a quick death. You have an hour.' Slaith glanced away, as if talking to someone off-camera, and then looked back. 'Slaves, dwellers in this place, hear me now. Search your habitats, your workplaces, your storehouses. Search your cellars and attics, your granaries and pantries. Find the uninvited Imperial vermin. It is your duty. Any amongst you I find to have aided them or sheltered them will suffer at my hands, and their kith and kin besides. Those that come forward to give up the Imperial vermin will be blessed in my eyes. Their rewards will be the greatest I can bestow. They will be honoured as my own blood kindred, for they will have shown true loyalty to my lord the Blood God.'

The screen view suddenly jolted and panned around, refocusing. The Ghosts caught a glimpse of a finely appointed chamber, backed by vast windows that looked out on a ruined statue. Then Slaith's fur-wrapped back filled the screen, the viewer following him across the chamber. He moved aside. The image blurred and refocused again.

The men of Larisel 2 caught their breaths.

Three bodies lay twisted on the floor under one of the windows. Two were unmistakably wearing Tanith uniform and unmistakably dead. Vast, ruinous wounds rendered them unrecognisable. Blood soaked the carpet under them. Sprawled across them was a mutilated man, naked except for Phantine-issue combat pants. He also looked dead, but he winced and writhed as Slaith slapped him with a steel-shod fist.

It was Cardinale. His face was a torn mask of blood. His wrists and ankles were bound with razor-wire.

'Sacred feth,' said Meryn.

'See how I know you are here, Imperial vermin. Your fellows are already discovered and broken. Your cause is lost.'

Slaith looked back at the screen. 'One hour,' he said and the picture went dead.

The screen fuzzed and rolled for a long while. They all jumped as another preacher suddenly appeared, howling out a stream of profanities.

Larkin's hands were shaking badly. His mouth was dry.

'They got Larisel 3,' Meryn said.

'Those bodies? Milo? Doyl?' Kuren asked quietly.

Mkvenner shrugged. 'Maybe. Maybe one of them was Adare.'

'So some of team 3 might have got clear?' Kuren pressed hopefully.

'Unless there wasn't enough left of the others to find,' said Mkvenner.

'I can't sleep now,' said Meryn. 'Not after that. Let's just get on. Let's find that bastard. Okay?'

Kersherin and Mkvenner nodded. 'Yeah,' Kuren agreed, his head bowed.

'Larkin? Okay with you?'

Larkin looked up at Meryn. 'Yes. Let's get on with it.'

THE STACKS OF Ouranberg's waste gas burners lay out to the north and west of the city, built up on slender crags of rock.

Heavy pipelines carried by vast trestle frames of ironwork girders, some over four kilometres long, linked them to the main city structure. The burners themselves were fat, kiln-like brick chimneys twenty metres in diameter, capped with blackened-metal ignition frames.

It was mid-morning on the 224th. The sky was a blinding bowl of topaz altostratus and the morning pollution banks welling up from the Scald were dissolving into yellowish vapours as the headwind gathered force. Ominous clouds gathered in the western distances.

Ouranberg was three kilometres away at the end of a vast span of rusty girderwork. The city was still immense. Sunlight flared and glinted off its ribbons of windows. Thin black smoke, like smudged thumbprints, rose from the domes.

Out of breath from the last stint of climbing, he sat back on a thin ledge of rock about fifty metres from the top of the stack, one boot braced to stop the wind sweeping him off. The burner high above him hummed as the wind blew through the cavities of its burner brackets and every ten minutes or so there was a gigantic whoosh as gas ignited and blistered up into the sky. Cinders floated down like snowflakes.

His air bottle had long since been spent, and he was forced to use the helmet's rudimentary rebreather. That meant every lungful came in moist and warm, and it was impossible to breathe deeply. This was a climb that would have been hard even in clean air conditions. He'd sweated off about two kilos already. His head ached from oxygen starvation. His hands and knees and feet, despite gloves, reinforced leggings and boots, were bloody and raw.

He started to climb again, and managed about ten metres. That put him almost on a level with the bottom spars of the pipeline's scaffold. He lifted his visor quickly to suck water from his flask, and then lowered it. The temptation to inhale the cold air outside was almost overwhelming.

He clambered to the edge of the scaffolding. It had looked slender from a distance, but now he was up close, he appreciated the titanic scale of the I-beams and girder spars. Climbing it wouldn't be easy. The spars were far too wide apart. He would have to belly along the girders, hand over hand.

And reach Ouranberg sometime next century.

The alternative was to keep climbing and cross the bridge along the pipeline. That meant going vertically up the increasingly sheer rock stack for another forty metres or so.

He tested the tension on the rope that played out beneath him. There wasn't much give, so he spent ten minutes hoisting the kit up to his level. Climbing with full kit on would have been out of the question. He'd been forced to lash it together and drag it up after him every time he reached the limit of the rope. If only his jump-pack hadn't been crippled in the drop. He keyed his micro-bead and tried another call.

'Larisel, Larisel, do you read?'

Nothing.

'Larisel, Larisel, over.'

Still nothing. He knew he was well out of range but still he couldn't resist trying every now and then.

'Larisel, Larisel… this is Mkoll. Do you read? Do you read?'

Three

THEY WERE ON the countdown for the invasion now. O-Day. Operation Thunderhead. Just over a day away.

Gaunt and Rawne joined Lord General Van Voytz and the officers of the Urdeshi and the Phantine to review the mustered ranks of the Krassian Sixth. They were a newly founded regiment, out of the recently liberated agri-world Krassia in the Rimward Marginals. Two thousand men in copper-coloured battledress and grey shakos. Their commanding officer, Colonel Dalglesh, was a PDF veteran with beetle brows and a spectacular handlebar moustache.

'A fine bunch of men, colonel,' Gaunt told him at the end of the inspection.

'Thank you, sir,' Dalglesh said, appearing to be genuinely pleased. 'May I say, it is an honour to be serving with you.'

Gaunt raised an eyebrow.

'Truly, sir,' Dalglesh said. 'The reputation of the Tanith First is considerable. Krassia was settled thanks to the Martyr's crusade. Your work in her name on Hagia Shrineworld is regarded with great esteem amongst my people.'

'Thank you,' said Gaunt. 'It's always nice to be appreciated.'

'It's always novel to be appreciated,' Rawne murmured behind him.

Gaunt's micro-bead trilled.

'Excuse me, colonel... Gaunt, go ahead?'

'Colonel-commissar, it's Curth. You'd better get up to the infirmary.'

ANA CURTH SET down the vox-mic and hurried back down the corridor to the intensive ward. She pushed her way through the crowd of orderlies, nurses and walking wounded that had gathered in the doorway.

Dorden looked round at her. 'Did you reach him?'

'He's on his way now.'

Dorden turned back into the room. 'Did you find him like this?'

She shook her head. 'I found his bed empty. He'd pulled the drips out. We started to search for him and Lesp found him in here.'

Dorden took a step towards the cot where Corbec lay half curled in a sleep that the doctor doubted he would ever wake from.

Agun Soric, naked except for a sheet and the heavy wrap of bandages around his bulky torso, was sitting on a stool next to the colonel's cot, his head on Corbec's chest. His skin was dimpled with blood-blisters where the drips had been attached, and with the puckered white marks left by the adhesive tape that had held them in place.

Soric raised his head as Dorden approached, and slowly lifted the laspistol so that it was aimed at Dorden's belly.

'Not another step.'

'Hey now, Agun. Easy. Calm yourself.'

Soric's one good eye was bleary. He'd been unconscious for many days. Given the extent of his chest wound, Dorden wasn't sure how he was managing to remain alive divorced from the life support apparatus.

'Doc,' he murmured, as if he was recognising Dorden for the first time.

'It's me, Agun. What's with the weapon?'

Soric looked at the laspistol as if he was surprised to find himself holding it. Then some realisation crossed his face.

'Daemons,' he hissed.

'Daemons?'

'All around. All around in the air. I had a dream. They're coming to take Colm. Coming for him. I dreamt it. They're coming for him. In his bloodstream, chewing like rats. Nnh! Nnh! Nnh!' Soric made a graphic gnawing sound.

'And you're going to fight them, Agun? With the gun?'

'If I gakking well have to!' Soric said. He swung his head round awkwardly and focused on Corbec. 'He's not ready to die. It's not his time.'

Dorden hesitated. He remembered, with an unnerving clarity, Sergeant Varl saying the same thing.

'No, he's not ready, Agun,' Dorden agreed.

'I know. I dreamt it. But the daemon rats. They don't know. They're chewing at him.' Soric made the gnawing sound again, and then coughed.

'I'd shoot them if I could,' he added.

'Where the hell did he get a weapon?' murmured someone in the huddle of onlookers.

'Who's that?' demanded Soric loudly, looking up alertly and raising the gun. 'Daemons? More daemons? I dreamt about daemons!'

'No daemons, Agun! No daemons!' placated Dorden.

'Get them out of here,' he hissed at Curth.

'Move! Now!' Curth ordered, herding the bystanders out. She drew the screen behind them and looked back at Dorden.

'How is he still alive?' she whispered.

'Because I'm a tough old bastard, lovely Surgeon Curth,' Soric answered. 'Vervun Smeltery One, man and boy, ahh. Hardens you up, it does, smeltery work. She's a lovely girl, isn't she, doc? A lovely, lovely girl.'

'I've always thought so,' Dorden said calmly. 'Why don't you give me the laspistol, Agun? Maybe I can shoot these daemon rats?'

'Oh no!' Soric said. 'That wouldn't be fair on you, doc. You don't use guns. Always admired that in you. Life-saver. Not a life-taker.'

'Why don't I take it then, Agun?' Curth asked gently. 'Back in basic PDF training, I was top of my class at small arms. I bet I could nail those rats for you.'

Soric looked at her. With astonishing deftness, he spun the pistol in his paw so that the grip was suddenly pointing at her. 'Off you go then,' he said. 'Lovely, lovely girl,' he added sidelong to Dorden.

'Oh, I know,' said Dorden, breathing out.

Curth took the weapon gingerly and tossed it into a laundry bin.

'Let me look you over,' said Curth.

'No, I'm fine,' said the old Verghastite.

'I just want to check the rats aren't chewing at you too.'

'Hnnh. Okay.' He coughed again, and Dorden saw the spots of blood that speckled the cot sheets. Soric seemed to slump a little.

Curth went behind Soric and did a bimanual exam of his torso.

'Feth! He's respiring on both lungs! How is that possible?'

'Clearly?' asked Dorden, unconvinced.

'No… there's a fluid mass.' She took out her stethoscope and pressed the cup to Soric's back. 'But not much. This is amazing.'

'Absolutely,' Dorden whispered.

'Forget me, I'm fine,' said Soric, rousing suddenly and coughing again. 'The dream told me I would be fine. The dream made me fine. Said I had to be fine so's I could get up and keep the daemons away from Colm. They want his soul, doc. They're chewing in.'

'The dream told you that?'

Soric nodded. 'Did I tell you my great grandmother was a witch?'

Curth and Dorden both hesitated.

'A witch?' echoed Dorden.

'Had the second sight, most peculiar it was. Earned her keep in the out-habs for years, telling fortunes.'

'Like… a psyker?' Curth asked.

'Gak me, no!' Soric spluttered. 'Lovely, girl, but very foolish, eh, doc? My dear Ana, if my sainted old grandma had been a psyker, she'd have been gathered up by the Black Ships, wouldn't she? Gathered up by the Black Ships or shot as a heretic. No, no… she was a witch. She had a harmless knack of seeing the future. In dreams mostly. My old mam said I'd inherit the talent, being the seventh son of a seventh son, but I've not had so much as a twinge of it me whole life.'

'Until now,' he added.

'You dreamed Corbec had daemons chewing at him?' asked Curth.

'Clear as you like, that's what the dream said.'

'In his blood?'

'As you say.'

'And the dream said you'd come back to life so you could prevent that? Prevent the daemons carrying Colm off?'

'Yes, lady.'

Curth looked over at Dorden. 'Find Lesp. Have him do a toxicological spread test on Corbec.'

'You're kidding,' Dorden said.

'Just find Lesp, Tolin.'

'No need. I can do a tox-spread myself.'

'I had other dreams,' Soric said. His voice was distant now, as if he had exhausted himself.

'We need to get you back to bed, Agun,' Curth hushed. 'The dream will only heal you if you help it by resting.'

'Okay. Lovely, lovely girl, doc.'

Curth helped Soric to his feet as Dorden stripped sterile wraps off the instruments he was about to use on Corbec.

'Bad dreams,' Soric mumbled.

'I'm sure they were.'

'I saw Doyl. And Adare. They're dead. Breaks my heart. Both dead. And the cardinal is in terrible pain.'

'The cardinal?'

'Terrible pain. But tell Gaunt… Mkoll's not dead.'

Curth glanced at Dorden. She saw the look in his eyes. Torn between hope and dismissal.

'Come on, Agun,' she said.

'Lovely, lovely girl,' Soric mumbled. He sagged and collapsed.

'Lesp! Lesp!' Curth yelled.

BY THE TIME Gaunt reached the infirmary, Soric was strapped into a cot and back on life support.

'He said *what?*'

'He said daemons were after Corbec. And that he'd dreamed Doyl and Adare were dead, but Mkoll was alive. And he said something about the cardinal being in terrible pain.'

'The who?'

'The cardinal.'

Gaunt stood with Curth in the shadows of a service door-way down the hall from the intensive bay. Curth was trying to light a lho-stick, her hands unsteady.

'Give me that,' Gaunt snapped, and plucked the stick from her mouth. He walked over to a flamer pack that had been dumped amidst a clumsy pile of kit along the corridor wall by crash crews and lit the thing off a blue pilot flame from the nozzle.

He crossed back to Curth and handed her the lho-stick.

'Those things will kill you,' he said.

'Better them than the warp,' she replied, sucking hard.

'His actual words were "the cardinal"?'

'That's what I heard.'

'The Phantine specialist assigned to Adare's team was called Cardinale,' Gaunt told her.

'No crap,' she said simply.

Dorden approached down the hallway and joined them. Without comment, he took the lho-stick from Curth's hand, took a deep drag, regretted it in a fit of coughing, and handed it back to her.

'Corbec will live,' he said.

Gaunt smiled. 'And Soric?'

'Him too. I dread to think what it would take to bring Agun Soric down.'

'You don't look happy,' Gaunt noted.

Dorden shrugged. 'On Ana's advice I ran a tox-spread. Corbec was in a terminal decline thanks to a nosocomial infection.'

'A what?'

'In his injured state, he had picked up a secondary infection here in the infirmary.'

'Blood poisoning,' said Curth.

'Yes, Ana. Blood poisoning. If I hadn't shot him up with twenty cc's of morphomycin and an anticoagulant, he'd probably have been dead by nightfall.'

'Damn,' said Gaunt.

'Daemons in his blood stream, chewing like rats,' Curth said, mimicking Soric's gnawing sound.

'Don't start with that,' Dorden said.

'But you've got to admit–' Curth began.

'No, I haven't,' said Dorden.

THE GHOSTS IN the main billet were packing kits and stripping down weapons when Hark brought the punishment detail back in. Trooper Cuu was cuffed and hobbled, and scurried to keep up with the guards. His face was drawn and pale from too many nights in a cell, and it made his jagged scar all the more prominent.

'Stand to!' Hark cried, and the detail slammed to a halt.

'Keys!' demanded Hark.

The nearest trooper handed him a fob of geno-keys and the commissar unlocked Cuu's restraints.

Cuu stood blinking, rubbing his wrists.

'Do you understand the nature of your transgression and renounce it utterly before the eyes of the God-Emperor?'

'I do, sir.'

'Do you accept your guilt and understand it as a measure of the God-Emperor's forgiveness?'

'I do that, sir.'

'Do you promise to stay right out of my damned way, from now on?' Hark snarled, pushing his face into Cuu's.

'You can count on it.'

'Sir?'

'Sir. You can count on it, sir.'

Hark looked away. 'Prisoner is dismissed,' he said. The detail turned on their heels and marched out, Hark behind them.

Cuu crossed to his cot. He sat down and looked along the row at Bragg.

'What?' Bragg said, looking up from the half-oiled firing mechanism he was stripping down.

'You,' said Cuu.

'Me what?' Bragg asked, getting up.

'Let him be, Bragg,' said Fenix.

'He ain't worth it,' said Lubba.

'No, Cuu wants to say something,' said Bragg. 'Cuu, I'm glad Gaunt got you off. I'm glad it wasn't you. Made me sick to think someone in our regiment could do a thing like that.'

'You thought it was me, Bragg. You told them where to look.'

'Yeah,' said Bragg, turning away. 'Those coins… that was your fault.'

'And this is yours,' said Cuu, pulling up his tunic so they could see his narrow back and the bloody welts the lash had made thirty times across his torso.

Four

IT WAS A long way down.

The late afternoon was bringing down a glowering weather pattern: low, dark nimbostratus swollen with rain and a stiff westerly wind. In sympathy, the Scald far below was seething up, churning with firestorms and electrochemical flares.

The driving acid rain was heavy enough to reduce Ouranberg to little more than a grey blur against the ominous sky. But it did little to reduce the scale of the yawning gulf beneath him.

Mkoll edged along the top of the pipeline. There was just enough room on the girders of the support cradle for him to put one foot exactly in front of the next, steadying himself with one hand against the side of the pipe itself. The rain was making everything slick: the metal under his feet, the pipe under his touch. There wasn't much in the way of anything to actually grasp onto except the occasional rivet. It was a matter of steady balance and total concentration.

For the first five hundred metres or so, he'd walked along the top of the great pipe, but then the weather had deteriorated and the rising wind had denied him that option. Walking along the edge of the cradle was much slower going.

He would have preferred not to look down, but it was essential. The girders were scabbed with rust and sticky lichens, and he had to place each step carefully. Below him was a sheer drop down into the toxic depths of Phantine. One slip, one patch of rust or moss, one rain-slick spar, and he would be falling without hope of survival. Mkoll was

pretty sure that if he fell, he would collide with one of the
span's cross members on the way, so at least he wouldn't
know much about it.

He'd already had two close shaves. A sudden gust of
updraft had nearly swept him off. And he'd accidentally trod-
den on one of the vile slug-like things that dwelt in this
dismal place. Thermovores. Bonin and Milo had told him
about them. The thing had squished and his boot had slid
right away in the slime. Too close. Too, too close.

Mkoll figured he was about halfway across. The rain was
getting heavier, sheeting down diagonally, and barks of thunder shook the air. It was almost twilight, and, apart from a
few lights, the city was now utterly invisible.

The rain had brought the slugs out. Mkoll presumed they
derived nutrients from the precipitation, or essential fluids,
or maybe fed on micro-algae dissolved out of the metal by
the rain's high acidity. Feth, he was no biologist! All he knew
for sure was that the metalwork was covered with the disgusting things, ten times the number that had been there at
the start of his crossing, before the rain. He tried not to touch
them and certainly not to tread on them. The latter was difficult. He had to take long strides regularly to step over
writhing piles of them. Twice, he had to use the stock of his
lasrifle to sweep particularly large masses out of his way.

The skinwing presumably mistook him for a rival predator.
Or perhaps it fancied bigger game. He saw it coming right at
the last minute, a scrawny, attenuated rat-like thing with a
ragged, two metre wingspan and a whip-thin tail four metres
long. It flew into his visored face, trilling ultrasonic squeals
frenziedly, and beating its wings at him. Mkoll stumbled,
swung at it with a curse, and slipped off the girder.

He caught the girder edge with his left hand. The impact of
arrest nearly dislocated his shoulder. Mkoll grunted in pain.
His legs pinwheeled, trying to find something to tuck against.
As his left fingertips began to slip off, he got his right hand
on the girder too. His first grab came away with a handful of
thermovores. He shook them off his fingers and got a better
grip. His legs were still dangling and his forearms were on fire
with the effort of gripping the spar and supporting his
weight.

The skinwing came back, attacking him from behind, shrilling so loud his steel helmet vibrated.

'Get the feth off!' he yelled.

Teeth clenched, grunting, he got one elbow up on the girder, then the other, then one boot. Finally, he rolled himself up onto the beam and lay, shaking and choking for breath, face down in a mass of crushed slug-vermin.

He lay there for a long time, trying to slow his racing heart, feeling like he was going to die.

He finally moved again when the skinwing landed on his shoulder and started to gnaw at his neck-seal. He jerked round, caught it by the head and held on tight as it thrashed and fought. He kept his grip on it long enough to pull out his knife and kill it.

Mkoll dropped it off the edge and watched it tumble away, wings and long tail trailing, into the depths. Wretched fething thing had nearly killed him.

Just before it vanished into the clouds far below, an indistinct shape, much, much larger than the skinwing and sleekly black, emerged briefly from the Scald and took it gracefully in mid-air before vanishing again.

Mkoll had no idea what he had just glimpsed. But he became suddenly glad it had only been a skinwing that had decided he might make a meal.

He got up, unsteady and aching, wiped the slime off his tunic front, and resumed his arduous progress.

NESSA PLACED HER hand over Milo's mouth before she woke him. It seemed unfair to disturb him. He was profoundly sleeping, like a child, it seemed to her.

But it was getting on for 20.00 Imperial, and the dusk cycle was beginning. They had to get moving.

Milo woke and looked up at her. She smiled reassuringly and took her hand away, uncovering an answering smile.

He sat up and rubbed his face with his hands. 'You okay?' he whispered.

She didn't reply. He lowered his hands and repeated the whisper so she could see his lips.

'Yes,' she said. Then added, 'Too loud?'

She had difficulty gauging the volume of her own speech.

'That's fine,' he said.

Sneaking away from the slave gang they had mingled with to cross the causeway, they had spent the earlier part of the day progressing across the main mill areas and work yards, avoiding the eagerly searching patrols of the enemy. In the middle part of the afternoon, weary from effort and the sustained tension, they had broken into a derelict tenement hab on the outskirts of Alpha dome to steal a few hours' rest.

Neither of them had mentioned the terrible events of the causeway crossing. Milo hadn't known Doyl well, but he knew the Ghosts had lost a valuable and gifted scout. Adare's death affected him on a more direct, emotional level. Lhurn Adare; sharp, confident and strong, had been a well-liked Tanith and a personal friend. He had been one of Colonel Corbec's sacra-drinking cronies, a die-hard carouser who liked to see the dawn come up with the likes of Varl, Derin, Cown, Domor, Bragg and Brostin. Part of the inner circle, the heart and backbone of the Tanith First. Milo had seen plenty of action at Adare's side, right from the early days. He remembered the relentless practical jokes Adare had played on Baffels and Cluggan. He remembered getting fabulously legless with him the night Adare made sergeant. He remembered Adare's frequent, sound advice.

Now they were both gone. Adare and Doyl. Dead, Milo was sure. Like all the others. Baffels, on Hagia. Cluggan, long gone on Voltemand. Mkoll, in the skies over Ouranberg.

How much longer, Milo wondered, until all the last pieces of Tanith were worn away?

He got to his feet and stretched, trying to shake off the sadness so his mind could be sharp. The bare room was lit by a single chemical lamp that Nessa had dared to ignite because the windows were boarded with sheets of pulp-ply. Her long-las was laid out on her camo-cloak, disassembled. She was using a thimble sewn from vizzy-cloth to polish and oil the firing mechanism.

Milo took out some foil-sealed bag rations and wolfed them down, swigging water from his flask. He noticed his hands were grimed with dust, but didn't care.

He opened the tissue paper schematic of Ouranberg they had all been issued with and studied it again, plotting routes.

'Did you sleep?' he asked, touching her arm first so she knew to look at him.

'A little.'

'Enough?'

'I had a dream,' Nessa said as she worked on her sniping piece.

'A dream?' he asked.

'I dreamed Colonel Corbec and Sergeant Soric came to find us. They were alive.'

'They probably are,' Milo said. 'I mean, we don't know.'

'No, but they were close to dying when we left. It's one thing to lose someone in battle. It's another to leave them dying and then never know... never find out...'

'We'll find out. They'll be waiting for us when we get back. Soric will be full of jokes and terribly proud of you. Corbec will have a bottle of sacra open and be demanding I dig out my pipes for a tune or two.'

'Why will Soric be proud of me?' she asked.

'Because you will have put a hot-shot between Slaith's eyes.'

She laughed. 'It's good to know you have such confidence in me. And that you can see into the future, Brin.'

'It's a gift I have.'

She shook her head with a chuckle and started to slide her long-las together. Her hands worked with economical practice, clicking the components together. Milo doubted he could have reassembled a lasrifle in twice the time.

He watched her. She was commonly regarded as the most beautiful woman in the Ghosts, though the men had their favourites: Muril, Arilla, Banda, Solia, Ellan, Criid and, when they were drunk or in pain enough to actually dare admit it, Ana Curth. Criid and Banda were thought to be the most alluring, though it often impressed Milo that Criid was firmly considered out of bounds even in terms of conversational fantasy because of her tie to Caffran. Nessa wasn't sexy in the same way Banda or Solia were. It was partly her quietness, itself a scar of warfare. But it was mostly her fine-boned, stunning face, the perfect angles of her cheeks and nose and the deep blue of her eyes. Her streaming, glossy hair had seemed to be a key part of her appeal. That was gone now, and she was still utterly beautiful. Her hair was just beginning to grow in again, a fine down-like felt. The lack of hair emphasised her sculptural features.

Her eyes came up and caught his. 'What's so interesting?' she asked.

Milo shook his head.

He looked away, and saw a small slab of pulp-ply leaning against the wall. A knife tip had cut the words 'Nessa Bourah, 341.748 to 225.771 M41.' into it.

'What the feth is that?' he asked.

'Just a habit,' she replied.

'It's a fething grave marker!'

'Relax, Brin. We did it every day during the scratch fighting. I never got out of the habit.'

Milo shook his head, puzzled. 'You'll have to explain more than that,' he said.

She put down her long-las and faced him. 'We were going to die. Every day, fighting the guerilla war in the ruined out-habs of Vervunhive, we were going to die. The death rate was awful. So we got into the habit of carving our own grave markers in what little downtime there was. If we died, you see, there would be a marker ready. Easy. Simple. A quickly dug slit-trench, a scatter of earth over the body, a prayer... and a marker ready and waiting.'

'That's terrible.'

'That's... the way it was.' She paused and cleared her throat quietly. Then she continued, 'It became routine, and people started putting the next morning's date on the markers, as if daring fate to take them. It was a joke at first. A bad, dark joke. Then someone, I don't remember who, pointed out that, as a rule, the fighters who carved the next day's date as their death date survived.'

'Survived?'

'The sensible ones who left the death date blank tended to die. Those that gleefully etched in that the next day would be their last... lived. So they'd have to scrap the marker and make a new one because the date was wrong. After a week or two, it became a habit, a lucky charm. We all did it, daring the gods, or daemons or whatever rules the cosmic order, to make our grave markers useless.'

'And you still do it?'

She nodded. 'At times like this, I do.'

'I feel like I should make one,' he said.

'Only works for Verghastites, I'm afraid,' she said.

'Damn shame...' he grinned.

And froze.

He could hear a knocking, scraping sound from the floor below. Seeing his look, Nessa got up and loaded a cell magazine into her long-las.

Slowly, listening, Milo lifted his cannon.

More knocking, a crash.

Let's go, he signed.

They gathered up their kit rapidly, keeping an eye on the door. Nessa extinguished the lamp.

In the sudden, blue gloom, Milo gestured to the back door with his thumb, they moved slowly, silently towards it, weapons ready, camo-cloaks draped around them.

Milo gently pulled back the pulp-ply boarding the nearest window.

Three platoons of Blood Pact were assembling in the square outside.

Another search-patrol. Ever since Adare and Doyl had been discovered, the enemy had been scouring the mill district for other Imperial interlopers. The public address system had broadcast imploring appeals to 'find the vermin', alternating with demands that the 'Imperial scum' give themselves up.

Milo and Nessa backed to the rear door. They were expecting Blood Pact.

But it wasn't.

The hab-room door splintered in, exploded by some powerful shotgun blast, and the first loxatl scurried through.

In the half-light, Milo got a glimpse of a sinuous, grey body with a flat, snouted head and a short, muscular tail. It came in and went up the wall, dewclaws ripped into the plaster to gather purchase. An augmetic limb-frame strapped around its mottled belly tracked around the pepper-pot nose of an alien scattergun.

A second loxatl slithered in through the door and clawed its way rapidly up the other wall. Milo could smell spearmint mixed with sour milk.

Its bionic weapon-frame clicked around, sweeping the room. It aimed at Milo, shooting out a dull green aiming light that splashed on his cloak.

Nessa's long-las roared.

The second alien mercenary was ripped off the wall by the hot-shot and smashed, convulsing, into the doorframe.

The other one fired its weapon. A huge hole was chewed out of the pressed-fibre panelling beside Milo.

He opened fire, lurched back for a moment by the U90's almost unmanageable recoil.

The hi-ex AP rounds blew the lizard thing apart and hosed the wall with its unwholesome blood. Its smoking carcass fell off the wall and slammed onto the floor.

'Feth!' he heard Nessa scream. The creature she had shot was lurching up again, sweeping its flechette blaster towards Milo.

Milo emptied the rest of the drum mag into the second loxatl, pulping its head and chest.

He looked round at Nessa.

Come on! he signed. She nodded and pulled him towards the doorway the loxatl had come through. Trusting her, Milo realised she was right. The Blood Pact squads were storming up the rear of the hab, intending to pick off any fleeing stragglers the loxatl had missed.

No one was expecting anybody to exit from the front of the building.

Nessa and Milo, hand in hand, raced out of the hab tenement, and sprinted away towards the forbidding shells of residence blocks on the far side of the square.

In the hab behind them, Nessa's grave marker lay crushed under the bulk of a dead loxatl.

THEY'D HAD TO wait the best part of the day for a chance to sneak back to the air wharf, where it took them just ninety seconds to commandeer the carrier. Banda's long-shot took out the driver, and Bonin and Varl did the rest with warknives.

Jagdea ran forward across the air wharf and heaved the driver's corpse out of its seat.

'Do we leave them here?' Unterrio asked, nodding at the dead bodies.

'No, get them aboard,' said Vadim.

They hefted up the heretics' corpses and threw them on to the carrier's cargo bed.

It was a light hauler, with a roofed cabin section and a tarp-covered payload bay. Jagdea got behind the controls as the rest of Larisel 1 finished lugging the dead onto the vehicle's bay and climbed aboard.

'Commander?' Varl prompted.

'Just familiarising myself with the layout,' she said.

Expertly, Jagdea launched them, and they flew down a canyon of habs towards the porta of Alpha dome.

AT JUST ABOUT the same time, far to the north-west, Mkoll was scaling the granite outcrop where the pipeline finally joined Ouranberg. It was dark, freezing cold, and the wind was fearful, but he felt triumphant. He had made it all the way across.

Now all he had to do was get inside.

CONVOYS OF TRANSPORT vehicles loaded with munitions for Alpha dome's air defences had been rumbling down the access routes non-stop for over an hour. Larisel 2 had been forced into hiding until the activity died down. They waited, with nervy impatience, in the basement of a burned-out Ministorum chapel.

Kuren watched the door, armed with Meryn's U90. In the course of the day they'd seen plenty of the vile loxatl mercenaries accompanying the Blood Pact patrols.

'This remind you of anything?' Mkvenner said. He'd been searching through the broken litter that covered the basement floor, and now held up a cheap plaster figurine, one of a dozen he'd found in a box.

'It's a memento of Saint Phidolas, who led the first settlers to Phantine,' said Kersherin. 'Every church on the planet sells cheap souvenirs like it. For the pilgrims.'

'Yeah,' said Mkvenner, 'but what else?'

'I don't know…' said Kersherin.

Mkvenner casually smacked the figurine against a pillar, smashing off its head and upper body.

'How about now?'

They all looked at it, like it was a joke and they were ready for the punchline.

'Feth,' said Larkin suddenly. 'It was behind Slaith.'

'Right,' said Mkvenner.

'What?' Meryn snapped. 'Behind Slaith? What are you talking about?'

'When he was on the screen,' said Larkin, 'when he… he showed us Cardinale… there was a big window behind him and a ruined statue outside.'

'I don't remember any statue,' Kuren said.

'There was a statue,' said Mkvenner. 'Ruined. Right outside his windows.'

The scout turned the broken figurine over and examined a label on the bottom.

'An image of Saint Phidolas,' he read, 'copied from the great statue that may be seen in the Imperial concourse, Alpha dome, Ouranberg.'

'Well, well, well…' Meryn chuckled.

'I DON'T LIKE the look of this,' Jagdea said.

'Keep going,' Bonin told her. He was riding next to her in the hauler's cab.

They had got through the porta into Alpha dome with remarkable ease, and joined an access route that had seemed busy enough for them to blend in. Varl hoped they might get as far as the dome's core districts by midnight.

But the traffic was slowing, and armoured Blood Pact airspeeders with rotating orange lamps were forcing all vehicles down to road level so that they could be channelled through a check station.

'We need to get off this route,' said Jagdea. They were barely crawling, following the tail of a large munitions truck.

'They'll see us if we try and break away. Besides, the route has no obvious intersections.'

'Well, I don't think going through that checkpoint is going to be an especially healthy idea!' she hissed.

'Sarge?' Bonin called back through the mesh partition to Varl. 'Any stunningly good suggestions from you?'

Varl peered down the line of near stationary traffic ahead and behind them. The six-lane route itself was open, with little cover, and thirty storey tenements rose on either side. Not the place for a firefight.

He cursed himself. Using the hauler had been a smart idea, and it had saved them a lot of time. But Jagdea and Bonin had advised him to ditch it once they were inside Alpha dome. Varl had wanted to press on, to see how far they could get. He felt stupid now, like he'd let them down. Even though Gol Kolea was nowhere around, the Kolea-Varl devil-dare rivalry had landed them in this fix. Gol had been the hero at Cirenholm. Shutting down the power plant like that had effectively won the battle for them. He'd triumphed that round. When Operation Larisel came up, all Varl had been able to think of was that this might be his turn. His turn to be the hero. Devil-dare, Kolea! How d'you like that?

So he'd pushed them on, far further than they should ever have gone out in the open like this. He had pushed them so they would reach Slaith and be heroes. 'Stupid' didn't even begin to cover it.

'There's a road to the left, about seventy metres up,' Varl said through the mesh.

'I see it,' said Jagdea dubiously.

'We keep rolling forward like this, up to the checkpoint, and then break left fast and exit.'

'Just like that?'

'Commander, I have absolute faith in your ability to drive this thing like it was a Lightning on afterburner. We get down there, ditch this cart and go to ground.'

'That's your plan?' asked Unterrio.

'Yes, it fething is,' said Varl. 'We all clear?'

'What happens if they rumble us before we reach the turn?' asked Jagdea.

'Okay…' Varl said. 'We pull out of the queue anyway. Fly straight at the tenement.'

'What?'

'I've got hi-ex loaded. I'll make a hole. We'll get inside the building and then ditch and cover there. Okay? Clear?'

The traffic line crept forward. The air was thick with exhaust fumes and the sound of dozens of engines. An airspeeder droned by overhead, flying down the queue.

Incomprehensible instructions boomed out of an amplifier at the checkpoint.

'Foot troops!' Bonin whispered sharply.

'Where?' asked Varl.

'Walking down the line towards us. On the median strip. There, by the crash barrier.'

'Oh feth.'

'They're checking papers,' Jagdea said. She tugged off her gloves, wiped her sweating hands dry on her jacket, and then gripped the wheel and the throttle lever again, tensed and ready.

'Wait for it. Wait for it,' Varl said. Banda, Vadim and Unterrio raised their weapons to their shoulders. Bonin put his laspistol on his lap.

'They may not come down this far,' Banda whispered hopefully.

The vehicles moved forward again, another few metres. A Blood Pact officer, standing on the route's central barrier, waved the three trucks immediately in front of them on with a torch stick.

Then he stepped out into their path and held up a hand.

'Shit!' said Jagdea.

Four more Blood Pact troopers and a slaver with a team of hate-dogs approached behind the officer. He walked towards the hauler.

'We're blown,' announced Bonin.

'I know!' said Varl. 'Wait to the last possible moment...'

The officer stepped up to the cab and peered in. They could smell his body odour and see his blood-shot eyes through the slits of his iron mask. He began to ask something in a language they didn't understand and then stopped as he saw Bonin and Jagdea and their Imperial combat gear.

'Go!' said Bonin, and shot the officer through the head with his pistol.

Jagdea threw the hauler out of the line, engaging the throttle so hard that Unterrio was thrown off his feet in the back. The air-truck screamed across the route towards the tenements as shouts, sirens and shots rang out after it. Heavy fire from an air-speeder stitched plumes of debris from the road surface as it tried to track them.

'Varl!' Jagdea screamed. The front of the tenement was approaching very fast.

Varl threw back the tarp and stood up so he could fire over the roof of the cab. He had to fight to stay upright. They were going to hit the wall in scant seconds.

He fired the U90 and created a rippling blister of overlapping explosions that blew the ground floor facade in.

They went through the hole.

Almost.

Varl had barely ducked in again when an overhang of brick caught the tarp of the speeding machine and ripped the entire cover frame off. That tipped the nose up and spun the back end out. The left rear engine mount sheared off against an exposed metal beam and a considerable portion of the hauler's underside shredded away.

The tenement's ground floor was one great, open space used for storage and presently empty, except for the metre square rockcrete pillars every thirty paces.

The stricken machine flew into the store-space almost sidelong. It hit the floor once with boneshaking force, bounced up under its own headlong momentum, and then impacted again, shrieking along the floor in an astonishing wake of sparks and fragmenting metal.

It hit the first pillar head-on with enough force to spin it off the ground and leave it crumpled and smoking, facing the way it had come.

Varl and Banda had both been thrown clear and lay unconscious on the ground nearby. Unterrio got to his feet and tried to get Vadim up. The young Verghastite had struck his head and was out cold.

'Come on! Come on!' Unterrio screamed.

Bonin came round. He was hanging out of the shattered cab section. It took him a moment to work out what was going on. He could hear Unterrio shouting.

Jagdea, saved by her harness belt, was alive but semi conscious. Bonin fought with her harness and began to drag her out.

Powerful searchlights lanced in through the street windows and the hole. Silhouetted against them, figures were surging in.

Unterrio leapt out of the carrier and opened fire with his lascarbine.

'Bonin! Get them clear! Get them clear!' he was shouting.

Bonin tried to work out how he could get four semi conscious people clear of anything. Banda was coming round, weeping with rage and pain, clutching a broken wrist.

Jagdea suddenly opened her eyes and looked up at Bonin with distant confusion. 'I keep crashing things,' she said weakly. 'I don't like it.'

'Jagdea!'

She began to pass out again, and murmured. 'I smell... milk. Bonin, I smell milk and mint...'

A flechette blaster roared and Unterrio's defiant stand came to a sudden, explosive end.

Something small and hard and metallic landed near to Bonin and came skittering to rest.

For a second, he thought it was a grenade, but then he realised it was a synapse mine.

'Run!' he howled, though he was pretty sure no one was in any state to obey.

The mine went off with a silent flash, like a falling star, that flared for a moment, bright and then went out.

And as he collapsed, paralysed, Bonin knew that his own lucky star had finally gone out too.

Five

IT WAS MIDNIGHT on the 225th. The massed forces of Operation Thunderhead were beginning to leave Cirenholm, streaming in convoy out into the night, heading for Ouranberg.

The vast bomber waves went out first with their interceptor escorts. It was a clear night, and up in the cockpits of the Magogs, it seemed to the aircrews like they were part of new constellations issuing from the city.

The drogues that would convey the main army forces began to depart, sliding up into the cold night air in the wake of the bombers, rotor blades chopping. Thunderbolt escorts cruised in beside them. The drogues *Zephyr*, *Aeolus* and *Trenchant*, heavy with Krassian and Urdeshi infantry regiments, headed out on a long path that would eventually turn them west to assault the main airwharfs and drome structure of Ouranberg.

The Ghosts were boarding the *Nimbus*, which, as part of a pack of six drogues, would convey the main assault force of Tanith, Phantine and Urdeshi to the southern face of Ouranberg.

O-Day. By dawn the next day, all hell would be unleashed.

Gaunt checked his despatch orders for a final time, signed them, and handed them to Beltayn, who hurried them off to Van Voytz. Rawne, Daur, Hark and the other senior officers waited for him outside the office. He rose, put on his cap, and led the Tanith commanders onto the main troop deck. No word had yet come from any Larisel group. He wondered how many of them might still be alive.

On the massive troop deck, thousands of battle-ready Ghosts were being conducted in prayer by ayatani Zweil.

Zweil saw the officers approach, and finished his reading from *The Gospel of Saint Sabbat*. He closed the old book and smoothed his robes.

'Let me say this, finally,' he projected, loud and effortless. 'To you all, so you know it and keep it in your minds through the danger that faces you. And let me say it now, before he does.' Zweil indicated Gaunt with a casual thumb and laughter rippled through the ranks. 'The Emperor protects. Know that, remember that, and he will.'

Zweil turned to Gaunt. 'All yours,' he said. He made the sign of the aquila and blessed Gaunt with a few words, and then went down the line of officers, repeating the same.

'It appears the venerable father has stolen my line,' Gaunt said, facing the Ghosts. There was more laughter. 'So let me tell you this. Colonel Corbec and Sergeant Soric are both out of danger.'

A considerable cheer went up. Gaunt raised a hand. 'They are expected to make good recoveries. So remember this. I'd like the first news they hear from their infirmary beds to be word that Ouranberg has fallen and that the Ghosts have acquitted themselves bravely. That sort of news will heal them faster than any drug Doc Dorden or Surgeon Curth can give them. What do you say?'

The cheers were deafening.

'Men of Tanith, men of Verghast–'

'And women!' Criid shouted.

Gaunt smiled. 'And women. I often ask you if you want to live forever. I won't tonight. I expect to see you all again this time tomorrow, raising the standard of the Tanith First above Ouranberg. Death is not an option. Fight hard and give the God-Emperor of Mankind the victory he asks of you all.'

Almost drowned out by the applause and the shouting, Gaunt turned to Hark.

'Viktor? Inform the admiral we're ready to cast off.'

THIS TIME, THE medics were going in with the troop assault. Curth's medi-pack was fully prepped, but she was struggling with the body armour Gaunt had issued.

'You've got the buckles misaligned,' said Kolea, coming into the drogue's hospital behind her.

'Really?' she said sourly, looking like a patient half-escaped from a strait jacket.

'Here, let me,' he said, stepping forward to fit her armour properly.

'Shouldn't you be on the troop decks?' she asked.

'Yes. But I had to see you first. I have a favour to ask.'

'Go on then.'

'How's that?' he said stepping back. She flexed her arms and patted the plated front of her armour vest. 'Excellent. Thank you. Now what's this favour?'

'You know I promised to tell Criid and Caffran about…'

'Yes.'

'That I'd do it after Ouranberg was done.'

'Yes.'

'And you know I'm not looking for that reunion round.'

'Yes, I do. Come on.'

'I don't think I'm going to be coming back from Ouranberg,' he said.

She gazed at his face. It was unreadable. 'What?'

'Listen to me, I'm not looking to find death, but I think it might be looking for me now. It's let me off too many times recently. I'm not saying I'm going to do something foolhardy, but it's a feeling I have. Now I've made up my mind to tell Criid, I think death might be hoping to cheat me.'

'Feth, aren't you the fatalist?' She gripped him by the shoulders firmly and looked up into his eyes. 'You are not going to die, Gol. You are not going to let death take you.'

'I'll do my best. But I have this feeling. This feeling Gol Kolea's not going to come back from Ouranberg. You've been gakking good to me, Ana. I have this last favour to ask.'

He took a sealed letter out of his tunic pocket and handed it to her. 'If I don't come back, give this to Criid. It's all there. Everything.'

She looked at the letter. 'And if you do?'

'Burn it. I'll be able to tell her and Caffran what was in that letter myself.'

'Okay,' she said, and slid the letter into her fatigue's pocket.

'Thanks,' he said simply.

She rose up on tip-toe, put a hand behind his neck to pull him lower and kissed his cheek softly.

'Come back, Gol,' she said. 'Make me burn it.'

IN OURANBERG, DRUMS were beating. Long range auspex had detected the mass formations of air machines moving out from Cirenholm, and the Blood Pact was preparing for war. There was a sense of relief, that the hour had finally come. The preachers on the address-systems spouted their last blasphemies and then fell silent.

The address screens fizzled with white noise.

The invasion was coming.

ON ALPHA DOME's Imperial concourse, a fifty acre rockcrete plaza in front of the central administratum palace, thousands of can-fires had been lit and the standard of the Blood Pact raised alongside the disturbing, semi-sentient fronds of algae the loxatl used as banners.

A rotund bronze cauldron, three metres across, had been set at the top of the palace steps, under the flags, below the desecrated statue of Saint Phidolas. Devotees of the warp-cult, Blood Pact troops and confused citizens were spilling into the concourse from all sides.

Blood Pact slavers led the prisoners out. There were fifty of them, all chained together, all beaten down and despairing. They were whipped to the base of the steps and ordered to sit.

Larisel 1 was amongst them. Bonin was chained up next to Jagdea, his head still swimming from the effects of the numbing synapse mine. She looked like she might pass out any minute.

Bonin could see Varl three rows away, and Vadim, both sullen and dazed. A little searching found Banda. The chains were chafing at her snapped wrist and she was ashen with pain.

Bonin and Jagdea were in the front row of the prisoners. At the head of their chain was Cardinale. Bonin barely recognised the Phantine specialist. Cardinale was very close to death.

The other prisoners were Imperial servants, captured aircrew or Ouranberg nobility.

Jagdea was staring at a man in the row opposite them. He was dressed in ragged Phantine flight-crew uniform, and his shoulder and neck were blotched with dried blood and signs of pollution burns.

'Viltry?' she said.

'Commander Jagdea?' he mumbled, looking up askance.

'God! I thought you were dead! What happened?'

'Lost my bird over the Southern Scald, thought I was windwaste… then one of Slaith's supply ships picked me up.'

'Golden Throne!' she said. 'It's good to see you!'

Viltry laughed darkly. 'Here? I don't think so.'

'We're not dead yet, Viltry,' Jagdea said. 'Someone once told me that death comes when it comes and only a fool would bring it early.'

'What kind of simple-minded crap is that?' Viltry said.

Jagdea looked across at Bonin and smiled. A weary smile, but not a defeated one. 'The best kind, I believe. All I'm saying is that it's only over when it's over.'

'Oh, for us, it's over,' Viltry said sourly. He gestured at the bronze cauldron.

'What is this about?' Bonin asked him.

'The invasion must be coming,' Viltry said. 'Slaith intends to symbolically renew his blood pact with Urlock Gaur so he can be strong when he meets the Imperial assault. We're the sacrifice. That cauldron… we're supposed to fill it. With our blood. Slaith will help, of course.'

'Feth…' murmured Bonin. 'I wondered why he hadn't killed us yet.' He looked at the huge bronze bowl. It was going to take an awful lot of blood to fill it.

Fifty prisoners, five litres each. That should do it.

THE CEREMONY BEGAN. Hundreds of Blood Pact warriors and dozens of loxatl flooded down the steps from the palace, passing the plinth of the shattered statue of Saint Phidolas, and stood aside as Sagittar Slaith descended.

They were beating their scarred fists against their weapons, and the clamour raised thundering applause from the gathered audience of thousands.

Slaith, magnificent in his armour and white fur, kissed the side of the bronze cauldron, and lifted the glinting, ritual adze.

Blood Pact troopers dragged Cardinale up the steps, pulling the chain of prisoners after him. Bonin and Jagdea found themselves yanked along closer to the foot of the steps.

Slaith raised the adze and bellowed arcane words. Cardinale was draped over the edge of the cauldron and held down by two slavers.

'BEFORE HE LOPS Cardinale, if you wouldn't mind,' Meryn hissed in Larkin's ear.

'Shut up and let me concentrate,' Larkin said. From the roof of the Ouranberg stock exchange, he had a perfect view over the Imperial concourse. There was zero wind, but the range was long. Larkin adjusted his sights, and wished he had been given the opportunity for a test round.

'Come on, Larks, you can do it,' Kuren said.

'I'd shut up, if I were you,' Larkin heard Mkvenner say. 'He's doing his thing.'

Below, Slaith declaimed something else and quickly raised the adze over Cardinale's exposed nape.

'Larks!' Meryn urged.

A hot-shot round sang out over the concourse and smashed into Slaith.

'Feth!' said Larkin. 'That wasn't me!'

Mkvenner looked up. Pandemonium had instantly overtaken the crowd below, and the Blood Pact were surging towards the eastern side of the concourse.

'It came from over there,' Mkvenner said, pointing to the Munitorium blocks that flanked the east edge of the square.

Larkin trained his long-las again, staring through the scope. He saw Slaith getting back to his feet beside the cauldron.

'Feth! He's got a personal shield!' Larkin said.

'Hit him anyway!' Meryn demanded.

Larkin fired, and Slaith was slammed over onto his back. At the same moment, a second hot-shot stabbed in from the Munitorium and clipped the edge of the cauldron. Then a third hit Slaith on the ground.

'Now we're in trouble,' Kersherin said.

Blood Pact and loxatl were tearing through the crowd towards the foot of the stock exchange.

Larkin fired again, hitting Slaith cleanly. But the warlord got up, assisted by his men. His personal shield had held.

'He's las-proof,' Larkin said.

'I suggest we get out of here,' said Meryn.

'No,' said Larkin, taking aim again. 'Wait...'

ON THE TOP floor of the Munitorium block, Nessa fell back from the window and looked at Milo.

'He's shielded! I hit him twice!'

'Okay, let's go. We did what we could.'

They ran to the exit door. Milo could hear boots thundering up the stairs towards them.

MASS PANIC HAD overtaken the square. People were fleeing everywhere. Bonin looked round at Jagdea and started to say something when he was lurched back by a powerful jerk on the chain. A pin-point las-round of extraordinary accuracy had severed the chain between them.

Bonin leapt to his feet and threw himself on the nearest Blood Pact guard, choking him with the dangling end of the slave-chain. As the red-clad warrior collapsed, Bonin grabbed his weapon.

It was a standard las. Good enough. Bonin gunned down three Blood Pact who ran towards him and then started firing at the enemy troops on the steps. Jagdea struggled forward and grabbed another of the fallen enemy weapons. She started to shoot away the chains confining the other prisoners.

'Death comes when it comes and only a fool would bring it early, eh?' Bonin yelled at her. 'What idiot told you that?'

'We get out of this mess alive, Bonin,' she shouted back, 'and I'll tell you!'

'And believe me,' she added, shooting a charging slaver through the head and shattering his iron visor. 'I intend to get out of this alive if it's the last thing I do.'

Bonin laughed aloud, and drove the fight towards the bewildered enemy.

FLANKED BY A bodyguard of three Blood Pact officers and two loxatl, Sagittar Slaith hurried back into the palace. He was cursing and swearing, bruised and shaken by the savage hits his personal shield had taken.

As he stormed back into his private apartment, the floor began to shake. It was nearly dawn and overhead the first waves of bombers had reached Ouranberg. Slaith turned slowly to his officers, smouldering with his infamous rage. The Blood Pact shook behind their iron grotesques, and even the xenos warriors closed their nictating han lids. Slaith opened his mouth, but it was not his fury that hit them.

A rain of shots from a lasrifle on full auto killed the Blood Pact officers instantly and exploded harmlessly off Slaith's screen and the reflective hides of the two loxatl.

There was a human standing in the rear doorway of the room. An Imperial soldier half-shrouded in a ragged camo-cape, his lasrifle aimed at them.

'Where the hell did you come from?' Slaith raged.

'Tanith,' said Mkoll, and fired again.

Slaith walked forward through the blasts unharmed, the flinching loxatl at his side, double-lids shut against the las-shots, armature cycling up their flechette cannons.

'A lasgun?' said Slaith. 'I'm shielded and the loxatl soak up las-fire. You're out of luck. You should have been better prepared.'

'Oh, this is just a distraction,' said Mkoll, gesturing with his lasrifle. 'The real surprise is under that table.'

The loxatl flechette guns spat their hails of lethal sub-munitions and exploded the doorway and the wall around it. Mkoll was already diving headlong out of sight.

Slaith stooped and peered under the table. What he saw was six tube charges wired together on a timer.

'No!' he screamed. 'Nooooooo!'

THE DETONATION TOOK the roof off the state room. Slaith's personal shield managed to hold for 1.34 seconds before it was overwhelmed by the blast force.

Sagittar Slaith was still screaming with rage as he vaporised.

Six

PHANTINE, WITH ITS oceanic skies and tempestuous Scald, was a planet of storms, but the greatest storm that morning was the human one that engulfed Ouranberg.

In the pale, violet light of dawn, columns of dense black smoke and spiralling fireballs crowned the city, and the air streamed with las-fire, tracer shells and streaking rockets. Swarms of attack craft, like plagues of insects, buzzed over the domes through the crackling blossoms of flak. Raging infernos glowed dull red through ragged holes in the main domes.

Preceded by diving packs of Shrikes, the main force of drogues and troop barges assaulted the Imperial landing platform and the expanse of Pavia Fields behind it, setting down thousands of Imperial Guardsmen under withering fire from the fortifications of Ourangate and the Alpha dome emplacements. The gun turrets of the barges chattered and flashed as they hovered in, their gate-ramps crashing down to disgorge charging troops or the clanking Chimeras and Manticores of the Urdeshi Seventh Armoured.

The noise was total. A dreadful blur of sound out of which individual noises could hardly be distinguished. As the ramp of his own barge came down, Gaunt led his men out with urgent waves of his power sword. They were never going to hear his voice.

Urdeshi units took the landing platform after a brutal series of firefights and horrific hand to hand encounters. The Ghosts of Tanith, led to the west by Major Rawne and to the east by Captain Daur, pincered the Blood Pact ground forces defending the Avenue of the Polyandrons, and opened the way to Ourangate itself.

The drogue *Skyro*, supported by Marauder gunships, manoeuvred in over Beta dome and roped Phantine and Urdeshi troops down onto the main vapour mill. A brigade personally led by Major Fazalur took and held the main mill complex against bitter resistance until Gaunt broke through Ourangate and moved Tanith and Urdeshi elements to relieve him.

To the east, the secondary assault poured into the city's main drome. For about an hour, the fighting there was the most intense and furious of the whole battle. The Krassians were driven back twice until the resolve of the Blood Pact finally snapped. After that it was a rout.

The cost was high. Nearly two thousand Imperial Guardsmen were killed, the majority of them Krassian and Urdeshi. Forty aircraft were lost. The drogue *Aeolus*, heroically staying on station to ensure that the Krassian units could get enough troops down for their third and final push into the dome, was hammered by Ouranberg's western batteries and eventually listed, rudderless and on fire, towards Gamma dome where it foundered and exploded. The entire crew perished. The colossal explosion shot a vast doughnut of burning gas up into the air and scorched the west face of Gamma dome black.

But Imperial victory was pretty much guaranteed from the moment that word of Slaith's death began to spread through the enemy forces. The Blood Pact kept fighting, and in many ways became more savage. They were lost, and that made them suicidally vengeful.

Slaith's demise certainly did not rob them of their courage. But their coordination and discipline were gone. Without Slaith, they were like a brain-dead body, still twitching with involuntary responses.

Van Voytz had known all along that Ouranberg would be hard to capture, nigh on impossible, in fact, if he was to keep the vital vapour mills intact. As fighting raged through the hab-domes of the city, and report after report came in of losses and casualties, he consoled himself with the knowledge that it could have been a hundred times worse. His gamble with Operation Larisel had paid off. If Slaith had still been alive at the start of the assault, chances were the

date 226.771 M41 would have been remembered as a tragic
Imperial defeat.

IT DIDN'T FEEL like victory on the ground in the streets of
Alpha dome. Fierce fighting continued until well into the
evening. Whole hab-blocks were on fire, and in places the
roadways had collapsed through into lower dome levels.

Gaunt led from the front, directly deploying his units into
the heart of the dome. Squads under Bray, Burone, Theiss and
Daur had secured a vital inner bascule and overrun a string of
well-made Blood Pact emplacements. There were rumours
that inside the domes the citizens of Ouranberg were rising
up against their oppressors. Gaunt saw nothing of that, only
hundreds of terrified civilians fleeing the main centres of
fighting.

His primary concern was not the overall victory. Van Voytz
could worry about that. As soon as he was within range, he
made repeated efforts to contact the Larisel elements and was
heartened to find that some of them at least were still alive.
Beltayn relayed broken transmissions from Meryn's team,
which had linked up with the survivors from Varl's Larisel 1
and were now besieged in the refectory of Ouranberg's
Scholam Progenium near the Imperial concourse.

Gaunt swore to them he would break through and secure
them. He pushed Rawne's elements to his left flank, supported by Urdeshi armour, and sent Haller, Maroy and
Ewler's units to the right.

The right flank approach was hopeless. Maroy reported
heavy resistance in the eastern market area. Rawne fared little
better. His forces – the sections commanded by Kolea, Obel
and Mkfin and a brigade of Urdeshi under young Shenko –
ran foul of the loxatl and got caught up in a period of ugly
street-fighting that lasted over two hours.

Gaunt himself managed to cut through eventually, leading
the platoons of Domor, Skerral and Mkendrick along with
forty-five Urdeshi pioneers and the units that had, until
Cirenholm, been led by Corbec and Soric. These last two
were temporarily commanded by Raglon and Arcuda, and
Gaunt kept the inexperienced leaders close. He needn't have
worried. Arcuda displayed a tactical gift that made Gaunt

wish he'd advanced the man sooner, and Raglon was as confident and assured as he might have hoped. Raglon had come a long way from junior vox-carrier.

They broke through a half-defended line of buildings and saw off a loxatl counter-attack with their flamers. Dremmond and Lyse led the flamer repulse against the vile xenos mercenaries. They had a fantastic resistance to laser rounds, but fled moaning from the flames. With Nittori from his own platoon still injured, Gaunt had allowed Lyse to take his role. She was the first female flame-trooper in the regiment, another notable achievement for the Verghastites.

Just after 14.00 Imperial, Gaunt's force caught Blood Pact elements on the Imperial concourse from the side, put them to flight and relieved the besieged Ghosts in the scholam. Despite the fighting that continued to rattle outside as the Urdeshi stormed the main palace, Gaunt took the time to greet them all personally, and thank them for their bravery and determination.

Of the sixteen Ghosts and their four Urdeshi Specialists who had gone in as Operation Larisel, they appeared to be the only survivors. Banda, with a shattered wrist. Scout-trooper Bonin and Sergeant Varl, both wounded badly in the mayhem of fighting that had followed Slaith's death. Vadim, seriously concussed from the truck crash. Larkin, crying quietly with the pain of the migraine that had finally conquered him. Mkvenner, Kuren and Sergeant Meryn, all battered but miraculously intact. Specialist Kersherin, the only Skyborne who had survived. Commander Jagdea, who praised in particular Bonin's efforts to free and protect the captives during the running firefight, including a pilot named Viltry and Specialist Cardinale.

Cardinale, Gaunt learned, had perished from his terrible wounds during the siege.

Gaunt called up immediate medicae support for them and tried not to think about the ones who hadn't made it. Rilke, Cocoer, Nour, Doyl, Adare, Nessa, Mkoll... Milo.

Fifteen minutes later, Arcuda voxed Gaunt to say his men had found Milo and Nessa alive on the roof of the Ministry of Vapour Export. Gaunt closed his eyes. The Emperor protects.

Almost as an afterthought, he turned back to the survivors and asked, 'By the way... who made the shot in the end? Larkin?'

'None of us did,' said Meryn. 'Larkin hit the bastard several times, and so did Nessa I think. But he was shielded.'

'Then how the feth–?'

Gaunt's unfinished question was finally answered late that afternoon, when Urdeshi units searching the ruins of the palace found a lone Tanith scout unconscious in the rubble.

His tags said his name was Mkoll.

RAWNE'S FORCES WERE being hammered by the loxatl in the palatial habs west of the Alpha dome heartland. The aliens were using some kind of heavy fragmentation mortar, perhaps a larger-scale version of their signature flechette blasters. Obel had pressed his unit forward, and Bragg had managed to hose one loxatl position with cannonfire, but the deadly shells were still whooping down.

With Troopers Lubba and Jajjo, Gol Kolea had broken through the back wall of a ransacked kitchen into some kind of service tunnel that allowed them to advance right up to flank the main loxatl dug-outs. Emerging from the tunnel, hunched low, Kolea could hear the regular *punk-shiff!* of the loxatl mortars, and a human voice screaming for a medic.

The trio ran low across debris-littered rockcrete and scooted behind an exploded water main that was weeping frothy water into the road.

Caffran was lying on his back in a nearby shell-hole. His leg was lacerated with loxatl barb shrapnel.

'Don't be daft, sarge!' Lubba yelped, but Kolea was already running.

Flechette shot winnowed the air around him and he threw himself into the shell-hole.

'How's it going, Caff?' he asked.

'Kolea. Feth, it hurts. The fething alien freaks have got the end of the roadway locked up.'

Kolea looked at the wounds. 'Nasty, but the medicae are on the way. You'll live, Caffran.'

'I don't care about that!' Caffran said. 'I care about Tona!'

'What?'

'Rawne sent us all forward. I got caught here, she went on with Allo and Jenk. I think they were hit too. I can't reach her on the vox.'

'Oh gak,' Kolea said, peering out of the shell-hole. 'Stay here,' he said, as if Caffran was in any state to move.

'Sarge!'

'What?'

Caffran swallowed back his pain. 'Why... why did you come to me when I was arrested? You were acting so... so strange. When Tona came to visit me she gave me hell for getting into such a stupid fix. But I knew she was just frightened. You, though... it was like you were really afraid I'd actually done that stuff to that poor woman. What was that about?'

Kolea smiled at him. 'Caff, it must be the parent in me. I'll tell you when I get back.'

He jumped out of the shell-hole and started to run.

ALLO AND JENK were dead. Criid was sprawled beside their remains, wounded in the arm and side. Enemy fire wailed around them.

Kolea half-fell into her foxhole, banging his knee against a broken pipe.

'Hold tight, Tona,' he said. 'Caff's missing you.'

He scooped her up in his arms, ignoring her moans of pain and started to run back the way he had come.

'You're crazy!' she wailed as flechette shot exploded around them.

'Not the first time I've been accused of that,' he said, struggling. 'You and Varl ought to form a gakking club.'

He reached the edge of the shattered buildings and almost threw Criid into Jajjo's arms as he fell down.

He was smiling, and only when he fell did they see the bloody mess where the back of his skull had been.

'Sarge!' Lubba yelled, risking his own life to drag Kolea's body into cover from the crossfire. 'Sarge! Sergeant Kolea! Please! Don't be dead! Don't be dead!'

BRAGG LOOKED OVER at Caill. 'Last box?' he asked.

'We've got two more,' said his loader.

Bragg sighed. He looked out of the nearest hole in the wall and shook his head. Loxatl flechette fire was sweeping the street outside. 'Not going to be enough to get through that. I'll stay put and lay down some cover fire. You run back down the line and get us some more, eh?'

Caill nodded. 'I'll be two minutes,' he said. 'Don't leave without me.'

Caill hurried away. Bragg looked over at the other Ghosts in the shelled out basement: Tokar, Fenix, Cuu and Hwlan.

'Any bright ideas?' he said.

'You give me a good spread of protective fire with that land-hammer,' Hwlan said, 'and I reckon I can get a group into that block opposite.'

'You're on,' said Bragg and hefted the big support weapon into place.

'On three,' he said. 'One, two–'

The cannon exploded into life, strafing the street with a devastating rain of shots.

Hwlan, Fenix and Tokar surged out, running the gauntlet of fire.

The cannon clicked dry.

'Need another box?' Cuu asked.

'Yeah,' said Bragg. 'That would be–'

The corner of the ammo box cracked into the side of Bragg's head. He slumped to the side, and passed out for a second.

'What the feth?' he spluttered, coming round. 'Cuu? What the feth was that?' Bragg felt blood pouring out of his scalp. He was dizzy and sick.

Lijah Cuu was standing, staring at him.

'You sold me out,' he said.

'Oh feth, Cuu! This isn't the time to settle some stupid feud!'

'No? When would be a better time, Tanith? I don't know, sure as sure.'

Bragg tried to get up. 'You really have lost it, Cuu. Gaunt got you off. You just got lashes. You were lucky.'

'Lucky?'

'I mean… feth, I don't know what I mean. Feth, you're scum. Gaunt will have you shot for this and–'

'He ain't gonna know, is he?' said Cuu. 'Is he, you big dumbo?' In Cuu's right hand glittered thirty centimetres of silver Tanith warknife.

'Cuu? What the feth are you–'

Cuu plunged his straight silver into Bragg's heart.

Bragg's eyes widened. His lips gasped for a second, like a fish.

Cuu wrenched the dagger out and leaned forward so his mouth was right next to the dying Tanith's ear. 'Just so's you know… it *was* me. I did her. And it was beautiful. She fought, oh how she fought. Not like you, you big dumbo.'

Bragg suddenly lurched up and swung the autocannon around by the barrel like a club. If it had connected with the lean Verghastite it would surely have crippled him. But Cuu had jerked out of the way.

'Try again, Bragg,' he said, and stabbed the blade down again. And again. And again.

EPILOGUE: THE GUNS OF TANITH
PHANTINE,
227.771, M41

*'I don't believe I had ever found a senior officer who appreciated
the Ghosts' particular skills before. Now I have, I don't really
think I'm any happier.'*

– Ibram Gaunt, C-in-C, Tanith First

THE DROGUE HAD docked just a few minutes before, but
already the children were running out and playing.

The Ghosts' entourage had reached Ouranberg as part of
the mass reinforcement wave. Surly wharf masters oversaw
the unloading of cargo freight, while men who would soon
become jugglers, mimes, fire-eaters and knife-sharpeners
haggled with them over the safe deposition of their worldly
goods.

And the children were loose. Laughing, chanting, scampering around the docking bay. Yoncy tottered forward and
half-threw a ball that Dalin went scampering after.

'Kids, huh?' said the woman behind Curth. The surgeon
looked round.

'Kids,' said Aleksa scornfully. 'The battle's won, the dead
are dead, and now the kids arrive to make us all soft and

sad. Well, I'm not gakking sad. Life sucks. Get a bloody helmet.'

'Agreed,' said Curth, taking a lho-stick from her pack and offering the box to Aleksa. The blousy older woman with her boudoir finery took one and lit them both from a chased silver igniter.

'Dalin! Careful with your sister now, you hear me?' she shouted. She dropped her voice and added, 'You're the one he told, aren't you?'

'The one he told?'

'Kolea said to me the only other person who knew was the lady doctor. That's you, isn't it?'

'Yes,' Curth sighed.

After a while, Aleksa asked, 'How's Gol?'

'He's alive,' said Curth.

'But what?'

'His primary functions are intact. He's conscious. But the damage to his brain was considerable. He has total sociotypal memory loss. I mean total. He doesn't even know his own name. Or that he has kids. Nothing…'

Aleksa smiled. 'So that solves a lot, really.'

'No,' said Curth, taking out the sealed letter and staring at it. 'Gol Kolea came back… but he didn't come back. I… I don't know what to do.'

'Honey,' said Aleksa, pressing the letter back into Curth's coat, 'take my advice. Thank the Emperor and walk away.'

Curth folded up the letter and slowly wandered back up the docking ramp into the city.

VAN VOYTZ HAD been effusive in his praise. He was full of talk of commendations and decorations. He spoke about petitioning Macaroth to officially change the Tanith First's regimental designation to reflect its specialist stealth and infiltration strengths.

'The next time the guns of Tanith sound, I want it to be in support of my advances,' Van Voytz had declared, pouring large snifters of amasec for his assembled officers.

Gaunt hadn't really been listening. The arch-enemy had been deprived of Phantine. A significant heretic leader had been eliminated.

The Crusade force would now benefit from the planet's massive vapour mill output.

And he had kept alive as many men as possible in the pursuit of those goals.

It was a victory, and duty had been done. Gaunt just didn't share Van Voytz's desire to toast the living and the dead and talk about it all night. He walked alone through the Imperial concourse. Clearance teams were still searching the surrounding buildings for enemy survivors.

Gaunt supposed that the curse of mid-ranking officers like himself was that they were still close enough to the sharp end to feel the loss. The Gaunts and Rawnes and Fazalurs of this galaxy were the ones who got to cope with the bloody aftermath of victory. The lord generals got to celebrate each triumph because, to them, the dead were just names on dataslates. The chain of rank insulated them from the emotional consequence. It made a generally decent man like Van Voytz seem just as heartless as some of the callous bastards Gaunt had been forced to follow in his time.

At least the perceived rift between the Tanith and the Verghastite that Hark and Zweil had chided him about appeared to be easing. During the fight for Ouranberg, the regiment had seemed much more of a single, integrated whole.

Maybe sticking up for Cuu had sent the right message.

GAUNT RETURNED TO his section and had Beltayn transmit his respectful thanks to all Tanith and Verghastites alike via all section leaders, along with the order for the regiment to pull out. Urdeshi and Krassian reinforcements from Cirenholm were coming in to supervise the occupation.

The guns of Tanith could fall silent for a while, and rest.

'Order and signal of thanks sent, sir,' said Beltayn.

'That'll do,' said Ibram Gaunt.

ABOUT THE AUTHOR

Dan Abnett lives and works in Maidstone,
Kent, in England. Well known for his comics
work, he has written everything from Mr
Men to the X-Men in the last decade, and
currently scripts *Legion of Superheroes* for DC
Comics and *Sinister Dexter* and *Durham Red*
for 2000 AD.

His work for the Black Library includes the
popular strips *Lone Wolves* and *Darkblade*, the
best-selling Gaunt's Ghosts novels, the
acclaimed Inquisitor Eisenhorn trilogy and
his fantasy novel *Riders of the Dead*.

More Warhammer 40,000 from the Black Library

THE EISENHORN TRILOGY
by Dan Abnett

IN THE 41ST MILLENNIUM, *the Inquisition hunts the shadows for humanity's most terrible foes – rogue psykers, xenos and daemons. Few Inquisitors can match the notoriety of Gregor Eisenhorn, whose struggle against the forces of evil stretches across the centuries.*

XENOS

THE ELIMINATION OF the dangerous recidivist Murdon Eyclone is just the beginning of a new case for Gregor Eisenhorn. A trail of clues leads the Inquisitor and his retinue to the very edge of human-controlled space in the hunt for a lethal alien artefact – the dread Necroteuch.

MALLEUS

A GREAT IMPERIAL triumph to celebrate the success of the Ophidian Campaign ends in disaster when thirty-three rogue psykers escape and wreak havoc. Eisenhorn's hunt for the sinister power behind this atrocity becomes a desperate race against time as he himself is declared hereticus by the Ordo Malleus.

HERETICUS

WHEN A BATTLE with an ancient foe turns deadly, Inquisitor Eisenhorn is forced to take terrible measures to save the lives of himself and his companions. But how much can any man deal with Chaos before turning into the very thing he is sworn to destroy?

More Warhammer 40,000 from the Black Library

THE GAUNT'S GHOSTS SERIES
by Dan Abnett

IN THE NIGHTMARE *future of Warhammer 40,000, mankind is beset by relentless foes. Commissar Ibram Gaunt and his regiment the Tanith First-and-Only must fight as much against the inhuman enemies of mankind as survive the bitter internal rivalries of the Imperial Guard.*

The Founding

FIRST AND ONLY

GAUNT AND HIS men find themselves at the forefront of a fight to win back control of a vital Imperial forge world from the forces of Chaos, but find far more than they expected in the heart of the Chaos-infested manufacturies.

GHOSTMAKER

NICKNAMED THE GHOSTS, Commissar Gaunt's regiment of stealth troops move from world from world, playing a vital part in the crusade to liberate the Sabbat Worlds from Chaos.

NECROPOLIS

ON THE SHATTERED world of Verghast, Gaunt and his Ghosts find themselves embroiled in a deadly civil war as a mighty hive-city is besieged by an unrelenting foe. When treachery from within brings the defences crashing down, rivalry and corruption threaten to bring the Ghosts to the brink of defeat.

The Saint

HONOUR GUARD

As a mighty Chaos fleet approaches the shrineworld Hagia, Gaunt and his men are sent on a desperate mission to safeguard some of the Imperium's most holy relics: the remains of the ancient saint who first led humanity to these stars.

THE GUNS OF TANITH

COLONEL-COMMISSAR GAUNT and the Tanith First-and-Only must recapture Phantine, a world rich in promethium but so ruined by pollution that the only way to attack is via a dangerous – and untried – aerial assault. Pitted against deadly opposition and a lethal environment, how can Gaunt and his men possibly survive?

STRAIGHT SILVER

ON THE BATTLEFIELDS of Aexe Cardinal, the struggling forces of the Imperial Guard are locked in a deadly stalemate with the dark armies of Chaos. Commissar Ibram Gaunt and his regiment, the Tanith First-and-Only, are thrown headlong into this living hell of trench warfare, where death from lethal artillery is always just a moment away.

SABBAT MARTYR

A NEW WAVE of hope is unleashed in the Sabbat system when a girl claiming to be the reincarnation of Saint Sabbat is revealed. But the dark forces of Chaos are not oblivious to this new threat and when they order their most lethal assassins to kill her, it falls to Commissar Gaunt and his men to form the last line of defence!